SHADOW OF A LION

By Anne Edwards

THE SURVIVORS

MIKLOS ALEXANDROVITCH IS MISSING!

SHADOW OF A LION

SHADOW OF A LION

by
ANNE EDWARDS

Coward, McCann & Geoghegan
New York

ACKNOWLEDGMENTS

For permission to reprint copyrighted material, the author wishes to thank the following: William Collins Sons & Company, Ltd., for an excerpt from "The Fisherman and His Soul" by Oscar Wilde, published in *The Complete Works of Oscar Wilde,* Vyvyan Holland, editor, reprinted by permission of the publisher; Random House, Inc., for excerpts from *Witness* by Whittaker Chambers, published by Random House, Inc., 1952, copyright © 1952 by Whittaker Chambers, and from "Hollywood" by Karl Shapiro, published by Random House, Inc., 1953 in *Poems 1940-1953* by Karl Shapiro, copyright © 1953 by Karl Shapiro, reprinted by permission of Random House, Inc.; Viking Press, Inc., for an excerpt from *After the Fall* by Arthur Miller, published by Viking Press, Inc., 1964, copyright © 1964 by Arthur Miller, all rights reserved, reprinted by permission of the publisher.

The author would like to acknowledge gratefully the assistance of Miss Eleanor Wolquitt and of Mr. Jay Schlein for help and support during the writing of this entire book, as well as the encouragement that was constant in those friends who knew the subject matter involved and had been a part of that time in history and who always gave her to believe that she could be trusted to deal with it in good faith. It is the author's hope that what follows is worthy of the support of all these good people.

for Leon

BOOK I

Luise

My children, when you were little, we used sometimes to go for walks in our pine woods. In the open fields, you would run along by yourselves. But you used instinctively to give me your hands as we entered those woods, where it was darker, lonelier, and in the stillness our voices sounded loud and frightening. In this book I am again giving you my hands. I am leading you, not through cool pine woods, but up a narrow defile between bare and steep rocks from which in shadow things uncoil and slither away. It will be dark. But, in the end, if I have led you aright, you will make out three crosses, from two of which hang thieves. I will have brought you to Golgotha—the place of skulls. This is the meaning of the journey. Before you understand, I may not be there, my hands may have slipped from yours. It will not matter. For when you understand what you see, you will no longer be children. You will know that life is pain, that each of us hangs always upon the cross of himself. And when you know that this is true of every man, woman and child on earth, you will be wise.

WHITTAKER CHAMBERS
"Foreword in the Form of a Letter to My Children . . . "
From *Witness*

MAXWELL ISAAC SEAMAN, AWARD-WINNING DIRECTOR, DEAD AT 54.

London 30 June, Maxwell Isaac Seaman, founder of Elektra Productions and twice winner of the Academy Award, died early yesterday morning in his London home. He was fifty-four.

As a Hollywood screenwriter he authored many of the films that ushered in the era of psychological realism in American cinema, among them *The Winner, The Woman Who Cared, The Frame-up, Little Angel, Escape to Tangier,* the controversial *Black in Eden,* for which he won the Academy Award in 1949, and the celebrated *Tiger in Heaven* (Best Foreign Film, 1951).

Mr. Seaman was born on 19 April 1915, in Bridgeport, Connecticut, the only son of Samuel and Berthe Seaman. Educated at New York University, he interrupted his studies in 1934 to go to war-torn Spain as a foreign correspondent, returning to New York the following year.

In 1937 Mr. Seaman joined the staff of the now defunct Liberty Press, a job that took him to Hollywood in 1939 to cover a long and bitter studio strike. He remained in California to write his first screenplay, a minor film entitled *The Cat's Meow,* which was followed by the highly acclaimed *The People's Case.*

Called before the American House's Committee for Un-American Activities in 1951, Mr. Seaman was declared an "unfriendly witness" and his Hollywood career came to an end. However, he elected to come to London, where within two years he had established his own production company, Elektra II, and released the gripping and commerically successful *Thunder in the East*. Mr. Seaman never returned to the United States although his films have been widely shown there.

Death came to Mr. Seaman early yersterday morning. According to Mr. Seaman's personal physician, Dr. Wolverley David, death was caused by a coronary thrombosis and was instantaneous. The body was found by Mr. Seaman's secretary, Miss Edyth Spalding of Kensington.

Mr. Seaman is survived by his widow, the former Luise Haydyn, who was in New York at the time of his death arranging a film festival of his work which will commence, as planned, on 4, July and by his two children, Anthony Haydyn Seaman and Anthea Seaman, who is also known by her stage name, Anthea Evans.

The Arj was a Jewish religious leader, who, like Christ, used to walk about the hills of Palestine, teaching and talking with his disciples. One day, the Arj suddenly said, "Let us go down to Jerusalem." The disciples began to murmur. Some thought of their wives at home. Some thought of their suppers. They said that they would not go. They walked on in silence. Then one of the disciples asked: "Why did you want us to go down to Jerusalem?" The Arj answered sadly: "That was a moment in eternity. If, at that moment, we had all been of one mind to go down to Jerusalem, the people would have been saved."

TRANSLATED FROM AN OLD PARABLE
BY WHITTAKER CHAMBERS

Chapter 1

"The barefoot girl in mink." That's what Max used to call her. Not in phase one of their thirty-two years together (well, "together" was not an honest word for the last seventeen years of their marriage, but the total togetherness of their first fifteen equalized things to some extent). If phase one had not been hypoed with happiness it had been rich with mutual purpose. Phase two had been the McCarthy period. Phase three had been all these long years since. In phase three she had heard those words often, could even evoke this moment, the sight of Max saying them to her.

"Sit in it, sleep in it, wrap it around your ass, Luise! What the hell do I care!" he'd say, smiling all the time, his slightly pugnacious face broadening, flattening, the steel mouth not melting much with the smile, the flinty-gray eyes mocking, laughing. "Lu Seaman," he'd chant in his low, nearly breathless way, *"the original barefoot girl in mink!"*

That was in the years after McCarthy. The years when they were still brutally flogging each other. But this was no time to think of those days. Eight hours of flying time stretched before her. She would do what she could to bring back some of phase one to her conscious in the desperate hope that by the time the giant silver ship set down in a summer's eve in London, she would know what she felt. Maybe she could even cry.

But as Luise Haydyn Seaman closed her eyes and sank back into the rough-textured seat, all she could bring forth as images in her mind were the status symbols of the compartment in which she now rode. A pair of red-knitted slippers stamped TWA danced before her lowered eyelids, but somewhere, very far back, she could hear Max again chiding her (phase three), "Who the hell ever told you it only costs ten percent more to go first class!"

She opened her eyes. The stewardess was at her side with a tray of drinks. The sun came streaming through the window nearest Luise, and she blinked hard, the light making her eyes tear. *(Dear Lord, maybe I am going to cry!)* She put on her sunglasses, took a scotch from the stewardess, put it down, and then stared ahead of her through the smoky darkness the tinted lenses created. It was now only 10 A.M. She was thankful that first class had been fairly empty and she was traveling without a seat companion.

Had it only been six hours since the telephone had jarred the dark in her bedroom and she had awakened not knowing if it was night or day? She had fumbled for the receiver rather than turn on the bedside lamp. It was always so difficult for her to sleep that long ago she had installed dark-green shades and used ear plugs to shut out the retchings of the city eighteen floors below. The telephone must have been ringing for a long time, because as she picked it up, the operator was about to disconnect.

"Mrs. Luise Seaman?"

Luise pulled the cotton stoppers from her ears. "Who is it?" she asked in a faltering, half-lost voice.

"International operator. Is this Mrs. Luise Seaman?"

"Yes, it is."

"Go ahead, please."

Luise lifted herself up onto her elbows and shifted the telephone to another hand and another ear. She searched the dark in the room for some clue to whether it was night or morning. She listened closely for the telltale traffic sounds. They were a gentle buzz, though the rasp of a siren could be heard off in the distance. Fear suddenly filled her consciousness. *It was the middle of the night.* Long-distance calls at such an hour had always terrified her. She sat bolt upright and with her free hand struggled to find the wristwatch she so methodically put on her bedside table each night.

It was 3 A.M. That meant 8 A.M. in England. It *had* to be

England. There was no one anywhere else overseas who would call
her at this hour. She was already braced for the worst by the time
Edyth Spalding was on the other end of the telephone.

"Luise?"

"Edyth? Is that you?" The siren was drawing nearer, and Luise
pressed the receiver as close to her ear as she could.

Edyth was suddenly convulsed with tears. That meant it was
Max. Then somehow Luise knew. *Max was dead.* For some
inexplicable reason, a reaction that would nag at her for years to
come took hold. She felt a great calm as though relieved of a
tremendously heavy burden.

"Edyth, control yourself," she said gently into the telephone,
and then, when that did not help, called sharply, "Edyth!" into
the instrument that would take her voice across the Atlantic.

"I'm sorry, Luise. Oh, God!" She was sobbing again.

"Is it Max, Edyth?" And then, because she knew she had to
have it over with: "Is Max dead, Edyth?"

There was a gasp as if Edyth had suddenly choked on all her
tears and then a long moment of silence. "You *knew*. You felt it,
too. Oh, my God."

Luise thought Edyth might have gone off the line, as the silence
was without life, without breath. "Edyth?"

"Yes, Luise. I'm here." Now Edyth used the calm, efficient
voice that had taken her through a lifetime of crisis. Why was it
that Edyth's life always seemed like a sea beset with hurricanes
and tornadoes, massive waves, thunderous vibrations, and Edyth
herself a ship gliding smoothly through the tumultuous waters?
"Well, you *know*. Yes. Max is dead."

"What happened?"

"He didn't suffer, Luise. I am sure he didn't suffer. Dr. David
said it was a heart attack and that death was instantaneous."

"Who called Dr. David?" Luise was sorry immediately that she
had asked that.

"I had one of my *feelings*," Edyth said surely, "as I did when
Mama died. I woke up at exactly three in the morning with this
terrible *feeling* and I walked around my flat until just two hours
ago and I tried reaching Max, but there was no reply, so I called a
taxi and went directly over there. I found him on the bed, and at
first I thought he might just be sleeping because he looked so *at
peace*. I've never seen Max look so at peace."

"You called Dr. David then?" Luise asked, trembling but aware that it was out of fear at the shocking calm in her voice.

"Yes. He came right over and he said—Luise, isn't this strange?—that Max had been dead for about four hours. That meant he died at three A.M." Edyth was quiet for a moment, and Luise, unable to question her anymore, fell back against the pillows, thankful for the soothing dark of her bedroom, and waited for Edyth to continue. "He always hated that hour. Remember how he *used* to quote Fitzgerald? About three A.M. being the dark night of the soul?"

Luise was irritated with Edyth's natural use of the past tense. At that moment she would have preferred a fresh onslaught of tears. "Is there a will and instructions?" she interrupted.

"A will"—Edyth's tone insinuated, "How could you ask . . . so soon?"—"but Max doesn't include any instructions. I mentioned that to him when I typed it and he just said, 'Hell, there's still time. I don't plan to die for another lifetime.'"

Luise's mind was now whirling. Tony and Thea had to be told and consulted. She decided she would not make any decisions until that was done.

"Edyth, where are you now?" she asked.

"At Max's apartment."

"Good God! Why are you still there?" she inquired with heavy distaste at Edyth's perennial morbidity. "Is Max still there?" Luise asked, unable to think of him as a body, speak of him as such, but having to ask the question.

"No. I had them take him to a reliable funeral home. But there are so many things to straighten up. Papers to go through. I'll pack his clothes if you like."

"Leave things as they are until I ring you back. I have to tell the children. Go home, Edyth. I'll ring you there in an hour or two."

"Yes, of course. *The children*. I hadn't thought about them." There was a touch of bitchiness in Edyth's voice as she said the words—*the children*.

"Give me your home number," Luise remembered to ask.

"Flaxman 7382."

"Now go right home, Edyth. Take a shot of brandy and try to get some rest until I ring you back."

"I'll try," Edyth replied, almost childlike. Then, "Oh, God, Luise, we've lost *our* beautiful Max."

"Go home, Edyth, and thank you for what you have already done." Luise quickly disconnected and fumbled to put the receiver back into place.

It was a long time before Tony answered his telephone, and when he did, he snarled into it, "Christamighty! It's three in the morning!"

"I know it is, Tony, but I have to speak to you."

"Oh. Mother." He seemed to have had all the air suddenly let out of him as he recognized Luise's voice.

"I'll wait until you are fully awake," she said. "You can go in and wash your face with cold water."

"You didn't wake me. I was just getting ready to go to bed," he replied.

Luise wanted desperately to be able to cry as Edyth had so that, perhaps, Tony would guess her news or at least that she was the bearer of bad news, but she felt as dry as her flower boxes must be on this hot June night. "Tony, I—I don't know how to say this," she began badly. "Your *father*—" She took a deep breath. "Your father, Tony, is dead." She was aware of the flat tone of her voice, then of the silence and then a sound—as if Tony had broken into sobs. "Tony, are you all right?" She recognized the sound now. Yes, distinctly, that was it . . . Tony was laughing! "Tony, you're hysterical. I'll get dressed and come right over."

"I'm all right. I'm . . . what happened?"

"Your father passed away at three this morning, London time. He had a heart attack, and Dr. David—"

"Wolfie David, *that* damned pill pusher!"

"Edyth called him. He—your father was already . . . had already . . . passed away." Luise's heart was pounding wildly. Not because of the strain of the last few minutes but because of the sound of her son's voice on the word "that." It had gone up and balanced there deliberately for several beats before returning to its natural pitch. She was certain that he always chose to do it purposely at least once in every conversation to distress her. He had been doing it since that horrifying afternoon two years before when they had met at the Plaza for lunch.

"Penela Jordan is such a nice girl," she had begun innocently enough.

"Don't! Not again. Never again. You know it, and yet you won't admit it. Not to me or yourself. I don't care about Penela

Jordan or any other of your friends' daughters. Nor will I ever. Not the way you want me to. I am a fag, Luise. A *fag*," he repeated, leaning in close across the table in the dark Oak Bar.

"I have to go to the ladies' room," she had replied in a light, conversational tone. "I'll be right back. Order a vodka gimlet for me, please." And she had left the table, gone to the bathroom, and returned to find her gimlet waiting and Tony apprehensive, but she had made no further comment and spoke instead about the Pinter play she had seen the night before, and never again had that ugly word passed between them, though Tony kept driving the knife a little deeper as a warning each time he spoke with the tip of his "thats."

"Tony, he—he left no instructions for his—"

"I'm sorry, Mother. I am really sorry." And the sobs came then, uncontrollable. It was almost too much for Luise to bear. She had hoped Tony would take over the situation, lift all the decisions from her shoulders, but she was aware now that that was not the case, would never be the case.

"Shall I go there, do you think, or shall I . . . have—" She was unable to complete the sentence, and she stumbled on quickly elsewhere. "Oh, God, Tony, please stop crying!"

There was a stabbing moment of agony when Luise realized Tony had hung up on her. She sat there in the moist dark now listening to the stuttering air conditioner. It wasn't working again. Couldn't be; otherwise she wouldn't be pouring with sweat. She pulled the nylon gown from her body and threw it on the floor as she got out of the bed and made her way into the bathroom. The cool tile felt comforting under her bare feet. She tried to block out everything but the sensation of the hard, cold tile, feeling with her toes the familiar crevices that created its design.

The telephone rang and she stumbled back to the side of her bed.

"Mother, I'm sorry. Don't say anything. Please don't say anything, just listen! I think you should go over there. Right away. I'll take care of the tickets for you. I can at *least* do that. Make all the arrangements there. I mean end it. Leave him there. Edyth will help. She's a gloom addict anyway. The scent of death works just like glue for that bitch. There are several flights around ten. I'll get you on one. You begin packing. It's half-past three now. I'll pick you up at eight."

"Thea . . ."

"I'll call Thea for you. No! I'll send her a cable. A night letter. She's in Puerto Rico."

"Where?" Luise was sure she heard wrong.

"With Bob. You weren't to know, though I don't see why. Hell, half the city knows she is having an affair with a married man and the other half doesn't matter."

"She may want to come," Luise said hopefully.

"She hasn't talked to that man in two years. Why would she want to go? Never mind," he went on quickly, "just believe me she wouldn't go, but I'll tell her you said to meet you there if she wants. OK?"

"Yes. Thank you, Tony."

There was a long silence, and for the first time since Edyth's telephone call, though she couldn't cry, Luise's eyes filled with tears.

"Luise," Tony said softly (he often, in moments of tenderness or deference, called her by her first name), "I just can't come over there now. I can't."

"I understand, Tony."

"I'll get the tickets and cable Thea and also call Edyth to tell her you are coming and to make a reservation for you at Claridges and to have a studio car pick you up at the airport. Do you have her number? Never mind, I remember now that I have it somewhere. I'll be downstairs in front of your building at eight."

"Yes, Tony."

He did not say good-bye, but he was slow, almost reluctant, in disconnecting.

Luise was now on the edge of the bed. It was impossible to think of going back to sleep. There was the press. She took the receiver off the hook. In a moment the exchange began its automatic signal, and the sound seemed to take over the room. She stuffed the receiver into the bedside drawer, cramming her nightgown into the drawer with it to muffle the sound.

She made her way through the familiar darkness and lifted her loose robe from the hook behind the bathroom door and then put it on as she crossed to the windows and raised the green shades.

The street was strangely silent. The siren had stopped, and the traffic was only an uneven murmur. Luise opened the window and looked up and into the night sky. It was a deep slaty gray with patches of dark clouds. The moon seemed to have disappeared, and the sun was not yet ready to rise.

She was thinking that Max had been alive in London this same night, and she was wondering what he had last seen and heard. He liked German music from Wagner to Weill, which had always disconcerted Luise, whose taste lingered on the more romantic composers. Often when they were still sleeping together, he would place the tape on his side of the bed, loving her to the strident cadences of *Die Walküre* and at last rolling off her and falling into an exhausted sleep before the tape ended. She would lie beside him, wide-eyed, unmoving, wanting desperately to wake him just long enough to ask him to turn off the tape, to hold her, to talk to her for a while, but she never did. Instead she would wait until his breathing was regular, then slide out of bed and cautiously tiptoe to his side, turning off the triumphant Brünnhilde.

Max had always been an ardent and demanding lover.

Perhaps his tastes and habits had changed these last two years. Perhaps he had mellowed. Could he have grown fond of more mystical sounds, like the gentle tapping of rain against a windowpane or the breath of the sea as it swept the shore? She did not even know what his current apartment looked like or what his bedroom window looked out upon.

There was so much she did not know.

She left the windows wide open and turned off the air conditioning and then, out of habit, went into the kitchen for some tea and brandy. The room appeared at once unreal, almost clinical. Her senses had become heightened so that each sound she made was sharpened and her eyesight not only magnified but clearer, making everything in the room more defined.

The kitchen had instantly become a laboratory, and the clink of her spoon against the stainless-steel drainboard filled her with sudden shock because it sounded like the sounds in an operating or autopsy room. Her sense of smell transformed the scent of brandy into the frightening odor of an anesthetic, or was it formaldehyde?

She just made it into the bathroom, where she fell to the floor, her arms cradling the toilet bowl as the heavings inside her began.

She remained there the rest of the night, retching. Then, though she could not remember when, she had fallen asleep sitting on the cold tile floor, resting her back against the wall.

When she awoke, it was half past seven. She went back to her bedroom, threw some clothes into a suitcase, paying little heed to her selection, and ran the water in the tub. She badly needed some coffee, but there wasn't enough time. She went to pour herself a drink, decided against it, took some soda water instead, and got into the tub of steaming water while it was still running.

Miraculously she was dressed and downstairs when Tony, ten minutes late, but more on time than usual, drew to the curb. He had not stepped out of the car but sat there as the doorman put the suitcase in the trunk and helped his mother into the front seat.

Neither of them spoke for several minutes. The streets were already thick with morning traffic. It was a morning blurred by layers of heat, everything misty, ill defined. The air was heavy and impregnated with chemical. "Close your window; the air conditioner is on," Tony finally said. "Edyth will meet you. She was positively ecstatic about it in fact. 'We should console each other,' she said. 'It would be exactly as your father would want it.' *Bitch!* However, she'll be very helpful, and at this time you need her."

"Yes, I guess so."

"I sent a cable to Thea and told her to contact you at Claridges."

"Thank you."

"I tried to call you, but your line was busy. I told you not to talk to anyone."

"I took the receiver off the hook."

They drove in silence for several blocks.

"You understand?" he asked unsteadily.

"I told you I did, Tony."

"I'll do anything you want me to do here."

"I know I can depend on you, dear."

He gripped the wheel with both hands. "And please, remember, leave him *there*."

She grew angry for the first time. "I'll do what has to be done, Tony." Knowing it would upset him, she opened the window on her side of the seat rendering the air conditioning useless and let the warm wind the car's motion stirred stab at her face.

"Excuse me." It was the stewardess, and she had a tray in her hand. "We're serving lunch," she announced.

Luise turned and settled her glance on the porthole window.

They were flying through a bank of clouds. The outside world was now solidly white, blotted out. There was not even a shape to the white, a line, a trace. It was as though they were drifting through a snowbank, slowly, because their motion did not seem to disturb the tranquillity surrounding them.

It had been a year since she had last seen Max. They had never been separated that long before. Throughout their anger and their bitterness they had, until that terrible night two years before, remained at each other's side, reflecting each other's pain and joy and disgust as if each were the mirror image of the other.

That night had been imprinted in her memory more vividly than any other experience. She could never let go of it, never allow it to fade into the blurred vision of dreams.

She had felt the cold air as it filled her lungs, for it had been late spring, but the thaw had seemed reluctant to come. They had had words upstairs. Bitter words. Her ears seemed not to hear what she was saying, shouting, for if they had, she knew she would have choked them back into silence. She had always prided herself on being temperate, measured, self-disciplined, and self-controlled, always bearing her hurts and her sorrows with a certain effacement she liked to call dignity.

On this night it had been different; she had run screaming after him, out of the apartment, down the five flights of stairs, bolted after him into the street.

She saw him now exactly as he had looked then, his coat left behind in his anger, so that he had huddled himself against the cold, moving into it as if he had a football tucked close to his body and as if Fifth Avenue, with its tangle of traffic, were a field of interference, the goalpost a taxi waiting at the curb on the opposite side of the street.

"Max! Max!" she had shouted, running, her fury warming her, driving her on until she caught up with him and tore at his arm, trying desperately to pull it away from his body to drag him back and away from the curb.

"Castrater!" he had spit at her.

She had fallen back as though mortally wounded and landed off-balance on one knee, and he had not stopped to help her up, but he had not continued on either and had stood there over her, his face beet red (so that she feared for his blood pressure) and his gray eyes sharp and narrow, stabbing points of ice.

"It's perverted," she yelled. "You're perverted! She's younger than your daughter. *She's a child!"*

Luise had never heard his full reply. All that ever reached her ears was the tag phrase "more woman than you'll ever be!" She had managed to get to her feet and stand erect before him. Her height had always disturbed him. He was a big man, but Luise was tall and their eyes nearly met.

"This is it, Max. I can't take any more."

"You? Why, damn you, you won't be done until you cut my balls right off me. You're a castrater, Luise. The worst kind. The *righteous* kind. You and your silent, unrelenting look of accusation, and you'll destroy me if I let you. Well, hear this, now. I damn well won't let it happen, because I'm leaving *you*, for good! I'm returning to England and this time *alone*. Don't come after me, Luise. Hear me? Leave me be. Take all the bread. Keep everything you want, including my name, but let me be!"

He had stepped into the street, and she had stood there screaming after him, "No one can destroy another person! No one! You're doing it to yourself! Damn it, Max, turn back before it's too late!"

But he had reached the other side of the street and stepped into the taxi, and her words were lost in the roar of the passing cars.

The stewardess tapped her on the shoulder. "Coffee or tea, Mrs. Seaman?"

"Oh. Coffee, please."

The stewardess was very young and very pretty. Twenty. Perhaps, twenty-two at the most. She had the kind of slim, small boyishness that Max had always appreciated.

Luise bit her lip so hard she could taste blood.

"Phase one," she prayed over and over to herself. "I have to think only about phase one."

They had passed through the cloud bank. The sky was now alive with the sparks that came from the wing of the plane.

She glanced at her watch. In seven hours she would be there. Two years ago Max had warned her not to follow him, but in seven hours she would once again be by his side.

Chapter 2

The six men sat around the poker table as they had every Monday night for the past ten years. They gathered at Burt Winters' as a sign of respect. Burt, after all, was the most successful of the group. He had, of course, been a successful agent in Hollywood before leaving the States in fifty-one and coming to England. *Correction.* He had been a *powerful* and successful agent, having under his aegis many of the top stars, writers, and directors in Hollywood. He was now owner and executive producer of Panther Productions, releasing through International Films (one of the five largest film companies in the world), and he was responsible for its most lucrative foreign releases. As such, no property, *no man,* was accepted and bought by the London office of International without Burt's nod of approval.

Only one man at that poker table could state he did not need Burt's paternal and approving yes from time to time, and that man was Burt's lawyer and a member of the board of directors of Panther Productions, Henry Green (Burt, his wife, Sylvia, Henry and two Englishmen on the payroll, making up the board). Without Burt as a client, Henry Green would have been back in New York City chasing ambulances as he once had chased the "creatively maligned" for cases to defend.

Though none of the men in the poker game thought it odd, they were all American (as opposed to being *all-American*), all in the business of making films, and all victims of the dark McCarthy days, the days of the hunts, the dark, *ever-dark* days of the House Committee on Un-American Activities.

Burt Winters, Henry Green, and the four other men at the poker table constituted six of the original political victims of the committee who had emigrated to Europe, based themselves in London, and not only survived, but were again actively involved in making motion pictures.

Not all were that lucky, or that talented, or that young, or that healthy. But these unfortunates were not present this Monday night.

Burt shifted uncomfortably in his chair, and the men fanned out around him looked toward him with concern.

"You shouldn't have eaten those pickles at dinner," Henry said, bending his long, lean torso forward. "An ulcer can't be ignored," he confided.

Burt got up from the table and walked over to the bar. He was a huge man, barrel-chested, his thick body drawn along on long legs and massive feet. He looked as if he once might have been a formidable halfback and as if he still might be able to throw his weight around a football field. The truth was he had never even made second string during his school days. Burt was never the man to be part of a team. It was the key to his success.

He poured himself a stiff shot of scotch, no ice. He stood at the bar, not offering his guests a drink, not even acknowledging their presence. Poker had suddenly bored him. The men had bored him. He gulped down the contents of his glass, knowing he would suffer the consequences later, refilled it, and went out and into the living room, closing the door tightly between himself and the poker players (who were, before he shut the door and when he did briefly glance their way, watching him and not playing their hands).

The room was furnished in what Burt called (but not for Sylvia's ears) *"nouveau Sylvia,"* much in the French style, though Burt would not have known what period. It was actually and fairly authentically Louis XV, mixed together with California Informal. The art, however, was Impressionistic, Sylvia's new and expensive hobby.

The house was always happier when Sylvia was not there. Right now Burt blessed the illness of Sylvia's mother that had called her back to California. It wasn't really a bad marriage as marriages go. They liked each other, respected each other's opinions, loved their two grown children, and accepted the fact that physically they had not been attracted to each other for more than twenty years. For Burt, the best hours were always spent in his office or at the studio or while he was on location.

Burt sank down into one of the deep couches that faced each other across the hearth of the paneled fireplace, now filled with dried flowers and green leaves. *Max dead.* He shouldn't have felt much reaction to that news. Though he had been seeing Max from time to time at the studio or at the White Elephant or the Curzon Club, they really had not spoken more than superficialities in—oh, God—he couldn't remember how long. Since they both first came to England. Well, it was a very long time ago.

Max had called for an appointment several times, and Burt had always politely managed to forestall it. Then on that day he was in the anteroom, and a flustered Shirley (who was his secretary then and now) came in and begged, "What shall I do?"

"Show Mr. Seaman in," Burt told her, but it was hardly necessary, for there Max was, standing in the doorway behind her, his face flushed but a sly cat smile plastered across it. Burt watched him appraise the office.

"Smells sweet," Max said, still smiling, unmoving.

"Come in. Come in. Thank you, Shirley." Burt nodded in dismissal, and Shirley left the room at a skittish gait, all too aware of the meaningful side glance Max bestowed upon her retreating figure.

The men were still nearly the entire room apart.

"Come in, take a seat," Burt said nervously watching as Max walked slowly, his pudgy body sure, almost . . . yes, defiant, a walk that seemed trained in a fight ring, in a straight line, never glancing to one side or the other, and coming to a stop just the other side of Burt's desk. He stood there for a long moment as if deciding something quite important and then sat down, his eyes never distracted from Burt's face.

"They call me an informer," he said quietly. "Vilify me. Turn away from me. Those of our number, that is. I'm not going to tell you that it doesn't disturb me. It damn well does."

"That's in the past, Max. We don't have to talk about that."

"The past? Now come on, Burt! You know, I know, there is no such thing as *past.* Yesterday, last month, last year—but not *past.* They won't forget. They can't forget."

"They?"

"The long and disquiet lines of witnesses." He leaned forward, and his voice grew softer yet, so soft that Burt had to lean forward to pick up every word. It was a trick Max had always used at decisive moments in story conferences and contract hagglings. "They can't forget because truth, after all, is only our own interpretation of reality." He sat back once again, but Burt remained inclined across the desk. "Really they would be desperate without me. I am their conscience and their pride. 'I betrayed *no* one,' they insist to themselves. 'It was tough, what I did, but as a human being, a *mensch*, it had to be done, and I did it!' But that's *their* truth. At the time of the hunts, you and I know, to *inform* meant you might someday work again. To be unfriendly meant you could be blacklisted for life, become totally unemployable in the only profession you ever knew, and in this age to be unemployable means the loss of everything, respect, self-respect, and, most important, bank credit. You and I both know that I did not give one name to the committee that had not already been given and that before that testimony, my own unemployable future smacked me right in the kisser, and I thought, *How the hell can I live through another day?* My life seemed utterly pointless. I am a creative man, not a businessman. I have a talent. I won't lie to you or myself. I have a *great* talent. To silence it was to die. I decided to find my own compromise and to live. That was my truth, my reality."

He got up then and breathed deeply, letting it all out in one great gasp as if he had (and of course, he *had*) removed a great heaviness from his lungs. He walked over to the window and gazed out aimlessly. "How's Sylvia?"

"Fine. Just fine. Busy decorating the new house."

"Life tastes good?"

"More often than not."

"For you."

"Don't play that game with me, Max. For you, too."

Max smiled. He came back to the desk and sat down again in the chair.

"The old school spirit," he said. "It's a pleasure to see."

"Can I help you in any way?"

"You have. I had to say what I said. You listened."

"Did I have a choice?"

Max laughed. "Burt, you're a big success. You *always* have a choice."

"OK, Max, let's push all this shit out of the way and get to the main event."

Max wasted no time, and his voice was now very audible. "I know, of course, that your closed session was not the brave testimony, the *shit*, Green publicized it as being. You gave plenty of names to the committee, and most *had not* been entered into the record before. And you got that closed session, no press, no coverage, no permanent record for libraries, because you won it fair and square. You held in your tight fist contracts to stars and directors and writers that meant millions to guys like Steiner and Warner and Louis B. You effected a trade."

"I don't have to answer any of that, Max."

"Of course not. Nor does it matter. I just had to let you know I knew for *my* record."

"You're wrong."

"You're a goddamn liar, baby—but I admire your guts." His head bobbed toward the closed door. "Attractive secretary."

"Good one, too. I plan to keep her."

"That means no hanky-panky, eh?"

"She's a big girl, Max. I don't care what the hell she does."

Max was glancing down at the polished desk top. "You keep in touch with Luise?"

"Something wrong there? Are you two separated?"

"No." Max was staring into the light from the window behind Burt, looking much like a blind man who had just seen a vision.

"I haven't been in touch, Max, not for a long time. Is Luise well?"

"Yes, very."

"Good. *Good.* I'm glad to hear that."

Max stood up then, his hands in his pockets disallowing the possibility of a parting handshake. "I'll see you around," he said.

"That's all?"

"What else! I made it back on talent, guts, and spit. I'm one of the few who don't need your help, Burt. That tastes good!"

And he had left. That had been the last time they had ever really spoken. The very last.

The five men in the other room had grown weary of their game and had moved away from the table and were helping themselves to drinks at the bar and some sandwiches the maid had left in the bar refrigerator (a weekly routine).

Except for Henry Green, the other four men had been writers in Hollywood. All victims of the committee and the blacklist, unable to work in the States, who had come to England as their one hope of employment. One of them, Merwin Bibbs, still remained solely a writer. He was a bitter man, now in his sixties and only eking a poor living from his trade. Of the men in the room he had been the only one to serve a jail sentence for his unfriendliness before the committee. He had never written a major film script before this occurred, nor since. Of course, he had remained blacklisted longer than most and only now, working for Burt, had hopes of seeing his name on the screen as film writer.

Gus Cone was now a producer of low-budget films. Younger than the others, he seemed, though in his late forties, still to have a boyish quality. As a writer, his contribution to the arts had merely been as a co-author of program Westerns. He had been married four times and was presently thinking of getting married again, but this very minute he honest to God could not think of the good woman's name.

Milton Stevens was about fifty-five. He had the look of a university don and was certainly the most erudite of the lot. His talent had always been on projects that were called block-busters—the big-budget, Cecil B. DeMille, wide-screen epics that came in and out of vogue like the length of women's skirts. He was an expert on research and data and trivia and indispensable in the making of such films. At present the vogue was out, which partially accounted for Milton's extreme nervousness; the rest could be attributed to the difficulties he was presently encountering at home with his wife and two daughters (and didn't they always seem to go hand in hand?

The last man to pour himself a bourbon and ginger ale (all the others drank scotch on the rocks) was Saunders Mayberry, called Sandy by all who knew him. Sandy had been born in Soft Bend, Georgia. He was a writer, an actor, and now hopefully a director, but he was also one thing the others were not. He was black.

Burt came back into the room just as all five men were lined up at the bar.

"Time for a toast," Merwin said, his face the vivid red of a man with high blood pressure.

"Seaman is dead," Gus intoned.

"Long may he rot," Sandy bit off.

"Ad infinitum," Milton said with bowed head.

Burt turned back out of the room. Henry started after him. "You all right, Burt? You look strange."

"I just want some air. Stay as late as you want. I'm going to take a long walk."

And he left them and went out into one of those damp and mistrustful June nights that London often offers.

Chapter 3

It was difficult for Luise to understand her mood. She seemed stifled, disassembled, not at all herself. She walked through the corridors to the customs hall surrounded by her own silence, feeling it press in on her. She supposed what she was suffering was despair, but since she had been through true despair so many times in her life with Max, this despair (if, indeed, it was) seemed numbed, as if an emotion had been anticipated and a drug taken to dull the effects.

She knew instead an excruciating terror in that one moment when she turned the last corridor and started down the long tiled stairway, the heel and toe tapping and foot scuffling sounding like a hundred typewriters as she made her way to the baggage conveyor in the great glass fishbowl that was the customs hall.

She felt as if she had entered a courtroom. Somehow her life was on trial, her future in the balance. Inwardly she cried for Max—not because of his death; she simply could not, would not at this moment think about that—but because these oh-so-many years afterward, she knew finally how Max must have felt (had felt) when he had entered that courtroom—that circus arena—in Washington and had taken the stand for the first time.

She supposed that out there beyond the wall of glass, Edyth was waving frantically to catch her eye, but she avoided looking in that direction and steadied her gaze instead upon the first baggage arriving from her flight. She had only reached the bottom of the stairway and taken perhaps two or three steps in that direction when the familiar voice brought her to an immediate stop.

"Oh, Luise, *Lu-ise*, I do hope this all wasn't too much for you." Edyth stood directly in her pathway.

Her first reaction was of anger and frustration; then she grew irritated as one might if not prepared for the intrusion of an early guest. Yes, Edyth being there prematurely—and quite without precedent, since no one except the passenger was permitted into the customs hall while the baggage was being checked, was an intrusion. It did, however, bring her out of her former state of lethargy.

"How in the world did you manage this?" she asked.

Edyth took her by the arm, led her to a bench where they paused, asked for Luise's baggage check, gave it to the porter, and then gestured for Luise to sit down. But Luise remained on her feet.

"The studio was helpful, of course, and the English are a most empathetic nation," Edyth said, but all the time her eyes were saying other things, and also, to Luise's great shock, Edyth was already in mourning, while Luise had been unable to think of such details and was wearing her navy and white checked traveling suit. Suddenly, the bright-red leather bag she clutched felt like a treacherous and alien flag. She hid it against her side.

"I'm sure it was your idea," Luise managed.

Edyth took this as a gesture of appreciation. "It was the least I could do," she murmured and lowered her head for a moment, the tears seeming ready to brim her eyes, but a brave smile on her face when again she raised it.

The baggage was now miraculously on a cart and at their side, and Edyth had Luise by the arm and was leading her, the porter following, through the great glass jaws that opened and closed automatically and up the rubber-carpeted and steel-railed aisle, Luise overconscious of the eyes upon her and so lowering her own (the bereaved widow), to the main concourse. A flashbulb exploded nearby. The suddeness of it caught Luise off-balance, and for a moment she thought she might fall.

"How dare you!" Edyth shouted to a retreating photographer, at the same time placing her arm more protectively around Luise and guiding her a little faster out and to the curb, where a black limousine waited, the door already open. Then she gently pushed Luise forward and into the dark interior, stepped in after her, and made sure the door was closed tight. But as the chauffeur and the porter deposited the baggage in the trunk several photographers crouched just outside the window on Luise's side.

"Just look down," Edyth muttered between tight lips.

And much to Luise's irritation at herself for obeying Edyth's instructions without question, she did. It was only moments before they were moving steadily, but slowly, as if leading a funeral procession, onto the main road to London.

Edyth finally relaxed. Luise noted the legs now stretched out, the one shoe surreptitiously and only slightly pressed down and angled to relieve their obvious tight fit. "I assumed you would want to go directly to the hotel," she said, her voice tinged with reproach.

"Of course."

"There was the possibility that you might want to go first to the funeral home."

"I have to admit, Edyth, that I never even thought of that possibility."

They drove along in silence, each looking away from the other, out her own window and thinking her own thoughts.

"Are the children coming over?" Edyth finally asked.

"Tony can't—he has business. Thea was away. I expect there might be a message waiting for me."

"I see."

"Yes, I'm sure you do," Luise said harshly, "but stop sitting in judgment."

"I'm sorry." Tight lips. Little contrition.

Luise weakened. "No. *I* am, Edyth." She placed her bare hand over Edyth's gloved one. "I understand. You were loyal. No one could have been more devoted than you." She stopped there, but the words still crossed her mind: *I know, I loved him as much but not more than you—and I had his love, his name, and his children, and you were never even given his acknowledgment, his respect, or his gratitude.* There was an uncomfortable moment when neither woman dared draw her hand away. Fortunately, the car stopped rather sharply at an intersection, and each had to reach for the strap near her window. An oppressive silence fell and remained until they had turned off the highway and were crawling laboriously through the streets of Earls Court.

"I do wish the driver would hurry," Luise said.

"I can ask him to if you want."

"No. We'll get there soon enough, I suppose."

"You must be exhausted, of course! You've had no sleep at all."
Luise smiled faintly. "I did, but not restful sleep."

"I'm sure not. Well, when we get to the hotel, you can rest for
an hour or two." Edyth glanced apologetically at Luise. "Arrangements do have to be made. I'm sorry."

"At this hour? They can wait until morning."

"If that's your directive."

Luise ignored the insult. "I couldn't possibly cope with the
arrangements tonight. I still haven't decided what exactly should
be done. What Max would want done," she explained instead.

"Naturally. It's too soon. It's been too great a shock. I know. I
know."

They rode on in silence through Knightsbridge, onto Rotten
Row, through Hyde Park, and then into Park Lane.

"When did you last see Max?" Luise asked, quickly adding, "I
mean before—"

"Friday afternoon. At the office. It was such a curious thing. He
left early, but oddly he returned about an hour later. He just came
back and sat down at his desk, the door to his private office kept
ajar. 'Can I do anything for you?' I asked. 'No, Edyth, I just want
to sit here for a while.' 'No phone calls?' I inquired. 'Just pretend I
never came back,' he replied. I started out, and he called after me,
'Edie, I don't ever think I've thanked you,' he said quietly. 'You
never had to, Max,' I told him. 'That's why, Edie—why I want to
thank you now.' "

She turned to Luise, her face lighted by a streetlight. Edyth was
an attractive woman. Luise only now recalled that she had been an
even more attractive young woman, no, she supposed Edyth had
been a girl when they first had met. How old was Edyth? Luise did
some fast arithmetic.

Edyth had come to work for Max directly from business school.
She had been no more than eighteen or nineteen at the time, with
a slim, lithe, almost boyish twig of a body, a shiny cap of short red
hair, no makeup, and magnificent pure green eyes webbed with
thick dark-brown lashes. If her face had been too angular, her nose
too broad, and her skin too splashed with freckles, those eyes had
still made her lovely.

That had been twenty-two years ago. Edyth was now over forty,
still trim, eyes even lovelier with their womanly depth, freckles

somehow gone or covered with makeup, and yet she was unmarried—alone. Luise reconsidered that. There was no way she could say for certain that Edyth had been and was alone. There could have been someone. No, Edyth was alone. Had been for years. It was a thing one woman could sense in another.

The car pulled forward, and Edyth rested her head back against the cushions. She sighed almost imperceptibly.

"Edyth, was there anyone—I mean—it's no secret that Max and I—" Luise began lamely.

"I guess so," she replied thinly.

"You weren't sure?"

"Oh, he was seeing some youngster. But it meant nothing. I really know that." She rested her hand on Luise's arm, her expression lost in the half-dark. "Don't worry, the press—no one will ever know."

"There was a girl then?"

"Her name was—*is* Bonnie. Bonnie something-or-other. She was—is a silly girl. About nineteen or so. I would guess. She was—was going to do a small part in the new film." She drew forward anxiously. "It is incredible! This is the first time I've thought about the picture. My God! There are so many decisions to be made!"

"Did they live together?" Luise persisted.

"No. Max was never that careless." She pressed in closer now, edging forward on her seat to make sure the glass partition between the chauffeur and themselves was securely closed. "You have to know this, I guess. She was with him when it happened. I only just found that out. They were in bed and— Oh, dear, I am sorry about this, Luise, but you can be sure no one will ever find out."

Luise sat back. She could hear Max's voice. The words filled her head, shutting out all other sounds: Edyth's heavy breath, the motor, the traffic. Years ago when a well-known actor had died in bed of a heart attack, but had not been alone, Max had said softly with that sly smile he used when pleased, "That lucky bastard. What a way to go!"

"Are you all right, Luise?"

"Yes. Yes." Then after a moment, meaning it: "That poor child."

"Don't waste your sympathy," Edyth snapped back.

The car pulled up in front of the hotel, and the door flew open, doorman and porters immediately on all sides.

"Don't get out, Edyth," Luise told her.

"What time tomorrow morning?" Edyth asked.

"Say nine?"

"That's not too early now?"

Luise smiled. "It's not too late, is it, Edyth?" she asked gently.

"This is a difficult time for you, Luise. I understand. I want you to be sure and always remember how much I understand."

"I do. I will." Luise allowed herself to be almost lifted out of the car by the chauffeur and the hotel staff. Then a thought occurred. "Edyth, do you have the key?"

"To the office?"

"No. To the apartment. Max's apartment."

Edyth stared up at her with some shock. "Why, yes—yes, of course, I do."

"May I have it?"

"Now?"

"If you have it with you."

Edyth fumbled in her purse, which seemed bottomless, but finally produced a key, which she handed to Luise.

"Thank you," Luise said weakly. "Thank you very much, Edyth." Then she quickly turned on her heels.

The manager was waiting for her as she entered the hotel, took her by the arm, solicitously led her to a side lift, and handed her several messages. He said nothing to her, his silence conveying his deepest condolences. He had already pushed the button for their floor when Luise sighted the familiar face across the quiet late-night lobby.

"Just one moment. One moment, please," she pleaded.

The manager instantly leaned on the Open Door button.

"I'm sorry. Thank you," Luise mumbled, as she got out of the lift and stood there staring ahead of her and up into the man's concerned and, yes, loving face.

"Burt," she said softly.

"Am I intruding?"

"No. *No.*" She took his outstretched hand and then looked up at him, her expression welcoming him back into her life.

"Are you too tired to walk?" he asked.

She just shook her head. They left the hotel and walked up the side street, saying nothing to each other for several moments.

"Where can we go?" he asked.

"Any restaurant, I guess," she said.

"No. That would be difficult, now and at this hour." He paused and turned to her. "I'm sorry, Sylvia is on the Coast, but I'm afraid the weekly poker game is still going strong at my place."

"How is Sylvia?"

"Oh, she's fine."

"That's good. And the children?"

"Well. Everyone is flourishing."

"You?" she asked gently.

"I'm a very successful man. Hasn't anyone told you that?" he replied with a trace of good humor in his voice.

"No one had to tell me. I read. And go to the movies," she added. "I'm happy for you, Burt. I hope it's at least part of what you wanted, and if so, I'm *most* happy for you."

"Would you come to my office? I can fix you an instant coffee there, and we can talk."

"Yes, of course."

"You are not too tired?"

"I am tired, but I would like to be with you for a time, a short time anyway," she replied honestly.

The minute she sat down on the couch in his office and kicked off her shoes and curled her legs beneath her, she was glad she had come. He made some hot coffee and then sat at his desk, not far from her, watching as she blew gently into the cup to cool the steaming liquid.

"Can I handle anything for you?" he asked.

"I don't know. Maybe. I won't be afraid to ask."

"Are you all right financially?"

"My goodness, yes!" Then with a twinge of bitterness: "Max was very good that way."

"I think he knew," Burt said evenly.

"About us?"

"Yes."

"I'm sure he did."

"You never told him?"

She looked over to him with mournful eyes. "He once said to me, 'If you've had an affair with Burt, don't tell me about it. It's the one truth I don't want to know.' " Remembering hurt her, and she put the coffee cup down on the table beside her and then nervously clenched her hands.

"Did it have anything to do with the split?"

"No. Nothing!" She got up as though to cross to him and then had to turn away. "I think I must be a very stupid and cruel—"

He was immediately beside her.

"Let me continue, Burt—yes, a *cruel* woman. You could not have harmed my life, you see? That is, my life with Max. But I know—oh, worse! I knew all along I had done something irreversible to yours." She faced him. "Forgive me, Burt. I loved him more than any woman should love a man, and the funniest thing is I am not the only woman to have done so, you can't understand this. I am aware of what you, the industry, the men and women he betrayed or took advantage of think—*oh, dear Lord—thought* of him, but Max . . . Max . . . was an exceptional man. I am oh, oh, so grateful I was able to share part of his life with him," she said squarely, "and yet I'm *relieved—my God . . . I . . . can't . . . believe . . . it*—yes, *relieved* he is dead." She turned away then, tears in her eyes, her shoulders trembling. "Oh, my messages. I haven't looked at them."

She moved away and to her pocketbook, which sat on the table next to her deserted coffee cup, and took out a fragrant handkerchief and the messages the hotel manager had given her. She dabbed at her eyes before she began to read them. Burt stood helplessly watching her. He was overwhelmed with feeling, well aware that she had aged; *yet,* he thought, *it suits her.*

"Tony called. I should call him back," she said.

"Use this phone."

"No, I don't think I can cope with it now. There's also a cable from Thea." She looked up at him with complete honesty. "She won't come. I'm sure of that. There was a terrible anger between them."

"You want to talk about it?"

"No."

He went over to her and took her narrow, high-cheekboned face in his large hands. She had allowed her naturally deep-auburn hair to turn gray, but it was still beautiful and fell voluptuously over his hands. "You never had to be alone," he said in a strong, positive voice.

"I chose it, Burt," she replied, not pulling away from him.

"And you don't have to be now," he continued.

She put her hands up to cover his tenderly. "Thank you." She broke away. "Thank you," she repeated with her head high and her shoulders braced. She was smiling. "There weren't many other messages."

"Max was not generally a well-liked man."

"I know." She never flinched. "A great many people thought he was a bastard."

"If it makes it any easier for you, one hell of a lot of people think the same about me."

She grinned that wise old grin of hers that always amused and pleased him. "I sure know how to pick them," she cracked.

"You sure do," he agreed.

She breathed deeply and reached for her pocketbook.

"Ready to go?" he asked.

"As ready as I'll ever be."

He took her by the arm and led her out of the office and down the corridor to the lift.

"Let's walk down," she said.

They went down the four flights at a healthy clip. Burt let them out, locked the door behind them, and went to flag down a taxi. She pulled back his arm.

"No. I think I'll walk."

"All right."

"Would you hate me if I said I want to walk back alone?" she asked.

He merely shook his head and laughed gently. "You are the damnedest woman, Luise," he commented.

"Yes, I know," she replied and then left him there as she marched off, lost to his sight within moments.

Chapter 4

The cable from Thea said: "Returning to New York immediately. Will call you on arrival. I love you. Thea."

Luise crumbled it and threw it into the wastebasket next to the small desk in her room. Then, reconsidering, she picked up the crumpled piece of paper, smoothing it out and placing an ashtray on it to iron the creases. It was a funny thing to do but the "I love you. Thea" seemed to bolster her spirits. She left it sitting where she could see the words.

The morning was crisp and azure blue, a totally unexpected June morning for London. It did little to lift the oppressive weight she felt as she dragged herself into the bathroom to shower and dress. In an hour Edyth would be downstairs to accompany her to the funeral home, but she had known since arising what else she had to do this morning. No, while sleeping, as her restive dreams had stirred the first thoughts in her. She could not recall exactly what the dream had been about. But she remembered—in fact, thought she could still hear—the dim echo of Max's voice, calling to her. Then she seemed to be opening doors. In the beginning they led nowhere, just great spaces filled with rising vapors, but when she had awakened, it had seemed she was about to open a door that would surely reveal to her some special and as yet unrevealed—what? Fact, she surmised.

She would go to Max's apartment as soon as she was dressed and had had some coffee. She would go alone—she instinctively felt that was one of the conditions, the terms, that her dream imposed—and further, she would not tell anyone she was going. (That meant Edyth, of course!)

Her absolute conviction that she was doing the right thing remained with her as she waited for room service, then a taxi and even as the taxi drew up before the building that had been Max's home the last two years, two years she had not shared, a building she had never entered, and a street, though she knew London exceptionally well, she was not aware existed.

It was a cul-de-sac off Kensington Church Street, a curious site for Max who in the past had always leaned toward—no, *insisted* upon—more elegant addresses. The short street itself was a surprise and a delight, and Max's building (a block of—Luise counted the names on the mailboxes—nine apartments) was at the far end. There was a garden dividing the two sides of the cul-de-sac. No cars could enter. It was really lovely, quiet, set apart, almost suburban in feeling.

She had not been able to contradict Burt the night before. No, Max was not a bastard. Max had been—God, the past tense had set in like rigor mortis!—a very neurotic, complex, deep, profoundly deep man. He had also been exciting, completely unforgettable, a force of life. She had tried from time to time, if not to forget the man, at least to weaken his hold on her. She had not succeeded.

Max had used the truth like a whip. Perhaps that was what made others consider him a bastard. It was after all *his* truth, not theirs, and she could never make him face the fact that unless you were dealing with a positive, like science or mathematics, truth was terribly ephemeral, since no two people ever saw things in the same light. But his was always self-flagellation, and it did not have its origins in masochism, not intentionally at least, but in an obsession of Max's that he had become (his words) "an honest historian of human emotions." "Honest" thereby being the key word, for it was *his* honesty or how he saw people and interpreted their reactions.

More than once she had heard people say, "There is no excuse for Max except his talent." Well, Max was one of the great film innovators of his time, one reason being that Max's own persona always became the essence of each of his films. He had made every Seaman film a step in his autobiography. One had to sit through all his films (except for one or two done for the studio—but not before terrible pressure—to honor the contract he later sued to break) to get the full, almost larger than life portrait of Max as an artist—*and as a man.*

It was curious that at this moment and for the first time a festival of his films was under way. The theater owner had come to her, and she had passed on his suggestion to Edyth to discuss with Max. For a year now this was how she and Max had communicated. Max had sent back word that it was agreeable to him. Luise was then invited to organize it. First instinct made her withdraw, but in the end she had lent her insight into what film should follow which, as their filming sequence did not necessarily follow, in fact seldom followed, the order of self-revealment of Max as man or artist.

Max was always concerned—personally and in his work—with ordinary people. He considered himself an ordinary man, and could never strive for baroque backgrounds—as, for instance, Burt did—but functioned best and most creatively in commonplace settings.

Some reviewer once said that Max's dedication to the common man in commonplace settings but in uncommon situations made his a cinema of the voyeur. Luise knew he had been mistaken. The festival would reveal that. Max was instead using film as one used a psychoanalyst's sessions. He was baring his most intimate self. A blatant sign of his megalomania and so perhaps to some of his colleagues though most suffered the same "disease" not to be admired.

But in spite of what Max believed, he was *not* an ordinary man. He was the opposite, a rare and extraordinary man (as were all his film protagonists) with extraordinary feelings, and the only thing ordinary in his life had been his backgrounds or settings. And because of this and because of Max's great talent for *seeing* a story, he always brought a brilliant touch of insight, of reality (Max would have said "truth"), to each of his films. And they were *his,* especially once he broke his studio contract as a staff writer and began to produce and direct his own screenplays as an independent.

Luise had to look on the mailbox for the number of the apartment. The building had three floors, Max's apartment occupying the top floor by itself, and the hallway had been decorated differently from the communal ones on the lower floors. There was a French hand-blocked fabric on the walls, alive with yellow flowers in an all-over design. Unusual cherrywood trestles lined in copper and filled abundantly with living greens stood against the baseboards. Next to the door itself was a unique and charming white wrought-iron umbrella stand that mushroomed up and out in the shape of a tree and was studded with pegs meant to hold coats and hats. There were finely etched black and white lithographs of famous composers, surprisingly all French and probably taken from an old book.

It was an inviting anteroom, but it was not in Max's style and did not reveal his hand. It vibrated with the nuances of a woman's touch—but not Edyth's—a woman with individual, though somehow too cultivated a taste.

The key was not an easy one to work. Luise tried it in several positions before the door gave way and she could open it and enter the apartment.

The entry and living room contained the same strong female vibrations. It was done in clear yellows and true whites with warm fruitwood furniture. There was a collection of antique glass set on glass shelves in the window that Luise could now see overlooked the yard behind the building. It successfully let in the light and still blocked out the unpleasant view. The other windows all overlooked the gardens and brought a melee of color and movement into the room, as the leaves stirred with the breezes.

A portrait dominated the room. It hung over the fruitwood mantel against a clear white wall and was subtly framed in antique white so that your eye moved instantly to the incredibly young woman, her long, straight mahogany hair shining beneath a full moon, her slim body sheathed in white satin. She seemed incongruously to have stepped out of the underbrush in some primitive land. A jungle of Gauguin-like greens backed her. Her feet were bare, and it looked as if they had been painted to intimate she was about to flee.

Luise did not walk all the way into the room. There was a door to the left of the entry. It was slightly ajar, and Luise could make out the shape of a bed. The shades were drawn in that room, and it was quite dark. She pushed the door open and stood there a moment, accustoming her eyes to the dimness.

There were massive Max-like pieces. A clutter of papers and books and newspaper clippings were strewn over the desk. Resting on the floor and propped up against one wall were various cross plots, a familiar, welcomed sight. They were strips of cardboard on slatted boards printed boldly with all the scenes by number and all the characters who must appear in each scene. Hours, sometimes days and weeks were spent moving those slats of paper about so that an actor's work could be lined up in a way that presented the greatest saving for the production.

The bedroom was very Max. And something else. There on the table next to his bed (his side obviously, for the telephone was also there and the pad and pencil he always left close by in case he should get an idea during the night), there was a framed picture of Thea. Luise sighed gratefully. The rift between father and daughter hadn't been irreconcilable then.

Luise closed the door securely behind her so that the rest of the apartment was shut out. The room was now close and very dark, and walking on tiptoes (she did feel she was intruding), she opened the drawn blinds and let in the light, the day, the living.

She could now see the objects obscured or unidentifiable before. The bed had not been made up since the discovery of Max's body and the covers were thrown back, the linen bunched in some places and pulled loose in others. The pillows had been tossed onto the center of the large bed.

Now that she was here, she wasn't sure why she had come or what she wanted or thought she would find. With the door sealing off the rest of the apartment, she did feel less an intruder, but an intruder all the same. Even so, she made her way to the bed, telling herself she just wanted to get a closer look at the picture of Thea, to see if it was signed in Thea's own hand, but the first thing she did was lean over to read the few words she could now see were written on the bedside pad in Max's precise and even script, the lead pencil having been pressed down hard. The four words inscribed seemed to form one exclamation mark. They read: "The game of truth!" He had underlined it three times and made the exclamation point with the broad side of the pencil so that its thickness made it look as if two such marks had banded together in a show of strength.

The words had an immediate impact on Luise. In fact, she was rather shaken by them and the intensity with which they had obviously been written. She felt weak in the knees and started to sit down on the edge of the bed, but then a reflex brought her to her feet again, for it seemed somehow disrespectful to sit on the bed in which Max had just died. Luise stumbled across the room and to Max's desk chair.

To anyone else, the phrase would mean nothing more than some philosophical comment that had come to Max's mind, but to Luise it was terribly clear what Max had been thinking not more than a brief few hours before he had died.

The game of truth had been quite simply exactly that: a game where any number could play. One person at a time would mount the "witness chair" (usually a straight-backed kitchen chair), and all the others would then have the right, in turn, to throw questions at the one in the "box." No matter how personal the content, the "witness" was obliged to answer with absolute truth.

They had played it for the last time two years after they had married and just before Max had been offered his "opportunity." It was not difficult for her to reconstruct the entire evening, so vivid was it still in her mind. It had been such a violent and frightening experience that neither of them had ever willingly exposed themselves to the game in public again, although Luise knew Max had often employed it through the years with her, attempting to intimidate her into revealing the truth "for the good of herself," he would say.

She had thought about the game when Max was in the witness box—this time for real—in Washington.

In the past two years the release from Max's game of truth was one of the few compensations for her being alone. Max had never faced the fact that there are times when the truth, *our own truth,* is simply too painful for us to face without self-destruction. To survive, one has to lie, mostly to oneself. That's how it was with Luise, with most people, but not with Max. The search for the truth, the battle to expose it (always *his* truth, of course), was what had kept Max alive and out there fighting and creating. It was at the very base of his monumental talent.

They had been living in Greenwich Village for nearly two years when Max managed to obtain the assignment to cover the film strike in Hollywood. They had, however, just signed a new lease on their apartment, and to avoid litigation before they left, or worse, the possibility of their possessions being "detained" in lieu of the rent they could not pay, they had been packing things up and letting friends take them singly, to avoid suspicion, out of the apartment and store them for them, so that by this particular evening (they were to leave in three days) the apartment's two rooms were barren except for one kitchen chair too humble to save, the double bed, which they had regretfully decided they would have to leave behind, and their suitcases, which they were using until departure as tables and chairs.

Burt and Sylvia had come over to pay their "last respects." Burt was an apprentice in the agency business at the time and though his take-home pay was not grand or his position exactly executive, he was already showing the enterprising spirit that would make him the success he would later become.

All four were young political animals. It was difficult for Luise to recall when she stopped being a political animal, when the apathy had set in, when she first noticed the same apathy setting in on the others. She was certain, though, that it was many years after—knew their involvement had lasted at least through the McCarthy period and into the first years of the blacklist. But that evening in the Village, when they all were young, she could never have believed that such a time of political apathy would ever come.

Sylvia held the only party card at the time and was the most militant. Burt and Max joined the party later when they were all in Hollywood, but Luise somehow never did get around to it. She put it off purposely she was sure because, though she could intellectually accept party membership, she found anything of an organizational nature repellant on a personal level. When the children were school age, she was even unable to join the PTA, and though for years after she and Max were married, she had planned to take time out to become a Jew, so that for the children's sake she and Max would be of one faith, she could never do that either because organized religion disturbed her.

Max, of course, was not a practicing Jew, professed, in fact, that he was an atheist. But regardless, Luise felt his faith was stronger than hers. (Her parents were Mormons, and when Luise left Salt Lake City at sixteen, she was confident that she had left all that behind her.) Max always claimed he was an American, not a Jew. Still, in all the years she had lived with him, she could not recall his ever working on Yom Kippur though there were many Fourth of July weekends in which he never left his typewriter. And he insisted Tony be circumcised for his health and welfare. He scorned such rituals as a Bar Mitzvah but, after Tony was thirteen, would always answer when Tony came to him for advice with, "Well, now you are a man you should be finding your own answers." And when Burt legally changed his name *for business reasons* from Weintraub to Winters, he had been incensed for weeks.

That had been the year previous to the evening of the last game of truth, and Max had by then been reconciled to Burt's name changing but not to many other things now showing themselves in Burt's personality.

It had all begun innocently enough, at least for the personalities involved who insisted on conflict in every meeting as assiduously as a producer insists on it in every film scene.

"Merwin Bibbs is having a helluva time getting milk for his kid," Max began. "Why don't you get one of Sylvia's friends out on the Coast to give him a job?"

"Merwin's a loser," Burt had replied.

"What the hell kind of a remark is that? He's an intelligent man. I've seen some good writing he's done," Max snapped back.

"He's a desperate man. Always will be. Desperate men compromise," Burt answered quietly.

"He's a writer, a *good* writer, and you're an agent, an *ambitious* son of a bitch agent at that, but both of you are supposed to be intelligent. Get him milk for his kid, and he'll stop being desperate," Max stated.

"I understand Burt's point of view completely," Sylvia interrupted. "The party is having the same reservations about Merwin. We certainly can't afford a desperate man."

"What do you think your husband is then, Sylvia? He is the goddamnedest most desperate man I have ever known! The only difference between Burt and Merwin is that Merwin is desperate to survive and Burt is desperate to succeed, and by his own admission desperate men compromise. Before you let your sacred party take your husband in, you had better figure out if they can afford his kind of desperation—because, baby, that's the first-class, go-for-broke kind!"

"Max." Luise gave him a restraining look.

Max got up, the anger seeming to have been throttled, a look of mild amusement on his face. Luise recognized the signs. He was now playing a scene.

"Okay. Okay, Burt. You say that there are two teams—winners and losers, eh?"

"That's right, two teams."

"And you're a winner, Burt?"

"Damned right."

"And so am I, because you wouldn't be my agent, my *friend*, if you didn't think I was."

"Max!" Luise chided.

"You're always so self-referent," Sylvia commented dryly.

"Right, Burt?" Max prodded.

"Sure, Max—right," Burt said easily.

Max smiled. "That's what I like about you, Burt. I mean sincerely, a man knows exactly where he stands with you."

"I think this could grow unpleasant," Luise said, "and since this is our last evening together for who knows how long, let's not quarrel."

"We're not quarreling," Burt assured her.

"Of course not. We are civilized, intelligent men in quest of the truth," Max said.

"Which is?" Luise asked.

"If in fact there is such a thing as winners and losers and if so which team is Burt on and which team am I on."

"Please don't, Max."

He ignored her.

Luise turned to Sylvia for assistance. "Sylvia . . ."

Sylvia balanced herself on an upended suitcase. "I think this promises to be very interesting," she said, smiling.

Max carried in the kitchen chair and set it down in the center of the empty room, white chips of paint flaking and falling to the bare floor as he did. "Have a seat, Burt?" he beckoned.

Burt sat down without hesitation. He was enjoying the turn of events as much as Max was. "Only one chair?" he asked Max.

"That's all that's left."

"Use a suitcase."

"I'll wait my turn." Max smiled.

"No. This time we're both on the hot box at one time."

"Okay, but I'll stand."

"Like hell. It's a psychological advantage."

"Why would anything be an advantage in a game of truth?"

Burt stood up. "We'll both use suitcases."

"Agreed."

They moved two suitcases facing each other and about five feet apart.

"And the girls don't play," Max said.

"That's not fair," Sylvia complained.

"A wife's testimony isn't worth a shit anyway," Max commented.

"Testimony?" Luise questioned. "Now promise, Max, *promise* this is to remain a game." But the men were too busy tossing a coin. Max won.

"Why did you change your name?" he asked.

"Hell, you know! Business reasons."

"More American? Easier to succeed?"

"Look at me, Max. Take a good look at me. Anyone going to think I'm not Jewish with *my* face?"

"Most of your business takes place on the telephone though, Burt. And then, of course, on the screen—"

"Agents don't get screen credits."

"But you don't plan on being an agent very long, do you, Burt?"

"Not everyone wants to be a writer."

"You didn't answer the question."

Burt sat there for a long and thoughtful moment. "Eventually I might like to produce," he said quietly.

"That's news to me!" Sylvia chimed in.

"And when that happens and I have no doubt it will happen, you don't want any obstacles, any obstacles at all, do you, Burt?"

"Winters has a ring to it, that's all."

"A *winning* ring?"

"Yeah. A winning ring." Burt was grinning now. "Burton C. Winters," he said. "It has a kind of class."

"Where the hell does the *C* come from?"

"I just invented it for my new cards," he replied as he handed one to Luise, who was standing behind him.

"Lining up all the help you can get, aren't you, Burt? A fine Anglo-Saxon name, only winners on your rostrum, and a political schism that keeps labor *and* management happy at the same time."

"Just a minute!" Sylvia shouted.

Max turned on her. "Wake up, Sylvia! Don't you know your husband is only on your side when it means he can win over the artists, the talents who are also represented in your ranks, but switches like those new razors—click, click—when he is within even *smelling* distance of a movie mogul's stooge? And we all know the studio heads are a tidy bunch of rabid reactionaries."

"Burt, speak up!" Sylvia commanded.

"I have to figure out the question. I think it went back to 'lining up all the help I can get.' That's show biz, Max."

"That's fear, baby. Desperation. Not enough inside you that says you can make it on your own. You're hung up on the fear of being a loser. I've known you a lot of years, Burt. You used to have to prove you were the bravest kid on the block, then the best lover."

"Why did *you* go to Spain?" Burt countered.

"I'm a true American. I believe in freedom and justice for all."

"How about justice for your landlord?"

Max laughed. "He's a reactionary bastard," he said.

"So not entitled to freedom and justice?"

"Sure he is . . ."

"But your welfare comes first?"

"Not my welfare, my talent."

"You're damned sure of that talent, aren't you?"

"You bet your ass!"

"Ever doubt it?"

"Never."

"But there have been times when it has been tough to feed that talent, hasn't there?"

"Look around you." He grinned. "Brother, can you spare a dime?" he asked sarcastically.

"You're not ashamed to ask, are you?"

"Not in the least," Max snapped.

"Even a bit arrogant?"

"I don't think the world owes me a living, but I do think I have to do what I can to keep myself going until I can write my talent into the open."

"How about marrying to get support for yourself?"

"Burt!" Sylvia warned.

"Luise is lending me these years. She'll get it back with full interest."

"And Spain? And if you join the party?"

"Experiences."

"But no commitments, because you are committed first and foremost to yourself—your talent. You're not even *really committed* to Luise. It's all to feed your talent, isn't it?"

"Burt, stop this," Sylvia begged.

"You said you were going to enjoy this, Sylvia, so just relax," Burt told her.

Luise had seated herself on the floor and was looking up at Max, waiting for his answer in stony silence.

"If Luise had a child, I would be committed because that child would be a part of me."

"Committed to the child or Luise?" Burt pressed on.

"To the child. But then the child would be part of Luise, too."

"And so your future?"

"Yeah."

"Your talent, eh?"

"Well, in that case, in the event of a child, *my balls*."

"Cocksure?"

"That's it, baby. *Cocksure*."

Luise had risen from the floor and disappeared into the other room, but neither man had noticed her departure. Burt was clapping ecstatically.

"Well, that's it, Max! I win! That's a winner you see—someone who's *cocksure*." He stood up then and leaned in close to Max. "You're a natural, Max. No way for you to go but up. Me—I was born a loser, but I had one thing others didn't. I knew it, and I concentrated every day of my life on surrounding myself with winners, beating the rap. And I'm going to do the impossible, Max. I'm going to become a winner. That takes a special kind of guts. A kind of guts that the Merwin Bibbs of the world don't have."

"Sit down," Max said quietly. Burt did not move. "Sit down, Burt. The rules of the game, remember?"

Burt sat down, but something had happened to him in the last thirty seconds. The skin on his face had grown tight as if drawn taut over a skull, and his lips were like two scars pressed tightly together to become two blade-thin white ridges.

"Burt, are you sick?" Sylvia asked, but it was as though he did not see or hear her. He was looking through dimly seeing eyes at Max. Sylvia grew furious. "I'll walk right out of here, Burt, if you allow him to ask you one more question!" she threatened.

"Yeah, you're tough, Burt, but are you tough enough to be the loser who wins? In the end, I mean?"

"In the end?"

"Sure, Burt," Max went on in a confidential tone, "when winning finally loses its sweet taste."

"That time won't come."

"Sh-it"— Max drew out the word as if it were a caress—"you know it will. And when that happens, what will you be left with, Burt?"

Sylvia hadn't left. She was now behind Burt, stroking his shoulder and whispering to him under her breath, "Burt . . . Burt. . . ."

"A loser," he said in a brittle voice.

"Yeah, but this breaks the ass out of your theory, baby, because that's what I'm going to be left with, too. *Me.* Maxwell Isaac Seaman. The born winner. The natural. Got to happen, Burt, because you can't win *all* your life. The odds are against it. Finally, up comes snake eyes." He smiled easily and then leaned over and patted Burt on the knee. "Sorry, fellow, but there aren't any winners in life. In the final chapter we're all losers." He got up then and stretched, as if completely unaffected by Burt's ghostlike pallor and Sylvia's face of mourning and the position of the bedroom door which meant Luise was listening.

"Lu," he called, "how about some coffee for our guests?"

"No, thank you," Sylvia managed as she helped Burt to his feet and then started across the room to the front door with him. She paused and turned back to Max once to venomously spit out the words "You bastard!"

"Ain't it the truth." Max grinned just before the door closed and his guests were gone.

The bareness of the room made Luise and the bed easy to find even in the dark of a bedroom without windows and so without moon or stars. She did not move or speak, but he knew she was still awake. His hands, his beautiful gentle, tender, feeling hands moved under the covers and over her nakedness.

"Don't try to understand me, Lu," he whispered in her ear as he held her body close to his, "just love me."

That night Anthea had been conceived, and when they left for the Coast and a new life together, they went as a family, and so for the first time in her life with Max, Luise knew a great security. He would never leave her, for she would be the mother of *his* child.

Luise thought she had heard a door open and then close, and so when she glanced up and saw the young woman there, she was not startled.

"You're Bonnie," she said softly.

"Yes, you're Luise," the girl answered. She looked as she did in the portrait, the sophisticated stance, the naïve face. Even her voice, which was well trained and carefully modulated and out of the finest finishing and theater schools in England, was to be expected. For a curious moment, though the two young women looked nothing alike, Luise thought it could have been Thea standing so surely and proudly in the doorway.

Luise got up.

"You don't have to leave," Bonnie assured her.

"I do. In fact, I have . . . someplace I must go. Someone is picking me up."

"I see."

Luise crossed the room to the door. She still held the key to the apartment in her hand, and as she passed Bonnie, she gave it to her. "I'm sorry. I think I may have been intruding," she said gently.

The girl smiled uneasily. "That was true of most people in Max's life," she said slowly.

"I'd like only one thing," Luise said.

"Yes, of course."

"The picture next to the bed."

Bonnie went over and brought it directly back and handed it to Luise.

"Thank you."

The girl didn't reply. Luise started out and into the front entry.

"Where is the funeral to be?" the girl called after her.

"I don't know. I'm not sure yet," Luise said nervously. She rushed to the front door, which she opened, and then turned around and glanced back one more time at Max's bedroom, the door now held open by Bonnie. "I'll let you know," she told her and then quickly went out, the door slamming by itself as she raced down the stairs and out into a blinding flood of sunlight.

There was a taxi just letting a passenger out, and Luise hailed it. On the ride back to the hotel she held Thea's picture facedown on her lap, both hands folded upon it. There were tears of gratitude on her face. The picture wasn't signed by Thea, but Max had had it by his bed. Thea had been there when he awoke. Thea had been there when he closed his eyes. *Thea.* A part of them both—the eternal flame of their love.

Chapter 5

"No calls," Burt ordered Shirley as he went past her and into his office, where, though not yet nine o'clock, five men waited for him to set into motion the meeting he had had Shirley call together at eight that same morning.

Henry greeted him at the door, walked with him to his desk, and then stood to his left beside him as he sat down. Sandy was in a chair to his right. Merwin, Gus, and Milton (who was never known to have been called Milt or Miltie) were lined up on the couch facing him. The air in the room was already dense with cigarette smoke and the tables sweating from the still-warm bases of the coffee mugs.

"What's up?" Sandy asked.

"I'm not going to ask an easy thing of you fellows," Burt began.

"Oh, Christ! He's expecting us to make a minyan!" Gus interrupted.

"Not that. Not that at all. But it does have to do with Max," Burt continued.

Merwin got up from the couch and went over to the window and attempted to appear disinterested in what else might be said inside the room, focusing his glance outside on the rear view of Piccadilly Circus. His face was flushed, though, and no one in the room was convinced that he was not listening, hanging on every word that was being exchanged. Still, he remained looking out and away until the very end, but Burt seemed totally unaware of his protest.

"Max never really considered himself a Jew," Burt continued. "Once he thought of himself first as an American, later as a writer, in the end as a man. But never a Jew. A minyan would be bad taste."

"Anyway, there aren't enough of us. It takes ten," Sandy commented.

Henry smiled. "You and Sammy Davis."

They laughed.

"The press is going to give complete coverage to this funeral," Burt prophesied.

"You've spoken to Luise? She's planning to bury him here?" Henry asked confidentially, so the others could not hear.

"I don't know if his widow has made a decision, but it seems logical he will be buried right here where he was happy these last years," Burt went on. "And for her and for our own public relations—I mean the American film industry here in London—we should make a good front."

"What exactly do you mean by a 'good front,' Burt?" Milton asked cautiously.

"Every burial requires pallbearers. Six is a legitimate number, and that's what we are. I'm expecting each of you to volunteer your services," he stated in a rather commanding tone.

"You don't expect us to agree to that?" Sandy questioned.

"Not without some inner searching, of course. I'll grant you, each of you men has a legitimate gripe against Max." Burt noticed the reaction of each of the men. "Well, maybe 'gripe' isn't the right word." He smiled expansively. "After all, you fellows are the writers—I'm only a producer." He was conscious of their averted glances and cleared his throat loudly to recall their attention, winning all but Merwin's.

"Granted, Max was an informer," he continued, "but not many in the world still remember that. Damn right, and damned right you do and the others he named do, and their families. All together about fifty or sixty people, I would guess. Hardly an overwhelming majority. The others, as they look at that front-page obituary"—he paused, smiling again—"I wish Max could have seen *that*."

" 'Unfriendly witness,' they said," Milton complained. "What publicity office issued that barefaced lie?"

"Unfriendly?" Sandy sneered. "Hell, he was so all Southern friendly he let the committee stick it right up his ass!"

"Gentlemen," Henry interrupted, "Burt was speaking."

"As I was saying, anyone outside your closed ranks is only going to notice his credits. Now, some of those films are still being exhibited in theaters around the world and still bringing in revenue—the later ones for International, who I don't need to remind you is responsible for the maids your wives have and the private schools your kids attend."

"Yeah," said Gus dryly, "and my alimony and child support checks."

"I hope, Burt, you're not saying what I think you are saying," Milton said, his face twitching somewhat nervously. "If so, that is tantamount to blackmail. As Tom Jefferson said, 'It behooves every man who values liberty of conscience for himself, to resist . . . ' "

"Oh, for God's sake, Milton, Burt isn't invading your liberty of conscience," Henry said with irritation.

"There are two ways to approach this," Burt began again. "You can protest Max's action before the committee twenty-odd years ago by not appearing at his funeral at all if you want, or—"

"Or?" Milton prodded apprehensively.

"Or, since the man is dead, you can remember the talent instead."

"As you say, still being seen through the courtesy of International Films, L-T-D," Gus said sharply.

"That's right Gus. But Max *was* a great talent. One of the greatest our industry has ever known. How many Pantheon artists have films had, after all? And of those how many were not only writers *and* directors but Americans as well?" Burt countered.

"And Jewish," Sandy commented.

"What the hell does that have to do with it?" Burt snapped.

"I'm remembering a famous story about Ben Hecht and David Selznick. Hecht was soliciting for funds for a Zionist cause as he always was and, after being turned down by all the movie big boys, went to Selznick who told him he didn't want to have anything to do with a Jewish political cause because he was an American, not a Jew and it would be silly of him to suddenly pretend to be a Jew with some sort of full-blown Jewish psychology, and Hecht challenged him to name three men, telephone them, and ask them if they considered him a Jew or an American and if even one of them answered 'an American,' Selznick would win. All of them said he was a Jew."

"That's as irrelevant as you can get," Henry commented.

"Don't you mean *irreverent*, Henry?" Gus asked.

"Henry means he thinks we are going off the track," Burt said. "I'm not sure. All right, let's add Jew, meaning belonging to a minority, which all of us in this room do."

"Not me, baby." Sandy smiled. "Don't you know anything about what's happening out there? One day soon you're going to look through that window Merwin's staring out and you know what you'll see? Black, baby. A black world!"

"You scare the shit out of me, baby," Gus said sarcastically. "The absolute *shit*."

"That *is* irrelevant," Burt commented. "Let's get back to the point."

Merwin turned into the room now, staring at them all. "I'll tell you what the point is because I'm the only one in this room who has nothing to lose. You see, Burt, I'm old, older than any of you here, and I know now I have nothing more to hope for, nothing at stake, because just before I left the house this morning, I got a call from the front office that I was being taken off the film and that Milton is going to continue on in my place, which means no screen credit in my own name at long last—because I know very well, though I broke the back of the script and Milton's job will be smooth sailing from here on out, that my work will be disguised to assure Milton his credit and—"

Milton jumped to his feet. "So help me, God, Merwin, this is the first I've heard—"

"As I was saying," Merwin continued, "and what makes you think it matters if you were told, Milton? As I was saying, the point is—"

"Let Burt make his own point," Henry told him sharply.

"Christ, Henry!" Merwin shouted. "You are such a cock-sucker, really you are! Don't you ever get your fill?"

Burt stood up, but his voice was calm and his hand steady as he raised it for order. "All right, Merwin," he said quietly. "What is the point?"

"You're a company man, Burt," Merwin replied quickly, "and that company is International. I can see you going into the next big board meeting, smiling, saying, 'It was nothing, boys, but I managed another fine public relations story for dear old International.' " Merwin had to breathe deeply for air to refill his lungs.

"If that were so, Mer, why would I include you? You were one of the ten. You the public remembers," Burt said—still calm, still in control.

"You never meant to include me, Burt. I realize that now. It was Shirley's error. You knew what my answer would be."

"What is it, Mer?"

"No. No dice. And you knew the others would all have to vote yes, no matter what kind of show they put on, because they need you, Burt, and you see they are only starting as compromised men and I have nothing left to compromise, haven't for years."

For a moment it seemed as though Merwin might cry. He heaved a deep sigh, and his body shook with it. The others in the room stood there, not knowing what to do, wishing they were elsewhere. Then Merwin walked across the room and, never looking to either side or glancing back when he reached the door, opened it and went out.

"I'm sorry that happened," Burt said. "I'm fond of Merwin. I'll call him as soon as I can have lunch with him."

"I really didn't know—" Milton began.

"I didn't think the boys would pass the word for a week or so. I planned to tell you both myself. Merwin's work was old-hat, old-fashioned. I wanted to help him, give him this opportunity, but it looks like it backfired," Burt continued.

He sat down again and looked around the room. "OK, fellows, are you with me or not?"

There was a long and painful silence that overtook the room. Merwin's situation was all too clear to these men who knew the business and Burt too well. The first draft of the script that Merwin had done was a thankless task, an adaptation of a complicated and uncinematic book that had nonetheless made the best-seller list and so because of its presold title had been purchased by Burt. Few writers could have been tempted to do the first treatment because no studio chief would have thought much of it, and the few writers who might have tackled it came at a high price. Merwin was paid minimum according to English scales (lower than American) and accepted it because of the hope that his name might reappear on the screen.

They knew as well that Milton would now add his know-how into a sensible but not yet fully cinematic script for more than Merwin's fee but less than standard. Burt would then hire one of the top writers around to do a polish for a good deal more than Milton did his piece, but because it was only a polish and could be done quickly, much less than the top writer's normal fee. And so the script went into the budget, even having had three writers on it, for much less than the accepted 5 percent of the film's budget usually allotted to the story.

It was one of the tricks that had ingratiated Burt so with the big boys.

And Milton was not displeased to know he was going on to the screenplay. He had hoped as much, though he had been honest when he said he didn't know the decision had been made. Even a shared credit on a Burton C. Winters production meant a few years' employment because Burt's films were *always* a success and every other producer in the business hoped some of it might rub off and so gambled on hiring his film writers.

"Well?" Henry asked. "You heard Burt."

"I say yes," Milton ventured. "Burt's right. He was a helluva talent. I take my hat off to him there."

"Sure," Gus agreed. "And Luise is one good woman. Wish I'd been that lucky."

"There's still time," Sandy kidded him.

"You, Sandy?" Burt interrupted.

"I'm with you." He looked Burt straight in the eye. "But I don't kid you or myself. I'm with you because I'm a greedy bastard who's wasted too much time already."

Chapter 6

Dr. Wolverly David, Wolfie to those who knew him even slightly, was a man who was confident of his attraction for women. He was certainly a man of considerable charm and even possessed tolerably good looks. He was tall and broad-shouldered and even at fifty had no paunch developing below his waist. He was constantly on a fitness course and spent a good deal of time in private gymnasiums. He much admired his nude leanness in the mirror in his bathroom, and though he enjoyed eating and drinking, he carried this image of himself in the corner of his brain as one would carry his driver's license in a sealed compartment of a car, knowing if it were abused, he might lose it completely.

His dark hair had begun to thin, and so he combed it forward, Caesar-fashion, and assisted the illusion that he was a man with a thick head of hair by growing full sideburns and then bleaching them to a distinguished gray. He had excellent even teeth, a Romanesque profile, and a clear and tanned complexion, by compliments of a nightly sun lamp treatment. The one flaw in his otherwise tidy good looks were his rather beady dark eyes, which were too small for the other features on his face and set too close together. He was not a careless man (after all, he had performed hundreds of abortions without serious consequences to either himself or the ladies involved) and he could see this flaw in his appearance and so he was most often seen—even on drearier days, even in the evening and especially in restaurants, clubs, and cocktail parties—wearing tinted glasses to obscure the defect.

His medical education had been both mediocre and provincial, his personal background distinctly middle-middle-class (his father had been an insurance salesman and his mother the daughter of an accountant). There had never been anyone famous or infamous on either side of his family tree.

He began performing abortions when he was still in medical school (he held each time that he was performing a truly humanitarian act) and considered himself something of an expert. Someone rather high up the executive ladder at International had found need for his very discreet services, and so his career was established and his practice guaranteed. He was put on the International payroll and thereupon called upon for abortions, the procuring of pills for addicted stars and personnel, for minor production ailments like sore throats, black eyes, and indigestion, and for such crises that called for a physician's signature on a health certificate for insurance purposes or on a death certificate for due process of maintaining a good studio image.

Edyth had asked him to come along just in case Luise found the ordeal too taxing and needed either reviving or calming down. Nine in the morning was a bit early for Wolfie. Nonetheless, he stood by the open door of the sleek black limousine in front of Claridges, smiling encouragingly as he helped Luise into the rear of the car, where Edyth already waited, and then got in himself.

He sat on the jump seat that faced her and took her hands.

"Edyth called me, but how fortunate. I have been racking my brains trying to figure out how I could be of some service to you," he said with a sincerity that convinced even himself.

"Thank you, Wolfie," she said quietly.

The chauffeur was driving slowly as if he were already leading the funeral procession. Luise leaned back and closed her eyes. After a few minutes of silence Edyth and Wolfie concluded she was asleep and began whispering.

Edyth wore a black silk dress, its severity broken only by a single strand of pearls. She had a black chiffon scarf over her hair, and as she spoke, she pushed it back, and it slipped down to form a collar of black chiffon, making her fair skin slightly gray from its reflection. "Luise is under great tension. I do hope this won't be too much for her to cope with," she whispered.

"Don't worry about our Luise," he replied.

"If it's too much, she doesn't have to go into the *room*. She can just talk with the director in his office."

"Yes, of course. No need to overexcite herself."

They were silent for a time. The car was being driven so slowly and smoothly that it seemed to lack motion entirely.

"We'll never get there," Edyth said with some irritation.

"You're not overwrought, are you, Edyth? Why, of course! This has been a terrible trial and a responsibility for you. I'll give you a prescription for some tranquilizers," he ventured.

"I'll take it, but I don't think I'll need to use it." She leaned forward, her voice even more faint. "I'm worried about Luise, that's all. I saw Max yesterday. I had to come. It may sound strange, but I knew Max was willing me to do so. We had this thing between us, you know? I always sensed when he needed me. It was a very special communication. He never had a sister, but I felt like *that*. Still do. Like a kindred spirit. A twin. A part of each other, you see?"

"Well, of course, you've worked together over twenty years."

"Yes. The best years of his life. Creating, that is."

"You were saying?"

"What?" She seemed distracted. "Oh, I went to see him yesterday. The coffin is too small. It's awful. Narrow. He looked all cramped . . ." Closer. Lower yet. "Do you think he had any pain, Wolfie?"

"Some. But only a moment."

Both of them darted looks at Luise, but she hadn't flicked an eyelash.

"Oh, God!" Edyth moaned, drawing all the blood from her lips as she did.

"I'm going to speak to Luise about having a proper casket flown over from New York. Or maybe Sweden. They *must* have large ones there. After all, all Swedes are tall."

She sat back then and clenched the window strap with her immaculately white gloved hand as she stared out the window, her eyes fixed but not seeing.

Wolfie shifted nervously to the other jump seat and sat with his back to the two women and looked straight ahead and through the glass partition.

Both of them heard Luise stir and were at immediate attention, but Luise had merely turned to one side and covered her face with her bare and noticeably unmanicured hand.

The director met them at the front door. He was an immediately likable little man with merry blue eyes and a handclasp that was vital and sincere. His name was Mr. Danby, and he led them through a flower-filled entranceway into a corridor with flocked paper on its high walls and fresh white paint on its ceiling.

"This is my office," he said, standing aside so that they would enter first.

Edyth and Wolfie went inside, but Luise stood indecisively in the doorway and then turned to Mr. Danby. "I think I would like to see my husband," she said quietly.

Edyth had heard her and turned back to her with surprise. "I'll go with you, of course," she said.

"I will, too." Wolfie agreed.

"No. You both stay here. I would like to . . . I *want* to be alone with Max." She looked down at Mr. Danby, who was a good six inches shorter than herself. "Is that possible, sir?" Luise asked without a tinge of condescension.

"Yes, of course. I anticipated that possibility. The late—" He stopped instantly and looked up at Luise almost tenderly. "*Your husband* is in the chapel. I'll escort you myself."

"Thank you."

He smiled at Edyth and Wolfie. "I've ordered tea. It will be here any moment. Please, feel free to help yourselves." Then he turned, offering Luise his arm, which was a bit awkward because of the difference in their heights.

"Shall I follow?" Luise inquired discreetly, allowing him to withdraw the offered arm with no embarrassment and to start on his course down the corridor, at the end of which Luise now saw a set of paneled double doors.

Mr. Danby paused as he reached to open them. "Would you like me to stand close by, madam?" he asked gently.

"No. I'll be quite all right."

"There is a bell directly inside these doors on the wall to the right."

"I shan't need it, but thank you."

"Shall I wait here then?"

"No, of course not, Mr. Danby. Please return and join the others for tea."

"As you say." He cleared his throat as he opened the doors and then stood aside for Luise. "The bell is on the right," he reminded Luise. Then he withdrew and closed the doors.

The surprise of the sunlight blinded Luise for a few moments, and she stood, not moving, only a foot into the chapel, waiting for the room to come into focus. Finally, as she was looking up (still a trifle too apprehensive to look down), she could see that the sunlight was streaming in from a high window exactly opposite the doorway. It overlooked a small private garden that appeared to be entirely enclosed. Luise's gaze shifted slightly to her left. There was a door that led to the garden.

She pivoted away slowly to study the room. There was a high, vaulted ceiling, a small altar garlanded with flowers and burning candles. It was not very big, nor were there any Scriptures or crosses or—Luise thought of it for the first time—Stars of David. This was not a Jewish chapel or a Catholic one. It was in all probability nonsectarian, and the funeral home must therefore be as well. Edyth had apparently not been sure Max would have wanted a Jewish burial.

Max.

Luise now forced herself to look at the coffin set on a pedestal in the center of the room. The top was open, but from where she stood and owing to its elevation, she could not really see in. The sunlight fell over its entire surface, completely filling the inch or so of space that was visible. It was quite narrow, and it was deeper than most coffins she could remember, and she realized Max must be sunken in it.

She did not move toward it to confirm this. Instead, she made her way over to a bench along the wall and directly under the bell for assistance and sat down.

She had suddenly been overwhelmed with the impact of recalling Max's last words to her: "Don't follow me!" But he could not have meant that. Not *now*. Not *this*. And in her heart she had felt, known, that in the end he would come back to her. She realized now that this had carried her through the two years' separation. It had been as if Max had been away at war (which of course he had been—a war with himself) and she had been the wife he would return to when all the battles had been fought.

Luise sat that way, cross-legged on the bench, as if waiting in someone's anteroom or perhaps outside someone's bedroom. She looked somewhat elegant. Max had been proud of that quality in her appearance. The elegance. The class. It was the first thing he had noticed about her. That and her legs. He always loved the long slimness of her legs. She nervously uncrossed them and then recrossed them.

They had met in violence and humor. It had been a Saturday night and she was having dinner in the Village with a young man she had once known in Salt Lake City. Accepting the date had seemed a disaster within ten minutes (in the taxi to the restaurant his hands began to wander). Now, of course, it all seemed like fate.

The restaurant had been small and crowded. It had added to the unwanted familiarity. They had their drinks before them and were waiting for dinner to be served when this man (it had been Max, and she recalled noticing his force of movement, the coordination of his body), apparently in a hurry to leave the premises, bolted past their table, knocking over her companion's drink. Her companion rose angrily to his feet.

"Son of a bitch Irishman!" he had shouted.

Max had whirled. He could have been Irish—broad, pugnacious nose, flinty eyes, solid chin. She had caught only a quick glimpse of him, though, for as he whirled, he swung and connected and her companion went sprawling across the narrow aisle. Max had smiled at her as he straightened, his glance rising slowly from her legs to her face.

"Are you Irish?" she had asked.

"No."

"Why, then?"

"They hate one, they hate them all." He had turned to go, paused. "Can I get you a taxi?"

"How did you know I wanted to leave?"

"I didn't." Her companion was getting to his feet, and Max took her by the arm and pulled her out of the restaurant, not stopping or talking until they were in a taxi. "You handled that with style," he had said. "And you have crazy legs."

"I wouldn't think you had time to notice."

He had grinned and settled back. "Give the driver your

address," he ordered. "We can discuss it more intelligently there."

She breathed deeply. It sounded like a sigh. Then she was silent. She seemed to be listening for something. Max's voice. She concentrated. Sighed once more. And closed her eyes.

Their friends had come down to Grand Central to see them off for California. Luise could always recall every detail of those last moments. Max with his back to her in the private compartment as he put some of the suitcases on the luggage rack. Sitting down then, smiling at her in that boyish, self-satisfied manner of his. They hadn't needed to exchange words. Each knew what the other was thinking. Max looked so young, so handsome, so vital. She sat there smiling back at him with pride. *You'll kill them dead out there*, she thought, her eyes conveying the message of faith to him. *This is it*, he was thinking. *I'm on my way.*

She had shifted, the heaviness of her pregnancy making her body feel a bit cumbersome. She could see that Max could hardly contain himself with all the crowded, rushing thoughts that occupied him. In his mind he was already in Hollywood, already killing them dead. She, on the other hand, was cherishing the prospect of sharing the next four days with Max. They would be alone and together. Four entire days! She smiled and closed her eyes as she leaned back against the starched white of the headrest.

She heard the shrill whistle, felt the lurch, the heaving forward; her nostrils filled with the acrid train smoke. She did not suppose she had ever in her life been happier.

"Crazy. I've been to France, Spain, even the Middle East, but I've never been farther West than Atlantic City," he said. He was like a child. He sat staring out the train windows, watching each inch of the country as it rushed past. At every stop he would prowl the platform, disappear into the station, exchange words with total strangers. "They look different, sound different," he told her. "I want to remember it all."

He wasn't interested in the other passengers, and so they remained in their compartment except for meals and the stops the train made. And they talked about things they had never spoken of before.

"Did you write your mother you were pregnant?"

"No."

"Doesn't every girl write their mother at times like that?"

"Not this one. I don't ever write mine. I haven't since we got married."

"Oh?"

"You never asked before."

"I'm asking now."

"I called before the ceremony. She said if I married a Jew, I wasn't her daughter anymore."

"You should have told me."

"It wasn't that you were a Jew. It was because you *weren't* a Mormon."

He laughed at that, and he never discussed it with her again or inquired during the succeeding years if she ever wondered about her mother. (She had but still had never contacted her and only heard about her death through a chance meeting with someone from Salt Lake years later in the shoe department in Saks Fifth Avenue.)

By the second day of the journey, she had noticed a change in Max's attitude. They had spent two hours in Chicago and had then begun the dismal stretch of land spreading south and west. "I didn't know," Max would say. Or, "Oh, my God," he would mutter. He was shocked by the poverty of the land. She was too, of course, but having come from Salt Lake by train to New York two years earlier, when the Depression had been at its worst, she was aware of conditions, and she was so content to have Max to herself for the days of the journey that she could not react in the same manner that Max did.

They passed caravans of migrant workers with their barefoot children and their junk heaps; gaunt, hungry faces at broken windows; dead animals—once pets—deserted, left to die, to lighten the burden. Women begged for milk for their babies on railroad platforms. Indian families performed war dances for pennies, dignity gone, pride vanished. Finally, they reached California. The land was green. The trees were laden. Oranges spilled onto the rich, fertile earth. A starving migrant family (newspapers in a car window) paused, and an old lady knelt to collect some fallen oranges just as a state trooper pulled up and took the oranges from her, magnanimously waving the hungry family on before tossing the oranges back on the ground.

They were to arrive on the morning of the fourth day. Max had been silent since rising. The suitcases were in the vestibule; the porter had been tipped.

"Los Angeles!" the conductor shouted.

The sky was azure blue. The day was warm and promising.

"We're here," she had sighed.

"I have to write about it."

"Of course, Max."

"I'm not even sure that will help."

She had taken his hand, and they had stepped off the train together. There was no one there to meet them, and they crossed the sun-splashed platform with its stucco arches and yawning trees to a taxi and rode in silence all the way to their new home.

The door next to her opened, and Mr. Danby stared ahead and then, not seeing her before the coffin or the altar (where she realized he assumed she should have been), anxiously searched the room until he found her.

"Oh, madam! You are quite all right?" he asked.

"Yes," she replied.

"Your friends were somewhat concerned."

"They needn't have been."

"Shall I leave you alone awhile longer then?"

Luise rose. "No. I'll come with you now."

He waited until she went past him, and then he followed her out and most carefully closed the doors behind them.

"Miss Spalding appears to be unhappy about the selection of the casket. I do want you to know, madam, that if need be, the extablishment can even make one to measure in a matter of, say, two days."

"I don't think that will be necessary," she said and then stopped.

Mr. Danby looked up at her with great concern. "Is anything the matter, madam?" he inquired discreetly.

She said, "No," and continued on, but she had only just realized that she had not seen Max.

Edyth and Wolfie stood in the doorway of Mr. Danby's office. They seemed relieved at the sight of her.

"I was *so* worried," Edyth told her.

"You shouldn't have been." Luise walked past her and into the office, directly to the tea tray and helped herself to a cup of tea.

The others stood timorously watching her, as if half expecting her to erupt into some new form of demimadness. "I would imagine there are some things you might want me to settle."

"Not now, Luise. It can certainly wait until this afternoon," Edyth said.

"Most certainly, madam," Mr. Danby agreed.

"Until you're up to it, Luise," Wolfie confided.

"I'm up to it now." She sat down.

There was an uncomfortable feeling in the room as the others sat down (except for Mr. Danby, who stood curiously at the closed door, a strangely foreshortened-looking guardsman).

"It is my decision," she cleared her throat. Everyone waited apprehensively. "In my opinion," she continued, her voice low and warm, the tone Max always liked her to use, "I think we should carry on as Max would have wanted. I must admit, Edyth, that you, perhaps, know what that would entail better than I. But I think, *yes*, yes, I know, that he would want the ritual quiet and private. I will turn the matter over to you, Edyth, if that is agreeable—"

"Naturally."

"But I would like to be consulted."

"Of course!"

"I really don't think the size—the casket—it can't possibly matter."

"Do you propose a closed casket, madam?"

"Yes. Decidedly." She turned to Edyth. "Agreed?"

"Ye-s," Edyth said tentatively.

"And the cemetery?"

"I've taken the liberty," Edyth began.

"It is like a small garden, madam."

"That's nice. Max always loved flowers," Luise said, realizing immediately how ridiculous that sounded, but remembering his great feeling for the earth, his pleasure when they bought the small ranch out in Encino after Thea's birth, and the sight of the large, awkward Max squatted to the ground, digging with his bare hands to plant their first tree. That garden had been a wild garden. The grass was never as closely clipped as the bordering ranches. Trees seemed to have heaved up into the air. The flowers grew in great masses, and the bougainvillaea vines were tangled with climbing roses.

They saw her mind was elsewhere. Wolfie rose immediately and came to her side. "I think that is enough for this morning, Luise. You've done just fine."

She rose silently and let Wolfie take her arm and guide her to the door. She shook Mr. Danby's hand (his grip was firm and *alive*). "Thank you very much for your kindness, Mr. Danby," she said.

"Not at all, madam. Not at all."

Edyth was now on the other side of her, and they walked cautiously and slowly out of the funeral parlor and into the bright sun of midmorning.

Luise stopped before entering the car, and Wolfie and Edyth stood there, concern marking their faces.

It was something she had remembered.

Max so caked with the mud from the back paddock after a rainstorm (they had had two horses, one for himself and one small pony for Thea, since Luise had not enjoyed riding) that it had taken her several hours to clean his clothes and scrape the mud from his boots. But he had delayed taking a shower and seemed to delight in the thick crust of mud on his body.

"Damn, that's beautiful!" He grinned. "And it's my earth. Mine."

There was no message from Thea when she returned to the hotel. But then it was hours earlier in New York. Still the middle of the night.

She had asked Wolfie to come up for a few moments, and he now sat on the large chair in the sitting room with his doctor's bag opened on the floor beside him.

"Would you like something to calm your nerves, Luise?" he asked.

"You certainly dispense those little pills of yours easily, Wolfie. No examinations, questions about history or background. Just 'Would you like something to calm your nerves, Luise?' "

"That was uncalled for, Luise," he said calmly.

She was pacing up and down. "I just had a *vision* of you at the premiere of Lucy Banner's last film about three years ago. There she was all radiant with excess energy, and there you were always two steps behind slipping her those ups or uppers, whatever you call them. Three weeks later there she was dead at thirty-nine of an overdose of sleeping pills prescribed by you to help her sleep after all those little pill boosts that she no longer could live without. And there you were at her funeral, wiping the tears from your eyes. 'So beautiful, so young,' you moaned." She sat down across from him. "I have to ask you something."

"Yes, of course, Luise. Anything."

"Was Max on pills of any kind?"

He stood up, bristling with irritation. "I don't know how you can ask me that."

"You were his doctor."

"You know damned well that's not the truth! He called on me from time to time. But I was not his doctor!"

"But was Max on pills?"

"Booze, yes. Pills, no."

"He had been drinking a lot?"

"Consistently."

"Since when?"

"Now, Luise. You know the answer to that as well as I do. Years."

"A drink or two before dinner."

"More often five or six and he would forget the dinner."

"Oh, Wolfie, would he?" she said, near tears.

"I'm not saying Max was an alcoholic. But a steady drinker, yes!"

"I see."

"But he never seemed to need sleeping pills. Never asked *me* for any, at any rate. And he never took Ritalin or Dexedrine or any of those."

"And the cause of death? I mean the *real* cause, Wolfie."

He sat down again opposite her and spoke to her in his most confidential tone. "At his age, drinking as he had been doing, working as hard as he was, with his history—well, you know he had a mild heart attack early last year?"

"No, I didn't know."

"I wasn't consulted, but it showed up on the tests for the insurance on the new film. The studio had to keep it hushed up and Max was most cooperative but with *that* history . . . " He looked at Luise and then straightened, as if suddenly deciding to give her the medicine as it came from the bottle. "A nineteen-year-old ding-a-ling. He must have either gone mad or had suicide as his intention."

"There was another nineteen-year-old before this girl," she said almost to herself and certainly never intending the words for Wolfie's ears.

"Why do you think he had the first attack?" he snapped, picking up every word.

She rose slowly, gracefully. "Thank you, Wolfie," she said in a controlled voice.

He reached into his case and took a bottle out, closed the case, and then handed the bottle to Luise. "You look very tired, dear. Take one of these and try to relax for a few hours."

Luise stood there looking at the bottle in her hand for a long while—until he had crossed the room and opened the door for that matter. Then she did a very unlike-Luise thing. She threw the bottle into the fireplace, where it shattered into many pieces. Then she called after him. "Never, never, in my presence dispense any of your calling cards, Wolfie—hear me?—for if you do, I shall report you to the authorities. So help me God, I will. You hand me an entire bottle of sleeping pills, and yet you see I could be exposed to the possibility of melancholia over the next few days or weeks. Suppose, Wolfie, just *suppose* I died from an overdose of your pills."

"There would be no record that they had been prescribed by me. I never dispense pills with my name on them. Prescriptions, yes. But pills themselves, never."

"Clever!"

"Cautious. But I know you would never take an overdose, Luise. Believe me. *You*, Luise dear, are one hell of a survivor." And he closed the door, all sound of him lost immediately.

She had given the telephone operators the names of only two people whom they could put through to the suite. The children. At exactly 1 P.M. the telephone next to her bed rang. It was Anthea, and she was calling from New York.

"Thea, *Thea*, it's so good to hear your voice!"

"Are you all right, Mother?"

"Yes, dear. Quite all right. My! What a wonderful connection!"

"I don't know *what* to do."

"How's that, dear?"

"I mean, there is *you* to consider."

"No, Thea. More important—yourself to live with."

"We had severed relations, Mother. *Truly* severed relations."

"You had done nothing of the sort. You were father and daughter. A part of each other."

"Oh, God, Mother." There was a silence for a moment or so, and then Thea spoke in a well-trained modulated whisper. "Have you made the arrangements?" she asked.

"Not really. I was at the funeral home this morning. But it was very difficult."

"I'm sorry, Mother."

"Edyth's helpful and I can call on Burt Winters if I have to."

"Yes, of course. That's good." A moment. "I love you, Mother," Thea said softly.

"Yes, I know you do, dear."

"This has torn me up terribly. I really don't know *how* I feel."

"Oh, Thea, Thea, I wish I could help you. I wish I knew the right things to say to help you. All I can say is that I love you, too. And your father did—always did, more than anyone else in the world, Thea, still loved you, had your picture next to his bed. He did inexcusable things, I know, darling. I'm not going to try to whitewash him to you. Not even now. But you mattered to him. A great deal. A great, great deal." She had to pause and catch her breath and fight back the wave of sobs that she felt rising inside her.

"Don't, Mother. Please, let's not. Mother?"

"I'm here."

"Okay?"

"Yes."

"I won't say no unconditionally as Tony did. I need a day to think about it. If I decide to come by this evening, I'll take the night plane and be there tomorrow afternoon, your time. But this very minute I can't promise you that. You understand that, Mother?"

"Yes, dear."

"And if I come, it may be for you—because I want to be with you. Do you understand that too?"

"Um," she managed, biting back the sobs again.

"You shouldn't be there alone. Shouldn't have to go through this alone. Tony and I are such selfish animals. I know that. But we're both fighting for our very lives, Mother. You'll just have to accept that. Our very lives."

"Edyth can be depended upon," was all Luise could reply.

"I know that. Edyth will always come through in times of crisis, though forever after she will seem to be languishing in her grief."

"How—how's Bob?" she asked, still fighting.

"He's fine, Mother. But we won't talk about that now. This is no time."

"All right, dear."

"Good-bye, Mother. Remember I love you. So does Tony. I'll either call you tonight—no early morning your time—or cable you my arrival time."

Luise was unable to answer. She had lost the battle. She hung up the receiver just a split second before the full onslaught of tears that had been building since Edyth's call had reached her in New York finally erupted, and for nearly an hour Luise lay there alone in the bed and heaved with the weight and depth of those tears.

Chapter 7

Luise was not to be spared the parade of the past. It marched through her head as relentlessly as the shabby but proud company of men who marched over the River Kwai. She could see Max leading them, even hear that nonsensical song. There they were—Max's company—all members in good standing of the Screen Writers Guild.

Max had joined the guild shortly after he began his first assignment for Omega. He had been assigned a project called *The Cat's Meow* after four other writers had failed. It had been a dreadful story and a depressing screen debut for Max, but Anthea had arrived by then and they had bought a small house. Also, Max was enamored with film as a medium and felt comfortable in it. He began to talk about film as art and of screenwriting as a vastly more satisfying means of communication than writing for newspapers or magazines. You could say volumes in one frame even without words. He practically lived in the studio in those days, spending his lunch hours and many of his evenings in the cutting room, and sound labs, and dubbing stages. When he could, he watched them shoot, riding the camera crane, standing in the sound booth, or sitting behind the director. The great love affair of his life had begun.

He had not let go of the images of the cross-country trip, either. On weekends he packed Luise and Anthea into the car and drove into Fresno and the Salinas Valley. He talked to the migrant fruit pickers and to the farmers. Or they'd take a longer weekend farther north to the fishing communities and canneries, to the forests and the CCC camps. No one seemed to resent Max. They spoke easily, though bitterly, to him. He was a stranger, and yet he cared. They sensed that.

America was still in the jaws of the Depression. Spain was under Franco's Fascist thumb, Portugal ruled by the dictator Salazar, Italy by Mussolini, Germany by Hitler; Czechoslovakia had been raped. There were whispers of concentration camps. In England the spineless Neville Chamberlain leaned heavily on the curved staff of his black umbrella, and in America there was apathy along with the unemployment. It seemed the only country that was progressing at all was Russia. One heard of the diminishing illiteracy there, of the help for the aged, the employment for all, the constant development of resources.

Many of their friends had joined the party. They were invited to secret meetings. Most of what they heard at these meetings made good sense, while what they saw happening around them did not. They discussed joining the party, but Luise could not bring herself to agree. She truly did not think joining was subversive in any way. To the contrary, anything that appeared to be for the overall purpose of bettering American life seemed very patriotic to her. But she was not a joiner.

One night Max came home late on a Tuesday night and showed her his card. For the next six months he was absent from home every other Tuesday night. They subscribed to the *Daily Worker*. They became socially involved with other party members and liberals. They joined the Anti-Nazi League, and Luise helped raise money for various causes. It seemed to be the one area in which she could work effectively.

The first note of discontent she observed in Max was at the start of his second assignment for Omega. Someone—he never told her who—was badgering him to slant the story.

"I'd slant the script any way I damn wanted," he told her one night, "if it was what I wanted to do. But no one's going to tell me in what direction I should slant my work."

He missed several Tuesday meetings after that.

One night a group of writers guild members met at their home. It had nothing at all to do with the party, and the majority of the twenty writers present were not members at that time (perhaps never were). There had been a schism in the guild between right-wing and left-wing factions, and the left wing had decided to break up and meet privately at ten different houses, twenty members at each house, to discuss a vote on the method of reorganizing a guild of their own. They had arranged this in a rather secret manner and split into smaller groups so that the right wing would not get wind of their plans. Two hundred members meeting in one place could hardly be kept secret. Secrecy also meant the studios would not have time to inflict reprisals, aligned as they were with the right-wing element.

Luise had organized everything she could for their comfort and thereafter attempted to stay out of the meeting room (her den), but she did peek in from time to time out of interest and because she liked to see Max in action. At the outset, he was in his stride. He was tentative chairman (it was his home, after all) and he ruled the group with a mixture of│father-*cum*-professor-*cum*-drinking buddy. There was a grin on his face in the beginning as he welcomed the men, pulled them to order. But then a little man—Luise concentrated—Prews, yes, his name was Prews. A smallish man, bald, red-cheeked, rimless glasses—but with a surprising bass voice. Harold Prews. He began to ask questions, suggest alternatives. He moved from the fringe of the group finally to stand beside Max. Max seemed to be taken off-balance. He stepped back, and the grin was gone from his face.

Prews had been a Communist and had also been a union organizer. He was a dynamic speaker, and although Luise had not recalled meeting him before, she did remember hearing his name in reference to a series of very avant-garde articles that had recently been published in the *Quarterly*, a magazine all the writers read and respected. She had heard he was in Hollywood to write a film script, but she hadn't known which one. It was obvious that his intent was to take over and direct this group, and all the men, except Max, seemed to be agreeable to this. None of them were really organizers anyway. They had elected Prews their representative by the end of the evening (Max the only dissenter) and allowed him to draw up the first charter of their own, making them a separate union to be dealt with in all matters concerning screenwriters. Max seemed impatient to get Prews and the rest of the men out.

Afterward he went into the den, closed the door, and was there a long time. It was late, and Luise finally interrupted his private meditation. It was a warm night, but he had built a small fire in the fireplace and stood watching it.

"I've burned it," he had told her.

"What did you burn, Max?"

"My card. That son of a bitch Prews. I don't trust him. He's a take-over man. I've watched those kind all my life. He can call himself a Communist, but I've watched those louses. Schneider, the rent man in Bridgeport. Veigel, the loan shark in New York. Franco, Mussolini, Hitler—hell, they can call themselves whatever they frigging want to, but they're take-over men and I hate them categorically and I'll be goddamned if I'll ever support them."

He had, of course, joined the guild. It was impossible for him to avoid it. But he had never again gone to a party meeting or renewed his membership. For a couple of years they dunned him for dues, and then it seemed they just decided to accept the fact that Max Seaman was no longer a party member.

Luise took a warm bath. She ordered a pot of tea. She closed the blinds and lay down again. It was no good. The film seemed to have been rewound. No. It was a new film. She held her head, closed her eyes. She was exhausted. She wanted desperately to sleep. But the memory-film kept spinning.

They had just returned from the premiere of Max's first film, *The People's Case (The Cat's Meow* didn't count), and the shock of what she had seen on screen was still with Luise. The film had revealed for the first time the growing megalomania that Luise would have to live with the rest of their lives together. Max had discussed the film with her, but she had never been offered a copy of the script to read or seen any of the film rushes. She had had some hostility about this, but since she had been busy with Thea and then pregnant with Tony, she had been distracted enough not to force an issue. But she understood the secrecy employed now.

Though masked by a brilliantly conceived plot ruse, *The People's Case* was the story of how Luise and Max had met and fallen in love, though it ended when the Max-like hero went off to Spain to help fight the people's case and his Luise-like heroine bade him adieu. There were entire dialogues that Luise could recall, incidents, twisted somewhat to fit into the story line, but nonetheless recognizable, and people in their lives, in the *public's* eyes, who could be easily identified. These people and she herself were not treated with any great kindness.

One had been the famous but then alcoholic and down-at-the-heels American novelist who was trying even at that moment to make a comeback in Hollywood as a scenarist. Max had shown him suffering from melancholia, dying, a drunk, no longer caring about the fate of the people or the condition of the world.

She was hanging up her beautiful satin gown (the first evening dress she had ever owned) with great devotion when Max entered their bedroom. Her silk negligee was tied loosely about her gently swelling middle (she was only in her fourth month). "How could you have done that to Grant?" she asked in quiet despair. "You know how hard he's trying to succeed again. It will cut him badly. Maybe throw him off the track again."

"A really good writer can always make a comeback," he replied and began to undress.

"You had no right—"

"*Every* right, Luise. A writer is a historian, after all."

"You left him hopeless, *lost*."

"Perhaps he is."

"And me, Max? You presented me as a yoke that had to be lifted for you to be free. Is that how you feel?"

"Most love is like that to a creative artist."

"You're beginning to think of yourself as a great artist, Max. It's frightening."

"To you. Not to me."

She began to cry, and he stood watching her soft, rounded belly tremble beneath the soft layer of silk. He came over to her and gently took her chin in his hand. He was nude.

"You are a beautiful woman, Luise, and you know what I love best about you? Your strength. The very thing I must fight, just as though we were two boxers in a ring and this were a championship match. You are a champion, Lu. A thoroughbred. A queen. And a king, Lu, needs a queen. But he also has to keep her there. In her corner, fighting but always losing the battle to the true crown."

He slid his hands down onto her shoulders and over her swollen breasts, untied the soft sash about her waist and then caressed her rounded belly. "The most beautiful hill in the world," he said softly and with pride as he took her into his arms and held her carefully to him. "I've immortalized you," he said with a smile in his voice. "Doesn't that please you?"

"Not really."

"What would?" His hands were stroking her body.

"No, Max."

"You can't get pregnant twice," he said, laughing.

And she laughed, and then they were laughing together, and then they were making love, and finally they were side by side on their fine new bed, in their lovely new home together, both of them listening to see if their night loving had awakened Thea and then deciding it had not, settling back into each other's arms and a long, happy sleep.

The telephone startled Luise out of her reverie. "Yes," she said nervously into the speaker.

"Sorry, Mrs. Seaman. I know you left explicit orders not to be disturbed except for overseas calls, but a gentleman has been insistent."

"What's the gentleman's name?"

"Mr. Merwin Bibbs."

"Good Lord, not now."

"Shall I tell him you are still not to be disturbed?"

Luise laughed sharply. "Mr. Bibbs knows just how long I *have* been disturbed," she said.

"Pardon?"

"I'll speak to Mr. Bibbs."

In a moment a voice that Luise hardly remembered, so like a true buried ghost of the past was it, was on the other end of the line.

"Luise, this is Merwin Bibbs."

"Yes, yes, I know."

"Can I come and have a word with you?"

"Merwin, please—please spare me."

"I was the one man he really destroyed, Luise. Did he spare me?"

"*Please*, Merwin."

"Just a few moments of your time."

"I can't go back, Merwin. I *won't* go back. It was a long time ago. A very long time ago. It simply can't help. I won't go back."

"Ten minutes, Luise."

"Oh, God! All right, Merwin. Ten minutes. That's all. But remember—I refuse to go back."

"Thank you, Luise," he said softly and then was gone.

He had never offered his condolences. Well, at least he was an honest man.

BOOK II

Hollywood

Farthest from any war, unique in time
Like Athens or Baghdad—this city lies
Between dry purple mountains and the sea,
The air is clear and famous, every day
Bright as a postcard, bringing bungalows
And sights. The broad nights advertise
For love and music and astronomy.

Heart of a continent, the hearts converge
On open boulevards where palms are nursed
With flare-pots like a grove, on villa roads
Where castles cultivated like a style
Breed fabulous metaphors in foreign stone,
And on enormous movie lots
Where history repeats its vivid blunders.

KARL SHAPIRO, "Hollywood"

Chapter 8

It was September 23, 1947. There was a sun in the midday sky, but it had to be seen through hoary ash-colored clouds. And even into the lazy hollow of star-studded Sherman Oaks the acrid smog penetrated, its pungent poisonous gases like the deadly nightshade, trapping them forever between ocean and mountain.

The day seemed to start innocently enough. Max had, in fact, awakened with a sense of well-being. He could hear the childish voices of Thea and Tony under his bedroom window. They were arguing as they often did, even at eight in the morning, even before going off to school. But Max was not displeased with these spats, for he felt they were good for Tony, who needed, in his opinion, to come up against a rock from time to time to sharpen his edges and educate his thrusts. Thea, who was eight, was such a rock, though her golden cap of hair and slim, almost twiglike body seemed to negate this. Max felt warmed as he thought about his daughter Thea. She truly pleasured him, as he would tell Luise from time to time. He was sure Luise did not understand his strong feelings where his little daughter was concerned, perhaps even misinterpreted them. He recalled how disturbed she was when he took Thea into bed with him on Sunday mornings. "She's too old for that, Max," she argued. But Max still let the child sneak into the bed when Luise was downstairs preparing breakfast. Though she would always interrupt her work at the sound of their laughter and good spirits. "You'd better hurry, I'm putting the pancakes on," she'd remind them and then stand in the doorway waiting until Thea got out of the bed and went with her, but not before the secret hand clenching beneath the sheets, their secret code that meant "I love you."

Max lay back on his pillow, happy for the moment that beside him was an empty pillow, content knowing Luise was downstairs already beginning the day's chores, pleased to be alone except for the sound of the daughter he loved. She would be a competitive bitch, single-minded, a hell of a lot of woman, of human being. It would take quite a man to fight the final battle with her. A man like him.

"I'll play you a game of pitch. There's time," she was saying sweetly enough to her little brother.

"I don't want to." The six-year-old Tony pouted.

"Don't scowl. You'll freeze that way. Like this, ugh! Why don't you want to?"

"You always win."

"That's no reason. You still have to try. Here—here's the ball. I'll let you go first."

"No," Tony said stubbornly.

"You have to. Otherwise you lose just because you didn't play."

"I don't."

"You do, too."

"I don't, I don't," he was crying, but he *had* pitched the ball.

Thea's voice rose dramatically. "Gotcha! I win! That was a lousy pitch!"

"Children—shhh," Luise said. "Clea," she said softly to the maid, "they are right under Mr. Seaman's window. Oh, well, never mind, it's time for the school bus anyway. Take them out front."

There was a fluttering like a pack of strayed chickens being shooed into another pasture. Then all was silent.

Max decided he would call Edyth and have her come to the house to work. He preferred that anyway and went into the studio only when he really had to, when there was a story conference, or a budget meeting, or casting interviews, or tests to see. He was a producer now and could go in when he damned pleased. He smiled. Well, he had finally been given the ball. He was writing, producing, and directing his next film. *His.* Like this house. Like Thea. Like Tony. Luise? Well, that wasn't the same thing. She was not really a part of him.

Before calling Edyth, though, he would take a fast dip in the pool. It was after eight, and there was still plenty of time to catch her before she left that crummy apartment of hers smack in the center of Hollywood, where one cracking plaster wall always shoved against another. He got out of the bed, stretched, and headed immediately for the john. Then he stepped into a fast shower and wrapped a towel around his nude body before taking the backstairs past the kitchen (Luise was thankfully not there) and once outside, heading slowly and with sensual pleasure, to the pool which was fairly private. He stood on the edge of the water for a long time after he threw his towel away from him, staring down at the rippling reflection of his nakedness.

He decided at that moment that he would insist on Edyth's moving into a small, new, cheerful place in the valley, near Sherman Oaks but in a working-class, not Hollywood-tainted, community. That would be easy to explain to Luise, since the studio was also in the valley.

He smiled when he thought about Edyth. *That* type always had the most pent-up passion. Sure, a man shouldn't engage in adultery so close to home, but Edyth was the kind of girl even Luise wouldn't suspect, and a lot had to be said for the undying loyalty the liaison created. Edyth's tight body and long legs flashed before his eyes, blotting out, no, intermingling with his own reflection. Max dived right into the heart of them both, and the water broke up around him as he thrashed his way to the other end of the pool and then turned and swam back to where he had dived in.

Luise now stood about ten feet away from him. She was wearing a shapeless housecoat that he thought had been left over from her pregnancy with Tony and had curlers in her hair. Still, she was a handsome woman.

"Dive in," he told her.

"It's the telephone. Edyth."

"Tell her I'll call back."

"I don't think I should. I think you'd better talk to her."

Something in the serious expression in Luise's beautiful face warned him. "It's here," he said, as he pulled himself out of the pool and wrapped himself in the towel Luise handed him.

"Merwin Bibbs received the first summons at eight this morning," Luise said flatly.

Max brushed past Luise and headed for the poolhouse, where there was a telephone extension.

"Shoot, Edyth," he shouted into the telephone as soon as he had lifted the receiver. "Don't wait to see the whites of my eyes."

"It's happened," Edyth began in her usual funereal tone. "At eight this morning."

"I know. Luise told me. Tell me something I don't know."

"It was given to Merwin at his house by a United States deputy marshal and it's a bright-pink subpoena signed by J. Parnell Thomas, chairman."

"Call the studio and tell them we're out scouting locations and then get your ass over here, Edyth."

"You could go to Mexico. Maybe there's time."

"I'm surprised you even suggested that, Edyth."

"I am, too." She sighed.

"What does that mean?" He slammed down the receiver. Luise was standing framed in the doorway.

"What did she say?" she asked.

"Nothing you don't already know."

She came into the cool dark of the room, its shades drawn, the floors tiled. "You could drive to Mexico and avoid being served. It's not an answer, but it might give you time."

"No, I won't do that."

"I'm glad."

He smiled at her. "You're quite a dame."

She passed that off. "Maybe you won't be subpoenaed, Max."

He grinned with a touch of malice. "Not frigging likely," he said. "The bastards have always been after my ass."

"How did the committee get the names in the first place?" She sighed.

"Everybody's afraid of being investigated. Even the most rabid reactionary has something to fear—some association, some past indiscretion."

"Someone informed."

"And he or she will have a good deal of company."

"Oh, God!"

"The industry will squirm now. Christ! Will it squirm!"

"You think you're in any real danger, Max? You did have a card, but that was so long ago."

"I'm in danger. More important, the film's in danger."

"I don't find that more important."

He lowered his head and shook it judicially at her. "You should,

Lu, you really should." He started out of the poolhouse, but she blocked his way.

"You think Omega will cancel at this late stage? You're almost set to roll. There's half a million invested."

"Yeah, Luise, I think Omega could lay the picture right on the shelf and let it rot there unless I can figure out by tomorrow morning what old man Steiner has to lose by doing that that adds up to a hell of a lot more than five hundred grand. I think a time may now be upon us when an honest story will be impossible to put on the screen. There's still time to fight it, but if Hollywood loses, the country's had it. This will only be the first medium of communication attacked. Next it will be the theaters, the publishing industry, radio, TV, newspapers, magazines, and, finally, sweetheart—education!"

"I'm frightened, Max."

"Don't broadcast it, but so am I."

They laughed nervously, and finally she stepped aside, but by then he had decided she had a good morning smell to her and that he liked her mouth raw and without lipstick and he knew the soft curves that were waiting for him beneath her loose robe. He pulled her back to him, but at that moment Clea appeared about twenty yards away and was shouting at him.

"Mistah *See-man,* there's a man to see you."

"Tell him to wait in the front hall. I'll be damned if those bastards will get me with my bare ass hanging out," and he brushed past Luise and swept past the startled Clea and stalked across *his* lawn, *his* hard earth, into *his* home.

"It's only Mistah Tanner," Clea called after him, but Max was already out of hearing.

Bob Tanner stood waiting for Max in the entrance hall. He was certainly not a young man who lacked self-assurance, but he never did feel comfortable in Max's presence or in any room that reflected Max's personality. He felt the same way in Max's office at the studio as he did in his home. Defensive. As if the years of apprenticing to Lou Whitehorn had meant nothing. As if he had not fought a war bravely, or made his own niche at twenty-nine in a killer industry. Yet he had left Lou Whitehorn without qualms to become Max's associate producer and supposed script collaborator. The war had used up vital years of his life, and when he had returned to Lou's employ, it was easy to see that the man he had admired as one of the films too few great masters was aging and that the industry was rushing past him.

He smiled as he thought about his campaign to win the job of associate producer, script collaborator with Max. It had been subtle and brilliantly carried out. The fact that he found himself more of an errand boy *cum* sounding board (Max talked the script a lot and listened to Bob's reactions but never let him write one word) did not negate the fact that he believed Max Seaman to be the biggest potential winner Hollywood had bred in decades.

Now there was this mushroom cloud of fear. Nothing was sure any more. No safe bets. Tanner blinked his eyes in the sudden brightness as the door from the den was thrown open and the sun streamed through its plate-glass walls. He hadn't slept well that night, and his eyes ached and his head throbbed. Still, he squared his well-tailored shoulders and snapped his freshly shined shoes to attention as Max stepped out into the hallway.

"Oh, Tanner. Hell, I thought you were the deputy marshal."

"You've heard then," Bob Tanner said as he approached Max. He cleared his throat and managed a cautious smile. "Well, of course, if I had, you *had to*." He laughed uneasily.

"Yeah," Max answered.

"What are *your* chances?"

"Mine?" Max laughed. "Son of a bitch—you're in this lottery, too!" Max turned his back and went into the den, leaving his associate producer to follow him.

Bob Tanner closed the door so that the two of them would have privacy.

"Luise is upstairs dressing, the kids are at school, and the maid couldn't care less. For all intents and purposes, Tanner, we're alone." Max sat down. There was hot coffee in a pot, several packs of cigarettes handy, and large, clean ashtrays at easy reach.

"Luise really knows how to make a man happy," Tanner commented as he sat down across from Max.

"Envy me?"

"Damn right, Max. You're the toughest and the most talented young lion in these Hollywood hills." And he believed that honestly. Also that Max was the strongest and the best equipped to battle the moguls and the studios. He wasn't sure he saw what Max did in *Cross Current*, the film that would serve as Max's debut as a three-headed man, but he was perceptive enough to know that it was a good, tough, tight script that would play like hell and that—oh, yes, indeedy—it had the touch of the master in it.

"You just keep your cool," Max said. "If I'm subpoenaed, Edyth will know, Luise, of course, *you*, and that's it. I want to tell Steiner myself when it happens and set my own pace."

"You have some plan of action in mind then."

"No, I don't, but just you and I know that, Tanner. Steiner doesn't, and if I can write a good enough scene for me to play," he said with a mocking grin creeping onto his face, "he never will."

"You will and he won't," Bob Tanner told him.

"From your mouth to God's ear." Max laughed.

Both men were quiet. Max was smoking, watching the smoke rise, a world apart, thinking, going over things. Tanner leaned forward and looked around him. Max, his house, his wife, even his kids, didn't exude the scent of well-being, of elegance, all right, class, that the world of Lou Whitehorn did, a world Tanner had much admired and slavishly aped for years. But Max's world demanded attention, too. It carried a vital charge. An electro-magnetic, hydroelectric, kinetic world that radioactivated all who came into the scope of its high-tension dynamism. Bob Tanner had grafted much of Lou Whitehorn's elegance and charm. It seemed to him then that if he could infuse Max's magnetic power with Lou's grace and his own talent and resources, he had the world—Hollywood at least—in his palm.

There was a picture of Max's two kids, Anthea and Anthony, on a desk against the one solid wall in the room. The little eight-year-old girl seemed to leap right out of the photograph. She had that same vital life quality that Max had. Tanner had been aware of that the many times he had seen her at play in the yard or just greeting guests in her father's home (for it was always Max's, *not* Luise's home). The boy had it too, but in reverse. The boy was somehow protesting—but even that was a vital, charged thing.

"Listen, Max. I just stopped by to say you can count on me." His voice was soft and confidential. "This is no time for a story conference—unless, of course, you want to have one."

"Not now—go home, Tanner. No. On second thought—don't do that. Go into the studio and get on the telephone and ride every damn ass in that place that needs riding to get our script launched.

I want a budget breakdown by tomorrow morning. Get on to casting and to camera. Get the scene, Bobby boy?" Max squinted right into the sun.

Tanner stood up. "I understand," he said quietly.

"And drop that hushed undertaker's voice you're using—you can even smell potted palms, for chrissakes!"

Bob Tanner started toward the hall door.

"Don't mind me, Bobby. I'm just a little edgy this morning," Max said. He got up and walked over to the bar and was pouring himself a drink when Edyth entered just as Tanner was leaving. Edyth muttered a greeting and then waited until the den door and the front door could be heard closing.

"I don't like him, you know," Edyth commented.

"I've noticed that."

"I don't trust him."

"He doesn't trust you either. Maybe he knows you're sleeping with the boss."

There was a wounded look in her eyes, then a frightened one as she glanced quickly over her shoulder. They were in the hallway, just inside the front door.

"Luise has gone to the market."

"Oh." *Relief.*

"Let's go into the den where we won't be disturbed."

Edyth followed a few nervous steps behind Max. Edyth never really felt comfortable in other women's houses. She had never liked being in her mother's house even when she had been a child and it was, after all, her house, too. Luise's house was all in such perfect taste, all sort of *American Home* crossed with *Town and Country.* Elegant but livable. Perfect. She was happier once they were in the den, which, because it served as Max's office away from his office, reflected much of Max as well as Luise and seemed less intimidating.

"I want you to call anyone you can to see if we can find out who has been served and how many, if there's a pattern, a particular studio involved, something like that. And I don't want to speak to anyone. *No one!* Understand?"

"Of course."

"And if that little man *does* ring the doorbell, you're not to tell anyone, you understand that?"

"I'm not an idiot."

He was sitting in a chair with his long legs up on the glass coffee table. He looked relaxed and reflective, the creative man at ease, but he was sweating badly.

"Max," she said slowly.

"Yeah?"

"You're really in love with Luise, aren't you?"

"Yes, I am."

"And I'm second best."

"The truth is brutal, Edyth. You sure you want it?"

"Sure."

"Not second best. Something else."

"Less than second best?" Her mouth quivered a bit.

"Just something else, Edyth. Let's leave it at that. This is no time."

"No, of course, it's not. I'm sorry."

"And for chrissakes, don't be humble, OK?"

"OK, Max."

"Now get on that telephone. I'm going to finish my swim."

He lowered his legs and sat there, studying her for a moment and then stood up, towering over her. "You're a good kid, Edyth," he said and then went out to the poolhouse to get his bathing suit.

By two o'clock in the afternoon, no sheriff's deputy had appeared. Edyth had the names of twelve men they knew for certain had been subpoenaed, and the three of them—Max was now back in the den with Luise beside him—attempted to put some logic to those singled out.

The majority were writers; a few were directors; they knew so far of only one actor. It was obvious that the vendetta was aimed at the men with words and pictures in their hands, not at the businessmen in the industry—the producers or studio executives.

The children returned from school at three fifteen, and Clea attempted to keep them busy in the yard. Some neighbor children joined them, and by four a war had developed, all sides it would seem directed against Tony, who came in crying bitterly.

"What is it?" Max asked.

"Stevie and Myron are beating up on me," the child whimpered.

"Where's your sister?"

"She says it's—it's not her fight."

"Is it?"

"N-no. It's because they want my f-frog."

"They have no right. That's *your* property. Go back and fight them."

The child looked terrified and Luise got up and went to his side and started to wipe his tears with her handkerchief.

"Lu, leave him be!" Max commanded.

"He's smaller than they are and outnumbered."

"That's the point. Stand away from him, Lu. Do as I say."

A look passed between the two parents. A hard, uncompromising look. Then Luise gave way and moved aside.

Tony stood there trembling.

"Where's your frog?" Max asked.

"I h-hid him." He glanced nervously over his shoulder and bit his lip.

"Are they getting close?" Max inquired.

Tony just shook his head.

"Well, you get out there and don't come back in until you make them leave this yard or I'll find the frog myself and give it to them because they would have won by default anyway."

"N-no . . . no . . . please . . . "

"Max—"

"Tony, did you hear me?"

The child nodded.

"Then do as I say."

Slowly, the little boy turned and moved without much animation back toward the glass doors of the den that led to the terrace and garden. At that moment he observed one of the neighbor boys coming uncomfortably close to the hiding place of his frog. Tony let out a loud cry, a scream of protest really, and began to run with desperation toward the glass doors, his arms flailing in front of him. Terrified of what was behind him and fearful of what was ahead of him, he didn't realize that the door was closed and that he was seeing *through* it. In a split second his screams were mixed with Luise's and with Edyth's and with the sound of breaking glass, now spattered with a coat of deep-red child's blood.

The two children outside stopped in their tracks and then turned and ran home. Thea appeared mysteriously from somewhere all motherly solicitude, giving courage—"It doesn't hurt; what happened? You musn't cry; please don't cry." And the maid fainted as she entered the room. She was still on the floor when Luise, holding Tony, ran past her, Max and Edyth right behind her, to take the child to an emergency hospital just two streets away.

Tony had had several very deep gashes in his arms and on the back of his hand, but as his hand had been clenched in anger and frustration, and his fingers therefore tightly protected, he had not lost any.

They all trooped exhaustedly back to the house an hour later, Tony now asleep on Luise's shoulder.

"It could have been terrible, Max, *terrible*," Luise said quietly as they came up the walk.

"At least he stopped them," Max replied with a soft smile. They had gone up the front steps, and Max was opening the door. "There's more than one way to skin a goat," he said and then stood in the entrance to his home, barring the path for a moment for the others. Then he snappily stepped aside, and they came straggling past him.

"You must be here to serve me a subpoena," Max said to the sheriff's deputy standing in his hallway. Luise, clinging to Tony's inert form, and Edyth huddled together as Thea ran to them crying.

"He's all right, isn't he, Mommy? He's all right?"

"Hush, darling. Tony's fine."

Thea wrapped herself around Luise.

"You Maxwell Isaac Seaman?" the ruddy-faced officer said as he took off his hat and mopped his brow.

"In the flesh."

The man then handed him the subpoena and got the hell out.

Max looked at the bright pink subpoena in his hand, on the front fold of which was written: "By authority of the House of Representatives of the Congress of the United States of America." Inside, the subpoena commanded him to "appear before the Un-American Activities Committee . . . in their chamber . . . in the city of Washington . . . and there testify . . . touching matters of inquiry committed to the said Committee . . . and not to depart without leave of said Committee . . . Herein fail not . . . . J. Parnell Thomas, Chairman."

Max and Luise went to Chasen's for dinner that night, taking

Edyth and Bob Tanner with them. Luise would have preferred staying home with Tony, but the little boy had been sleeping, Clea was with him, and Max felt it was important for him to make a show, and *keep those bastards guessing*.

It was a curious, almost surrealistic evening. Already fear, like some leprous gas, had permeated the industry. There was an awesome terror of being guilty by association. Except for Dave Chasen no one came over to their table, though some called out a courteous "Hi, what goes, how's the film?" from their own table or as they passed. They didn't want to make a social slip, either, a slip that might later cause them a loss of an assignment, job or client.

By eleven Max and Luise were in bed and the children sleeping fitfully. It was a clear night, and they both studied the heavens on their backs, through the glass skylight that had been the *pièce de résistance* when they had bought the house years back.

"What do we do now, Max?" Luise asked gently.

"Fuck, baby," Max whispered, and in a moment he had had his way.

Chapter 9

Hollywood is a land of false illusions and of grand and small deceptions. It is a seriocomic land through the looking glass where nothing is as it seems. In Hollywood the president of a large studio is pseudonymous, whereas the man who holds the title Vice-President in Charge of Production is all-powerful, virtually a supreme being, infinite, eternal, personal God to the thousands in his employ. His disapproval can smash the career of any one of them. And in the case of Omega Films and its vice-president in charge of production, H. M. Steiner (sometimes referred to as His Majesty, but not in his presence), a Christmas greeting sent as a telegram and signed "Harry and Grace Steiner," signified approval and meant the actor, writer, or director had at least achieved a stay of execution.

At Omega, where even the brightest stars were made to punch a time card and the studio police force operated like the FBI, power was seldom allowed except to the Godhead, Steiner. If a star became too difficult, he or she was placed on suspension. If a writer became too individual, he was demoted to fourth writer on a second-class film. Seldom did a man or woman overcome these impediments to his or her future. If one did, it meant that H.M. considered him or her like a son or daughter and also thought the party so favored could substantially increase the sixty-five-million-dollar personal fortune already amassed.

Max was one of the chosen. *God's own.*

H.M. had been partially responsible for bringing him to Hollywood and to Omega. He had wet-nursed him, seasoned him, put him in the little leagues and then the big. Max was a big talent on a studio lot that had nurtured many big talents. H.M. then saw a good deal more in him than that. Most big talents were defiant when crossed or stymied. Max, instead, treated each setback or roadblock with cool statesmanship before initiating a course of action, which was not always attack and was seldom defy. He was a worthy adversary, and H.M. enjoyed having him around.

None of Omega's other producers, except for one of H.M.'s son-in-laws, was ever given full reins to produce, write, and direct a film. Of course, none, especially H.M.'s son-in-law, was capable of carrying such a load. Max, though, had had the temerity to purchase a best-selling novel with his *own* money, a book the author had refused to sell to Omega in the first place. Now Omega owned the property jointly with Max, but Max had been given the sanction to produce, direct, and adapt the film under his own aegis, giving Omega, of course, more than its slice of the pie, more than was general with an independent working through a studio. And since H.M. had sublime faith in Max's ability and felt Max would be able to turn *Crosscurrent* into very big box office, Maxwell Isaac Seaman had joined the ranks of those in power in Hollywood, which made him a much envied and terribly disliked man. "Hated" would be a better word.

Max dressed carefully for the morning meeting he had just arranged with H.M. Let H.M. wear the business suit and feel like the executive; he would wear an Italian sports shirt and knit tie and a softly tailored jacket and just slightly creased trousers—soft blue, to contrast with the dark grays H.M. perpetually wore.

H.M. had sounded friendly on the telephone. But Max didn't kid himself. He had also noted something in the trained voice (H.M. had always considered himself a public speaker) that was cautious. The one thing Max had learned from the conversation was that H.M. did not know for sure at that time that he had been served. Max knew he was right this minute trying his damnedest to find out for sure, but if he didn't, Max then had a slight advantage. He decided he couldn't count on that.

Max always liked to think of himself as shrewd, not devious, nor did he care if anyone thought he was was a bastard. In the jungle he had grown up in, the bastards were to be respected. "Wow! Is he a bastard!" on the side of Bridgeport he lived in meant "Man! Is he tough! Don't tangle with him!" He was born in the slums, and the fact that Mama fought a constant battle with the cockroaches and rats coming from neighboring apartments that were not so cared for didn't make the memory any softer. Nor did the fact that he couldn't understand why his father allowed them to keep on living there, year in, year out. He thought about the daily sight of Mama' back, curved and tired, bent over, the scrub pail by her side, the brush being used to flail the hidden creatures from between the rotting floorboards. He would always bear in mind that memory of her and of the soft skin at the back of her neck and the neat gray hair in its rich, full bun, the hair he so loved to see loose and free. He would never forget his father's death, either, or the six thousand dollars they found concealed in his prayer shawl and prayerbook which, while his father lived, his mother was never allowed to touch. His father had left no insurance and Mama was being evicted when they discovered it. Six thousand dollars! A fortune to them then. But for his mother it came too late. She died—just simply gave out—three months later.

But the six thousand dollars had put Max through school.

"Don't ever let your Papa down," his mother had said just before she died.

Those words had haunted him and twisted something irreparable inside him. Whatever he did, he did for himself, Maxwell Isaac Seaman. Yet no matter how he tried to intellectualize or rationalize, the nagging, irritating, nihilating truth that nothing could stop it working toward—*not letting that son of a bitch, his father, down.*

Tony was lagging in the hallway when Max started out to get the car.

"Some kind of a holiday?" Max asked.

"Mommy said I could."

"It's your left arm and you're right-handed, and otherwise you look fine to me. Slept more than usual, too."

"Mommy said—"

"I'll drop you at school, on my way to the studio."

The small face puckered as if to cry. "I'll be late. I'll have to walk in late."

"So?" Max said and began hustling his son forward.

Luise had entered the hallway and stood there with some shock. "Max, he really doesn't have to go to school today. After all, yesterday was more than a little traumatic."

"This day, above all other days, he *does* have to show his face, Luise."

"I can't make you change your mind?"

"Get into the car, Tony."

The child ran out of the house and could be heard opening the car door.

"Pretty good for a one-armed kid," Max beamed.

"Will you take him into the classroom?"

"I'll see."

"Please, Max."

"I'll see how *Tony* feels about it."

He kissed her lightly on the cheek.

"Good luck, Max," she said.

"Hell, luck won't help, baby. This is war."

And he was gone.

Father and son drove in silence until they reached Sherman Oaks Elementary School's daisy-lined front gates.

"Now, what shall it be," Max asked. "It's your decision. Do you go into the class by yourself like a man, or do I take you in like you're a baby?"

"I'll go myself," Tony said, finally without tears or a quiver in his voice.

"Good!"

"But don't watch me. Promise—honest injun?"

"Promise."

Tony scrambled out of the rear seat of the car, where he had selected to ride, and stood at the front gate of his school. He waved his father off.

"You promised," he chided.

Max waved back and released the brake and continued on his way to the big meeting.

Harry Steiner's offices would have intimidated even Eleanor Roosevelt—and they were meant to. They occupied the entire third floor (which was the top) of the executive building of Omega. There was no elevator, except a private one that H. M. controlled and that came up directly into his private chambers. All but the most privileged had to walk up three flights of stone stairs, be greeted by an elderly receptionist who had once been a character actress, give their credentials, and be made to wait on an elegant hard antique bench surrounded by hundreds of framed English hunting scenes. Then, as though being led into an examining room, the caller was ushered through an electrified gate, past the elderly receptionist, and into one of a series of anterooms and left alone. These rooms were a little more designed for comfort. There was the hard antique chair or bench to be sure, the same hunting scenes on the walls, but the floors were now deeply carpeted, and there was a table with an ashtray and several copies of the *Reader's Digest* and often a copy of an old *Wall Street Journal*. Never was a *Hollywood Reporter* or a *Variety* visible anywhere.

A younger secretary would now come to fetch the caller and lead him or her this time to the anteoffice directly outside H.M.'s sanctum sanctorum, where she would hand the visitor over to H.M.'s *private* secretaries (there were three), who thereupon sat him down for the last wait (now in a leather armchair that was so deep as to be impossible to rise from without feeling ludicrous)—unless, of course, the caller was so in favor, or so out of favor, that he or she was ushered instantly into H.M.'s presence.

It often depended on H.M.'s whim, not his time schedule, how swiftly this process would transpire.

In Max's case, he had had no time to sit anywhere along the line, but still had to make all the stops and goes, having yet to reach the studio summit, which meant entrance by that private elevator.

He now stood across Harry Steiner's gargantuan desk and looked straight at him, not at the two tiger-head trophies on the wall directly behind and to either side of H.M. The desk was too broad to permit a handshake, though H.M. did rise a few inches from his throne chair (a set piece from one of the Henry VIII films) in greeting. He was a surprisingly dapper little man, attractive in a neatly clipped way. His hair was graying in a distinguished manner, and his mustache suited him. He was a man in his late fifties, still with no need for glasses and not yet suffering high blood pressure. He wore one of the hundred or so dark gray suits he owned, a monogrammed French-cuffed silk shirt, a maroon pure-silk tie. His only ostentatious touch was a mammoth star ruby he wore on his right pinkie finger. On his left hand, he wore a wide gold wedding band.

They exchanged simple pleasantries.

"I want to take Bob Tanner off the project," Max opened with. "Is that what you wanted to speak to me about?"

"Among other things."

"Like . . . "

"Can we take first things first?"

"Naturally, my boy." The vice-president in charge of production sat back.

"Tanner has talent, but he's too polished. He learned a lot from Lou. He's a great 'learner.' For that matter, I always have the uneasy feeling that he's got me pinned under a classroom microscope. He's not *today*. He's where the winners, not the action is. I need someone who has a grasp of the young people today. After all, that is what *Crosscurrent* is about. The veteran who returns from bloody battle and says: 'Is this what I risked my neck for?' I'd like someone who could bring me a few ideas for a change. And someone who I know, if I gave him a tough time, would then give me the best that's in him, unafraid that I might disagree. I need a boy who's not afraid of tigers."

"Who did you have in mind?"

"Your son."

Harry Steiner's son was indeed a returning veteran, who, however, had fought his battle in Special Services—film division in Hollywood, California. He was Steiner's great hope, his pride and his joy, though at twenty-six years of age, others might question the great man's faith that his son, who was renowned for being a great whoremaster in a town filled with whoremasters, would ever become more than that.

He smiled at Max—pleased. He had wondered how Max would parry, made some speculations—this wasn't one of them.

"It won't work, Max," he said.

"You can't mean *you* don't believe in the boy?"

"I mean I know you've been subpoenaed and I've already made up my mind."

"Who says it's your move?"

"I do."

"OK, Harry, I'll listen."

"They have us by the short hairs. They can destroy all the talent it has taken me years to build. They can rip our product right off the screen, block production on all our projects, yours included.

Omega could collapse, Max. I could lose my shirt. Remember that whatever happens to you, to all those in my employ, means my life, too." He stood up and came around his desk, which took many long seconds, and then perched himself on a corner, looking down at Max.

"We shelve the picture, Max, until this blows over, as it will. We shelve it because it does have a few things in it the committee could misinterpret. We'll transfer Tanner to the Western as you suggest, and since Frank is an old dog anyway and needs a little pasture, you take over the Western. And you go into Washington with the best lawyers money can buy and power can command, and you tell those bastards the truth, but you do it in closed session—that much I am sure I can get for you. Then you go to Europe or South America, wherever you like, six months top before returning to Hollywood and, I am confident, to the final shooting on *Crosscurrent*. You know I love that story, Max. Trust that. Trust *me*." He waited patiently for Max to answer.

"I'll think about it," Max finally said, giving no clue whatsoever to how Steiner's words had hit him.

Steiner got to his feet. He was beaming from ear to ear. "We think alike, Max. I've always felt that. A great communion. I always felt like a father to you. I'm old enough to be, you know." He laughed. "Hell, I was a boy wonder. It could have been true!"

Max stood up and Steiner put his arm around his shoulder, though he had to reach a bit to engineer it. "The Western is a dog, Max. I admit that. But I have a feeling you could make a respectable picture of it."

He was leading Max to the doors of his private elevator. He lowered his arm from Max's shoulder and pushed the button, and the doors opened. "I'll call you tomorrow. We'll discuss the next steps." Then he held out his hand and Max took it and, as there seemed no place else to go, stepped into the carpeted, antique-paneled, fur-cushioned elevator and began to descend.

"That bastard," he said silently (having heard the elevator—in fact, the entire studio—was bugged). "That bastard!" and then he laughed.

Chapter 10

Within a few days it became common knowledge that forty-five men and women had been subpoenaed and that they fell into two categories: "friendly" and "unfriendly." The "friendly" witnesses were those who planned to testify that they stood ready to rid Hollywood of any Communist-inspired men or women. The "unfriendly," nineteen in all, Max being one of their number had belonged to or supported what the committee considered Communist-inspired organizations or groups. Max reacted without surprise on learning that Harry Steiner was to be a "friendly" witness.

"He's always liked public speaking," he told Luise. "He'll shoot off his mouth like a three-headed parrot."

The "unfriendly" nineteen, as they were now referred to, met for the first time as a group less than a week after being subpoenaed, for the express purpose of deciding upon legal representation to defend them before the committee in less than a month's time. There were, among the nineteen, twelve screenwriters, five directors, a producer, and an actor. On every one of their minds was the question: "Why *me?* Why *us?* Why were *we* singled out?"

There was one common denominator: None of the nineteen had seen American military service. The committee was perhaps attempting to avoid the touchy subject of the returning veteran. Two of them had not been inducted because they had served with the Lincoln Brigade in Spain. The others, however, had simply been too old, or had been exempt for medical reasons, or had had too many dependents. A look at their conglomerate film credits did not enlighten them much further. Those credits constituted some of the most patriotic films produced in Hollywood in their time and certainly among the most successful, artistically and financially. However, Mr. Thomas and his committee could take any film and interpret any given scene, any scrap of dialogue, as an idea or theme that was "Communist-oriented."

Max looked slowly around the smoke-filled room. The men gathered with him were not men he would have thought his life would hang with—and hang, instinctively he knew it did. He knew all of them fairly well, though not intimately. He had worked from time to time with a few of them, been on committees with others, either for the writers or directors guilds, been at party meetings with three of them, and been to bed with the secretary of one, a sister of another, and two of their wives. He had attended premieres, restaurants, and large parties they had been to as well, but of the eighteen other men in the room only Milton Stevens and Lou Whitehorn had been at his home socially, and, of course, Merwin (though Max had attempted through the years to keep Merwin at arm's length)—Merwin and his wife were invited when he and Luise were throwing large parties and not when they were hosting small informal dinners.

Of all the men in the room, Max admired Lou Whitehorn the most. He didn't really like him. He just admired him, for he thought Lou, who was also a writer, was one of the only real talents in Hollywood. Certainly, and without any false modesty, Max was able to say to himself that he and Lou represented the only writing guts in the room. Surely, they had to be the only two whose words the committee could feel were strong enough to sway an audience, and Lou's last picture had been ludicrously enough a splashy musical based on the life of one of the most reactionary bastards in show business and his current project a remake of a Bible story.

If J. Parnell Thomas had begun this Hollywood inquest to reveal subversive, Communist, and un-American influence in motion pictures, on the face of it, the men he'd leveled the committee's attack against dissipated the accusation almost entirely. What he had in his corner was the ill-gotten confidence that the masses could be stirred into a mob—a lynch mob at that. What he had *not* bargained for was the staying power of their opponents.

Lou Whitehorn took over immediately as speaker. "We all have our own private lawyers, I'm sure. God knows, in this business we overwork and overpay them, but I think we will all be in accord that this time we need a good deal more than a good theatrical lawyer, a divorce lawyer, or a copyright and libel man. We need men who can impress the committee and who can impress the nation as well, because we won't be spared constant press coverage," Lou said in his clear, theater-trained voice, his soft blue eyes sharper than usual. "And we don't want any militants. I've made up a list of men here in California whom I consider possible. Each of you add whoever I may have overlooked." A slip of paper was passed to each man. "Several of us," Lou continued, "have already agreed that we will need at least six. Before we leave here, we can vote on who we want those men to be. Then comes the problem of convincing them to represent us."

"How do we pay them?" Merwin asked.

"Between us we've solicited funds for almost every hardship case or group that has come to our attention. We sure as hell should be able to solicit funds for our own defense," someone called out.

"Well, those of us who can will give what they're able," someone else shouted.

"What does *that* mean?"

"We have to figure out a way of protecting our dependents. It could be a long time before we work again."

"Ridiculous!"

"We could be imprisoned."

"For what?"

"Let's get the matter at hand settled."

"Good idea."

"Agreed."

Very shortly thereafter six men became the attorneys for the nineteen men. One had been a former elected state officer, all were men with impeccable law records, and all accepted the awesome responsibility suddenly thrust upon them.

As well representing producers and studio interests, was the president of the Motion Picture Association and two attorneys. Opposing them would be Chairman Thomas' committee consisting of four Democrats—John S. Wood, J. Hardin Peterson, Herbert C. Bonner, and John E. Rankin—and five Republicans—Thomas, Karl

E. Mundt, John McDowell, Richard B. Vail, and Richard M. Nixon.

"You have to watch Richard Nixon," Lou Whitehorn told the nineteen. "He asks the most dangerously ambiguous questions."

Chapter 11

There was always something disconcerting in the sound of Lucy Banner's voice on the telephone. It was a voice that agent and studio proclaimed had the greatest contact in the world. But isolated that way, like some rare and closely incubated virus, it had a way of becoming rather awesome. Lucy Banner had more than a sex-charged voice, however, more than a set of beautiful legs (for which she was almost as famous as for the voice), more than her large talent to sing and dance. Lucy Banner had that indescribable something that could transform a performer into a star, a third dimension, something that only seemed to burst into aliveness before a camera and on the screen. On the telephone, however, you were reminded uncomfortably that the voice belonged to a near-nympho, frustrated, neurotic nineteen-year-old girl who had been peddled as a body by her mother to the studio executives when she was only thirteen and whose every hard-earned buck was continually and as fast as she could make it being filched by agents, managers, mama, mama's boyfriends, her own boyfriends, and whatever quack doctor would prescribe the pills for her that kept her awake, asleep, thin, sexy—name it, Lucy took it.

"Oh, Max, Max, *Max!*" The words shot into his ears. "What can I say? What can *anyone* say? It's what they *do* that counts now. Right? Did anyone tell you about the meeting at Lucey's? We're *all* behind you, Max—all the *thinking* people in Hollywood. Have you seen the list of names? Wouldn't H.M. like to have *those* names on cards above his time clock!" She took time out to laugh.

A low, unsettling, nearly hysterical laugh. Max waited for it to end, for Lucy to continue. "We're flying into Washington right after the nineteen of you arrive. We have time on national radio and an auditorium."

"That's wonderful, Lucy," he said artfully.

"Is it, Max? I mean, is it what we should do? Is there something else we—*I*—should be doing? It sounded right to me. Protest seemed the only thing. But is it, Max? I mean, I knew you'd tell me. You know, I've really never been very politically oriented. Not because I wasn't, *am not*, interested, it just all seemed so—so beyond me." There was now a small quiver in her voice as though it had stretched itself as far as it would go and was about to break. When she had had too many ups, too many diet pills, the famous voice would sound like this.

"Right now I can't think about anything more you could do, Lucy," he assured her.

"Oh, thank you, Max—and God bless." The words were usually a sign-off, but she hadn't disconnected.

"Lucy, are you all right?" he asked tiredly.

"I haven't slept, that's all, and I'm out of pills."

"Where's Irv?" Max inquired of her latest lover.

"In Petersburg, Texas, on location. Can you imagine anyone in Petersburg, Texas?"

"Why don't you hop a plane and join him?"

"But I'm going to Washington day after tomorrow."

"Yeah, well, that's the day after tomorrow. I know if you were my broad and I was in Petersburg, Texas, on location with a lot of sweaty Western types, I'd sure as hell expect you to get your ass down to me, even for one night," he told her confidentially.

"You would, Max? *Really?*"

"Damned right."

"Thanks Max. Thanks." She started to hang up: "Oh and, Max, good luck."

She was gone, and Max breathed a sigh of relief. He smiled to himself, for the first time that long, difficult day, and thought, *That poor son of a bitch Irv. I hope he hasn't got some busty squaw shacked up!*

"Who was it?" Luise asked as she came into the room with some coffee and cake, setting the tray down on the cocktail table and then sitting down on the couch to pour.

"Lucy Banner."

"You shouldn't be bothered with calls like that."

"I give her five years."

"Was she in bad shape?"

"Usual. Five years and she'll take an overdose."

He sat down stiffly on the couch beside her and helped himself to coffee and a generous slice of chocolate cake.

"Max, I want to go with you," she said in an even voice.

"You know that's impossible. It's no place for a wife. No place for a man to have his wife to worry about."

"You always minimize my facility to cope, Max." She spoke, not in an injured tone, rather coolly for that matter, with measured detachment.

"I just don't want you hurt," he countered.

"If I would be, it would be a shared hurt. Anything shared has to help. And being left behind in Sherman Oaks won't keep me immune."

"The children will need you." He pushed the cake aside and then stood up, pacing slightly, a few steps and then a pause, hands on hips, eyes in the distance, as he did when he was writing or dictating. "It won't be easy," he said.

"They're too young to know what it's about."

"I want them to know." He wheeled toward her, pointed at her. "I make you responsible for that, Luise. I want them to know it's their country, their future. You think I want them to end up sponges or wet mops? They carry the name of Seaman and there's no damned reason to be ashamed of that."

"Of course not, Max. Of course not."

"Where are they?"

"In bed."

He began to pace again—stopped. "It will be in the newspapers—Thea can read. And the other kids—they can be brutal. They can make them believe that 'Communism' is a dirty word, not an ideal we once believed in and that 'once a Communist' is synonymous with being 'once a spy'—a *traitor.* I hope Tony has the guts to slug that one out."

"Max, he's only six years old." She had to turn away then because she was having a hard time fighting back the tears.

"You employ *smother* love, Luise. You'll ruin that kid. You sure as hell can ruin men, baby."

She turned her head slowly and looked up at him. "I'm trying very hard, Max, very hard not to lose my control. Not tonight. Not this night."

"Not before your man goes into battle, eh?"

"Yes, I suppose that's it." She got slowly to her feet.

"Where are you going?"

"To see if the children are asleep."

"You have to learn to face things, Luise, fight it out, say what's on your mind."

"Not now, Max." She started past him toward the door, but he swung around and grabbed her by the arm.

"*Now*, Luise."

"Let me go, Max. For *you*, for *me*—please, Max, let me go. *Not tonight*."

"There's something eating at your gut, causing a small ripple in that great calm you wear as proudly as Chanel Number Five. It's been there for months now, building up, ready to goose you into a normal reaction at any given moment. *Now*, Lu . . . "

She pulled away from him and tottered uneasily on the high stiletto heels she always wore as a badge, never condescending, never coming down from her height until she was ready for bed.

"Yeah, I sleep around," he called softly after her.

She paused in the doorway and threw the words back over her shoulder. "You have from the beginning, Max. But you always come home."

Max laughed, and she turned to look at him. There was about ten feet of hostility between them.

"You hate me, you hate yourself, Max," she said. "You want to strike me, make me suffer, feel pain, break. You're just testing yourself, and you know it. Well, I know it, too, and that's how it is. We've been together so long we've taken on a part of each other. In my case I think that's love. In yours, you believe it's possession. Perhaps we're both right. Perhaps the two are one—interchangeable. Perhaps we are interchangeable now, as well. But the children, that's a different matter."

Max grinned nervously. "Brush a mother cat the wrong way . . . " he began.

"The way you push that little boy isn't natural. A man your age expecting a child of six to act as he would. No, *worse*, to act as he *wants* to act. As he thinks he should act. Talk about me ruining his manhood. You've created a situation where a six-year-old believes he's already failing as a man because he doesn't have the initiative or the reactions of a man thirty-seven years of age—a man who is an exceptional talent, an accepted genuis, famous, infamous, a fighter . . . warped, warped . . . warped!"

Max started walking toward her and Luise instinctively braced herself, expecting him to strike her, knowing she was, in fact, provoking him to do so, thinking, *So this is how a perfectly respectable man is moved to strike his wife!* But instead, he slammed the door shut behind her with a rather violent shove and walked away from her and to the bar and poured himself a stiff drink.

"I think I'm going to need this," he said.

"A normal man would have struck me. Can't you see that? You're not normal. You prod and ram and flog people into revealing all their private hurts; then, oh God, then, Max, you *study* them." She came closer to the bar, looked into those cool, cool gray eyes of his. "I'm going to tell you something." Her voice became suddenly calm and very cold. "We fight and pick and torment each other over Tony when Thea is the real problem. Tony's fighting you. Oh, yes, he is—he's fighting with tears and frustration and small tantrums because that's the only fight his six-year-old mind can come up with. But *Thea*—she's in love with you. Yes, I said in love. She's only eight, but it's no child's game for her. You say, 'Be a fighter,' and she fights. You say, 'This man has no talent,' and she believes you. You say, 'Strong people don't cry,' and she doesn't cry. 'Wear your hair long,' and she won't cut it. 'Red's my favorite color,' and she'll wear nothing else. You belittle everyone in her presence, including Tony and myself, and then share private looks and secret words about it. You made yourself out as a God to that child, and you had better stand ready at all times in the future for the responsibility that involves."

"You're overwrought," Max whispered and drank down the scotch.

"I'm going to tell you something else. You know it's true. Every word I've said. You would have struck me otherwise. There would have been no alternative. But you know I spoke the truth. And you are a man who does, heaven knows, respect the truth."

She stood with her arms crossed in front of her, as if holding herself together. She had no look of triumph. Instead, she seemed ill, desolate, and about to cry.

"I'll check the kids for you," he said and, not able to bear looking at her, turned away as he went past her. And not able to pass her without feeling her misery, bolted to the door, opened it, and took the stairs to the children's nursery three steps at a time.

Neither was sleeping, and so he took Thea from her room and carried her in his arms to Tony's room, where he sat down with her on the edge of Tony's bed.

"Kids," he said, "your old man is in for a tough time of it. But I'm not alone. There are all kinds of tragedies. All kinds of battles. You're going to hear them call me some pretty dirty names. Like those bully kids from next door sometimes call you. They'll say 'Communist!' and make it sound like 'dirty rat,' or 'ratfink.' You're going to have to face many pairs of unfriendly eyes. And you'll ask yourself: 'Was my daddy what they say?' The answer is no! Your father is a man whose life and faith are now on the witness stand. He has been called to testify in history's defense. And in doing so, he has had to accept such consequences as his children's being bullied by the ignorant, the foolish, and the naïve. Do you understand?"

Neither of them really did, but Thea clung to him, and Tony nodded his golden head solemnly.

"I love you both very much. And your Mommy. I'll only be gone a couple of weeks, but I'll expect you to take care of Mommy during that time. OK?"

"OK," they both whispered in frightened voices.

He leaned over and kissed Tony and Thea, picked up Thea again, and carried her back to her own room, placing her in her bed. He turned out all the lights in the nursery and then edged his way through the playroom. As he reached the stairway in the hall, Thea came running out of her room.

"Daddy! Daddy!" she cried, her voice static with tears.

Max turned back and caught the slim, trembling figure in his arms.

"Daddy! Daddy!" she sobbed.

"Don't, Thea. You'll upset your mother and Tony," he whispered as he held her out a short way from himself.

The little girl fought for control and stepped back, biting her lip, grasping one hand with the other.

"Go back to bed, Thea," he told her and then started once again down the stairs.

"Daddy! Daddy!" the screams fighting their way out.

"Thea!"

"Don't ever go away," she cried.

"Even death won't make that come to pass," he said.

"Daddy!"

"Don't worry, Thea, I'll never, *ever* go away."

Luise was standing, waiting for him in the opened doorway to the den. She let him go past her and then closed the door so that the children wouldn't hear. "I'll go up to them in a moment," she said.

He went straight to the bar and poured himself another stiff drink.

"It's been a ghastly night. It's mostly my fault. I'm sorry."

"Don't apologize, Luise."

"I've never let myself go like that before, and it will never happen again."

"Let's not talk about it."

She went over to the cocktail table and began to put the cold coffee cups back on the tray.

"I won't leave the house in the evenings, Max. Please call. And if you change your mind . . . "

"I won't."

"You sure Edyth won't prove more of a problem than a help?"

"We have to keep up with the correspondence and so forth. Take notes. I've more or less donated her for the cause."

"I packed your suitcase this afternoon. You're leaving so early in the morning."

"Yes, I saw. Thank you."

He took his drink and crossed with it to a chair and eased himself, exhausted, into it.

Luise perched on the arm for a moment.

"It will be all right," she said. "I just can't believe otherwise." Then she kissed him on his forehead and rose carefully and went out of the room and up to her children.

BOOK III

Washington

It behooves every man who values liberty of conscience for himself, to resist invasions of it in the case of others; or their case may, by change of circumstances, become his own. It behooves him, too, in his own case, to give no example of concession, betraying the common right of independent opinion, by answering questions of faith, which the laws have left between God and himself.

THOMAS JEFFERSON

Chapter 12

Max paced the unfamiliar room as if attempting to memorize every corner, every spot on the rug, each glass ring on each table. Washington seemed to be waiting for an impending execution. When Max, the remaining eighteen men, and their attorneys had arrived at Washington Airport, planes had arrived before and after them, bearing the highest deacons of journalistic aristocracy in America. The fact that it was Sunday had not dimmed the midnight oil. The men had been housed at the Shoreham Hotel while the attorneys had filed a memorandum challenging the authority of the Un-American Activities Committee to issue subpoenas and maintained that the committee aimed at censorship of the screen by intimidation. The producers' representatives had agreed that they shared their feelings and would support their position.

"Tell the boys not to worry," the producers' envoy said. "There will never be a blacklist in Hollywood. We're not going totalitarian to please the committee."

Max, now alone in his hotel room, was not sure. He knew the production end of the industry somewhat better than most of the other men. The money men, the moguls like Harry Steiner. They were fighting for their lives, too. They had worked many hard years for those bank accounts, the power; they wouldn't chance ruin, court the possibility of decline that easily. If the committee pushed a blacklist, the producers might consider themselves obliged to concede.

Max nervously lighted a fresh cigarette from the burning stub of the one he had been smoking, then squashed the old one violently out in a glass ashtray. No one knew when he would be called. How long the wait would be—hours, days. Right now it was impossible to judge how much time would be allotted or consumed by each witness. The unwritten, unspoken, but tacitly understood commandment among the nineteen was that no one would reveal any names. No one would inform. What was happening to them was unconstitutional, un-American. Unlike most Germans at the beginning of Nazism, they would fight. To stand up to the committee was the first giant step. Defy it. But Max at this moment felt like the small boy with his finger in the dike.

He looked at himself in the contortion of the cheap mirror over the bureau. He could not shake the look that met his stare. Once he had gone hunting as a boy in Bridgeport and cornered a young rabbit. What he had seen in that rabbit's eyes was in his own now.

"He who is about to die," he said in a cynical whisper. He flicked off the light and stood in the strange darkness, wishing morning would come swiftly even though with it might come the loss of life and freedom for him forever. Anything was better than this purgatory he was now in.

So the producers were assuring them that there would not be a blacklist, and he had cheered the news along with the others, but alone, with time to question, he was not sure that they were being dealt from the top of the deck. There could be the possibility of a gray list—shadowy, screened, an invisible blacklist. He measured what that would mean to him.

He had made enough money to hold out for a while. But not that long. Two, three years, maybe. Five or six, if they sold the house. A blacklist could last longer than that. It could go on forever. Well, of course, he was a healthy man. There were other jobs to hold, other fields to enter. But he was a writer, a creative man. A man who dealt in ideas and words. A man to whom those very ideas and words meant life. To be silenced *forever*. Max shook slightly. Then he began to tremble uncontrollably. He felt cold, deep in the center of him. He was unable to warm himself with a shot from the bottle he had in his room. Outside, it was Indian summer in Washington, and the city still steamed under sweaty sheets. But inside this room at the Shoreham Hotel, inside himself, it was polar temperature. He got into one of the single beds in the room and stripped the other bed and piled those blankets on top of himself. He tried to sleep, but it was impossible.

The telephone rang in Milton Stevens' room, which was directly next door. It rang only once. Max could hear Milton's muffled voice. He sat up, pulling the cover around himself, and lighted a cigarette. He thought about calling Luise, since it was still several hours earlier in California, but dismissed the thought. He was sorry he hadn't had Edyth come on the same flight instead of having her arrange a flight for herself the following morning; then he was thankful he had. He smoked the cigarette to the end and then lighted another from the burning tip. The voice in the next room was now gone.

Moments later his bedside telephone rang.

"Yeah?" he muttered into the speaker.

"Mr. Seaman?"

"Yeah?"

"Don't ask who this is. I'm just a friend."

"Friends are seldom anonymous." He went to disconnect.

"Mr. Seaman. Please."

"Look, it's the middle of the night, and I have a long day ahead of me."

"Yes, I know. One night I had the same day ahead of me. Mr. Seaman, I only called to warn you."

"I don't need warning. A man stands on the edge of a cliff, and he knows damned well he can fall."

"I think you should know what you are in for, Mr. Seaman."

It was only now that Max realized his caller was a woman. She paused, and he thought perhaps she had changed her mind or the telephone had gone dead. "Are you still there?" he asked. Then he heard a strange sound on the line. He sat up, straightening in the bed. He had suddenly grown warm, and he threw the top covers off. His head was spinning, but he was clear-thinking, and he managed a cool, indifferent, guarded tone, though his words were sharply edged. "You're not suggesting I inform, are you, baby?" he asked.

"I'm saying you could get a closed session if you were smart—smarter than I was. You're safer with the committee than the studio. They'll throw you all to the lions, Mr. Seaman. You can expect that."

Max felt a strange emptiness in the pit of his stomach where right now it was truly the middle of the night.

"Are you there, Mr. Seaman?"

"Yeah." Cool. "Go on."

"You're only pin money. One picture in preproduction state—a half million loss to the studio at most. You have no pictures currently in release and no expensive properties that the studio has bought for you in the future. But Omega has big stars, directors, producers who have *millions* of dollars' worth of product in the cans and ready to release. Men and women worth millions to them. Men and women unwittingly—some, perhaps, even wittingly—who joined the same organizations you did. Someone has to be the goat. The others aren't any more or less guilty than you, but you are going to get it for them."

"Drop dead," Max said smoothly and then hung up.

He tore out of the bed, grabbing his pants and stepping into them, stumbling barefooted, attempting to zip his fly as he crossed to the door to the corridor. He left his door wide open and began to knock wildly on Milton's door. It was only a moment before Milton, carefully sashing his Japanese kimono, opened it and let Max in, not that it would have been possible to stop him, and then closed the door tightly after him. Max was prancing around the room, pulling up cushions, removing pictures from the wall, sticking coat hangers behind the radiators and over the windows.

"Have you gone mad?" Milton asked.

"We're bugged. Those sons of bitches have bugged us," Max roared.

"You'll wake the entire hotel." Milton found his glasses on the bedside table and carefully put them on.

Max had paused, having found nothing, and stood panting in the middle of the room. "Did you get a telephone call?"

"Yes, I did. From Betty"—that was Milton's wife—"not that it is any of your business, Max," Milton said nervously.

"So it wasn't from Betty. Who the hell cares if it was a broad? I'm only interested in one particular broad—she has an oily, curling voice, and she's out to seduce informers."

"I believe you are really quite mad. I received no such call."

"Well, I did. And if I did, *you might*— and the others too—and when that happens, just slam the receiver down." Max started back toward the door again. "I wish to hell I could believe you,

Milton. I just wish to almighty hell I could. You always were a cock-sucker, and I don't like you any better just because we're in this together." Max stood with his hand on the door handle.

Milton's nose was nervously twitching. "This is no time, Max. It's damned insensitive—*stupid* of you. This is no time at all." Milton looked as if he might cry.

"Well, just don't say anything you wouldn't want to hear in court, on the telephone *or* in this room." Max opened the door but stood there a moment. "And you might as well ring that broad back on the telephone and tell her to get her ass over. Hell, even Spartacus got laid before he was thrown to the lions."

And he went out, slamming the door after himself, and went back to his room, where he ordered another bottle of scotch and nursed it until daylight finally came.

Chapter 13

The corridor in the old House Office Building leading to the offices and hearing room of the House Committee on Un-American Activities was already lined with press and spectators when the chairman made his way past them, through the heavy oak-paneled door and into the committee's outer office. It was not quite nine in the morning, and although he might have thought he arrived early, the outer office was already packed with many secretaries and men gathered in small groups. It was a bright room with many windows. One could see the Capitol just a short way to the south.

The committee's chief investigator sat behind a very impressive desk, his cool dark-blue eyes taking in everyone and everything. He was a tall man who looked imposing even while seated. Most of the nineteen had seen him in action during the Hiss trial and knew the lean Southerner would be the man wielding the whip, although the chairman, naturally, was his superior.

It was thought that Milton Stevens would be one of the first witnesses, and he had prepared a written statement (many, *many* pages—typical of Milton's tendency to ponderous overwriting) which the attorneys now handed to the chief investigator, who did not even glance down at it as he slipped it into a briefcase on his desk.

There was a hushed, muted feeling in the room, as if a radio had been turned down too low to distinguish the words of the speakers. The carpets were thick so that even footsteps were muffled. After a short uncomfortable time, the men and their attorneys were led from the outer office into the caucus room.

No matter what the men expected, they did not anticipate the battery of newsreel cameramen standing side by side, waiting for them, their cameras whirring as the men entered and were led to their seats. Dozens of photographers ran close to them, bunching up, crouching for angle shots, their flash cameras raised, turned, armed like artillery, bursting into brilliant flashes of light in the men's faces.

The room was beginning to fill up with spectators, who crowded into a bank of seats to one side. Across the front of the room was a platform where the committee sat, brass plates before them, to identify them for the cameras. Below the platform was the witness table and flanking it, to right and left, were tremendous tables set up to accommodate the ninety-four members of the press who would finally be accounted for. There were large windows in this room as well, but the eastern sun was deflected by the massive broadcasting equipment and rows of control panels situated there. In every corner of the room were loudspeakers for the public address system. There were microphones on the committee and witness tables.

There was a distinct feeling of a circus or an entertainment that was about to begin. An overwhelming sense of unreality that even all of Max's years on a Hollywood sound stage had not diminished. It seemed impossible that this could be any form of legislative hearing.

Nowhere in the room was there an American flag.

There was a long wait and then a long silence as the short, red-faced chairman entered the vast room. It was as though the chief surgeon had just entered the operating theater. His balding, gray-fringed head was bright and shiny beneath the intense light of the huge crystal chandelier as he drew closer to the arena. The flashbulbs exploded around him, and he stood there calmly, with the air of a man well acquainted with the limelight. Then he raised a small white hand, and all activity stopped as he made his way to the chairman's seat. There was a slight commotion before he sat down. A District of Columbia telephone book and a red silk cushion were placed on his chair so that the diminutive man could be seen by cameras and audience alike. A man then took a tape and measured the distance from his face to the cameras and thanked him for his cooperation.

The cameras began grinding; the radio microphones were switched on.

"Testing, testing. Mary had a little lamb . . . "

The chairman lowered his gavel.

CHAIRMAN: . . . I cannot emphasize too strongly the seriousness of Communist infiltration, which we have found to be a mutual problem for many, many different fields of endeavor in the United States. Communists for years have been conducting a relentless "boring from within" campaign against America's democratic institutions. While never possessing a large numerical strength, the Communists nevertheless have found that they could dominate the activities of unions or other mass enterprises in this country by capturing a few strategic positions of leadership.

This technique, I am sorry to say, has been amazingly profitable for the Communists. And they have been aided all along the line by non-Communists, who are either sympathetic to the aims of Communism or are unwilling to recognize the danger in Communist infiltration. . . .

The question before this committee, therefore, and the scope of its present inquiry, will be to determine the extent of Communist infiltration in the Hollywood motion-picture industry. We want to know what strategic positions in the industry have been captured by these elements, whose loyalty is pledged in word and deed to the interests of a foreign power.

The committee is determined that the hearings shall be fair and impartial. We have subpoenaed witnesses representing both sides of the question. All we are after are the facts.

Now I want to make it clear to the witnesses, the audience, the members of the press, and other guests here today that this hearing is going to be conducted in an orderly and dignified manner at all times. If there is anyone here today or at any of the future sessions of this hearing who entertains any hopes or plans for disrupting the proceedings, he may as well dismiss them from his mind.

COUNSEL: Mr. Chairman.

CHAIRMAN: Just a minute—

COUNSEL: I am attorney for the nineteen subpoenaed witnesses. You recall that we submitted a telegram yesterday on a motion to quash. It seems to me the most orderly way that we can present this would be to do so before a single witness has been sworn as the motion would be identical for any witness. If the committee is without constitutional authority to proceed . . .

CHAIRMAN: Counsel, these witnesses of yours will not be called until next week. They will not come up today at all or any day this week. So if you present your statement to the committee, we will take it under advisement, and then you can argue the question, if the committee sees fit, when your witness comes up next Monday. I believe the first witnesses are to come up Monday or Tuesday or Wednesday of next week. So if you will just present your statement to the committee.

COUNSEL: Mr. Chairman, may I file—

CHAIRMAN: Present your statement to the committee.

COUNSEL: Thank you. I would like to file with you, Mr. Chairman.

(A paper is handed to the chief investigator.)

CHAIRMAN: That will be filed. You may discuss the matter further when you present your witnesses to the committee.

INVESTIGATOR: The first witness today—

COUNSEL: Mr. Chairman.

CHAIRMAN: That is all.

COUNSEL: May we have the right to cross-examine?

CHAIRMAN: You may not ask one more thing at this time. Please be seated.

COUNSEL: Certainly American.

(Counsel, though, sits down.)

(It became immediately evident that the first witnesses were to be "friendly" ones who could pass into the record the names of "unfriendly" elements in the industry.

Among the first of these to take the stand was to be H.M. Steiner.)

CHAIRMAN: The committee will be in order.

INVESTIGATOR: I would like to call Herschel Meyer Steiner to the stand.

(H.M. came forward. He wore a dark gray suit and a maroon pure-silk tie. Curiously, the star ruby ring was absent from his right pinkie, though he was wearing his gold wedding band on his third finger, left hand. He did not look at the men at the witness table as he passed them and sat in the witness chair, looking straight ahead and at the chief investigator, not to left or right. Occasionally he would turn and stare into a camera as he spoke, as if this were meant to be an aside for the world to make special note.)

CHAIRMAN: Mr. Steiner, will you raise your right hand, please?

(H.M.'s right hand was raised high for a camera's close shot.)

CHAIRMAN: You solemnly swear the testimony you give this committee shall be the truth, the whole truth, and nothing but the truth, so help you God?

MR. STEINER: I do.

CHAIRMAN: Have a seat.

(H.M. sat down in the witness chair with considerable dignity as a clerk fluttered about him to carefully adjust the microphone. The chief investigator waited until the clerk had dissolved once more into the anonymous audience behind the cameras before beginning his questioning.)

(TESTIMONY OF MR. HERSCHEL MEYER STEINER)

INVESTIGATOR: You are Mr. Herschel Meyer Steiner?
MR. STEINER: Yes.
INVESTIGATOR: When and where were you born?
MR. STEINER: New York City, August 4, 1889.
INVESTIGATOR: What is your present place of residence?
MR. STEINER: 34589 Belagio Road, Bel Air, California.
INVESTIGATOR: What is your present occupation?
MR. STEINER: Motion picture executive.
INVESTIGATOR: You are, in fact vice-president in charge of production at Omega Films?
MR. STEINER: That's correct.
INVESTIGATOR: Will you identify your counsel?

(H.M. put forth his counsel's name before the committee, and the gentleman stood up when asked whom he would be representing at the hearing.)

COUNSEL: I represent the Motion Picture Association of America, Inc., and the Association of Motion Picture Producers, Inc., and their member companies. Mr. Steiner's company is a member of both associations.
INVESTIGATOR: You will be appearing then with various witnesses?
COUNSEL: Yes.
INVESTIGATOR: Do you represent in any way the nineteen witnesses, not members of the organizations you entered into the record?
COUNSEL: I do not.
INVESTIGATOR: Have a seat, sir.
CHAIRMAN: Counsel, the chair would like to inform you that it is the policy of this committee to permit counsel to advise his client, the witness here on the stand, of his constitutional rights, and only on the question of his constitutional rights.
COUNSEL: I understand, Mr. Chairman. Of course, I should like to make a request to be permitted to cross-examine witnesses.
CHAIRMAN: You will not have that permission. It is not the policy of the committee to permit counsel to cross-examine witnesses. You will only have the right, the solemn right, to advise your client, the witness, on his constitutional rights. Nothing else.
INVESTIGATOR: Mr. Steiner, approximately how many pictures does your company, Omega Films, produce a year?
MR. STEINER: On an average, twenty to thirty full-length films. We also film short subjects, of course. Over a hundred of those a year.

INVESTIGATOR: Mr. Steiner, as the chairman has stated, the purpose of this hearing is to determine the extent of Communist infiltration and influence in the motion-picture industry. Since you have been in Hollywood, has there ever been a period during which you consider that the Communists had infiltrated the studio?

MR. STEINER: If I may , I would like to read into the record a statement I have prepared.

INVESTIGATOR: Mr. Steiner, it is not the policy for this committee to permit witnesses to read statements. However . . .

CHAIRMAN: May I see the statement, please.

(The paper is handed to the chairman.)

CHAIRMAN: It will be all right to read this statement. The only reason we questioned it was that we wanted to make certain that it was pertinent to the inquiry.

MR. STEINER: Yes, sir, it is.

CHAIRMAN: And also will you read it into the microphone, Mr. Steiner.

MR. STEINER: Yes, sir.

CHAIRMAN: And speak just a little louder.

MR. STEINER: Yes, sir.

(STATEMENT OF MR. HERSCHEL MEYER STEINER)

It is my belief as an individual and Omega Films as an organization of American citizens that we must be on the constant lookout for any subversion that could endanger the American way of life.

Omega knows well its responsibilities to keep these influences out of its products. I personally oversee the production and planning of all of Omega's product and am confident that no Omega film has ever been released that contains any Communist undercurrent or propaganda.

We believe at Omega in freedom of expression, of course, but do not concur that this gives anyone a permit to betray our American way of life.

There is no positive guide to determine whether or not a person is a Communist, and the laws of our land, which are in the hands of you gentlemen, offer no clean-cut definition on that point, but subversive germs breed in dark corners and I agree wholeheartedly with you, that light should be shed there.

As a spokesman for Omega Films, I pledge to rid our organization of any subversive germs and will establish, if necessary, a fund to ship to Russia the people who don't like our American system of government and prefer the Communistic system to it.

I want all you good and dedicated men to know that I am happy to have this opportunity to testify.

Thank you.

(The above is possibly a classic of sorts, being the shortest statement H.M. had ever made for publication in his lifetime.)

MR. STEINER: Do you want this statement for the record?

INVESTIGATOR: That will be made part of the record, Mr. Chairman?

CHAIRMAN: So ordered.

INVESTIGATOR: Are there any Communists in your studio, Mr. Steiner?

MR. STEINER: There are those with un-American leanings, primarily writers.

INVESTIGATOR: Do you mean un-American because they are Communists or un-American because they are Fascists?

MR. STEINER: Un-American because what they attempt to put into their scripts, though I always cut it out, is in my opinion un-American.

INVESTIGATOR: Can you give us some examples of this.

MR. STEINER: Un-American things I cut out, you mean?

INVESTIGATOR: That's correct.

MR. STEINER: Well, of course, some things are just innuendo, double entendre, and hard to catch. You'd need a Harvard law degree to define each thing. One just feels it.

INVESTIGATOR: They are very subtle.

MR. STEINER: Exceptionally so. Sometimes they do it in a joking way—the rich man is the villain, a banker. One script had a scene in which the hero said to his rich girlfriend, "Your father's a banker. Mine lives over a grocery store—we're doomed." I took it out. That sort of thing, though.

INVESTIGATOR: You feel, Mr. Steiner, it is your patriotic duty as a motion-picture producer to oppose as well as you possibly can at any time the infiltration into your industry of writers or others who in some way or other would attempt to put into those pictures certain lines of propaganda which have as their aim and their purpose the setting up in the United States of a totalitarian system of government, be it Fascist or Communist?

MR. STEINER: I am for everything that you have said.

INVESTIGATOR: You agree with that statement?

MR. STEINER: I agree wholeheartedly.

INVESTIGATOR: The statement was a little long.

MR. STEINER: It was a very good statement; it was the statement of a real American, and I'm proud of it.

INVESTIGATOR: Now, would you say that the writers in the industry have been the ones to seek to inject their Communist propaganda into films?

MR. STEINER: Yes, I would say ninety-five percent.

INVESTIGATOR: Ninety-five percent is through the writers?

MR. STEINER: I would say so.

INVESTIGATOR: And some were entrenched, so to speak, at your studio?

MR. STEINER: When I found out about it, which was always the case, the writer was let go at the end of his contract and kept off assignments until that time.

INVESTIGATOR: And have you gotten them all out?

MR. STEINER: There are a few—Milton Stevens, for one, Merwin Bibbs, Sol Levitz, Louis Whitehorn—that this committee has also uncovered. If there are any others, they will be ferreted out and dealt with accordingly.

INVESTIGATOR: And all these men injected Communist propaganda into Omega films?

MR. STEINER: Endeavored to inject it. I took out all that I found.

INVESTIGATOR: You recognize the fact that Communsim is a very definite threat to our government today?

MR. STEINER: I do.

INVESTIGATOR: And you recognize the fact also, that the motion-picture industry, paying high salaries to actors and writers and directors who support Communist causes and organizations, is thus lending its support to the Communistic effort?

MR. STEINER: If you have that proof, undoubtedly that is what they are doing.

INVESTIGATOR: I feel you are more informed about the situation in Hollywood, Mr. Steiner, and could help this committee immeasurably by putting before it any names of persons other than your own employees who have been substantial contributors to the Communist Party and their causes.

MR. STEINER: I will cooperate fully with the committee and, to the best of my knowledge, withhold no name that is known to me as a Communist sympathizer.

The naming had begun.

Milton Stevens and Merwin Bibbs sat in the latter's hotel room at the end of the day and discussed what had happened, what might happen, and what they were fearful would happen. Uppermost in their minds and conversation was Steiner's testimony. Other "friendly" witnesses had taken the witness chair during the long first day of the proceedings and had revealed names. But Steiner's allegations and testimony clearly established the fact that in spite of the producers' previous denials, the studios would hold by a blacklist—a list that would outlaw all men and women who had been named (guilty by insinuation) from working at their livelihoods.

"I'm a poor man. A poor man," Stevens wailed as he wrung his freshly manicured hands. "This will ruin me."

"Haven't you ever held another job?" Merwin asked in a curiously paternal tone. Merwin, of course, would be affected as greatly as Stevens. The only difference was that he had been serving a long apprenticeship in hardship and ruin.

"I was a real estate salesman once. God! A real estate salesman."

"I haven't even had *that*," Merwin confessed. "I started in films when I was fourteen. I worked for Chaplin and Sennett as a callboy. Went on as an extra for Griffith and DeMille. That was when they were still shooting films in New York. I began writing in the thirties for the various government workshops. When I came to Hollywood in thirty-seven, it was to write. I've never worked outside the industry in my entire life."

"A year or two—it could pass over," Stevens speculated. "It's possible."

"No, Milton," Merwin said quietly, "from the time I received the subpoena I've known with a certainty. I can't explain it, but it's there. It won't go away. *Milton, we're doomed.*"

Edyth sat huddled up on the couch in Max's room, cooling her warm, sweaty hands on the outside of her cold drink, rolling the glass between her palms, pressing it against her forehead. "He didn't name you," she repeated once again. "It's incredible. He didn't name you. Why, Max? *Why?*"

Max was smiling. "The bastard wants me to know he still holds the strings," he said.

"He's going to offer you a way out, even now," she said.

"Yeah."

"Will you take it, Max?"

"What do you think?"

"I hate people who answer a question with a question."

"You hate me, Edyth?" He grinned.

"Sometimes," she said quietly. "Yes, sometimes, I do, Max."

"Hate's a pretty strong emotion, Edyth. Passionate, some would say."

"You?"

"Yeah, I'd say that."

"You think Steiner hates you?"

"Hell, no! Steiner hates *no one*. He can't afford the luxury of such emotions as love and hate. But authority—power—that's something else again. We're playing a small game for high stakes right now. *My neck*. He's got it down pat. The power game. You have to admire that bastard. He's an expert at it."

"You're not so bad yourself." She had swung her legs out in front of her and propped a cushion beneath them and her skirt had ridden up, allowing the white flesh of her thigh above her nylon stockings to be revealed. Either she hadn't noticed or she didn't care or she cared a lot.

"Not now, baby," Max muttered, and she tugged at her skirt rather discreetly.

She had been watching him closely all day, admiring his calm, his impeccable coolness. Not once had he allowed himself to be seen reacting. It had been a remarkable performance since what was going on in that caucus room was like a game of Russian roulette: *One more click and the name that is put before the committee may be yours!* She had even noticed relief in the other men when they had finally been named (and all but three of them had been labeled "Communist sympathizers" that day).

Right now, though, Edyth saw nervousness rise to the surface of the man. It was impossible for her ever to consider Max's being intimidated, but she could recognize the alarm in the brightness of his eyes and the pallor of his skin. Often in the year she had been working for him there had been moments like these. Times when he was remote, separated, un-get-at-able. *Most of the time*, Edyth admitted sadly to herself. Often he would mock her. Usually he spoke to her as if listening to himself. When he made love to her she knew he was never aware of her as Edyth. No. Not as herself. Sometimes when she was truly low, she would consider the idea that she was Max's moral concession to masturbation. Yet she loved him desperately. He occupied her every thought, her every feeling. He kept her emotional temperature feverish.

She got up and put a few more ice cubes in her glass and stood there about three feet away from him.

"I think I'll call Luise now," he said, his eyes elsewhere, his voice detached. He went over to the telephone next to the bed and stood as he placed the call. He turned away, his back to Edyth, when the call was finally completed.

"Hi, baby," he said softly into the receiver of the telephone, cupping it sensually with his hands.

Edyth thought she might cry, but somehow the moment passed, and instead she walked to the window of the hotel room and looked out as the encroaching night sky pushed her first day in Washington forever behind her.

His hotel room was dark, but Lou Whitehorn stood quietly in the corner smoking one cigarette after the other. Through the window he could see the lights of the hotel where many of the "friendly" witnesses were staying. *The enemy camp.* Most of them were men and women he had known the best part of his adult years. The majority were right-wingers for whom he had small respect. One of their members he had respected, sponsored and loved—Bob Tanner.

By now, nearing the seniority of his sixtieth year and having achieved most of what he had set out to in his life and then lost what was dearest to him—his wife and daughter—in an auto crash, Lou had less than the others to fear in terms of the jeopardy of his future. He was known as one of the deans of Hollywood film writers and had for years commanded one of the top paychecks. He was a very rich man whose financial future was assured.

He had been a card-holding Communist and still paid his dues. He believed sincerely that the Soviet Union was peace-loving and devoted to the good of all people. He did not see how believing that made him less of a loyal American or, since the Communist Party was legal in the United States, holding a card or paying dues discredited his citizenship. There was honest fear in his heart for the fate of America. To him, at that time, Communism seemed the answer. What was happening to him, to the nineteen, to the men and women whom he had known for years and were now in the enemy camp, only worked to convince him he was right. He felt his country was swinging toward becoming an aggressive Fascistic country. *The America he loved!* A potential police state! Again, Communism seemed the answer. If it was not, if Communism was as the committee said, then there seemed no answer and God help them!—they were all lost.

The enemy camp. Bob Tanner was over there now preparing to testify the next day against all he had claimed he had believed in for years. Against the men and women who had been his comrades. Against Lou, who had been his mentor, his friend, as near as an older man could get to being a father to a younger man who was not his true son.

Lou turned away from the window and stood there thinking for a long time. He knew the telephone was tapped and that he was being watched. He had been conscious of the men constantly surveying him and the others at the airport, the hotel, and the restaurant where they ate lunch, and he knew several men would be positioned right now in the lobby. He had decided he must see Bob Tanner even though it might place him in jeopardy. After a few more moments of careful deliberation, he snuffed out his cigarette in the ashtray at the bedside and picked up the receiver of the telephone sitting there.

The monitor was immediately audible to his sensitive ears. The operator came on the line.

"The Washington Hotel," he said distinctly. "Mr. Robert Tanner."

It had given him hope that Bob had finally agreed to a meeting in just the time it would take Lou to leave the Shoreham and cross the street. They were to meet in the coffee shop of Bob's hotel. When Lou arrived, he rejected the table he was being offered by the hostess and took another one near the pantry so that should even this table or Bob himself conceal a microphone, the clatter of the dishes and the chatter of the busboys would interfere.

He sat watching the young man enter the restaurant. He had always had a sense of pride whenever he had previously viewed Bob entering any room. He came in then as now, head high, shoulders back, a soft courteous smile on his face as he edged his way through a crowd. He looked so much older suddenly to Lou, his short defiant body slightly thickened, the bronze tennis tan he had no matter what the season looking curiously like Technicolor makeup on an aging actor. Lou rose slightly as he approached the table, and then the two men sat down together.

Bob looked around. "There are better tables than this, Lou," he said in mid-Atlantic tones he had developed since his recent year in England.

"This will do fine."

Bob looked straight into Lou's soft blue eyes. *What a good-looking devil he was*, he thought. *Still is*. He always thought about that when he saw Lou, as he always recalled Lou's background: the prominent doctor father, the scientist who had been his mother, the Harvard degree, the contacts, the publication of a book at age twenty-two, the immediate success as a film writer, the beautiful film star who had been his wife and had quit the screen at the height of her career just to be Mrs. Lou Whitehorn, the wife who had so obviously adored him until death did them part.

"I understand you've made arrangements with the committee, Bob," Lou began in even tones.

"I went to them. I told them I had been a Communist but was

one no longer and that I didn't want my loyalty to the United States misunderstood. I told them I would discuss the workings of the party but would not discuss my former associates," Bob told him quickly, the dryness in his mouth an audible recognized thing.

"I want you to give me your assurance that you won't give any names. *Bobby?*"

"I can't do that."

Lou leaned in closer across the table. "All you have lived for, *built* for, will turn to ashes. *An informer. Bobby, Bobby.* Do you think either side could have any respect for an informer?"

"This last year has been a nightmare for me. I know I've been considered a Communist by almost all Hollywood, all Washington—and a renegade by you, the others. And I've had this terrible fear, this nightmare, that in the event of a war with the Soviet Union, I would be considered a friend of the Soviet Union. That would mean, Lou, my own country would consider me an enemy."

"If there is a war, Bobby, it could only be because the States have been the aggressors. I'm sure of that. You were, too."

"Not anymore. So I'm the odd man out, but I don't believe in the Soviet's presentation of the world anymore. I don't believe it's a paradise." He pushed back on the hard frame of his chair as if having to put distance between himself and the older man. "It's just not for me, Lou. Russia, may be a fine country, but it's not for me."

"How can you be sure?"

"I was a Communist seven years, Lou, and having lived through that, I can tell you—I'm sure."

"I want your assurance, Bobby, your personal assurance, and after ten years of fatherly interest and friendship, I believe I have the right to ask that, your personal assurance that you will not give names."

"I'll give it to you, Lou—if you, in turn, give me yours that in the event of a war between the United States and the Soviet Union, you will do nothing to aid *them*."

"If it's an aggressive war of the United States, I could not support it."

"I'm not interested in whether it's aggressive. I still want that assurance, *your personal assurance*, Lou."

"I can't do that," Lou said stiffly.

"Then neither can I."

Lou rose from his chair. "We never could lie to each other, Bobby," he said in a distinctly paternal tone. "Thank God, at least that much remains." He bowed slightly, a habit he always had when he was leaving anyone's presence, and then, without ever glancing back, walked out of the restaurant in a truly majestic manner, a manner Bob Tanner had worked to imitate for the last ten years of his young but no longer tender life.

Chapter 14

At this moment Bob Tanner felt alone against the world. He knew that the testimony he was about to deliver would bring ruin upon many lives and that he himself would find his own company difficult from this time forward. There is, after all, an unwritten law that states that one man may not inform upon another, especially if *the other* is one whom he has broken bread with or known as a friend.

Bob Tanner was violating that unwritten law. He was doing it fully aware that a penalty followed. Life would never be quite the same for him. The sharpness, the focus, would be somehow forever dimmed.

CHAIRMAN: I would like to call Mr. Robert L. Tanner.

(The polished, tanned, brisk figure of the witness moved past the witness table. He did not glance to either side, apparently distracted by his own thoughts. His hair had been freshly trimmed, and he exuded the odor of talcum and men's cologne. He sat down with great dignity, and never once during his testimony did he shade his expressive dark-brown eyes from the cameras' glares or the chief investigator's unrelenting glance.)

CHAIRMAN: Mr. Tanner, will you raise your right hand, please? You solemnly swear the testimony you give this committee shall be the truth, the whole truth, and nothing but the truth, so help you God?
MR. TANNER: I do.
CHAIRMAN: Have a seat.

(TESTIMONY OF MR. ROBERT L. TANNER)

INVESTIGATOR: You are Robert L. Tanner?

MR. TANNER: Yes.

INVESTIGATOR: When and where were you born?

MR. TANNER: San Francisco, California, November 18, 1918.

INVESTIGATOR: What is your present place of residence?

MR. TANNER: 144 South Spalding Drive, Beverly Hills, California.

INVESTIGATOR: What is your present occupation?

MR. TANNER: Screenwriter.

INVESTIGATOR: Will you state for the committee, briefly, your educational background.

MR. TANNER: I attended public schools in San Francisco, then one year at Oxford in Great Britain. My parents had financial reverses, and I was called home.

INVESTIGATOR: San Francisco?

MR. TANNER: Yes. I went into my father's business then, for another year.

INVESTIGATOR: That business being?

MR. TANNER: Leather goods. I worked there for a year until my father discovered he was totally bankrupt.

INVESTIGATOR: And how have you been employed since then?

MR. TANNER: I came to Hollywood in 1937 and for several months was unemployed. Then I got a job as an outside reader for Universal, then for Twentieth Century-Fox, then I went to work as a reader in a large literary agency. That would be 1938. Mr. Louis Whitehorn was a client of theirs, and as he was forming a production company of his own, he took me with him as a story editor. I remained in that capacity until 1942, when I went into the service, where I remained until 1944. Mr. Whitehorn had dissolved his company by then and was working instead solely as a screenwriter for Omega Films. He spoke to Mr. Steiner on my behalf, and I was hired for the first time as a screenwriter.

INVESTIGATOR: Is that where you are still employed?

MR. TANNER: Yes.

INVESTIGATOR: When you first arrived in Hollywood, did you become affiliated in any way with any Communist groups?

MR. TANNER: Well, I met a man who was a fairly well-known film writer and he had been to Russia and was very enthusiastic about it. His name was Stephen Lomberger.

INVESTIGATOR: I didn't get the name.

MR. TANNER: Stephen Lomberger.

INVESTIGATOR: Will you spell that please?

MR. TANNER: L-O-M-B-E-R-G-E-R. He took me to a smallish building—I believe it was a guest cottage behind someone's house—where they were conducting classes in Marxism. There were only about seven or eight people there.

INVESTIGATOR: Do you recall their names?

MR. TANNER: It was a long time ago. I can't even recall the teacher clearly.

INVESTIGATOR: Was it then that you became associated with a group of writers?

MR. TANNER: No. That was later, when I was employed by Louis Whitehorn. I was in reality a story editor, but I did work on screenplays that our company produced. Mr. Whitehorn always wrote all the final drafts, but I often helped on the first draft. The beginning. Mr. Whitehorn thought it might be helpful if I was a member of the Screen Writers Guild.

INVESTIGATOR: And was this a Communist organization?

MR. TANNER: There were Communist and non-Communist members.

INVESTIGATOR: Would you say the group was organized because of the efforts of the Communist Party?

MR. TANNER: You mean the Screen Writers Guild?

INVESTIGATOR: Yes.

MR. TANNER: Yes, it was. But first I have to explain something about the Screen Writers Guild.

INVESTIGATOR: Very well.

MR. TANNER: Just before I joined the guild, there had been two strong factions: the Screen Playwrights, which was a right-wing writers' group, supported by the studios, and the Screen Writers Guild, which was left-wing. The Screen Playwrights had—this was just before I joined the Screen Writers Guild—smashed the left-wing group, so to speak, and so this group splintered off and met privately for the purpose of reconstituting the Screen Writers Guild. But the writers had very little experience in organizing a union. At that point, a Communist member who was so experienced took charge.

INVESTIGATOR: What was his name?

MR. TANNER: Harold Prews. That's spelled P-R-E-W-S. One night a number of different meetings were held at various writers' homes—twenty to thirty writers at each meeting—and at the end of the evening, the Screen Writers Guild, as it presently stands and as I belong to, was formed with about two hundred members so that then, since there were that many writers, the fear of reprisals and blacklisting on the studios' part was abated.

INVESTIGATOR: What was the purpose of holding separate meetings?

MR. TANNER: So that there wouldn't be any publicity. Two hundred writers meeting would be one thing—twenty to thirty, entirely another.

INVESTIGATOR: Were you one of the initial members of the reorganized Screen Writers Guild?

MR. TANNER: Yes.

INVESTIGATOR: And has that Communist influence remained in the Screen Writers Guild to this day?

MR. TANNER: No. The Communists were proud that they had helped in the reorganization of the guild, but the majority of writers were not Communists. They simply wanted a noncompany union. One that really reflected the wishes of the screenwriters. And we—the Communists—helped them. The Communists, of course, had something to say about the running of the guild because some of them were officers and because the line they pursued was not far from what the members wanted and so they were able to exert some influence.

INVESTIGATOR: When did you join the party, Mr. Tanner?

MR. TANNER: In 1938. I can't recall the exact date.

INVESTIGATOR: When you became employed by Louis Whitehorn?

MR. TANNER: About that same time.

INVESTIGATOR: And before you joined the Screen Writers Guild at Mr. Whitehorn's suggestion?

MR. TANNER: Yes, that's right, except that I was pleased to get the opportunity to join the guild. I wanted to be a screenwriter more than anything else in the world. It seemed to me this brought me closer to my goal.

INVESTIGATOR: Which was?

MR. TANNER: Being a successful and producing screenwriter.

INVESTIGATOR: Did the Communist Party exercise its influence over a writer's work?

MR. TANNER: That's not an easy question to answer. The late thirties and the war years were a time of social change, and certain of the questions the Communists asked, such as the question of race discrimination, were of great concern to writers. And the writers also felt it kept them in touch with labor. Then, of course, there were the attitudes toward the Spanish Civil War and the anti-Nazi feeling that most writers and Communists were united in, so influence was not difficult. I myself felt all they preached was reasonable as I was both anti-Nazi and for Loyalist Spain and the Communists were the most active opponents of Franco and Mussolini and Hitler at the time.

INVESTIGATOR: Will you state to the committee the extent of your contributions to the Communist Party while you were a member?

MR. TANNER: About sixty dollars a month in the beginning, about three hundred dollars at the end.

INVESTIGATOR: A month?

MR. TANNER: It was based on four percent of my salary.

INVESTIGATOR: Are you now a Communist?

MR. TANNER: Last year I took a writing assignment in England. I considered it my chance to break with the party. I haven't paid dues since then or been to a meeting and do not consider myself a Communist. I am certain, after my appearance before this committee, the Communists will concur.

INVESTIGATOR: To whom did you pay these dues?

MR. TANNER: A financial secretary.

INVESTIGATOR: Who was?

MR. TANNER: During the years there were many.

INVESTIGATOR: Try to recall.

MR. TANNER: Maria Perkins, Solomon Lemmins—that's L-E-M-M-I-N-S, Michael Horder—H-O-R-D-E-R. That's all I can recall.

INVESTIGATOR: Can you remember other executives of the Communist Party in Hollywood?

MR. TANNER: I remember Maury Schulman.

INVESTIGATOR: Would you spell that first name?

MR. TANNER: M-A-U-R-Y.

INVESTIGATOR: Were you acquainted with a person by the name of Merwin Bibbs?

MR. TANNER: Yes.

INVESTIGATOR: Was he known to be a member of the Communist Party?

MR. TANNER: Yes.

INVESTIGATOR: Were you acquainted with Milton Stevens?

MR. TANNER: Yes.

INVESTIGATOR: Was he a member of the Communist Party?

MR. TANNER: Yes.

INVESTIGATOR: Burton Winters and his wife, Sylvia Winters?

MR. TANNER: I can't say that I was ever at a meeting with them.

INVESTIGATOR: Sol Levitz—L-E-V-I-T-Z. Was he a member of the Communist Party?

MR. TANNER: Yes.

INVESTIGATOR: Have you mentioned in the course of your testimony the name of Stanley Caplan—C-A-P-L-A-N?

MR. TANNER: No. I worked with him on a screenplay for Louis Whitehorn.

INVESTIGATOR: Was Stanley Caplan known to you as a member of the Communist Party?

MR. TANNER: At that time.

INVESTIGATOR: Were you acquainted with a person by the name of Maxwell Isaac Seaman?

MR. TANNER: Yes, I was.

INVESTIGATOR: And was he a member of the Communist Party?

MR. TANNER: Yes, he was.

INVESTIGATOR: And did you know a Luise Haydyn Seaman?

MR. TANNER: Yes, I did, but I never knew her in the party.

INVESTIGATOR: You did not?

MR. TANNER: No.

INVESTIGATOR: Were you a member of the Anti-Nazi League?

MR. TANNER: Yes.

INVESTIGATOR: Can you name any other members of the Communist Party who were members of that league with you?

MR. TANNER: It would have been difficult to know, as the Communists were only a small fraction of the membership. Thousands of men and women who opposed Hitler were members of the Anti-Nazi League.

INVESTIGATOR: The Hollywood Committee for Social Exchange?

MR. TANNER: Are you asking if I was a member of that group?

INVESTIGATOR: Yes.

MR. TANNER: I recall attending one meeting, but I can't recall at this time what it was about.

INVESTIGATOR: Were you affiliated with the Hollywood Writers Mobilization?

MR. TANNER: Yes.

INVESTIGATOR: And was this truly a Communist-front organization?

MR. TANNER: The membership contained many Communists.

INVESTIGATOR: Can you name them for this committee?

MR. TANNER: Louis Whitehorn, Sol Levitz, Merwin Bibbs, Milton Stevens, Max Seaman, Stephen Lomberger, Harold Prews . . .

INVESTIGATOR: Are there more?

MR. TANNER: I would have to think back.

INVESTIGATOR: I believe, Mr. Chairman, this is a good place for a break.

CHAIRMAN: The committee will take a recess now until two o'clock.

(Thereupon, at 12:05 P.M., the hearing was recessed to reconvene at 2 P.M. with the same witness, Robert L. Tanner, to testify.)

The men met for lunch in a restaurant near the old House Office Building. They knew that microphones could be concealed anywhere and were aware of the familiar but shadowy figures hovering nearby. They still refused to conduct any meeting, any gathering, as if it had the melodrama of a cloak-and-dagger film.

By now the extreme pessimism that only Merwin originally felt had begun to permeate the entire group. No matter what the outcome of the "investigations," they were certain that no refutation of the libelous charges hurled against them could counteract the tremendous circulation those charges had received by the press. Scheduled as "friendly" witnesses for the remainder of the week were several famous actors. The public were certain to tune them in and listen to their revelations and their roll call of names, but by the time the so-called "unfriendly" witnesses were called the public would have grown weary of the extravaganza, and any honest attempt to counteract the defamation of character already heaped like piles of dirt upon the nineteen men would have been a lost cause.

"We are going to draft a brief," the attorneys told them, "placing the illegality of the committee as evidence that the committee is unconstitutional. Stating that films, in the same way as the press, are entitled to the full protection of the First Amendment. That the committee is attempting to control the contents of films to accord with the views of the committee and that Congress is without power to censure the thinking and expression of the American people. We'll try, in this way, to quash the subpoenas."

"What are your chances of succeeding?" Max asked.

"Not good," one of the attorneys leveled. "The committee is without constitutional authority, but it seems to be working autonomously."

"I can't believe Tanner. I just can't believe him," Milton moaned.

"You're a child, Milton. Tanner has always been a company man," Sol Levitz replied.

No one looked at Lou. He sat very straight, one hand in his lap, as he finished his bowl of soup with what seemed the most intense concentration.

Chapter 15

By the Friday afternoon, just five days and twenty-three witnesses after the hearings had opened, more than a hundred men and women who had spent their lives employed by motion pictures had been named as un-American, and their professional lives had been shattered. Life and limb had been regarded no more dearly than the days when Christians were fed to the lions. There was no recall for the men and women who suffered this barbaric character assassination, as the witnesses "friendly" to the committee could not be cross-examined and could not be reproached by the law since their testimony was given under the protective cloak of immunity. Yet these same men and women condemned the nineteen for refusing to surrender their own constitutional immunities before the committee.

Max excused himself from the others and met a lawyer, Henry Green, for lunch. Green was a young New Yorker, a liberal, who had achieved the minor status of becoming a junior partner in the small law firm of Levenson, Kahn & Manheim. He had initiated a theatrical department in the firm and lured two major clients. One was Burt Winters, who had a West Coast firm of attorneys as well, and the other was Kate Steiner, H.M.'s spinster daughter, who thought of herself as a stage producer, but who, though she had financially supported several plays, receiving program credit as a co-producer, had never physically entered into the productions themselves.

Henry had called Max the night before from New York. "Burt

Winters suggested I get in touch," he explained. "He thought I might be of service to you."

"Yeah? How?"

"I'll drive up to Washington in the morning and we can have lunch and talk," Henry replied, paying no attention to the indifference in Max's voice.

"I'm very happy with my counsel. Don't waste the gas," Max said.

"Another opinion never hurt," Henry continued with the thick sincerity of a man selling insurance.

"Except in the bank account." Max laughed.

"Lunch—one o'clock?"

"I don't call the shots in the recesses. The chairman does."

"Of course. I'll wait at the Shoreham for you," Henry replied, with sympathy and understanding underlining each word.

"How will I know you?" Max asked.

"I'll know *you*," Henry assured him.

But now, as a man walked across the Shoreham lobby, toward him, Max knew he would have known Henry Green anywhere. Though he was not more than thirty, his hair was thinning, and he combed it forward in an effort to cover the spareness. He was tall and lean and carried himself in a Lincolnesque manner and was dressed so conservatively he gave a first impression of meagerness. On closer examination, one had the feeling not so much that the man might be Lincoln, but rather, he might be a man imitating Raymond Massey playing Lincoln. Max distrusted him immediately, while all the time knowing that if he represented Burt, Henry Green must have a cunning and a perceptiveness well worth his probable retainer fee. *Definitely a five-figure man,* Max thought.

Henry said nothing until he had his arm entwined in Max's arm and was propelling him back outside with him. He was much taller than Max—*much taller than most people,* Max thought. Clearly an advantage in any courtroom. He had to be six feet six or seven.

"We'll take a walk in the park out back," he said and then pushed Max slightly forward, to go through the revolving doors first.

He walked with tremendous concentration, hands pushed deeply in his pockets, shoulders slightly hunched, eyes off in the distance or to the toes of his outsized shoes. *Young Lincoln,* Max thought, as he kept up with Henry's loping steps. There was no exchange between them until they had stepped onto one of the paths of the park.

"There." Henry sighed. "Now we can speak freely." They walked silently for a few moments. "You're not hungry?" Henry asked with the concern of a good host.

"Not at the moment."

They continued on in silence until they reached a park bench. Henry sat down, and Max followed suit.

"It's a grave situation," Henry began.

"I hope you don't know something I don't," Max quipped.

"I have nothing but the utmost respect for your counsels. I want you to know that. But I only see disaster at the end of the road they're taking."

"You know a detour?"

"You see, your counsel is assuming constitutional immunity will either work for you, as it did for your accusers, or will get the hearings quashed entirely. The assumption, however, is faulty. I cannot ethically inquire into counsel's advice to you; that is naturally sacrosanct between you and counsel. If you are going into the witness chair, however, or stand on constitutional immunity to your right to private religious and political affiliations—even if you stand on the Fifth Amendment—you are very probably heading toward a contempt of Congress charge. Of course, we both know the committee is not constitutional and therefore cannot place you in contempt of Congress. But what we *know* and what would be possible to *prove* at this time in our history are not one and the same thing."

From somewhere in his pocket, Henry brought forth a small bag of peanuts and began cracking the shells and throwing the nuts to two squirrels near to them. After three or four peanuts had thus been disposed of and the shells put back with the uncracked nuts, Henry sealed the bag and put it back in his pocket.

"Contempt of Congress could carry a pretty stiff sentence with it."

"Like?"

"A year. Depending." He leaned back, closed his eyes to the sun, and stretched out his long legs in front of him. "What you have to be aware of is that you don't necessarily have to take the Appian Way to get to Rome."

"I'm not a natural martyr, Green. I admit that—but I'm not an informer, either." He stood up. Henry was at attention immediately and had him by the arm.

"Upward of a hundred names have already been entered into the record. I could spit on each and every man who introduced each one of those names. I'm a liberal. Hell, I was brought up on the WPA. And the firm of Levenson, Kahn & Manheim is known to be a liberal firm. I suggest only that you play the committee's own game. A private audience could conceivably be obtained, in which the only names given would be those *already* well known and recorded by the committee. You would be hurting no one, and you would be free to fight the committee with the one means in your power—films."

Max stood there calmly. He had to squint because Henry was standing with his back to the sun and Max was staring right at Henry and into the sun. "You're not a free crusader, are you, Green?"

"We wouldn't have to worry about fees at this time."

"When would we?"

"Never, really. My firm would only expect to represent you and your company. And let me say, we all believe you are a great talent and have a great future. Just the usual company retainer fees. And you know, if we represent the old man's daughter, we must be pretty good."

"To say nothing of Burt Winters, a very shrewd operator."

"And a first-class filmmaker."

"Yeah. Well, you're a first-class heel, Mr. Green. An absolutely prima-class son of a bitch," Max said quietly, spit on the ground again, and then turned and walked back the dusty path to the street the Shoreham faced.

He never looked back and sincerely hoped he'd never see Henry Green again, to save him busting him in the jaw. Or Burt Winters either.

He stepped into the street without glancing to either side or at the traffic light which was green. A car swerved and narrowly, perhaps only by a matter of a few inches, missed Max. The driver stopped the car short and stuck his head out the window.

"Damn it! Why don't you look where you're going!" the driver screamed.

But by this time the light had turned red and Max was safely across the street.

It was a stifling hot day, and Luise had switched the air-conditioning unit on in the bedroom and had closed the door, shut the blinds, and gone back to bed after the children had eaten lunch and returned to school. She was now watching the small TV set beside the bed. The hearings were about to convene again. It was 3 P.M. in Washington.

She was suffering from a painful headache, and her eyes were aching. She had been glued to the tiny seven-inch screen for five days, watching in the evenings as well, when highlights would be rebroadcast and commentary made. She had tried to keep some degree of normality in the house, but it hadn't been easy and the children were too perceptive. By this morning she had given up the battle and allowed the children to see her with red eyes.

She did not know how it was going to be possible to get through even the rest of this day, not to mention the grueling week to come and the lonely weekend that was almost upon her. The telephone, of course, had not stopped ringing. Most callers were fellow sufferers or well-meaning sympathizers, but there had been threatening calls and foul-mouthed callers, as well, and Luise now let the answering service pick up all the calls. Still, when the phone rang, she would nervously wait for a small amount of time to pass and then ring the service back to find out who had called. Always, there was in the back of her mind that there might be some news, even though she was watching Max that very moment on the TV screen.

The hearings were now in session, and a well-known but generally light-minded actor had stepped into the witness chair. As he did, the cameras swept past the long witness table, and for a brief moment Max was discernible, but his head was turned away and Luise, strain though she did to uncover some small sign in his attitude (the slope of his shoulders, the tilt of his head) that would give her some fresh insight into what he was feeling that moment, could not.

Clea was using the vacuum cleaner in the upstairs hallway and the noise was directly outside Luise's door. Luise turned up the sound, but then there was static and the picture began to slide. For a moment it seemed the set would clear itself, then it went dead, the air conditioner went off, and the vacuum cleaner stopped.

"Clea," Luise yelled and then stumbled out of the bed and to the doorway, opening it only a slit. "Clea, you've blown a fuse."

"Yes, ma'am."

"Well, do you know where the fuse box is?"

"Yes, ma'am."

"Do you think you could fix it?"

"Yes, ma'am."

"Good God, Clea. Can't you say anything but 'Yes, ma'am'?"

"You sure am irritable," Clea replied and then kept on muttering as she descended the stairs.

Luise stood there in the doorway. Her first instinct was to follow Clea to the basement and change the fuse herself, knowing Clea was always frightened of anything electrical. Then she reasoned that she might miss Max or an important piece of testimony once the TV was on again. She started back into her bedroom when she heard the front door open and then slam shut and muffled sobs in the downstairs hallway. Luise ran to the head of the staircase.

"Who is it? Tony?" she called down with a terrifying premonition that it *was* Tony and that something god-awful had happened to him. "Tony?"

There was no reply, but the soft cries continued. Luise stumbled over her long robe as she ran down the flight of stairs.

Tony was huddled in a far corner. He was covered with mud and grime and his clothes were torn and his hair was disarranged and a stream of dark blood oozed from his mouth, down the front of his shirt, which had been spotless an hour or so before, and onto the thick hallway carpet.

"Tony!" Luise screamed and ran to the child and went down on her knees and held him to her, unmindful of the mud or blood. "Tony! Oh, dear God, what happened? A car? Tony, tell me. Clea! Clea!" she yelled.

But the wind, as the front door had slammed shut, had also slammed the basement door, and Clea was out of earshot. Luise pushed the sobbing child gently from her. "Can you tell me? You'll *have* to tell me. Tony? What happened? Where do you hurt?" she said in an even, soothing voice as she wiped the child's face with a corner of her soft flannel robe. "Was it a car, Tony? An accident? What hurts, Tony?"

She lifted him in her arms as she rose to her feet and started up the stairway with him. She could feel his blood soaking through the shoulder of her robe, as Tony rested his head there. It was warm and sticky against her bare flesh under the robe. *I must be calm,* she thought. *I mustn't frighten the child more. I'll wrap him in a blanket and dress quickly and take him to the emergency hospital.* "It's all right, Tony. You'll be all right," she said aloud.

Luise labored up the stairs, hanging onto Tony desperately. She managed to make her way rather blindly to the top, across the hallway, and into her room, where she gently deposited him on her bed and wrapped a blanket quickly around him. Then she tore off her robe as she crossed to her wardrobe and grabbed a dress that was easy to get into and required no bra, and stepped into it.

"Mommy will take you to the doctor, Tony. It will be all right."

"I ·don' wanna g-g-go to the—" Tony broke up in convulsive sobs.

Luise hurried back to the bed, where she sat down on the edge. "Tell me what happened, Tony," she said quietly as she brushed the child's hair from his face and took some soft tissue from her bedside table to wipe away the blood and dirt.

"It was My-my-*my*ron!" Tony sobbed.

"Myron? Myron, next door?"

"He beat me a-a-a-up." Tony threw himself against Luise and clung to her.

"Why, Tony, why?"

"Da-da-daddy was a spy!"

"He said Daddy was a spy? Is that what you mean?" She could feel the child nod his head affirmatively against her breast. "Wasn't there a teacher in the schoolyard, Tony?"

"M-mr. Schneiderman. He sent me home . . ."

"Like this! Good God! Did you walk all the way, Tony?" She tore the child's arms from her and held him there slightly away from her. She was talking to him and listening to his answers, but now that the first shock had passed, she realized that Tony had not broken anything and that the blood came from a gap where once a tooth had been in the front of his mouth.

"Y-yes."

Luise now got up and went into the bathroom and returned with a damp cloth. She began carefully to wash the blood and dirt from the child's face. "You lost a tooth, that's all, Tony. That *is* all, isn't it? You don't hurt elsewhere?"

"N-no."

"You were very brave. I'm proud of you. *Daddy* would have been proud of you. You are a very brave little boy."

Tony began unaccountably to sob again.

"Myron isn't completely to blame, Tony. He doesn't understand. His parents are really to blame."

At this moment Clea had obviously had success in the basement, and the television, the air conditioning, and the vacuum cleaner all came on at once. The TV picture jerked in and out of focus and then came clear. The newsreel cameraman had just moved in for a close-up of Max, tight-lipped anger in every muscle of his face, obviously reacting to some comment of the "friendly" witness on the stand.

"I h-hate him!" Tony sobbed convulsively and threw himself facedown on the bed.

Luise wasn't sure her son meant the small boy who lived next door *or Max*—and she was too fearful of the answer to ask.

"I think we'd better get those muddy clothes off you, Tony," she said gently. And then as Clea had just appeared in the opened doorway, "Clea, please run a bath for Tony—he fell into some mud in the schoolyard."

Luise calmly rose and turned off the TV and then lifted Tony from the bed and handed him to Clea. "It's only that loose tooth that fell out, Clea. That's all the blood is from. I'll be right in. In the meantime, I'll strip the bed for you."

Clea took the child's hand.

"And please turn off the vacuum, Clea. You can do that later."

"Yes, ma'am," Clea said and led the little boy gingerly out of his mother's room and to his own bath.

Chapter 16

Lou Whitehorn woke up with a severe pain somewhere deep in his gut. It was indescribable. A living thing. It didn't gnaw or lacerate or stab. No. It sucked. It was as if a suction had been sunk deep down in his gut and was pulling the rest of Lou into it with a mighty force. He managed to stumble out of the hotel bed and into the bathroom. He knew this would be the day he would be called upon to testify. He had known it the day before. Had gone to bed knowing it. By the close of the day he expected to be found in contempt of Congress and to be facing a prison term. He considered his Hollywood career a thing of the past. Dead now, along with his wife and daughter. He knew somehow that even at his age, he would be able to stand up to what he had to face, that he was strong enough to go on, more than that—that he loved life, the battle, dearly enough to continue to involve himself actively in the act of living even with the eventualities that faced him. He took a towel and soaked it with cold water and wrung it dry, wiped his face with it, and then held it to his forehead.

Perhaps there are no brave men, he thought, *only stubborn ones.*

He went back into the bedroom and sat down on the edge of the bed studying the anonymous surroundings. It was like the caucus room. All things innominate—the press, the audience, the committee, all looking at him with one anonymous eye, speaking with one anonymous voice, the room itself cloaked in anonymity, like a morality play out of context in time, having no time locality and yet becoming, as it ensues, tenaciously real.

155

He closed his eyes and recounted the plot line in its most basic terms, as he had done so many times when trying to lick a screenplay that was worrying him. The main character in *this* story was the committee, and the committee was the leader and coordinator of the ultrarightist forces in the country. To exist, the committee had to exercise its power—and at frequent intervals. Continuity was vital. The committee had to find *someone* to expose. Not to expose would mean there was no need for the committee. Therefore, it was *expose or die.*

Exposure required more than identifying a witness as a subversive. The identification had to be made in a climate of pervasive hostility. Fear was used to overcome reason. As the committee worked to destroy the subversive, it also discredited and smeared as many liberal causes and groups as possible. The end result was meant to be a political overkill.

Right now "Communism" was the dirty word. The subversive to be uprooted. In Germany it had been the Jew. In the future who? *Anyone.* The Negroes, the Catholics, possibly even the youth of the nation. All the opposition had to be was a minority that was widely hated, different, and that constituted little voting strength and was in direct opposition to the committee's views. A President who relied upon the committee tactics could smash the country beyond repair. Or for that matter, any of the committee who were trained in this political technique.

A very valid one, Lou admitted to himself, *for where a man is fearful that* any *past association might bring him before the committee and lay his life open to ruin, he treads softly and shies away from involvement in any controversial matter.*

Lou got up and looked around him. He had the feeling that he must overcome the unreality of his surroundings. He went over to the window and looked toward Capitol Hill, but the hotel where Bob Tanner was staying blocked his view. The pain in his gut grew again, and he leaned against the cold radiator beneath the window. There would be a parade of Bob Tanners from the film industry now that the producers had made it clear that approval by the committee's demands called for the witness to name others as a price for escaping a contempt citation.

He had watched with a mixture of horror and disgust and, yes, fear the day before as Sol Levitz had been put through the circus hoop. No question of the committee was wasted, and all questions asked—even the opening identifying questions such as residence, occupation, and place of employment—were directed toward the witness' ruin. The committee knew damned well where each witness lived and worked. It was on the record. Public identification, however, was the committee's only insurance that a witness would lose his job and that his neighbors could be reached. The threat of contempt was from the first oath an element of blackmail, and the questions were phrased in such a way that to answer was to incriminate yourself, while to stand on your constitutional right *not* to answer, because of the innuendo in the question, incriminated you anyway.

It all echoed ominously of the grilling of the Jews by the Nazis and the seventeenth-century witch trials.

Sol Levitz had stood up admirably and with dignity to his inquisitors. He had refused to name anyone, no matter how innocent or ambiguous the question seemed. ("Who was your landlord?" could lead into "Who were the other Communists living in the house?"—which implied the landlord was a fellow traveler at least and possibly a Communist. Once the man's name was even mentioned, it went into the cumulative index the committee published and sent to firms, etc., which meant the probable loss of the man's job and harassment by his neighbors.) In the end, Sol had been refused the right to read a statement he had prepared. He had been ruled in contempt of Congress and now faced the ruin of his career and a prison term.

There was a knock on the door, and Lou thought at first he would ignore it, would have to ignore it. Whoever it was became very insistent, however, and Lou, with great difficulty, managed to cross the room.

"Who is it?" he called out.

"Sol, Lou. You OK?"

Lou drew himself up to his full height and squared his shoulders and opened the door quickly.

"Sol, come in. Come in."

He ushered him in and closed the door.

"Shall I order us some coffee?" he asked with his old charm and calm once more forcibly restored.

"I don't mind, Lou."

"Good. *Good*."

The two men stood there looking at each other in mutual

understanding. Finally, Lou turned away and went over to the telephone to order some coffee. His hand shook, and he was unable to lift the receiver. Sol was instantly at his side.

"It's OK, Lou. That's why I'm here. I just wanted you to know you're not alone."

CHAIRMAN: Let the committee be in order.

INVESTIGATOR: Mr. Louis Whitehorn.

CHAIRMAN: Mr. Whitehorn, will you please raise your right hand and be sworn.

(Let it be noted for the record that the witness' hand did not shake as he raised it in solemn oath.)

CHAIRMAN (continuing): You solemnly swear the testimony you give before this committee shall be the truth, the whole truth, and nothing but the truth, so help you God?

MR. WHITEHORN: I do.

(TESTIMONY OF MR. LOUIS WHITEHORN)

INVESTIGATOR: You are Louis Whitehorn?

MR. WHITEHORN: That is correct.

INVESTIGATOR: Are you represented by counsel?

MR. WHITEHORN: Yes, I am.

INVESTIGATOR: Will you please state your full name, place of birth, and your age?

MR. WHITEHORN: My full name is Louis Loenstein Whitehorn, though I have been known my entire life personally and professionally as Louis Whitehorn. I was born in Syracuse, New York, on April 17, 1887, and I reside at 1469 Bennington Crescent, West Los Angeles, California.

INVESTIGATOR: Will you give the committee a brief statement of your educational background.

MR. WHITEHORN: I attended public schools in Syracuse until I was nine. Then I was sent to a lycée in Paris for six years. From there I attended Cambridge University. I received my BA from Harvard, my master's from Columbia and my PhD from Princeton.

INVESTIGATOR: Will you give the committee a statement of your employment record, please?

MR. WHITEHORN: It is a lengthy one.

INVESTIGATOR: Summarize it.

MR. WHITEHORN: While I was obtaining my PhD in the humanities at Princeton, I used my own background as a basis for a novel published under the title of *A Loss of Innocence*. That would have been 1909. I was twenty-two years of age. The book was purchased by a New York film producer—films were then centered in New York City—and filmed under the title of *Innocence*. The experience engendered a lifelong association with the film media. I have been employed by almost every studio in New York and Hollywood and have written over a hundred film scripts and produced several of them as well. I have also been employed as an executive producer at Paramount, Columbia, and Omega Films. During the First World War, I was not drafted owing to a back injury sustained when I was a child in Syracuse, but for a period of twenty-six months I worked exclusively in the presentation of entertainment for the troops.

INVESTIGATOR: What was the last screenplay on which you were employed?

MR. WHITEHORN: I must protest at this point. The question seems to me a direct attempt to create a film blacklist in Hollywood. Once my name is entered into the record, and the film title as well, exhibitors will be forced to withdraw this film, upon whose revenue a good many people depend for their future livelihoods.

INVESTIGATOR: By what company were you employed?

MR. WHITEHORN: Independent Artists.

INVESTIGATOR: Who employed you?

MR. WHITEHORN: Independent Artists.

INVESTIGATOR: There must have been *one* official representative in making the employment. Who was he?

MR. WHITEHORN: I am afraid I shall be forced to protest again. There is the possibility that there might be a basis of guilt insinuated in the mere fact that you employ a man. I was employed, I am sure, because I was the best man for this particular project and not on the basis of my political beliefs.

INVESTIGATOR: Were you engaged at one time in a working arrangement with Robert L. Tanner?

MR. WHITEHORN: I was.

INVESTIGATOR: You were present in this hearing room during the giving of his testimony last week?

MR. WHITEHORN: I was.

INVESTIGATOR: I suppose you heard his testimony in which he stated that you were a member of the Communist Party?

MR. WHITEHORN: I heard Mr. Tanner place an *assumption* before this committee that such was the case.

(Another member of the Congressional committee stands up.)

CONGRESSMAN: I have a question or two for the gentleman. The statement that you are a resident of California—so am I. We are both American citizens. I assume, Mr. Whitehorn, that you would be interested in helping this committee uncover any person or any groups of persons who were subversive in their attitude toward the constitutional form of government in our nation. Is my assumption correct?

MR. WHITEHORN: Congressman, I should be happy to aid this committee in uncovering subversion, but one man's subversion is another man's patriotism. I consider the activities of this committee subversive of the American Constitution.

CONGRESSMAN: I assumed you did when you refused to answer a minute ago. But you have now made a statement that this committee is un-American. According to Webster's dictionary, that means we are undertaking to overthrow the foundation of our constitutional government. Now, in what way are we doing that?

MR. WHITEHORN: This country, Congressman, was founded on the doctrine of freedom, the right of a man to advocate anything he wished—advocate it, agitate for it, organize for it, attempt to win a majority for it. And I think that any committee that intimidates people, that makes it impossible for people to express their opinions freely, is subverting the basic doctrine of the United States and its Constitution.

CONGRESSMAN: Do I understand you as saying that an American citizen has the right to advocate the forceful overthrow of our constitutional form of government?

MR. WHITEHORN: I am *personally* opposed to any use of force and violence. However, President Lincoln said that the people of this country have the right to revolution, if necessary, if the democratic processes are clogged and if the people can no longer exercise their will by constitutional means.

CONGRESSMAN: Do *you* know of any organization that advocates the overthrow of the constitutional form of government?

MR. WHITEHORN: This committee.

CONGRESSMAN: Do you know of any such organization?

MR. WHITEHORN: According to this committee, every organization that has advocated peace in this country.

CONGRESSMAN: I am asking you whether or not, under the definition of *Mr. Webster*, you know of any organization in this country that advocates what *Mr. Webster says* is subversive conduct.

MR. WHITEHORN: You have had my answer.

CONGRESSMAN: You refuse to reply?

MR. WHITEHORN: The committee has my reply on record.

CONGRESSMAN: Let us go back to your allegations that this committee is responsible for blacklisting. I want to make it very clear that if people are being deprived of any rights or privileges of employment because of their appearance before this committee, it has been because of matters that they themselves have brought out, and not this committee. If being a member of a subversive organization and admitting such membership causes a man to lose some employment rights, that is his responsibility, and not this committee's. This committee has never yet been responsible for any man's being a member of any organization, subversive or otherwise. The only thing on earth this committee has ever attempted to do or is attempting to do now is to ascertain, under the functions it is charged with carrying out by the very act of the Congress that created it, what activities in the realm of subversiveness in this country are going on and who is responsible for them.

CHAIRMAN: I want to thank my learned colleague for this clarification.

(The Congressman is seated.)

MR. WHITEHORN: Mr. Chairman, I have a written statement—
CHAIRMAN: We would like to see the statement.

(Statement handed to the chairman.)

CHAIRMAN: Mr. Whitehorn, this statement is clearly out of order. It is just another case of vilification, as Mr. Levitz's statement was yesterday, and the statement will not be read by you.
MR. WHITEHORN: Do I not have the same rights as the witnesses who appeared before this committee last week?
INVESTIGATOR: Mr. . . .
MR. WHITEHORN: This statement is particularly pertinent . . .

(The chairman pounds gavel.)

MR. WHITEHORN: In that I am accused—
CHAIRMAN (pounding gavel): Ask another question.
MR. WHITEHORN: I beg your pardon—
CHAIRMAN (pounding gavel): Ask another question.
INVESTIGATOR: Mr. Whitehorn . . .
MR. WHITEHORN: I accuse the members of this committee of being . . .
CHAIRMAN: You will not accuse anybody further . . .
MR. WHITEHORN: I do accuse them . . .
INVESTIGATOR: Are you a member of the Screen Writers Guild?
MR. WHITEHORN: This is the same sort of loaded question put to the witnesses yesterday. It involves a question of my association.
INVESTIGATOR: Do you refuse to answer?
MR. WHITEHORN: I have not refused to answer the question, but I must answer in the only way in which I know how, and that is, that I believe that such a question violates my right of association and does not properly fall—I do not believe it falls properly—within the scope of this committee's inquiry and that the question being asked is done so with full knowledge that membership in any trade union is of concern only to the member and the union.
INVESTIGATOR: We will move on to the sixty-four-dollar question. Are you now or have you ever been a member of the Communist Party?
MR. WHITEHORN: Unless it has been changed since yesterday in our country, we have a secret ballot, and I do not believe this committee has any more right to inquire into my political affiliations than I believe an election official has the right to go into the voting booth and examine the ballot that has been marked by the voter. General Eisenhower himself has refused to reveal his political affiliations, and what is good enough for General Eisenhower is good enough for me.
INVESTIGATOR: Mr. Chairman, I ask you to direct the witness to answer the question whether or not he is now or has ever been a member of the Communist Party?
CHAIRMAN: Mr. Whitehorn, in order to save a lot of time, we would

like to know whether you are or have ever been a member of the Communist Party? We would like a very frank answer. *Yes or no.*

MR. WHITEHORN: May I ask if you would have General Eisenhower here and ask him . . .

INVESTIGATOR: Just a minute.

CHAIRMAN: Just a minute.

MR. WHITEHORN: And ask him if he is a member of the Republican or Democratic Party?

CONGRESSMAN: I must object.

INVESTIGATOR: Mr. Chairman . . .

(The chairman pounds gavel.)

MR. WHITEHORN: The question here relates not only to the question of my membership in any political organization, but this committee is attempting to establish the right . . .

(The chairman pounds gavel.)

MR. WHITEHORN (continuing): Which has been historically denied to any committee of this sort, to invade the rights and privileges and immunity of American citizens, whether they be Republican or Democrats, whether they be Protestant, Methodist, Jewish or Catholic, or anything else.

CHAIRMAN (pounding gavel): Mr. Whitehorn, just quiet down. I ask you again whether or not you have ever been a member of the Communist Party.

MR. WHITEHORN: You are using the technique used in Hitler Germany, to create a scare here . . .

CHAIRMAN (pounding gavel): Oh . . .

MR. WHITEHORN: In order to create an entirely false atmosphere.

CHAIRMAN (pounding gavel): We are going to get the answer if we have to stay here a week. Are you a member of the Communist Party, or have you ever been a member of the Communist Party?

MR. WHITEHORN: I have written Americanism for years, and I shall continue to do so and to continue to fight for the Bill of Rights which you are trying to destroy.

CHAIRMAN (pounding gavel): Stand away from the stand.

MR. WHITEHORN: I would like the list of my films—*all* of them—entered into the record. They represent some . . .

CHAIRMAN (pounding gavel): Excuse the witness.

MR. WHITEHORN: Of the most pro-American films the industry . . .

CHAIRMAN: Officers, take this man away from the stand.

(Applause and boos. The witness rises on his own, however, and with braced shoulders and an open stare directed to anyone in his path of vision, walks unescorted to his seat. From the rear of the room whispers are heard. Then the cry "Jew! Jew!")

CHAIRMAN (pounding gavel): There will be no demonstrations. No demonstrations for or against. Everyone will please be seated. Now. Proceed.

INVESTIGATOR: Mr. Chairman, the committee has made exhaustive investigation and research into the Communist affiliations of Mr. Louis Whitehorn. Numerous witnesses under oath have identified Mr. Whitehorn as a member of the Communist Party. I have here a five-page memorandum detailing at length his affiliations with the Communist Party and its various front organizations. I now ask that Mr. James E. Roland, a former member of the Federal Bureau of Investigation and an investigator for this committee, take the stand.

(END OF THE TESTIMONY OF MR. LOUIS WHITEHORN)

(James E. Roland, a former investigator for the Federal Bureau of Investigation, investigating for the committee, entered the dossier he had put together on Louis Whitehorn. The list of his films was entered into the record, and an impressive list it would seem to be. Louis Whitehorn was found to have had a Communist Party card from the years 1944-45. He had supported several Communist candidates for the Senate and belonged to a list of organizations that witnesses had testified were Communist-front organizations, had given money to these groups, and written testimonials on their behalf, and he had had an article on the possibility of Russo-American film production published in the *Daily Worker*.

At the end of Roland's testimony, the chairman pounded the gavel.)

CHAIRMAN: The evidence before this committee concerning Louis Whitehorn clearly indicates that he has been an active Communist Party member. Also, the fact that he followed the usual Communist line of not responding to questions of the committee is definite proof that he is a member of the Communist Party. Therefore, by unanimous vote of the members present, the committee recommends that Louis Whitehorn be cited for contempt of Congress and that for his refusal to answer the pertinent question "Are you a member of the Communist Party?" and his refusal to answer other questions the committee recommends appropriate action be taken by the full committee without delay.

Chapter 17

"My God, Lou was wonderful! Wonderful! He could have had any woman in Washington last night. My God, he could have had *me!*" Lucy Banner declared in a voice that was all breath and exclamation. "What are *you* doing this evening, Max?"

Max was in the hotel lobby, standing at the desk telephone. Lucy's page had caught him just as he and Edyth were leaving the hotel. He shifted uneasily from one foot to the other. "What happened to Irving?"

"Irving? He's in Texas. And don't tell me I should get my ass down there. I'm a star, you know. I shouldn't have to travel all the way to Petersburg, Texas, to get well and truly futtered."

Max laughed. "You're quite a broad, Lucy," he admitted.

"I know. So what are you doing tonight?"

"Planning my future. I always could barbecue a good hamburger. Might be something there. Seaman the Hamburger Man." Max's laugh was brittle.

"Oh, Max! I'd like to do something to help. Really *need* to do something to help. I want to understand, Max. Be a part. You heard our radio broadcast?"

"They've been keeping me pretty busy."

"Frank, and Freddie March and Myrna, Gene, Bob Ryan, Garfield—I could go on and on."

"I heard about it."

"And the others?"

"Yeah, they heard about it, too."

"Good. Good. Max, you're one of the most talented writers in Hollywood. I want you to know I believe that. And one of the most intelligent men, too."

"Yeah? How about Irving?"

"We're talking about brains, not futtering. Irving is a true genius in that department. That I *know*. But, after all, Max darling, where you're concerned—futtering-wise, that is—all I can rely on are rumors."

"You know, this call is being monitored, Lucy?"

"Good God! You mean the committee may hear *this?*"

"That's right."

"Roses are red. Violets are blue. May your peckers all shrivel and *futter you!*" Lucy recited in her inimitable voice.

"What are you laughing about?" Edyth asked as he came back to where he had left her before Lucy's call.

"Lucy Banner," he explained.

"You know, I think she's a sad girl, Max. I like her, too. Like her and feel sorry for her."

"Yeah. Let's get out of here."

They made their way out of the hotel, avoiding a reporter who had sighted them, and ran all the way up the street to where Edyth had parked the rented car. They didn't talk until they were on the outskirts of Washington.

"I thought we'd have dinner in the country," she said.

"Fine."

"You don't want to talk about it. I understand. I respect that."

"You're wrong."

"I'll listen then."

"Those sons of bitches won't cow me," he said. "Ten men have already walked the plank, but not me."

"You're not suggesting they were wrong?"

"Hell, no. It was the only thing they could do. There was no way to foresee that we would be denied the right to counsel and confronted by witnesses who would be permitted to smear us with innuendos, and suspicion and prejudice, without being permitted to cross-examine. It seemed inconceivable, to me at least, that those same men and women could be permitted to enter statements into the record and expound on any question asked, while none of us were permitted to do so. They weren't asked what guilds *they* belonged to—what political affiliations *they* had. Sons of bitches," he said under his breath, clamping his lips down hard on the cold cigarette dangling there. He pressed the car lighter in and leaned forward as he waited for it to heat.

"They leveled charges against us with full national publicity and with full legal immunity as well, and none of the ten men so far cited for contempt of Congress—contempt of Congress! Good God!—none of the ten were permitted to rebut those charges, were even allowed to see such so-called evidence as their Communist Party card." The lighter popped back, and he grabbed it and held it. "Well, hell! All the cards introduced into the record so far were allegedly issued in November or December, 1944, to cover the year 1945 and were read off as stating that they were 'Communist Party registration' cards. Yet during the time they claim those cards were issued, the Communist Party of the United States wasn't even in existence. It had dissolved and reorganized under the name of the Communist Political Association. Any card issued then would have had to have *that* name on it."

He relighted the cigarette and inhaled deeply. Then his voice rose, his face grew puffed and agitated. "You can't fight those sons of bitches with anything less than they fight with. *Power*. The power's on their side now. Hearst. Thomas, Rankin. And they couldn't have picked a better and easier target than Hollywood. Where the hell else would you find so many frightened, insecure men and women! You know where the power is, Edyth? *Our* power?" He leaned back, relaxed for the first time, smiling at his own thoughts, a tentative smile, a weary one. "On the screen. Those dumbheads aren't quite that dumb that they don't know Hollywood hasn't been producing much Communist propaganda, and in fact, even to get a *worthwhile* film made has always been a difficult task. But, baby, *they* could sure use control for the Ministry of Fascistic propaganda."

Edyth drove on in silence. Quiet. Waiting. Because she knew he didn't want her to comment. Not even to agree. He just wanted her to continue for the time, driving in silence.

"Now, let's see, tomorrow's Thursday. Brecht is scheduled to testify in the morning. The rest of us haven't been scheduled in. Maybe they're planning to break early for the weekend. Who the hell knows? I want you to make reservations in New York under your name and keep the car. And call H.M. Keep trying all day until you get through to him *personally*. If I call, it will be monitored. Explain that to him and that I have to see him for a few hours on the weekend. Think you can do that, Edyth?"

"I'll try my best, Max."

They drove on again in silence. Max had closed his eyes as he often did when he was thinking.

"Max . . ."

"Yeah?" he said under his breath, his eyes still sealed.

"What are you planning?"

"A little blackmail of my own. My own little grab into the power game," was all he ventured. Then he slumped down into the seat. Only his occasional tapping of his forefinger on his chin indicated to Edyth that he was not asleep.

The lush green summer grass had turned to brown, and although the stiff line of trees along the highway was glowing with autumnal color, their leaves were loosing themselves and baring the branches. There seemed to be no farmland, no hills. They were still on the outskirts of the city, and gas stations and cafés blotted out the countryside every hundred yards or so. Edyth had the window on the driver's side open, and the air was crisp and cleansing. The heat of the first week had passed. It was now almost November, and a first promise of winter was in the Washington wind.

Edyth followed along the highway as if it were a course upstream and she had lost her way and were groping, using instinct, like a blind person. She leaned forward against the hard wheel of the car and felt it press against her chest. Suddenly she turned off the main road onto a narrow dirt road. It was as though she wanted to lose all familiar landmarks, were set on getting lost.

The car bumped and thumped as Edyth doggedly held the wheel. She glanced at Max, but he seemed content, not caring where she was taking them. In her way Edyth was another-world person. Not truly psychic, but believing in the psychic. At this moment she felt driven by some unknown psychic force. She had been *directed* to take this particular highway out of town, directed to see this road and turn onto it. Wherever she and Max were headed would hold some clue, some omen, some explanation. Of that she was certain.

There was a small stream to the left of the road. Somewhere the stream would widen into a river, and as Edyth could now see, farmland and houses in the distance, perhaps a restaurant in what might be a summer place.

Edyth had been under great strain the last few months. More strain than Max had realized. There was, of course, Max's plight, the country's plight, for that matter. Edyth was after all a thinking person, a concerned person, and an informed person. She considered herself a real liberal, but though to look at her, one would assume she was twenty-four or twenty-five, Edyth was not twenty-one and so had not yet voted. She wasn't sure she would be a Democrat, though there seemed little alternative. She knew that she would have voted for Franklin Roosevelt, and Helen Gahagan Douglas, even though she didn't approve of Roosevelt's third term (but then again, she would have had to vote *against* Dewey).

There was as well the terrible knowledge that she was having an affair with a married man. This was not an easy situation for Edyth to cope with. She had been born and raised in the comparatively small-town atmosphere of Salem, Oregon. Her father had been dead for years, since the day when as a forestry worker for the CCC in the thirties he had been pinned to the earth by a falling tree. Mrs. Spalding had raised Edyth and her brother, Edward, with more tenacity and will than money and comfort. She made and sold jams in the summer, picked walnuts, and during the war years worked in a local factory that was turning out boots and leather goods for the services. Edward had been killed on Guadalcanal, and neither Edyth nor Mrs. Spalding had ever recovered from the shock. They had both adored him. He had been their only hope, their future.

Even at this moment, Edyth could not reconcile herself to the fact that Edward was gone. Somehow she was certain in her heart that he would reappear, come alive, *at least make himself felt again.*

It now seemed inconceivable that Mrs. Spalding had allowed Edyth to leave Salem after high school and one year at Willamette University to go to Los Angeles and to Sawyers Business School. Her mother was always on Edyth's mind, and she sent home as much of her paycheck each week as was possible. Still, she felt an overwhelming guilt that her mother, who had been ailing, lived all alone. In the last three months her mother's ailment had been diagnosed as progressive leukemia. Mrs. Spalding was a dying woman, and if Edyth did not bring her down to Los Angeles or leave California herself to return to Salem, her mother would spend the next year or two *dying alone*. It seemed impossible to discuss this with Max at this time, to get his advice and perhaps his help. Edyth loved her mother very much. She really did. She had a great knot of anxiety right now in the pit of her stomach, and she felt she would burst into tears as she thought about her mother's plight. But her own had been keeping her awake nights for months now. If she brought her mother to her apartment in California, where, oh, where would she and Max be able to be together?

The road plunged downward into a deep valley, and the stream became a fall. The sky had turned from ash to violet and now into a dark isolated blue. There were few stars and an unpeopled silence, though the rush of the water and the whop of the wheels of the car as they ground their way over the dirt road broke the stillness.

At this point Edyth thought perhaps she should look for some place to turn the car around in so that they could head back for the main road again. The car's headlights picked up another turnoff a few yards ahead and to their right.

"Lost?" Max asked, a smile on his face, undisturbed.

"No. We can turn back and get onto the main road again."

She swerved the car into what was obviously a private road.

"Right at this moment I wouldn't mind being lost," Max said.

"I would. I'm hungry."

The car dipped down, and then the wheels spun around and the car refused to go forward.

"Oh, God!" Edyth got out of the car and stepped right into a muddy ditch.

"There's a house ahead," Max yelled out the window.

"It looks deserted," Edyth said as she tried to pull herself up the side of the ditch.

"Well, we can't stay here," Max said as he opened the car door and, stepping widely onto a stump on the side of the ditch, managed to get up onto the bank without getting too muddied. He started toward the deserted building, which looked to be no more than a shack.

Edyth began to cry.

"Don't you dare," Max screamed at her.

She seemed to swallow a sob whole. She valiantly fought back the tears, and by the time they reached the door of the shack, she was no longer tearful, but, instead, curiously excited.

The door was unlatched, and inside, the construction was not as derelict as either had supposed. With his lighter to guide them, they found candles on a table near the center of the room. The place was electrified, however, though only one light fixture, an old ship's lantern, was in evidence. Max turned it on.

They had happened onto a guest or caretaker's cottage and were at the back end of a large estate. There was obviously another road that led to the main house. Through the rear window of what constituted the living area of the old cottage could be seen a gravel road winding and lost in the dark night, but a road all the same, lined with pruned and well-kept walnut trees. Their scent was familiar to Edyth, one she could never forget. For outside her bedroom, and shared by Edward in his adjoining room all their childhood in Salem, had been a massive walnut tree. They had entered each other's rooms by climbing out their windows onto the branches of *their* tree.

"We'll have to walk up to the main house and see if anyone's there," Max said.

"Can't we stay here for a while?"

"I thought you were hungry?"

"There are canned goods here. I've already taken inventory. I can fix us something."

"Cooking is not one of your true talents, Edyth."

Edyth was investigating the closets and stores of the cottage. "Someone truly lives here. We're intruders. We could probably get ourselves arrested."

"That's just what we need. Come on, Edyth." Max held open the rear door.

Edyth was in the one other room in the cottage, a small bedroom. "There's a telephone," she called out triumphantly. On the bedside table was, indeed, a telephone, as well as a huge old book on English history. "*The History of Edward the Third,*" she read aloud to Max who now stood in the doorway. Between the pages of the book a dried rose had been placed at the beginning of the reign of Edward III, as though to mark a place.

Max was by her side. "It's a telephone connecting the cottage with the house. Hell, let's try." He pushed her aside and picked up the receiver and clicked the dial.

"Hello?" someone finally replied with some surprise. "Who is this?"

"Just someone who got stuck in a ditch outside this cottage, trying to turn around to get back to the main road. I'm really not trespassing, but I'm with a young lady, and we need to get a taxi or a garageman. But I'll tell you, honestly, we don't know where we are."

"This is Walnut Grove. I'm the caretaker. You're in my cottage."

"I'm sorry, but there didn't seem to be any alternative."

"I'll call the garage from here. What kind of car?"

"Chrysler. White. New model."

"OK. Then I'll be down." He hung up.

"Walnut Grove! And this rose and the book—it says *Edward the Third.* So was my brother. Edward was my father's and grandfather's name, too! And today is October thirtieth! That was Edward's birthday. When we were kids, I always gave him a rose—" Edyth broke off. She looked up with huge believing eyes at Max. "Max, it's a sign. An omen. I know it. I was *directed* here." *Sent.*

"Your brother's name was Edward Spalding the Third?" Max said curiously.

"Yes. Edward Spalding the Third."

"It has a good ring."

"It's a *beautiful* name. He was a *beautiful* person. I loved him a lot. He had so much talent. So much potential. He wanted to be a writer, you know."

"Yeah?"

"Um. He won a contest. Patriotic speech, kind of thing. He wrote poetry. His letters—I'll show them to you sometime, if you think you would be interested."

"Edward Spalding the Third."

"What are you thinking, Max?"

"I won't be able to write as Max Seaman for a while, Edyth, and at this time it is more imperative that I write than ever before. How would you feel if I called myself Edward Spalding the Third?"

Edyth held the pressed rose gently in her hands. Her eyes were moist. "Just beautiful, Max," she said.

Headlights now flashed outside the rear windows. A car door slammed shut.

"Hello!" the caretaker shouted as Max and Edyth went out to greet him.

Chapter 18

It was Thursday morning, October 30. The second week in Washington was moving toward a close at a tempo that seemed like a film that had been accelerated. The nineteen witnesses sat waiting at the long table. Playing his scene with the greatest of theatricality, the chairman called the eleventh "unfriendly" witness, Mr. Bertolt Brecht, to the witness chair.

Brecht was a mild, smallish-looking man who might have been easily mistaken for a professor or scientist except for the deep, dreamlike quality in his expressive eyes and his soft, deliberate manner of speaking English which was an attempt to overcome his broad German accent, and yet made one conscious of his reverence for words.

CHAIRMAN: Mr. Brecht, will you hold up your right hand and be sworn. You solemnly swear the testimony you give before this committee shall be the truth, the whole truth, and nothing but the truth, so help you God?

MR. BRECHT: I do.

(TESTIMONY OF MR. BERTOLT BRECHT)

INVESTIGATOR: Mr. Brecht, will you please state your full name and present address for the record, please? Speak into the microphone.

MR. BRECHT: My name is Bertolt Brecht. I am living at 34 West Seventy-third Street, New York. I was born in Augsburg, Germany, February 10, 1898.

INVESTIGATOR: Mr. Brecht, the committee has a—

CHAIRMAN: What was that date again?

INVESTIGATOR: Would you give the date again?

MR. BRECHT: Tenth of February, 1898.

CHAIRMAN: 1898?

MR. BRECHT: 1898.

CHAIRMAN: The Immigration records state *1888*.

MR. BRECHT: 1898.

INVESTIGATOR: I beg your pardon.

INTERPRETER: I think the witness tried to say 1898.

INVESTIGATOR: I want to know whether the immigration records are correct on that. Is it '88 or '98?

MR. BRECHT: '98.

INVESTIGATOR: Would you please give this committee a brief history of your progression to the United States.

MR. BRECHT: I left Germany in 1933 when Hitler took power and went to Denmark. War seemed imminent, and so in 1939 I went to Stockholm, Sweden. One year later, when Hitler invaded Norway and Denmark, I went to Finland to await a visa for the United States. I arrived here in 1941 and applied right away for my first citizenship.

INVESTIGATOR: What is your profession?

MR. BRECHT: Poet and playwright.

INVESTIGATOR: Are you currently employed?

MR. BRECHT: No.

INVESTIGATOR: Have you worked in Hollywood?

MR. BRECHT: As a film writer?

INVESTIGATOR: Yes, as a film writer.

MR. BRECHT: My only connection with films has been through the sale of a story of mine, *Hangmen Also Die*, to an independent producer and another story that has not yet been produced.

INVESTIGATOR: You did not write the screenplay?

MR. BRECHT: I did not.

INVESTIGATOR: Mr. Brecht, are you now or have you ever been a member of the Communist Party?

MR. BRECHT: May I be permitted to read a statement?

CHAIRMAN: Let me see the statement.

(The statement is handed to the chairman, who glances through it.)

CHAIRMAN (continuing): Mr. Brecht, the committee has carefully gone over the statement. It is a very interesting story of German life, but it is not at all pertinent to this inquiry. Therefore, we do not care to have you read the statement.

INVESTIGATOR: Mr. Brecht, I ask you again, are you now or have you ever been a member of the Communist Party?

MR. BRECHT: Mr. Chairman, I have heard my colleagues when they considered this question not as proper, but I am a guest in this country and I do not want to enter into any legal arguments, so I will answer your question as fully as well I can. I was not a member or am not a member of any Communist Party.

CHAIRMAN: Your answer is, then, that you have never been a member of the Communist Party?

MR. BRECHT: That is correct.

INVESTIGATOR: You were not a member of the Communist Party in Germany?

MR. BRECHT: No, I was not.

INVESTIGATOR: Mr. Brecht, is it true that you have written a number of very revolutionary poems, plays, and other writings?

MR. BRECHT: I have written a number of poems, and songs, and plays in the fight against Hitler and, of course, was for the overthrow of that government.

CHAIRMAN: We are not interested in any works, Mr. Investigator, that he might have written, advocating the overthrow of Germany or the government there.

INVESTIGATOR: I understand.

(A rather long exchange followed here, among Mr. Brecht, the investigator, and the committee's own interpreter, regarding Mr. Brecht's works. The investigator read several excerpts which seemed positive proof that the works quoted followed a Communist line. However, the committee's interpreter interrupted these readings to state that the investigator was *misquoting*, and then Brecht was asked to verify which one was correct. Brecht's translation was not the same as either man's and showed clearly that the works were anti-Nazi. The investigator asked him about associations and meetings in the long ago—twenty, thirty years past—with men believed to be Communists.)

MR. BRECHT: Yes. I recall those men. They are old friends. We played chess and spoke about politics.

INVESTIGATOR: Politics?

MR. BRECHT: Yes.

CHAIRMAN: What was that last answer? I didn't get the last answer.

INVESTIGATOR: They spoke about politics. Mr. Brecht, did you ever make application to join the Communist Party?

MR. BRECHT: Never.

INVESTIGATOR: Did anyone ever ask you to join the Communist Party?

MR. BRECHT: No. No. I think they considered me just a writer who wanted to write and do as he saw it, but not as a political figure.

CHAIRMAN: Did anyone ever suggest Mr. Brecht join the Communist Party?

INVESTIGATOR: Did anyone ever suggest you join the Communist Party?

MR. BRECHT: Some people might have suggested it to me.

CHAIRMAN: Who were those people who asked you to join the Communist Party?

MR. BRECHT: Oh, readers.

CHAIRMAN: Who?

MR. BRECHT: Readers of my poems or people from the audiences.

CHAIRMAN: Some people did ask you to join the Communist Party?

MR. BRECHT: In Germany? You mean in Germany?

CHAIRMAN: No, I mean in the United States.

MR. BRECHT: No, no, no.

CHAIRMAN: He is doing all right. He is doing much better than many other witnesses brought here.

INVESTIGATOR: Mr. Brecht, did you write the following poem? [reading] "Forward, we've not forgotten. We have a world to gain. We shall free the world of shadow; every shop and every room, every road and every meadow. All the world will be our own." Did you write that, Mr. Brecht?

MR. BRECHT: No. I wrote a German poem, but that is very different from this.

(There is laughter.)

CHAIRMAN: Thank you, Mr. Brecht. You are dismissed. We will now adjourn for lunch.

The same ex-FBI man who had appeared ten times previously and following the testimony of each "unfriendly" witness was called to the stand after lunch. He had nothing to add or subtract from Brecht's testimony. In fact, he did not mention Brecht at all. Instead, he went into a detailed and very convoluted story that began with an official of the Soviet government's being sent to Hollywood as a film representative and from there jumped to various places in the United States where Communists were suspected of being active, ending up at the atomic bomb project at Los Alamos, New Mexico, indicating there might be some link from the beginning of this daisy chain to the end.

The witnesses sat there, sharing much of the same surprise as the audience and the press. There had been no revelation. Only innuendo. The audience rose before the chairman had dismissed them. He pounded the gavel. They stood waiting.

CHAIRMAN: The hearings today conclude the first phase of the committee's investigation of Communism in the motion-picture industry. While we have heard thirty-nine witnesses, there are many more to be heard. The chair stated earlier in the hearing he would present the records of seventy-nine prominent people associated with the motion-picture industry who were members of the Communist Party or who have records of Communist affiliation. We have before us eleven of these individuals. There are sixty-eight to go. This hearing has concerned itself principally with spotlighting Communist personnel in the industry.

I want to emphasize that the committee is not adjourning sine die but will resume hearings as soon as possible. The committee hearings for the past two weeks have clearly shown the need for this investigation. The prominent figures in Hollywood whom the committee had evidence were members of the Communist Party came before us and refused to deny that they were Communists. It is not necessary for the chair to emphasize the harm done by the presence within the industry's ranks of known Communists who do not have the best interests of the United States at heart. The industry should set about immediately to clean its own house and not wait for public opinion to force it to do so.

The hearings are adjourned.

It was over. Ten men were to be indicted for contempt of Congress and face a year in jail. Brecht had been smeared with innuendo, and the other eight men faced future inquisition. But for the time being, the ordeal of possible testimony was behind them. What was before them none of the men could be sure. Except that the blacklist that the studios had said they would not inaugurate had, in fact, already begun.

Chapter 19

It was Saturday. The first day in November, which meant it should have been bleak and cold outside, cold autumn—it could come, of course, at any moment. Max could glance away, distracted, look back, and there it would be, a dark gray, threatening November day through the window behind Harry Steiner. But instead, the sun was high as New York coped with the last hot day of an Indian summer. In the park the flowers had faded, but the leaves and grass were motionless, as if exhausted from the long summer drought, and though the air was still, it was heavy with damp scent and the sky seemed to be quivering. In Steiner's hundred-dollar-a-day suite overlooking Central Park, all the windows were sealed and the room was filled with the whir of the air conditioner, and this air was also heavy with its own damp scent intermingled with the too-sweet odor coming from the several dozen roses sent by the management to welcome the great man to their premises.

Right now Harry Steiner stood with his back to the window as he turned the star ruby ring on his little finger and looked across the large impersonal and elegant hotel room at Max, his glance seeming detached, deliberate, and cool. As Max talked, Steiner appeared to be listening, but it was difficult to be sure. Max thought so, thought that the constant turning of the heavy ring indicated intense concentration on Steiner's part.

It was reasonably cool in the room, but Max was still sweating uncomfortably under his blue serge suit. "I'm aware," Max heard himself say, "I'm well aware it will be most difficult to get *Crosscurrent* off the ground."

"Impossible." *He was listening, then.*

"That's what I thought. It's a crime. Omega would have had a hell of a film and a money-maker as well." Max edged forward on the deep couch. He felt at a disadvantage sitting down while Steiner stood there facing him so implacably.

"I'm also aware that Omega has, by shelving the project, dropped half a million down a sewer." He decided to stand and the hell with it. He got to his feet. That was an advantage. He was a full six inches taller than Steiner. He took out one of his own cigarettes—though a bowl on the otherwise naked coffee table contained a package of every brand in triplicate—lighted it with his solid gold lighter, and, holding the cigarette in one hand and the lighter in the other, began to pace slowly while Steiner waited.

Max paused. He was now close enough to Steiner to blow smoke in his face if he wanted, but as he stood facing him, eyes cast downward to the shorter man's level, he held the cigarette loosely between his fingers, casually, and smiled at him instead. "Harry, I can make you back your five hundred grand . . . and then some. OK with you?" he said.

"I'm listening, Max."

Max waited a moment as if to be sure. He never shifted positions. He stood as implacably as the man he faced. His smile broadened. "I have a story that's a natural." He grinned. Then he lifted the cigarette to his lips and inhaled deeply, holding the smoke in his lungs and walking away a few feet before sending it up in a long spiral to the vaulted ceiling.

"You know I told Grace once you could have been Scheherazade in another life," Steiner cracked.

"She told dirty stories. This one's clean. It's about an eight-year-old kid. Doesn't even masturbate. He's lived on an island all his life—a tourist's paradise. Only to him it's a cold-water shack and a bed he has to share with six other brothers and sisters. He stows away on a private boat and manages to get, undetected, into the city," he said.

Max studied Steiner's face for a moment. *Interested. Not yet hooked.* Max continued. "We see the city—this harsh cement jungle that the tourists on the kid's island have run from—from the kid's point of view. To him, though, it's beautiful. He sees all the beauty they can no longer see, just as they see beauty in his island where he can't. He finds a friend, a blind kid, and tells it to him as he sees it. The blind kid's family and neighbors fight back with the truth as they see it. The two boys argue bitterly. Our boy has to go back to his island paradise. He's broken up. The two kids meet again. The blind kid has stowed away, but our boy sends him home. This time the blind kid *believes*—through the beauty his friend sees, *he believes*."

Max leaned over a table and flicked his ashes. He casually threw away the next few words. "The entire film could be shot here, with no professionals, for under two hundred and fifty thousand dollars." He straightened. Steiner was interested now. "It's a camera and cutting job, really. We'd need a kid with an expressive face—soulful."

Steiner was interested. "Got a title?" he asked.

"Black in Eden."

"Damn it, Max! A colored kid! It can't be a colored kid. And you know damn well you can't call him black, if it could be a colored kid." Steiner had lost his calm now. His face turned red, and he was scowling unhappily.

"Black is the kid's name, and Black is what everyone calls him. Hell, Harry, we're saying in this film that beauty is where we see it and this kid *Black*, he sees it in the toughest city in the U.S.A. Talk about Americanism!"

It was a long moment before Steiner spoke. Something seemed to be clicking in his brain. "You'd have to have one major adult role—a Negro. Male. Tailored for someone like Saunders Mayberry, and I could let you script it, that's all. Just the screenplay. You'd have to take someone like Frank or Tanner as producer," he said.

"How about you, Harry? How about you doing this one yourself. Produced by H. M. Steiner himself. The boys would never question that!"

"I'd like to, Max. I might just surprise you." He looked away and then back. "You couldn't use your own name, Max. You'd have to use another name," he said.

"I'm prepared."

"And it has to be just between us. You understand that? I'd have to have your written word on that."

"Agreed."

"And money, Max, I can't pay it to you or to Luise for that matter."

"You could buy off my old contract, Harry, if I was prepared to sell. You could make a settlement. No one would question that."

"How much?"

"A hundred grand. Payable over five years."

"Seventy-five."

"Over three."

"It's a deal." Steiner extended his hand for Max to shake. The ruby ring cut into Max's flesh. Steiner's grip was a powerful one.

"Coffee, Max? I can't offer you lunch. I have an appointment with some of our Wall Street boys. In fact, that's really why I'm here."

"As soon as the rabbits are in the trap, they prepare the stew, eh?" *The blacklist is upon us*, Max thought.

"Max, I couldn't do anything but what I did. I have my pressures, my responsibilities, too. Omega's a big business. A lot of people depend on my keeping the gates open for their support. Thousands. You think I could afford all that personally? Max, I *need* Wall Street."

"Yeah, I understand, Harry."

"Coffee?"

"No thanks. I have to run."

"When will you start?"

"Right away."

"I'll arrange the settlement." He had his arm linked through Max's and was leading him through the hallway to the door. "I'll tell you who to give the pages to, Max. Someone here. Someone we can trust."

"You have a short memory, Harry. I don't give pages. You'll have to wait for a first draft."

"OK, Max. As you say."

The door was open now. Steiner extended his hand again, and Max took it, avoiding the ring as well as he could.

"Son of a bitch!" he cursed aloud as he waited for the elevator, demoting Harry Steiner forever from the honorary ranks of "Bastards."

Max decided to walk back to his hotel, though Steiner was

staying at the Sherry Netherlands and Max and Edyth all the way midtown. He felt choked and hot but he needed the time to himself.

Loosening his collar, untying his tie, he stooped a little, putting his hands deep into his pockets, and walked swiftly, staring straight ahead. He knew New York well. Like the back of his hand. He didn't have to glance to either side of him to know what he was passing. The dust beat up beneath his feet. He could smell and taste it.

He walked down Fifth Avenue past the lean buildings, the magnificent shops, the sights that people came from all over the world to see. He didn't stop until he reached Rockefeller Plaza. He stood for a moment or two watching a street crew at work. The men worked silently, spreading dust and despair on all sides of them. Max leaned against a wall and looked up at the sky. Black clouds were closing in fast. Just as he thought. The end of summer. Everything was getting set to die a little. He lighted a cigarette, crossed over the street, conscious of and irritated with the rushing people surrounding him, and turned off Fifth Avenue, heading toward Park.

It was going to rain. It didn't seem to matter to him. He was unprepared, but he didn't care. Everyone else on the crosstown street began to rush. They all seemed personally persecuted. Hell! It was the first of November. What else could you expect but a skyful of wet clouds? You could smell the coming wet now. The sky was the color of slate, and the sidewalk turned leaden. There was no longer any sun at all. Max slowed his gait. He was in no hurry to see Edyth.

If there was one thing Max hated about Edyth more than another, it was her incredible ability to inflict her gloom on other people. It was as though she did it purposely to establish her own interpretation of intimacy. Why had he started an affair with her anyway? He had asked himself this many times but had never been able to satisfy himself with an answer. He supposed it had a good deal to do with her pathetic quality. She was the half child, half adoring fan, and yet, as he had originally suspected, in bed she was also part untamed animal.

She was also the best and most devoted secretary he had ever had. For some curious reason, though unable to cope with all the sordid details of her own existence, Edyth could handle the affairs of others with a competence that was almost frightening. She also had no sensitivity to insult, neglect, or detachment. That was perhaps the thing he liked about her most.

He liked the way she looked, too. Lean and tight. He hated fat. Worked every day to keep himself from turning to fat. And she had that marvelous burnt-amber hair and white, finely textured skin. She wasn't a beautiful girl by any stretch of the imagination, but she did from time to time please him, and her demands were seldom difficult to meet. Had she been a clever woman, she would have kept her damned glooms to herself, and they could have gone on forever.

Last night had been decisive for him, though. She had languished all evening in a kind of secret sacramental depression. She had, of course, accomplished everything he had asked her to and more. Steiner had been contacted (after several dozen tries), arrangements for New York taken care of, notes on *Black in Eden* transcribed and ready for him, Luise informed where he was to be, and his bags packed.

But all evening, except in the passion of lovemaking, she had sat with grieving eyes, small sighs punctuating the silence from time to time. And this morning there had been tears on her cheeks, and she had employed that most annoying gesture, the face turned half away—the *I-shall-suffer-alone-it's-my-sadness-not-yours* gesture.

Max didn't know what the problem was, nor did he plan to ask. He just prayed that Edyth would not reveal it. It was curious—he was always compelled to drag the truth out of Luise, but from any other woman, he merely wanted service.

The rain had begun to fall. Max began to hurry, more out of deference to the suit he wore and was fond of than any other reason. He moved at a slightly more accelerated pace, but still a walk. *No one, nothing, will make me run,* Max thought. Then he crossed Park, turned and, staying under the canopies of the buildings lining the avenue, reached his hotel with a minimum of wetness.

When Edyth opened the door to the hotel suite and saw Max standing there, her pleasure was extreme.

"You don't mind me being here?" she asked. "My room was rather dark."

She was wearing Shalimar, his favorite scent, and had on a soft pajama outfit in a dusty rose, a marvelous shade for her skin and hair. He was surprised to find as he followed her into his own suite that he was happy that she had been there to greet him.

"Shall I order some coffee?" she asked.

"I haven't had lunch."

"Oh," she said as if shaken by this a bit. She crossed immediately to the telephone and without asking him ordered a rare hamburger, a slice of onion, a dish of raw vegetables, and a large pot of coffee. It was exactly what he felt like eating.

She waited until he had taken off his jacket before pouring him a straight shot of scotch.

"You aren't expecting anybody?" she asked.

"No, nobody."

"That's nice."

She drew a small table up to the most comfortable chair. "You can eat here," she said. "I think you'll find it cozier than those room-service carts." She looked up at him. "You're not longing to be alone, are you?"

"No. Not longing."

"May I ask?"

"It went better than I hoped."

"Oh! Max!"

"I'll only be doing the screenplay, though." He sank down into the chair.

"But it will be a great screenplay! That makes all the difference."

"And I can't use my name."

"You'll use Edward's name?"

"Yeah. I think so."

"It will be great, Max. You'll see. When do we go back to California?"

"I'm going to let you go back to help Luise and to get my things in order. I'm going to stay here."

"In New York?" she asked with surprise.

"Yeah."

"You always hated New York."

"That was before Washington. Now I hate the sun spot *more,* that's all."

The joy had suddenly left her face. "Max, what about me?"

"You'll come here, of course."

There were tears of relief in her eyes. Her narrow shoulders quivered, and she had that small-child look about her. He got up and took her by the hand. "Come on. Let's go in the bedroom," he said quietly.

"Room service . . . " she protested weakly.

"It will take them a good fifteen minutes."

He led her into the bedroom of the suite and closed the door to the living room. There was an office building facing their windows. Lines of girls were sitting at small tables typing busily. He drew the blinds and then stood there, watching Edyth as she painstakingly turned back the covers on the bed and then as she nervously undressed, away from him, slipping into the bed as fast as she could. He went into the bathroom before joining her, taking his time, knowing Edyth would be all the more ardent for the waiting.

"Oh, Max. Oh, God. Max, Max, I love you. I've *always* loved you. I always *will* love you," she said between grateful, lingering kisses after their passion had been spent.

The bell to the suite rang.

"Room service," he assured her.

They both were silent as a door beyond opened. They listened to the sound of the cart being wheeled in and lay there on top of the covers wound still in an embrace until they heard the waiter, finished setting up Max's meal, close the door.

"Max," Edyth said softly.

"Yeah, kid." He ran his hands down her back and over her buttocks and then let them rest between her thighs.

"There's something—"

"Yeah?"

"Very personal—"

"Umm."

"That has been on my mind."

"Uh-huh."

His hand was moving, and Edyth pulled away, sitting up, drawing the cover over her. "I never told you about this because you have had so much."

Max slid off the bed and headed for the bathroom. She had to talk over the sound of the running water.

"It's my mother. She's very ill. She's—she's dying, Max. Leukemia. And she's all alone. I said she's—" The water had been turned on with greater force, and Edyth got out of the bed and, putting Max's shirt on to cover herself, went to the open bathroom door.

Max was taking a shower.

"Can you hear me, Max?"

"Sure, kid."

"I said my mother's very sick with leukemia. She's dying—and—" Edyth began to cry. "Max, I can't leave her alone to die. I just can't. And the hospital says they haven't room for her and that there is really nothing they can do anyway."

Max turned off the water. "You want her with you?" he asked.

"I—I guess—oh, Max, I don't really know what to do!"

Max stepped out of the shower and came over to her. He looked her straight in the eyes and with great sincerity. "She *should* be with you, Edie. I tell you what. You make arrangements for her to come here with you."

"Here? New York?" Edyth was so shocked she stopped crying.

"Yeah. They have the best doctors here and in Boston. I'll pay for her trip and help where I can. You know it isn't great financially with me now, but I'll try to help. You find a nice apartment for the two of you."

"That will make it more difficult for us, Max, won't it?"

"Edie! This is your mother we're talking about, and she's a sick woman. First things first."

"You're right, of course, Max. You're really wonderful."

"Before you leave for the Coast, you'd better look into apartments and try to find someone to help you with your mother. You won't have to worry, Edie. I can at least pay for that."

"That would be a tremendous help."

He wrapped a bath towel around himself, stepped into his slippers, and started past her. He paused to give her a parting pat on the rear.

"You know, that's the best part of you, Edie," he said. "Now get dressed so you can get a head start on finding that apartment." He went into the living room and, instead of sitting down, took two slices of bread, put the hamburger and the onion between them and ate standing up.

That settles that, he thought. *She'll be busy nights. That was one way to walk away a hero.* He walked over to the window and looked into the typing pool across the way. *And still keep a dependent secretary—the best kind of secretary to have.*

Chapter 20

It was simply not possible for Max to work in the apartment he and Luise had taken uptown off Fifth Avenue. It had no segregated area for him to use as an office, for one thing. For another, the children had never lived in an apartment before or in the winter weather. It wasn't their fault or Luise's, but the din forbade concentration. He took two rooms midtown, in a small office building that housed a large theatrical agency on the first three floors. Max was on the fifth.

In a short time his life fell into a familiar routine. The present had eroded the past. Luise had adapted immediately to this new way of life. That was part of Luise's uniqueness, her ability to cope, any time, any place, her stability, her reality. In those ways Luise was an anchor for Max. Without her he felt a good deal like a spaceship without radar, marooned, abandoned. But her special genius for hanging on and dispatching normality as she did was also devastating at times in its quiet demand that he exorcise all abnormality in himself, lust, bad taste, his own character. She would have normality at the cost of his own livingness. Perhaps, that was why he whipped her with the truth so often and abused her with his lust. Luise pushed order, dispensed constancy, administered nonbetrayal.

There was something too perfect about Luise, her beauty, her control, her majesty, her health, her adjustment. Yet in bed he enjoyed this most. Took great pleasure in releasing the strange winged creature that was housed inside her and then rendering it wingless, marooned, as he often felt when not in bed.

The children were attending public schools and seemed all right. There was no less bigotry, no fewer reactionary parents, but there was less concentration on film personalities. The other children might have taken notice of Gary Cooper's or Tyrone Power's children, but the name Max Seaman carried no weight. The parents of these children had no reason to read film credits.

Only in truly inclement weather would Max taxi to his office. Walking down Fifth Avenue shortly after nine had become a welcomed prelude to his day. The office was on Madison and Fifty-ninth, thirty blocks from the apartment, and just over thirty minutes, walking.

Edyth was already there when he arrived.

"You had a telephone call," she greeted him.

"This early?"

"Saunders Mayberry. I took his number and said you'd ring him back."

"OK. Do it now before I begin work." He started into the room he used for himself. "Did he say anything to you?"

"Just that he'd left Hollywood and was thinking of New York if he could find work."

"How did he know how to find me?"

"I didn't ask. Still want me to get him for you?"

"Yeah."

He went into the back room and closed the door. There were fresh cigarettes on the desk, sharpened pencils, a new legal-sized yellow pad—the kind he always worked on—and the typed transcript of the previous day's work. The scent of Edyth's Shalimar lingered in the room and intermingled with the fumes from the lighter fluid she obviously had just used to fill his table lighter.

He sat down and began to read the script pages. He found it difficult to concentrate. He lighted a cigarette and leaned back, waiting. The intercom rang.

"Yeah?"

"Mayberry."

"Put him on."

"Max?"

"Yeah. Welcome to New York, sweetheart."

"How's it going?"

"Not bad. With you?"

"I'd like to talk with you," Mayberry said.

"Now?"

"If possible."

"You know the address?"

"I'm aware it's the secret of the Sphinx, but I do."

"Who told you?"

"Tanner."

There was a moment's silence.

"I'll be waiting," Max said. He put the receiver down and leaned back in his chair. It wouldn't be possible to work until Sandy Mayberry had come and gone. He decided to enjoy the half hour or so of privacy.

"Don't interrupt me until Mayberry gets here," he told Edyth over the intercom.

"Right, Max."

He leaned back again and plotted the scene that would soon unfold.

Saunders Mayberry was a good-looking bastard, and he knew it. He sat, no, sprawled in the chair opposite Max with deliberate casualness. His pants were tight, hugging a slim waist, trim hips, a sizable piece of equipment, and taut legs. His skin was light for a black man, smooth, the color of malted milk. He had been born in Jamaica, and the bone structure of his face, the aquiline nose, the broad but not full mouth, the rounded green eyes and the straight, close-cropped hair on his perfectly shaped Rodinesque head immediately announced a legacy of mixed bloods. He had a voice like sweet crystals dripping from a honey pot.

"What do you expect, Max, baby? They won't make a picture out there about the American Negro. It took them all these years until the word 'Jew' was used in a film. Those are *frightened* men, baby. Always first-choice pickings for Judas goats." He tipped his chair backward, balancing it precariously. "I won't play those Uncle Tom roles they offer me. That makes me a Communist right now, though you and I know the party would have no part of me. Hell, they'd throw me right out on my tight, liberal ass." He laughed, a line of evenly capped teeth revealed as he did. "Hollywood? They can put it you-know-where. Right up that committee chairman's ass."

The chair creaked as it jerked back into position, and Mayberry—

then tilted it forward, leaning with it, looking as though he might fly right over Max's desk and into his lap. "But I'm a big talent. *Big.* You know that. I know that. It eats me, Max, baby. Eats me up each time I think about it. Burt Lancaster—I got what he's got and more. And I eventually want to direct. You think they'll give a colored man a film to direct?" He laughed again. This time harsh, bitter, no song of the islands. He waited, then laughed a softer laugh, a mocking laugh, really just an echo of his thoughts, and, tipping the chair back on all fours again, pushed himself up to his full height, crossed his legs almost defiantly, and folded his hands in his lap. "I hear you have a role in the script you're writing I could get my Chiclet teeth into," he said.

"Where did you hear that?"

"Bob Tanner."

"You're one of the few speaking to him, I gather. And how the hell did *he* hear?" Max could not cover his own curiosity.

"Kate Steiner. That's the new, big 'twosome.' Haven't you been reading Louella?"

"Not lately."

"Anyway, the grapevine has it that your script's a beaut and that there's a part that makes a Negro a human being for a change."

"That's right. A sailor on a private boat that a kid stows away on. Three scenes. Best I've written."

"So they say."

"Tanner and Kate Steiner?"

"I'll let you in on a secret, Max, baby. Once it was Mayberry and Kate Steiner. I understood that one is meant to be kept like the secret of the Sphinx."

"I have to hand it to you, Sandy. You sure as hell are a shrewd bastard." Max smiled, but a kernel of disapproval still showed.

"I dig that chick, Max. Still do. She's a real lady. I checked out. That's how it had to be."

"Tanner know?"

"Not from me. But Kate might have told him." He looked Max straight in the eye. "How about it, Max?"

"Well, yes, Sandy, I wrote the part with you in mind. But I'm only the writer on this one and the mystery guest, as well. I swing no weight."

"Would you let me read the script?"

"When it's finished."

"When will that be?"

"Three, four weeks."

"Fair. I'll try to be patient."

"Decent of you." The two men sat in an awkward silence. Mayberry retained his stiff, professional posture. "Bob Tanner, Sandy. I don't get it."

"I'm not going to tell you I don't hate his guts. Kate's in love with him, though. I think they're plotting marriage. I told you, I really dig that chick. She asked me up to her apartment . . . *begged me* to meet Tanner, be polite. I'll give her that. I know her old man's buying me off with this part. He didn't have to, Max. That's the truth. If it's not as good as you say, I'll be stupid enough to turn it down. And Kate's secret is still with me."

"And me—and Tanner."

"Yeah, right. I think I'd better start shutting my rubber mouth." He laughed nervously.

"When did you leave the Coast?"

"Week before last."

"Any frontline news?"

"None you probably don't know. The ten have been fired and blacklisted. When they finish serving their time in jail, there's nothing to come back to. The fear's like some creeping cancer out there. They're not making films; they're shooting scenery. I don't know how you got this one off."

"That had puzzled me, too."

"Had?"

"You pick up fast."

"You think H.M.?"

"Yeah, I think H.M. found himself the payoff when he heard the basic story of *Black in Eden*."

"Damn!" Mayberry roared with laughter. "That's *got* to be the wildest thing that ever happened to me. And, Max, baby, take it from me, my life has not been dull."

Edyth came into his office with a cup of coffee just as soon as Mayberry left.

"Sandy was certainly in good humor when he left," she said.

"Sit down, Edyth."

"Coffee time?"

"Not really."

"I'll get my pad."

"Sit down."

Edyth did as she was told. "Yes, Max?"

"That son of a bitch used me," he said between tight lips.

"Sandy?"

"H.M."

"Oh. This *is* a serious conversation."

"Now, I don't mind being used, Edie, but I like to know it when it's happening—be able to put it in my asset column." He looked up over Edyth's head. "I could have pulled a better deal. Maybe I still can."

"Can I ask what happened in the early reels?"

"Mayberry and Kate Steiner."

"No!"

He gave her a sharp look. "And now Kate Steiner and Bob Tanner. It all fits. That Tanner is one shrewd son of a bitch. And I was an easy sucker. *Black in Eden* would never have been bought if the old man hadn't needed a payoff. He still needs it, Edie. *Thinks* he does, which is one and the same. It's really pretty funny at that—the only reason he penciled in a meaningful script at this time was that he didn't want the world to know his only daughter had been having herself a piece of black ass."

"I feel sorry for Kate. I don't really know her, and I don't know exactly why I feel that way. But I do."

Max was standing now, pacing, away. "Edie, when a man's at his lowest, that's when he has to come on strongest. I'm going to form a company. What's more, Steiner is going to give me the front money to get it rolling." He walked over to the one window in the room. It looked into a court, a cement wall directly facing. It was a dark day, and even with all the lights on, the room held onto the gloom.

"You're good on names, Edie. Come up with one," he said turning back, looking seriously at her.

"For a company?"

"Yeah."

"I just can't think of one like that. Maybe a combination of the children's names."

Max sat down again facing Edyth. "You really had a thing for your brother, Edie, eh?"

"You're always insinuating something incestuous, Max. It really does disturb me." She pushed her hair back from her face with injured pride. "And what made you bring Edward up now, anyway?"

"You mentioned the kids. I think about them along those lines. Wonder if they have your problem."

"Max . . . "

"If I'd had a sister, I might not have married Luise."

"Max . . . "

"As it is, I guess Mama was a fair substitute. I've been thinking a lot about her lately. She was really a pretty strong dame. I've always thought it was my father who had the strength. I'm not so sure about that anymore. You know, I think if she had found that son of a bitch's bankroll about five years earlier, she would have lifted it, and neither one of us would have ever seen her again. She had no alternatives, though, until after he died. No alternatives. That's like taking a life rap."

"You thinking about doing a story about your mother?"

"Yeah." He grinned. "How'd you guess?"

"It wasn't difficult. You've been talking about families all week. Especially mothers."

"How's yours?"

"Not good. Getting weaker. I've done a lot of digging around. I understand there's a doctor at the Leahy Clinic in Boston who's done wonders, performed miracles with leukemia."

"Maybe you wouldn't be doing her a favor to prolong it."

"I can't think that way."

"Perhaps you should force yourself."

"Max!"

"I'm thinking about you, Edie."

"Yes, I know it."

"I can't help you too much more financially."

"You've really been marvelous, Max."

"Why don't you take a couple of days and go up and speak to this guy in Boston?"

Edyth's face lighted up. "Could you spare me, Max?"

"I'll struggle through."

"I might do that."

"Give me a day's notice."

"Of course."

"Elektra."

"What?"

"I think I'll call the company Elektra Productions. Yeah. That's it. Elektra."

Edyth went out of the room and closed the door softly. Max sat there, the minutes dragging by. It was not going to be easy to work this day. The telephone rang. He picked up the receiver.

"Yeah?"

"Bob Tanner."

"OK."

"OK?"

"That's what I said, Edyth."

"Hello, Max. I know this call will take you unaware."

"Very little does nowadays, Bob."

"I don't know how else to say this to you except straight out. Max, Harry Steiner has put me on *Black in Eden* as your producer."

"Yeah?" The receiver felt leaden in Max's hand, but what Tanner had just told him he had guessed from his first few words with Sandy.

"What I've read of the script I think is beautiful, Max. I'll try to be as loyal to it as I can."

"That's encouraging."

"Could we meet?"

"When?"

"You say."

"Next week. Toward the end. I'll have my secretary check with you."

"Fine. Max . . . "

"Yeah?"

"I'm sorry it has to be done this way. If it was possible to use your name, I'd do everything in my power."

"Save it, Bobby."

"OK. Thursday or Friday. I'll check with your office."

"You do that."

He lowered the receiver without saying good-bye and sat there quietly. It was a long time until he was able even to pick up the typed copy on his desk and read it.

Chapter 21

Max sat alone in his office. He welcomed the moments, savored them, had truly been desperate for them. The situation at home had become increasingly more difficult. It was not just the children, nor was it the lack of privacy in such small quarters. It was New York as well. Having been away for so long, Max was no longer comfortable in the city. His ears could no longer take the cacophony. It grated, it scraped, was untuneful, musicless to him. Crowds unnerved him; the loss of greens depressed him. It disturbed him that the interiors of all restaurants were unfamiliar to him, that headwaiters did not know him, nor clerks in stores. He would walk thirty streets and never see a familiar face. He enjoyed privacy, but his ego, in order to exist, had to have certain tidbits, reassurances from time to time.

Like Saunders Mayberry, he now hated Hollywood. But he knew it would always be home. Someday he would want to go back, would need to return, for in those hills the roots of his talent were deeply implanted.

Something had happened, of course, to Luise and himself. A great deal had to do with Luise's change since the day the subpoena was delivered. Never as politically inclined as himself, interested always to a greater extent in his writing, in their home, their children, never the promoter of causes, Luise had suddenly—at least it seemed sudden—become a martyrologist. Every morning as she opened the mail or read the newspaper, the death roll would toll.

So-and-so has been named. You-know-who has been fired. What's-his-name can't find work.

She read all the literature that she could find that might pertain to witch-hunts and blacklists. Russia, Spain, the United States in the 1600's, no country, no history escaped her attention, and she would discuss it endlessly in the evenings, on Sunday afternoon, Saturday mornings—no free time was ever overlooked.

Luise had come to believe (he did, too, of course, but that was different) that they were living through a time in U.S. history that would make the Dark Ages, the Inquisition pale in comparison. And each person named, therefore, became a martyr to the cause.

Worse was her bitterness when anyone became an informer. He shared these feelings and yet resented Luise's right to her violence in the matter. It was, after all, his life, his career, his name that were now in jeopardy. He realized he felt as a Jew might have felt married to a non-Jew in Nazi Germany. *It's my death they are tolling,* he thought. *You can escape. My life, my career, my talent, mine—mine—mine!*

Edyth was no better. Though, to her credit was her single-mindedness. Her attention was wholly on injustices to *Max*, impediments to *his* success, slights to *his* ego and pride. He did not question his love for either woman, as love in Max's mind was completely interchangeable with need, and right now, this minute, he needed both women mightily.

He grew angry at Edyth now for going to Boston this week when he needed her most, even though he had told her to go. It was a damned fool thing for her to do. Futile. Expensive. Hard on Max. She should have refused his offer. She should have placed her mother in a hospital right in the city where she could have divided her time between office hours and visiting hours. He could have raised her pay twenty a week. That would have made more sense than Boston. Mrs. Spalding could conceivably hang on forever. She was a strong dame. A real survivor. She could outlive Edyth and in a comatose state as well.

It was five minutes to ten. Bob Tanner would arrive precisely at ten. Max was certain of that. Tanner had punctuality pressed into every precise trouser crease. The thought of the approaching meeting had kept Max up most of the night and had been at the back of his head since waking from the few hours' sleep he did catch. There was his distaste for Tanner as an informer, coupled with his loathsome use of people—Lou Whitehorn, for one. Now Kate Steiner, whom Max had met only twice in his life, both times at the Beverly Hills Tennis Club. The first time had been when he had just arrived in Hollywood and came as someone's guest. She had only been a girl of sixteen then. She had played a man's game and afterward had contributed intelligently to adult conversation over iced beer and pretzels. The second time was only a year before, just before her departure for New York. She still played a man's game and had become an even more adroit conversationalist. She was no beauty. But she was lean and tight and long-legged, with alert eyes and a full, very sensual mouth. Max had found her attractive, and though the fact that Sandy Mayberry had had an affair with her did not bother him one whit, Bob Tanner's conquest did.

Something far more disturbing about Tanner made Max restless, keyed up. He was a younger man with far less talent than Max, in fact, no spark of genius at all, and yet he was momentarily arriving in Max's office as Max's superior.

The doorbell rang, and since Edyth was gone, Max had to get up from his desk chair and answer it himself.

Ten on the button.

Trousers precisely creased.

White monogrammed shirt, French cuffs an exact inch below the sleeve of a custom-made gray flannel suit. Tie from Sulka's. Smelling of the barbershop and French cologne. Shoes polished, spotless (and it was raining outside. That meant taxi or limousine from and to the door), nails manicured, cuff links—real star sapphires.

"Max! Good to see you."

"Come in." Max turned his back on Tanner and led the way into his office.

"Are the children all right?"

"Yeah," Max said and dropped it.

They were in Max's office, and Max went to his desk.

"Shall I close the door?" Tanner asked.

"Edyth's not here. We're alone."

Tanner sat down facing Max. "I realize this is not easy for you, Max. It's not easy for me either. I'm a sensitive character, and I like to think I'm intelligent. You resent me. No other way for you to feel. You hate me, too. In defense of that, I can only say I don't expect you to like me any better after today. You'll probably hate me more—but maybe you will, somewhere deep down, understand."

"You're not here to discuss politics," Max snapped.

"In a way I am."

"Yeah?"

"First, I have to tell you I read the script. It's brilliant. You know that. Now I know that too, and so does Mr. Steiner."

"But?"

"No buts—no reservations. It's one of the best scripts I've ever read, and I am honored that I will produce it. I'm thinking of bringing Albertino over from Italy to direct. Do you like that idea?"

"It's not bad."

"The Italians know how to get reality into these things. I think we will have a real first. An American art film."

"But?"

"Why are you so antagonistic, Max?"

"You're coming on too fast and beautiful, sweetheart. Experience with your type—"

"What does that mean?" Tanner said evenly.

"Well, on one hand we have the wheelers and dealers, on another, the talent. But it doesn't end there. Then there are the takers and the users. That's you, Tanner. And the only thing you know how to give is compliments, but they're only skin deep and cost nothing." Max smiled all the time he was talking, a slow, wry, mocking smile. His voice remained even, almost too low. In spite of himself, Bob Tanner had to lean closer to Max to hear himself insulted.

Tanner laughed too easily. "It's like that in your script," he said. "You had a sentimental subject, but you allowed no sentimentality into the action or the dialogue. It breaks your heart, but it comes right to the point. Tough. Uncompromising."

Max pointed to Tanner's tie. "Those your school colors, Tanner? Some school. I should make a note of that."

"All right, Max. We'll never be friends. That might give us a better crack at honesty."

"I don't spare my friends, either."

"I'll remember that. Misery loves company."

"OK. Albertino. Not bad." Actually, Max was very pleased, excited. Albertino was the director who had brought a new realism to the Italian screens, and he was one of the few living great directors in the world Max really admired. There weren't many. Here there was Welles—he stood alone—Chaplin, maybe Ford and Hitchcock. In Europe there was Ophuls and Renoir, Rossellini and Albertino. Yes, *Black in Eden* was Albertino's meat. He'd serve it up without a compromise.

"I don't see any script problems at this point, Max. And if I did, I would be smart enough to let Albertino bring them to your attention." A smile darted tentatively across his handsome face. "There is the credibility of the coincidence that the same sailor that helps Black get to the States helps him return to his island, but we won't bother about that now."

Max had a sour taste in his mouth. He took some Dentyne from his pocket and offered Tanner a stick.

"No, thanks. Not one of my vices."

"Oh, you have vices, Tanner? Who would have thunk it?"

"Yes, Max," Tanner said, his voice deadly serious. "I have vices, too. Who hasn't? Greed, ego, envy . . . "

"Oh," Max said lightly. "*Those* vices."

"*Those* vices." There was a static silence. Only the motor of the air conditioner was audible, intrusive. Tanner rubbed his hands. "Air conditioning in the winter? Always knew there was hot blood under that cool exterior, Max."

"It's to cut out the street sounds." Max reached behind himself to the control panel of the machine and clicked it off. It droned to a halt. The traffic sounds now entered the room—horns, screeching brakes, a pneumatic drill. "Better?" he asked.

"Yes, thanks." Tanner stood up and turned away. "You want some coffee? We're not far from the Pierre."

"I'm happy. Aren't you?"

"Not completely."

"Spit it out then."

Tanner leaned forward on the desk, in close to Max. "We really have a serious problem, Max."

"Yeah?"

"Mr. Steiner." He straightened. Waited. Then he slowly sat down again. "He's had second thoughts owing to the content of the script. I mean, after reading the final version. Come right down to it, sum it up in one line, and *Black in Eden* will have to say that visually there's no longer any such thing as Eden."

"I suppose you might sum it up that way."

"That could be interpreted as a Communist theme."

"Possibly."

"Mr. Steiner still believes the film should be shot except—"

"Yeah?"

"Though you won't be using your name, there is always the chance of revealment. Theme coupled with sympathizer—the combination could be deadly. In that case Mr. Steiner could conceivably be forced to shelve the picture. That would be an expensive oversight."

"Oversight?"

"It could be provided for before we roll."

"How? I'm not being snotty, Tanner. I'm just asking a civil question, though I realize my civil rights may have regressed some since you entered this office."

Tanner ignored the sarcasm. He was sweating now.

Max smiled to himself. *You could use that cold air now, you son of a bitch*, he thought.

"Testify."

Max bolted out of his chair. "Are you asking me to *inform*, Bobby boy? Because if you are, I want you to get your cute ass out of this office before you find you can't even drag it after you." The drill five stories down grew louder, and Max shouted to be heard over it.

"Not inform, Max." Tanner stood his ground. "Over a hundred names have been given. The committee would be satisfied if you only *repeated* those names. You can't hurt anyone that way. I agree it's a lousy thing. But you don't have to put one new name forward, and *Black in Eden*, Max, can help the cause more than your silence, more than a hundred men's silence. And if you don't agree, Mr. Steiner has no recourse but to shelve the project right now. You and I know *Black in Eden* was your one hope. Lose that, Max, and you're *hung!*"

"Like Lou?"

Quietly. "Like Lou."

"Get out, Tanner! Just get the hell out of here." Max went over to a window and opened it. "It's foul but still an improvement."

He stood there and watched Bob Tanner turn and walk out of his office, through Edyth's, open the door.

"You have Steiner under that hot microscope of yours now, Tanner, eh? From Lou, to me, to Steiner. About time for you to try it out on your own, isn't it?" Max said.

"My best regards to Luise and the kids, and say hello to Edyth for me," Bob Tanner replied and then was gone.

Max felt his heart pounding, the anger building inside him. The telephone rang.

"Yeah?" he shouted into the mouthpiece.

"Max—"

"Edyth, you'd better get your ass back here."

"Oh, Max, she's dead. Mama's dead. And before she died—"

"You'll tell me another time, kid. Get back here. I'll handle the rest for you."

He disconnected and then left the office before she could call back.

Chapter 22

Luise hadn't said a word to him all evening. Her silence was eating at his gut. Didn't she know that what he had to face the next day was gut-tough as it was?

The kids were already asleep and they were watching television. An old film. One of Milton Stevens'. It was something about the Conquests. Everyone spoke in stilted pseudo-Shakespearian phrases, their armor clanking for emphasis. It was about war and the men inside the armor were dying and they were talking to each other in stilted Shakespearian sentences, for God's sake! Stevens might know a lot about history, but he sure as hell knew nothing about men. Particularly dying ones.

Max had been a child in the First World War, over thirty and a father at the beginning of the Second. He had been to Spain, though, in the thirties, before he married Luise, before Hollywood, before purgatory or hell. He had been young, a correspondent, inflated with ideals, and he had been eager to get to the front, get where the action was at.

He was never sent there. He was sent to a hospital instead.

When he approached the hospital in the car supplied to him, he had noticed first the red-tile roof, rosy in the early-morning sun. There were farms spreading out from all corners. The farmhouses were ugly, squat, pockmarked blocks of adobe. Dirt floors. Dirt farmers. But each house had a cow, some chickens, lots of kids hanging around. He had not been prepared for the inside of the hospital. He had been told what to expect, but still he had not been prepared.

The stink was so bad he had gagged, fought to hold consciousness without breathing in the stinking air, felt his legs buckle. Legs—well, hell, he at least had legs. The smell was of gangrene. He didn't really know, but he knew. Moldering, rotting, putrefying flesh. Max had looked around the one large room, beds a hodgepodge, a maze. What did they do with all those arms and legs? Where did they throw them?

A kid's eyes pleaded for him to come near. No more than eighteen. Probably still a virgin. Big black Spanish eyes. Wounded. Smooth olive skin. Young—younger than eighteen. Sixteen. Seventeen tops. He had felt as if he were swimming as he made his way to the side of the kid's bed.

The kid couldn't speak to him. The lower part of his face was swathed in bandages. His mouth and chin had been shot away—no more sweet kisses. There was no hand to hold. No more tender embraces. The bottom part of the bed was flat. No legs. No hopes for sweet conquest. Eyes that could see and ears that could hear. A heart that was beating furiously and a brain that was overcrowded with emotions, thoughts desperate for release.

"Hi, kid." Well, what the hell did you say? He had stood there, looking down, smiling, trying to smile, at least his nausea had gone, but something worse had set in. A kind of frozen panic. He thought he might never be able to move from the side of that bed, never be released from the accusation in those eyes.

Eyes that said: "I can smell soap and talcum, the cigarette you just smoked. You had a woman last night. I can see by your eyes. I've learned much this way—from eyes, from smell—from voices, even words in another language. What are you here for? War is hell. You knew that before you came. So what are you here for? Guns kill, maim. You knew that too. So why did you come? Live, damn you, live. Why else—oh, God—why else? What other reason could there be? Is that why you're here? Is that why you've come?"

"Forsooth, I am feebled of heart and weary of foot. The enemy draweth nearer. Leave me here. Escapeth with your life—the cause—"

Max turned off the TV.

"You don't want to watch that crap, do you?" He got up. Luise was still staring mutely. "I don't know where Milton gets his dialogue," he added.

"Got," she said. "Maybe prison sharpened it a bit."

Caustic. A sigh would follow. It did.

"Luise, it is not my fault the ten served time."

"I never said it was." She had moved from the couch that faced the TV to a straight-backed chair that faced him.

"Every silent breath," he snapped. "It would not have helped anyone if I had served time, too."

"I never said that either."

"You haven't said much of anything this week, and yet you've made things pretty damn clear. You *sweat* accusation, Luise."

"I haven't accused you of anything. A man does what he thinks he has to do."

"And a woman?"

"It depends on how much she loves a man."

"How much, Luise?"

There were tears in her eyes. "Enough to find reasons. Too much to dare losing you."

"I've been fighting a hard battle all week."

"I know that, Max."

"*Black in Eden* will be able to reach a lot of people—touch them, move them. I have another story. I haven't told you about it. We can shoot it in Europe. That will be a great experience for you. Good for the kids. It's important I do this film, Luise—very important to me—not my existence, *my life*. I told you once, if you really love me, don't try to understand, just accept."

"I am trying. Accept that, too."

"OK. I buy that."

"I'm not selling, Max. Anything I have for you I *give*. I don't sell." She pushed herself up on her feet and headed toward the bedroom.

"Want to change your mind and come to Washington with me in the morning?"

She turned in the doorway to the bedroom. He was standing there looking at her in a soft, almost small-boy manner that he mockingly adopted from time to time.

"Do you need me, Max?" she asked, almost hopefully.

"Edyth's coming, and it will only be overnight, but I can ask her to stay here with Tony and Thea. It hasn't been easy for Edyth since her mother died. She's been taking her mourning a bit too seriously. The kids might get her out of herself."

"I'll be here when you come back."

"Oh, like the wars, eh?"

She came back a short way into the living room. "You said you were fighting a battle."

"Yeah. Yeah." He turned away, lighted a cigarette.

"Max." She was crossing the room. Nearer. She paused only a few feet from him.

He slowly faced her. Calm. "Yes, Luise?"

She ran into his arms, threw them around his neck, held her body close to him, closer.

"Max, I'm frightened."

"Luise, Luise."

"Please don't go, Max."

"I know what I'm doing."

"It will kill you. I know it."

"I'm a tough bastard, Luise. Hard to kill."

"I love you."

"That's right, Luise. Love me. I need your love, baby."

She pulled back slightly and looked into his eyes. "I think it's better if I wait here with the children. If we're all three here for you to come home to."

"Fine."

"You don't mind? You think that's right?"

"I'm no damn judge, Luise. Do you think that's right?"

"Yes, yes, I do."

"It will be good to see you when I get home."

He gently pushed her arms down and to her side. "I think we'd better get some shut-eye," he said. He began to turn off the lights.

"Max."

"Yeah?"

"I have something very difficult I must say."

"Spit it out."

"I accept what you are about to do. I accept it, Max, but I can't—*I don't condone it.*"

There it was then. There they would always be—the deep, black, soulful, accusatory eyes.

Gus Cone had come into the hearing room with him. They had spoken.

"Gus."

"Max."

But they had not exchanged glances. Max never averted his own, but Gus had a way of looking to one side, or the other, or down at the polished tips of his shoes.

The word was out. Gus knew.

Gus had preceded him into the witness chair. Max wasn't sure. He had never really known Gus Cone well. They had met on the lot a few times, at some parties, at guild meetings. "Gus." "Max." That's all they had ever really exchanged. He had seen some of Gus' work and respected it. He wrote good, hard, true dialogue, and he never wasted a chance for a visual bit of action. He was an economic writer, not exciting, but better than most. What he never had liked about Gus was the open way he womanized and the fact that he had changed his name from Cohen to Cone. Well, he didn't know that for sure, but it had to be.

CHAIRMAN: What is your name, please?

MR. CONE: Gustave Sebastian Konig. But I am known professionally as Gus Cone.

Son of a bitch!

Max sat restlessly, listening to Gus recite his statistics, his education, his Army record and his film credits. Within a matter of minutes, the first loaded question was tossed at him.

INVESTIGATOR: Were you a member of the Screen Writers Guild?

MR. CONE: I am going to refuse to answer that question, sir, and claim protection under the Fifth Amendment, the right against self-incrimination, the right not to testify against myself, and insofar as the First Amendment is relevant to it, I would like to use that, too.

Cone was standing on his constitutional rights. He would not reveal names or organizations. He would walk away from the hearing room a free man, morally righteous, unemployed and unemployable.

INVESTIGATOR: Mr. Maxwell Isaac Seaman.

CHAIRMAN: Mr. Seaman, will you raise your right hand and be sworn, please? Do you solemnly swear the evidence you give this committee shall be the truth, the whole truth, and nothing but the truth, so help you God?

MR. SEAMAN: I do.

CHAIRMAN: Have a seat.

(TESTIMONY OF MR. MAXWELL ISAAC SEAMAN)

INVESTIGATOR: What is your name, please?

MR. SEAMAN: Maxwell Isaac Seaman.

INVESTIGATOR: Are you represented by counsel?

MR. SEAMAN: Yes, I am, sir.

INVESTIGATOR: Will counsel please identify himself for the record?

MR. GREEN: Henry Green, 1572 Broadway, New York City.

INVESTIGATOR: Mr. Seaman, will you please state for the committee your educational background?

MR. SEAMAN: I was educated at public schools in Bridgeport, Connecticut, and in New York City. I attended and graduated from New York University.

INVESTIGATOR: What year?

MR. SEAMAN: I believe it was 1936, 1937. I'm not sure. I interrupted my university work to accept a job as a reporter. Then as a correspondent I was sent to Spain for a time.

INVESTIGATOR: When and where were you born?

MR. SEAMAN: Bridgeport, Connecticut, April 19, 1915.

INVESTIGATOR: Did you go from New York to Hollywood and engage there in your profession?

MR. SEAMAN: I was a newspaper reporter first, then a correspondent. As I said, I was in Spain during that war.

INVESTIGATOR: Fighting?

MR. SEAMAN: No, as a correspondent. When I returned to New York, I graduated from the University—that was in 1936 or 1937—then I wrote a play, and a series of articles. Then I went to Hollywood and to work for Omega Films.

INVESTIGATOR: Mr. Seaman, are you now a member of the Communist Party?

MR. SEAMAN: I should like to state emphatically that I am not a member of the Communist Party. I am not sympathetic with it or its aims. I don't believe in any divided loyalty, and in the event this country goes to war, I stand ready now, as I always have, to bear arms in its defense and to serve in whatever capacity the country may call upon me, against any and all its enemies, including the Soviet Union.

INVESTIGATOR: You state you are not sympathetic with the aims of the Communist Party. Has that always been true?

MR. SEAMAN: No. I was a member until 1944, holding a card and assigned to Club Sixteen of the Valley Section of the Communist Party, in Los Angeles.

INVESTIGATOR: At that time, were you acquainted with an individual by the name of Louis Whitehorn?

MR. SEAMAN: Yes, I was.

INVESTIGATOR: Was he a member of the Communist Party?

MR. SEAMAN: Yes, he was.

INVESTIGATOR: Merwin Bibbs?

MR. SEAMAN: Are you asking if Merwin Bibbs was a member of the Communist Party?

INVESTIGATOR: I am.

MR. SEAMAN: He was.

And on and on for one hour and forty minutes. A roll call of exactly one hundred and five names. A record. That was a laugh. He had never broken a record before in his life! Hey, Gustave Sebastian Konig, I broke a record. Hey, you son of a bitch, stop staring at me with those damned black eyes of yours. Hear me? Stop staring.

CHAIRMAN: The witness may be excused.

BOOK IV

Anthea

O city running with blood,
I too will make a great fire-pit.
Fill it with logs, light the fire;
*   make an end of the meat,*
pour out all the broth and the
*   bones with it.*
Then set the pot empty on the coals
so that its copper may be heated
*   red hot,*
and then the impurities in it may
*   be melted*
and its corrosion burnt off.
Try as you may,
the corrosion is so deep that it
*   will not come off;*
only fire will rid it of corrosion
*   for you.*
Even so, when I cleansed you in your
*   filthy lewdness,*
you did not become clean from it,
and therefore you shall never again
*   be clean*
until I have satisfied my anger
*   against you.*

THE NEW ENGLISH BIBLE

I, the Lord, have spoken; the time is coming, I will act. I will
not refrain nor pity nor relent; I will judge you for your conduct
and for all that you have done. This is the very word of the Lord
God. . . .I am taking from you at one blow, the dearest thing you
have. . . .

EZEKIEL 24

Chapter 23

Anthea stood before the long mirror in the bedroom of her father's suite in the George V and admired the young woman who stared candidly back at her. She had piled her long, thick tawny hair on top of her head. It emphasized the majestic length of her neck, the chiseled bones in her angular face, and it gave her a sophisticated look. But still she was displeased. Her father was waiting for her in the lobby, probably irritated and impatient by now. She began to remove the pins in her hair rather frantically. She shook her head to make sure the pins were all out and then brushed her hair to one side, so that the long curve of her neck and one ear could be seen. Better. She clipped a dangly pearl earring on the one exposed ear. Better still. She smiled. There was lipstick on her teeth, and she wiped it off, smiling again. Her lipstick was too dark. She blotted it and patiently smiled again for her own final approval. There.

She turned away from the mirror and walked carefully toward the door aware that the mirror now caught the high arch of her foot created by the stiletto heels she was wearing, the backs of her long, lean legs that her tight nylons tinged with bronze, the small curve of her bottom so snug in the jersey skirt, the leather-bound slenderness of her cinched waist, and the bra straps that caused small ridges in her sweater-blouse. At the door she glanced back over her shoulder. "Yes," she breathed and hurried out of the room into the next, never pausing even as she lifted her shoulder-strap bag from a chair and went out into the corridor. There was another large mirror by the elevator, and as she waited for it to reach her floor, she studied herself again, wetting her lips, shifting the strap of the bag from one shoulder to the other.

Today was her sixteenth birthday, and she had flown from London to Paris to celebrate the occasion with her father.

The family had been living in Europe for five years now, headquartering in London with Max making frequent trips to the other two film centers in Europe—Paris and Rome—seeking and most times finding financing and distribution for his films. *Black in Eden* had been made with Max able to use his own name, after all, and he had won an award for the screenplay. Saunders Mayberry had, however, refused to appear in the film. Sandy, for that matter, had been blacklisted that same year and was currently living in Paris and working in French films.

Max had spent a good deal of the last five years filming on location, places in the south of Spain and islands off the coast of Greece. At holiday time, Luise and the children would join him. Otherwise, Luise remained in London, where Anthea had been attending first the Eton Square School for Girls and now the American School where next year she would receive her high school diploma. Tony, who would soon be fourteen, had been boarding for the past three years at a school in Switzerland, at Max's insistence and without Luise's approval. However, Max appeared to be right, for Tony was steadily improving in his studies and seemed to be making a small niche for himself at the school.

Anthea did not truly miss Tony, for when he was home, the atmosphere invariably thickened. But she did feel an overwhelming guilt that he was away while she was at home. That guilt caused her to write him very often and to think of him oftener. She adjusted the earring, one of a pair Tony had sent her for her birthday. She loved them, loved all presents Tony bought her, which were always superfeminine and superglamorous. The perfume she wore he had given her at Christmas. And the long flowered chiffon scarf tucked now in her bag (probably costing Tony a full month's allowance) he had brought home as a gift for her at Eastertime.

It seemed the elevator would never come. Anthea decided to take the stairs. As she started down them, a thought occurred to her, and she paused and taking the scarf out of her shoulder bag, tied it loosely to the strap of her bag so that it seemed to float by her side as she continued on, the perfume she'd sprayed on it earlier billowing about her.

Max stood by the front desk.

Anthea paused before her father saw her. She was always filled with a sudden and disturbing emotion when she caught sight of him. She found herself conscious of her body inside the restriction of her clothes, always feeling overdressed, too warm.

She was shocked to discover how much older her father looked. It moved her to the edge of tears. Anthea had been well aware that things had lacked a certain harmony at home. Her mother had been irritable and often appeared depressed, and her father had been away from them quite a lot—the reason, Anthea was sure, that Luise had permitted her to make this trip. She found herself resenting her mother now, blaming her for the gray which seemed suddenly to streak her father's hair, the lines on his face, the added flesh that had accumulated under his chin. It was as though a curtain had fallen, hiding everything that was familiar. It was as if she were seeing her father for the first time. His appearance was different, his attitude, his stance. Deep inside it made her feel different—happy to see him and yet sad.

Max saw her then and smiled, and she began the slow walk across the lobby of the hotel, conscious of his steady glance and nervous that her outfit might not win his approval.

"Black," he said and pursed his mouth in that special crooked mocking way, his eyes narrowed and laughing so that no insult could be felt.

"Black," she snapped back with a small touch of arrogance, sounding sure that the black jersey skirt and sweater were exactly what a sixteen-year-old young woman would wear at lunchtime in Paris, but happy at that moment that Tony's chiffon bouquet of muted pinks and greens and violets floated at her side.

"*Très charmant.*" Max grinned and took her by the arm and led her out onto the street. A doorman rushed up. "I thought we'd walk," he told Anthea. She nodded in agreement. The doorman shrugged his shoulders and walked away.

May in Paris. A clear blue sky over the Champs-Élysées, over the shops, the cafés, the girls already dressed in their summer dresses. The air filled with new smells. The colors all seeming fresh, virginal. It was still cool, breezes stirring on the shady side of the street, a soft wind at corners to lift a skirt hem and disarray a hairdo. A mild sun, still warming.

Max walked with an even step, his arm linked through Anthea's. He hadn't realized how tall she'd grown. Of course, she was wearing those skyscraper heels, but she had to be about five feet six or seven in her bare feet. Max remembered her that way just the summer before—barefooted on the hot sands on the coast of Spain. Jumping up and down to ease the burning on the bottom of her feet, her topaz hair honey-pale in the sun and the wind. Running, long-legged, arms flying, into the frothing waves, going under, coming up. Laughing, squealing, golden skin wet and shiny, tawny hair stuck to her face, her neck, her shoulders, still laughing and smelling of salt and suntan lotion and heat and girlness as she splashed him with water.

"I thought we'd have lunch outside at the Café Arno, all right?" he asked.

"Could we eat inside? If it's no extra bother. It's more elegant. We can find a secluded corner." She giggled, reminding him she was still a girl.

"It's your birthday."

"I haven't forgotten."

"Neither have I," he said mysteriously.

"Really? You didn't have to—this trip, and Mom bought me the luggage from the two of you."

They were at the corner of the Champs-Élysées, ready to cross and walk toward the Café Arno, which was close to the Crillon. She couldn't help it. She had to ask. She pinched his arm closer to her body. "What did you get me?"

"You'll see."

"That's not fair."

"You'll see." He smiled. He loosened her arm and changed sides, shifted her to the inside position.

"Have you got it with you?" she asked.

"Can't tell."

"Are we going to pick it up?"

"Who knows?"

"You're mean."

"You're too eager."

"Umm. You bet." She laughed, throaty, controlled, playing the coquette.

She clung to his arm as they walked down the boulevard, her head back, feeling the sun on her face, squinting up at the blue sky.

Outside the restaurant, the tables were already crowded. Inside there was a line. They had to wait a few minutes as Arno himself searched his premises for a table. Arno's was a regular for the film crowd. Most of the faces were familiar to Max. Men and women from the theatrical agencies, the distribution offices, overseas offices of the studios, and the writers, producers, directors, and actors who were about to, or were hoping to, film soon. Max smiled at them but did not introduce Anthea.

Young chick Max has in tow. Good-looking, he figured they were thinking, and it inwardly pleased him.

The table was anything but secluded. It was in a corner but against the plate-glass window at the front of the establishment, looking onto the terrace and directly into three familiar faces. Max turned his back to the window and concentrated his attention on Anthea.

"Can I have a drink?" she asked.

"If you like."

"A martini?"

"No, I think a Cinzano on the rocks or a Dubonnet and soda."

"Oh—"

"A pernod?"

"No."

"Frozen daiquiri then," he finally suggested.

"Yes!"

"Shall we order?"

"Not yet."

The waiter brought a Campari for Max and a frozen daiquiri for Anthea. Anthea leaned across the table. "They never asked my age," she confided.

"So I noticed."

"Shall I be subtle?"

"Yeah."

"OK. Then I won't ask you about my present until we've finished lunch."

"That's a deal." He watched her as she sucked at the straw in her drink, her small sharp, even white teeth not sparing the delicate plastic. "How's your mother?" he asked.

"Umm. Great. Very busy."

"Oh? With what?"

"Arrangements for the summer. You did know we were all going to Italy?"

"Yeah, I heard."

"And the committee she's heading for the charity premiere. Korean orphans."

"Oh?"

"Mr. Winters' new picture. I forget the name. In fact, I even forget the stars. It's all very forgettable."

Max laughed. "When did your mother get involved with Korean orphans?"

"Oh, weeks and weeks ago. Could we order now?"

"If you like."

"What's *foie de poulet?*"

"Chicken liver."

"Ugh. I'd like to have something really extravagant—like cold lobster—something like that. Would that be all right?"

"Hell, the sky's the limit."

"Then I'd like a side order of asparagus and hollandaise sauce, too."

"No *pommes frites?*"

"I know what *they* are, and they are aimed at destroying my twenty-two-inch waistline. No, thank you."

Max ordered.

"About Italy—" he began.

"Isn't it marvelous! You should see the pictures of the house. Straight out of Julius Caesar. Fabulous. Swimming pool, orchards, staff. Just great. It belongs to a Contessa Something-or-Other."

"De Miralda."

"You know all about it, then?"

"Not really. I just sent in the *fabulous* deposit."

Anthea giggled again.

"About Italy," Max began again. "I feel I have to warn you about a few things."

"Don't. Mom already has. Consider me sufficiently warned."

"The men are what might be termed as slightly aggressive."

"They pinch."

"The ones who pinch are not the ones I'm warning you about. It's the ones who look."

"Lasciviously?"

"Look lasciviously and *don't* pinch."

"I'll beware of all dirty old men."

"The old ones aren't the only ones."

"I'll beware of all young and old lascivious-eyed men."

"Has your mother told you much of anything?"

"Not much I didn't know or am not in the process of learning."

"Oh?"

"Daddy, that 'Oh' was uncalled for."

"I hope so."

"Let's face it. I'm not being brought up in the Dark Ages. I know about things like rape and babies and diaphragms and rubbers, and what a French kiss is and what it can lead to. I also like boys, but prefer men, am still a virgin, possess what might be called a 'good reputation,' and know why some girls have bad ones. Look at that lobster! It is simply incredible! You didn't order *foie de poulet*? My God, Daddy, how could you!"

The laughter spilled out of her. Max watched her as she ravished the white meat of the lobster and the pale-green tips of the asparagus. There was a great vitality about his daughter that his son had never seemed to possess. Whatever she did—eat, walk, swim, even sleep—she did with an aliveness that was breathtaking. He could see her now, a small girl, her tangled hair golden on her pillow, the covers kicked aside, legs positioned in sleep as if she had been running and had simply fallen asleep that way, arms out, grasping, reaching. He had walked into her room in Spain, just last year, to awaken her and found her still in that animated sleeping position.

"I want very much to invite Lissa to Italy with us, but Mom says no."

"Lissa?"

"Melissa Bibbs. We're in the same class at school. We've been friends all year, but it has been difficult."

"Perhaps this celebration shouldn't take this serious turn."

"There it is. Glumsville every time I mention Lissa's name to

Mom or you. And Lissa doesn't even *dare* to mention mine at home. She lies. 'I was with Sally Kornbloom,' something like that. It's ugly. I hate it. I hate deception."

"Melissa's father is a bitter man. It can't be helped. I don't blame him. I've explained it to you before. You know all about it. Mr. Bibbs served a year in prison, suffered humiliation, the loss of his job, and still, after all these years, remains blacklisted, unable to pull a fair deal on a job, not permitted to use his own name. It would be difficult for him to be anything but bitter."

Anthea glanced down at her plate. "Lissa says her father called you an informer. Is that true?"

"No. It's not." Max glanced away. It was the first time he had lied to his daughter, and it hurt.

"Could we have remained in the States, though?"

"Yes, but what you have to understand, baby, is that the studios had gray lists as well as blacklists. Even informers unless they were reactionary and right-wing made these lists." He raised his glance and leveled with hers. "All of us, Mr. Bibbs, Burt Winters, myself—most of your mother's and my friends could have remained in the States but not in the same circumstances as the past. I might have had an easier time than Mr. Bibbs, but I still would have had to fight those damned lists."

"I thought if you called Mr. Bibbs. . . ."

"No good, baby."

"Well, it was worth a try." There were tears in her eyes. "I do love Lissa so. She's my best friend. They're having such a rough time. No money at all. I thought it might be great for both of us if she could come to Italy with us."

"I can't call her father, and if I did, I assure you the answer would still be no."

"You could try."

"No!" The sun grew brighter, stabbing at them through the plate-glass window. "How about a *glace*?"

"I don't think so."

"Your present, then?"

A small smile played at the corners of her mouth. "The subject's closed?"

"It is."

She sighed. "The present, by all means then."

Max took a small jewelry box from his pocket and put it on the table in front of Anthea.

"It's a ring, isn't it?" she asked staring at the tiny box.

"Open it and find out."

The excitement had slipped back into her face. Her eyes danced, and she pushed the hair back from her face and pulled impatiently at the ribbon around her gift almost in one movement.

"A *diamond* ring! Mom will kill you!"

"Do you like it?"

"It's fabulous!" She put it on her finger and waved her hand in front of her. The men at the table outside were staring, and she turned her hand around and beamed as she waved it at them. "A diamond ring. *My first!*"

Max laughed. "You expecting more?"

"Of course," she said surely. And giggled.

"Well, happy birthday, baby."

"It is. It really is," she said, softly thanking him with her eyes as she did.

Chapter 24

Burt Winters regarded all travel as a necessary evil to be endured only for the sake of one's livelihood or health. Yet he had hardly stepped out the front door of his flat when an impulse, too fantastic and too upsetting to be seriously considered, swept over him. At that moment had there been a taxi on the street (Sylvia was using the car) he might have hailed it and gone directly to Heathrow Airport, leaving London, Sylvia, and his work for . . . where? A trip, leisurely, time-consuming, around the world, finding new and distant scenes, freedom, release, forgetfulness—flight. The daily struggle between his tenacious will and his growing fatigue had this morning simply seemed lost. The great hunger he had never before been able to satisfy, acquisitive, omnivorous ambition, had been satiated some time between his daily glass of grapefruit juice and his usual second cup of breakfast coffee.

The impulse had left him by the time he had reached the Bayswater Road and crossed the screeching traffic-convoluted thoroughfare and entered the park. He knew that what was truly worrying him was the knowledge that no one must know that his ambitions had flagged—not the office or Omega, not his peers or the industry. Certainly not Sylvia or her mother. It was a thing he would have to bear secretively.

It was already the second week in May, and after months and months (when had it begun? Sometime last October most certainly!) of penetrating cold and unrelenting wet there seemed today to be a promise of summer that should have buoyed his

220

languishing spirits. But Burt dreaded the thought of the approach of summer, dreaded the well-scanned seaside at Angmering, where they had a summer cottage, the rocky beach, the constant attendance of his women: Sylvia, their two daughters, now teen-aged, and Sylvia's mother, who arrived every Fourth of July and departed every Labor Day like some sort of American assault on Anglo-American relations.

Hyde Park was thronged with people. Burt should not have been surprised, as this was a rare and festive occasion—a sunny day in May. Couples sprawled on the grass, entwined, the men bare-chested, the girls bare-legged. The nannies packed the banks of the Serpentine with their carriages and tots. Dogs tore around the bushes and the trunks of trees, terrorizing the duck families. The boatkeepers of the Serpentine, the chair men and the ice-cream men were already selling their wares. And the old folks paused and strolled, strolled and paused. The ducks would be well fed, the squirrels as well, but the grass would need replanting and the littermen would be working late. A sunny day in May. A beginning. An end. Or were there such things as beginnings and ends?

Burt took a path out of the park, ending on Park Lane. Traffic was snarled and angry, morning shoppers, early tourists, late officeworkers, revving their motors, tooting their horns, yelling obscenities. Burt rejected the idea of the underground passage, however, and, with a seldom-exposed abandon, wove his way through the thundering, stampeding herd of automotive idiocy to the other side of the thoroughfare, ending up by the Hilton Hotel and cutting down Hertford Street to go the back route through Shepherds Market to his offices in Curzon Street.

It was still not half-past nine, but Shirley would already be in the office, working furiously, diligently, her perfection at her job a constant reminder to the men who passed by her desk that they had also passed up the great opportunity to marry a woman who could be proficient, intelligent, economical (just note how the pencils are used to the stubs, the carbon carefully guarded, and how all old·scripts, time schedules, location sheets, and interoffice memos are turned over on their blank sides and used for notepaper and first drafts of letters and memoranda), hygienic (take one peep into the immaculate office kitchen with its instant coffee, instant cream, instant service, and disposable cups, plates, spoons and serviettes), and attractive as well. But Shirley, the queen of the IBM's, was still a bachelor girl at thirty-two.

Shirley looked up from her filing as he entered. She had the air of someone terribly inconvenienced by an interruption. "Oh, Mr. Winters," she said as if vaguely remembering him.

"Good morning, Shirley." Burt started past her into his office.

"Oh, Mr. Winters!" she said testily.

"Yes, Shirley?" he paused, smiled blandly at her, waited.

"You forgot Mr. Bibbs' appointment. Nine o'clock." She let him know by her voice that she had come early—not forgotten. "He's waiting in your office. I've made coffee if you'd like a cup." She softened a bit.

"No, thank you, Shirley."

He had completely forgotten Merwin's appointment. Or had he? Was that perhaps one of the things he had felt he could not face today? Merwin had called the day before, enthusiastic. He had a marvelous film idea. Burt would love it. Could he see Burt right away? That afternoon? Burt had suggested nine the next day, though it meant coming into the office early to prevent Merwin's confronting any of Burt's other visitors. Merwin had become terribly antagonistic, and one was never sure who would suddenly receive the brunt of his vituperation.

Merwin sat on the couch, legs close together, hands folded, pinched, ready to spring. When Burt entered, he jumped to his feet.

"Good to see you, Merwin." Burt smiled warmly and took Merwin's eager hand in his. Merwin's palms were wet. "Sit down, sit down." Burt went to his desk and began to putter around. "Coffee?" he asked.

"Your secretary was good enough to bring me a cup already."

"That Shirley. Someone's missing out on a damned good wife. Well, how about another cup?"

"No, thanks."

"Sorry I'm late. Sylvia needed the car, and there were no taxis. Walked all the way."

"It's getting as bad in London as New York."

"That it is." Burt sat down, leaned back, looked steadily and with true friendship at Merwin. "You want to tell me the story?" he asked gently as a doctor might inquire after symptoms.

"I hope you don't mind it this way, Burt. I just hate outlines.

Never could do them. Always lost every assignment I had to do an outline on. I'd rather speculate on an entire script than do an outline."

"I understand. Outlines are insults to creativity," Burt commiserated.

"Exactly." Merwin drew a deep breath. He took a crumpled handkerchief, wiped his forehead with it, and then jammed it back into his pocket. "You have to believe I trust you sincerely, Burt, because this is a story based on something in the public domain. A story that has haunted me for years."

"Classics are responsible for many of the industry's best films," Burt agreed.

"This is not an American classic. It's a Russian classic, though not well known. The last English translation was in 1896, and that's a collector's item. I located it in the British Museum. The book is by Brznovski and is called *The Fate-Maker*. That's a lousy film title, though, so I call my version *Revelation!* with an exclamation. I always hate such devices, but it insinuates sexual revelations and has a ring of action to it."

"Umm."

"I've always wanted to write a film with an authentic Russian background. It's really never been done before. Not by an American film company, that is." Merwin took out the handkerchief again and dabbed at his forehead and then at his neck. "This is the story of a man, a Brando type—Brando as a Russian, it would be fascinating—a man who marries the woman he took away from his best friend. He loves her more than his life, but because of her faithlessness to his friend, he is always fearful she will be unfaithful to him. The idea possesses him, takes over every waking minute of his day and night."

Merwin was watching Burt closely for any clue to his response. Whatever Burt was thinking, however, he managed to conceal behind an expression of detached interest. His hands rested quietly on the arms of his chair. His fingers did not drum.

"Whenever he looks at his beautiful wife, our Brando type is tormented, wondering what she is thinking, whom she is thinking about. He begins to spend most of his time trying to trap her in a lie, in a tryst, a rendezvous. He sets things up for her to make it easier, to catch her. But to no avail. He thinks, of course, that she is wise to him, that she anticipates his plan. Never will he allow himself to believe her innocence. His business, his estate is neglected; his friends are avoided; he is near ruin. At last he believes he has discovered who her lover is—his own brother. Actually what she has done is go to the brother to confide her fear that her husband is losing his mind. Our Brando discovers them together and threatens to kill his own brother. His wife is now beside herself. He has come close to driving her to madness, for she loves him dearly and would not think of being untrue to him. She kills herself, and he is like a different man. Alone in his home, he now builds a shrine to her and dedicates his life to being constant to her memory."

Merwin took a deep breath. Burt hadn't moved.

"The action all takes place in and about St. Petersburg in all its beauty before the turn of the century. It is a picture of the aristocracy but in the background we have the feeling, the beginning, the murmurings of the peasants' revolt. Our Brando's house and office staff—the workmen in the town—I'm not so sure we couldn't succeed in getting a co-production." He was sweating again. Nervous. He coughed uneasily. "What do you think, Burt?"

"It's a good story. A classic, as you said, Mer. It has integrity. Class. You could attract a big star like Brando, I'm sure. But an audience—now I'm not at all sure. It's depressing, downbeat—and Russian at a time when Russian backgrounds are definitely out of vogue in the States. And after all, that's what we're talking about—Omega, an American release." Burt took time to fill and light a pipe, concentrating on the final task as he continued, "Look at the big money-makers last year. *Gentlemen Prefer Blondes, Roman Holiday, The Moon Is Blue . . .*"

"How about *Shane* and *Moulin Rouge*? Both downbeat, studies of men at odds with the world and themselves," Merwin said defensively.

"True, but in *Shane* you had the secure background of the Western, and in *Moulin Rouge*, the accepted glamor of Paris and the cancan." Burt drew slowly on his pipe. "I couldn't recommend it to Omega, Mer. But if you believe in the story, then I think you have to write it. There are French outfits that might be interested—or an independent. I'll give some thought to it."

"I can't afford to speculate, Burt. I couldn't even afford the time to write an outline." Merwin dropped any pretense of pride.

"I know. I know, Mer."

"You don't. You can't. I had one job last year. *He* was an independent, of course, he had to hire me sub rosa. Didn't matter that my fee used to be a thousand dollars a week. Or that minimum—minimum, mind you—was three hundred and forty-five a week at the time. He hired me sub rosa. I got three thousand dollars for sixteen weeks' work. A little over a hundred and eight bucks a week, for crissake, and then the script carried *his* name, not mine. And I haven't worked since then. I *can't* speculate, Burt."

"I didn't realize it was quite this rough with you."

"Well, it is," Merwin said angrily.

"If you need a loan . . ."

"No, thanks!" Merwin grew red, fought back the fury. "I'm sorry, Burt. Truly sorry. But no, thanks. I don't want a loan. I want a job. Desperately need a job. Have to have a job."

"I'll speak to a few people. See what I can do."

"It won't help. The blacklist has them all castrated. They're frightened men. I'm a leper, Burt. An untouchable. Hell, I can't even get anything sub rosa anymore."

Burt stood up and came around his desk and put his arm around Merwin's shoulder. "It's a good story, Mer. I'm really going to see what I can do. In the meantime, there's the BBC. They do a lot of classics over there. I think you should speak to them. I'll speak to them for you." He was walking to the door with Merwin. "How's the family?" he asked.

"It's not easy for them, Burt. It's worse for them, I think."

"I understand." Burt opened the door. "Shirley."

"Yes, Mr. Winters?"

"What is the name of that man we know at the BBC?"

"Cyril Donnelly?"

"Yes, that's it! Cyril Donnelly! I want you to write Mr. Bibbs a letter of introduction to him—I'll dictate it to you in a few minutes—and send a copy to Mr. Bibbs." He looked down on Merwin who was shorter than he. "Does Shirley have your address?" he asked.

"If she sent out the Christmas cards, she does."

"Check that, Shirley." He now walked with Merwin across the front office to the corridor. "You have a tough cross to bear, Mer. No one knows that better than I do. But you shouldn't let yourself get bitter. You can't afford that. It will show in your work. Now, look"—out in the corridor now—"if you do need—"

"For crissakes, Burt, does a duck need water?"

"Then . . ."

"Thanks, Burt. I appreciate the audience," Merwin said calmly and extended his hand.

Burt took it. "Anytime, Mer. Anytime."

He knew Merwin had felt the folded bills the minute that Burt had passed them from his palm into Merwin's. Knew he would not acknowledge them, knew that as soon as Mer would reach the privacy of the elevator, he would open his hand and look at the bills, knew he would be surprised, resentful, and thankful at the same time, because Burt had happened to have two one-hundred-dollar bills that one of the boys had lost to him at poker the night before in his pocket.

"Jesus," Burt said as he went back into Shirley's office. "What's next?" he asked sarcastically.

"Mrs. Seaman at ten."

"Oh, yes."

"And there is a list of calls from yesterday and the day before. The mail is opened. You'll find the personal letters in your top drawer. I thought with Mr. Bibbs . . ."

"Yes, thank you."

"Shall I bring in my pad?"

"No. Not until after Mrs. Seaman's appointment."

"You have advertising here at half past ten and Paul Levit with the breakdown on the new film at half past eleven. You have a luncheon engagement with that film interviewer at one. Shall I reserve at Claridges or the Dorchester?"

"The Dorchester."

"And—"

"Spare me the rest until later." He started into his office.

"Hello."

Her voice always unsettled him. The throatiness, the lilt. He turned. She stood in the doorway. "Hello, Luise."

"Shall I wait?"

"No. Please come in." He stood aside and let her pass by him, conscious immediately of the fragrance of her loose hair and subtle perfume.

He closed the door after them and motioned for her to sit down on the couch. "Shall I get you a coffee?" he asked.

"I don't think so. Not yet."

Burt sat down at his desk. "You've done a marvelous job for your charity on this premiere, Luise. I understand the tickets are all sold out. And at ten pounds a seat, that's incredible."

"I have another favor."

"The next film won't be ready for exhibition for six, eight months yet." He smiled.

"Not that kind of favor."

"Oh?"

"I need some advice."

"If I can help in any way, of course."

"You're my oldest friend in London. I can't count Sylvia because we have never really been friends. I always have the feeling Sylvia doesn't like women much or views them always as competitors. But that's beside the point."

"What isn't?"

"Max. Me. I think we're in danger of going on the rocks."

Burt knocked the cooling ashes from his pipe and refilled it. He worked to conceal his feelings, fought to control the small muscles on the side of his face that were dead set to betray him. *I am madly in love with you*, he thought. *It is insane, but I have been for years now. I'm as uncontrolled as a boy of sixteen when you're in a room, near me.* "I hate to hear you say a thing like that," he said out loud.

"It's not a thing a woman would normally discuss with a male friend."

"You know I would want you to feel you were free to come to me."

"Yes, I know that. That's why I'm here."

She began to search frantically in her purse.

"Can I get you anything?"

"A cigarette."

He reached into a desk drawer and pulled out a pack and crossed with it to her, offering her one, lighting it, standing there awkwardly. "I'm trying to stop—therefore, the pipe."

"Good idea," she agreed.

She was not really nervous. Luise seemed always to retain an outward calm. But she did appear inwardly disturbed. He sat down on the couch next to her. Took her free hand in his. "Is that better?"

She smiled. "It helps." She looked up into his rugged, uneven face, making him immediately conscious of his broad nose and his early receding hairline, and his beard, which, no matter how close he shaved, always looked heavy. "Dear Burt," she said, and he thought he detected a mist of tears rising in her beautiful eyes. "Help me. I think I'm losing him, and I love him unconscionably." She turned her glance away, withdrew her hand.

Burt patted her on her shoulder and, not knowing what else to do, stood up and went back to his desk. By the time he sat down and faced her once again she was in full control.

"I'm listening," he reminded her.

"It's eating at his gut, Burt. He knows they all regard him as an informer, and it is eating at his gut. Somehow he's placed me right in the enemy camp. I love him, oh, my God, I do love him, but I'm not one of those women with no opinions but their husband's. I would have fought the battle with him. On his side. He's a great talent, Burt, a real life force. I know that. You do, too. He would have survived as an artist and a man. What could I do? Should I have lied to him? Told him he was right?"

"Of course not, Luise."

"I could never have done that. He's always valued the truth so. I just could never have done that." A small shiver ran the length of her arm, which was bare, and caused her shoulder, her breast to quiver beneath the soft white wool of her sleeveless dress. "I know that's the cause of it—the pulling apart—and Burt, I just don't know what to do."

"There's nothing you can do, Luise. It's something Max has to settle in his own way, in his own time."

"He believes you informed, too, Burt."

"He's wrong. I suppose he'll never accept that because he doesn't want to. Max needs company to share his private guilt. But he is wrong. Men like Sol Levitz and Lou Whitehorn, Merwin, Milton Stevens—they *know* it. They simply know it. But more important, Luise, *I* know it. I'm sorry now Henry Green was able to get me that closed session. Truly sorry." Luise's expression did not change. "I was never what one might call a politically oriented man," Burt continued. "I believed in people, not countries. Still do, whatever philosophy I have—that's it. The States, England—all the same. The people, though—they are individual, different." He stopped, actually blushed. "Sorry about that." He grinned.

"Please don't apologize. There's nothing you have to apologize for." She mashed her cigarette out in the large glass ashtray on the table beside her. "Here it is. The real favor."

"Go ahead. You're close enough to see the whites of my eyes."

"You seem to have the boys all on your side, so to speak. I thought if you could champion Max a bit—if some of the antagonism could be softened . . ."

"You've asked a tough one, Luise."

"You could. I know you could."

He was thinking of Merwin Bibbs. "Impossible."

Luise stood up. She smiled wanly. He noticed she was pale and thinner than usual. "At least I tried."

He got to his feet. "Don't go," he said.

She turned and looked at him quizzically. He came around the desk and held her two bare arms with his hands.

"Don't let him destroy you, Luise," he said solemnly.

"One person can't destroy another unless he wants it."

"Yes, I know that."

They both stood there, looking squarely at each other.

"I'm very much in love with you, Luise. I have been for years," he said, shocked at how easy the words had been to say.

"Yes . . . yes . . . I hope I haven't taken advantage of that, Burt. I hope I never shall."

And she drew gently and easily away and left him standing there as she let herself out of his office.

Chapter 25

Lissa breathed in the salty warm air and dug her bare toes further into the dry, shifting sand beneath her feet. Thea was riding the waves, and Lissa enviously watched her. Lissa envied Thea, not her good looks, her fine clothes, her beautiful homes, but her incredible body coordination and her ability to do anything sportive immediately and without fear as if she were a professional athlete in training. Thea would climb, dive, skim, race, jump, ski, swim, her long tight legs never slacking, her head set just right, her arms poised and sure, and with that winning smile always on her face.

Thea waved as she came up on the wet sand and then turned right around and swam back out beyond the point where the waves were breaking. Lissa took off the sleeveless beach coat she had fashioned from an old voile curtain, spread it out carefully on the sand, and sat down on it to wait for Thea to tire. She was wearing a bathing suit of Thea's, and it was too large and she had to bind herself with the ribbon she had brought (thinking to tie her hair back) so that she could sit without fear of losing the top and exposing her small girlish breasts. Not that it really mattered— this stretch of beach was private, belonging to the contessa's villa, and a high fence to the far left and the far right of her guarded her from anyone's sight. It was purely an instinctive, inbred thing for her to do, a Victorianism that maddened her and yet restricted her from simply allowing the top to fall if it should happen to.

Melissa Bibbs was not exactly a beauty. She was nearly a year older than her friend Thea, making her not quite seventeen. Yet she had a way of seeming, from a distance or in repose, like a little girl. And she had in her manner the restlessness, the wonder, of a small child. She had a constant soft, surprised expression, as if she were always awed and vaguely intimidated by whatever or whoever came into her view. And she spoke in a very special once-heard, always-remembered voice—low and breathless, quick and in confidential whispers. Her lips were thin but tender-looking, never rouged, and when they nervously parted, a small pink tongue would dart out and caress her upper lip. She had undisciplined overly curly dark hair that fell in wisps about her slender face and in unwanted curls upon her narrow shoulders. She had a habit of shaking her head almost convulsively to force the unruly hair back, but in a matter of moments the hair would once more fly into disarray. But two features set Lissa entirely apart from girls her own age. First, her dress. Her sense of style was at once unique and yet old-fashioned. Unable to afford new clothes, she had set a vogue for buying old ones and remaking them and for adding odd touches—a velvet rouche about her neck, a snake necklace recoiled to crawl the length of her entire arm—that could make her one day a Brontë heroine and Cleopatra the next. Then her eyes. Once caught in the gaze of those wide, questioning, disbelieving opalescent eyes, one felt drowned by an undertow too overwhelming to struggle against.

She had lied to her father and hated having to do so. Hated even more implicating her mother in the lie. But her need to spend the summer with Thea had been a detonated charge about to explode within her. Life at home had become suffocatingly oppressive. Her father was a beaten man, and she could not bear to see him that way. She was constantly humiliated for him. And her mother had suddenly aged, lost her elasticity, any livingness she once had had. Their three claustrophobic rooms left no space for any privacy whatsoever. It seemed to Lissa that the most terrible sound in the world was the heaving of her father's breath as he stalked their home in the daytime and labored in the bedroom at night. She had begged, pleaded, threatened her mother with vague plans to run off, and finally her mother had relented and become a conspirator. Her father was told that Lissa had accepted a job through an agency as an *au pair* girl on the southern coast of Italy to a Contessa de Miralda. To both Lissa and her mother's relief, Merwin had not even questioned the validity of his daughter's first job.

The idea of going behind Merwin's back, deceiving him this way, having to do so to make his own daughter happy, had at first angered Max and made him oppose the idea of having Lissa join them. But in the end Thea won out, and Lissa had followed Luise and Thea within a week of their departure from London. Tony's school did not break until July, several weeks after the girls' school ended for the year, and Max had been detained in Spain, where he was scouting locations for his next film. So at present only Luise and the two girls were occupying the contessa's villa.

Lissa was suddenly showered in cold water as Thea, tiring finally of her water sports, shook herself out like a wet animal. The cold felt good on Lissa's sun-moist skin and she didn't flinch.

"You should have come. It was fabulous," Thea panted. "Fabulous!" She dropped down on the sand, not caring that her body was now covered with it. Then she absentmindedly began to brush the sand from her legs. "We could sunbathe nude here. Who's to see?" she said squinting out to the dazzling blue ocean glimmering with blinding light from the sun.

"Airplanes. People on boats," Lissa said.

"Airplane? No one's eyesight's that good."

"Well, a yacht came awfully close to shore this morning."

"It did? Where was I?" Thea asked.

"Still sleeping."

"You didn't tell me you went walking." She took a terry-cloth robe she had tossed onto the sand earlier, wadded it up, put it beneath her head, and fell back on it, stretching out her arms on the sand around her, closing her eyes, breathing deeply. "Is it very beautiful then?" she asked.

"Very."

"Wake me up tomorrow, and we'll come out here together."

"OK."

They both let the sun warm their bodies, sharing an intimate silence.

"What kind of yacht?" Thea finally asked.

"I haven't a clue."

"Big, small, medium?"

"Big."

"English, French, Italian?"

"It had a flag I didn't recognize."

"Oh? Anyone on deck?"

"I couldn't see too well. There was a morning mist, and the wind kept blowing my hair in my eyes."

"You simply *have* to do something about your hair, Lissa."

"There were two figures."

"Male?"

"I think so."

"Maybe they'll come back tomorrow morning."

"Maybe." Lissa giggled.

"You're thinking the same thing I am." Thea laughed.

"No, I'm not."

"How do you know what I'm thinking?"

"How did *you*?"

They laughed merrily, turned over on their bellies, and, with their knees bent and their bare feet wiggling like antennas over their bottoms, raised themselves up on their elbows and looked at each other squarely.

"We could pretend you're drowning and I'm signaling for help," Thea suggested.

"The way I swim, let's hope they could reach us fast enough," Lissa said.

"Never fear. I'd never let you die a virgin," Thea said.

They laughed again, both of them blushing. Then Thea rolled over on the side facing Lissa, her back and shoulders taking the full assault of the sun.

"Do you think we'll get into the Royal Academy of Dramatic Arts next year?"

"I think we have as good a chance as anyone—getting in, that is. But I'm not sure I can go, Thea."

"Last week you were sure."

"Occasionally I allow myself dreams."

"Fees, you mean?"

"Umm."

"You'll get a scholarship. You really are very talented, Lissa. I guess you're what they call a natural. You're a wonderful actress. I never can believe it's you on the stage when you do anything at school."

"I'm also American. I'm not sure RADA gives scholarships to Americans."

"We'll investigate first thing when we get back."

"Yes, of course. We could do that."

Thea ran her finger along the narrow rivulet of sand between Lissa and herself. "You know what frightens me most for you, Lissa, that you might do something really insane. I mean I know how unpleasant it is for you at home. Promise me you won't just run off and get married to some poor schnook."

Lissa sat up. "I can promise that. Believe me the one thing I *won't* do is marry a poor schnook."

"Or a rich one."

"Or a rich one. I'm not marrying anyone for a long, long time."

"How about having an affair?"

"That's different."

"A *lot* of affairs."

Lissa scooted around so that her back was to the sun and hugged her legs to her body. "Isn't it funny that Gale Nathan can sleep around and everyone thinks she's liberated? And Doris Steinman does it and they think she's desperate."

"Gale's pretty and Doris isn't. She's a cow, in fact."

"I guess you're right." Lissa sat reflectively for a long time. "Thea . . ."

"Umm?"

"If you knew, absolutely knew for certain that you would be dead next week, what would you do this week?" she asked in a tiptoe voice.

"That's a morbid thought."

"No. It's not. It's real. Reality. By next week war could be declared against Italy. A bomb could be dropped right here."

"Not bloody likely."

"More so than you think. All it would take is one trigger-happy Italian pilot and one pushy American bombardier. *Pow!*"

"Still not bloody likely."

"Death could be a more intimate thing then. Probably will be. We could get an incurable disease, or we could fall down a flight of stairs or drown then."

"I'm going to live until I'm a hundred and ten," Thea proclaimed.

"Not me." Lissa's face clouded. "I'm going to die young."

"Don't be silly, Lis."

"Really, Thea. I've always felt that." She smiled wanly.

"Anyway, the world's too old. Already overpopulated. Twenty-five's as old as anyone should live."

"Shhh. I hate to hear you talk that way." Thea stretched out flat on the sand and turned her face away.

"I think that's how one should live one's life. As if they might die tomorrow. You're right, Thea. I don't want to die a virgin. And there is so much I want to feel. Love. That corny?"

"No," Thea mumbled.

"But there's also so much I don't want to see anymore. That I wouldn't miss. Cold anger. Detached apathy. Self-pity. Self-abuse. I think," she said slowly, "if I knew love once, I could die without regrets."

Thea turned over and sat up. Her figure threw Lissa into shadow, making her gray and somber while behind her was a world of glimmering blue sea, dazzling golden sand and a clear azure sky. "Don't talk that way, Lis," she said softly, her voice suddenly older. "Never. You are going to know a great deal of love and loving in your life. Once you can unbottle all that love you have stored up, you'll see. You're a very special person, Lis. I can feel that. When you're on stage, an audience can feel it. You just have so much to give. You communicate just by *being*, Lis. That's a very special quality. I know it's difficult to accept now, but someday it won't matter about your mother and father or about your father and mine. I don't mean it won't matter. That's wrong. It will matter less, because something else will matter more. And we don't know— do we, Lis—that something might not be a very wonderful thing."

The cloud shifted, grew wistful. "All things beautiful, eh?"

"All things can't be."

"They will be. For you they can be, Thea."

"You, too." Thea stood up. The sand clung to her body, making land patches on it. "Let's take a dip in the beautiful sea." She smiled.

"OK."

Lissa got slowly to her feet. She stood there watching Thea run eagerly toward the oncoming waves, shouting unintelligible words over her shoulder, screaming with delight as she crashed into the cold water, beginning immediately to swim out, rushing to meet the next wave.

Lissa walked to the water's edge, extended one foot slowly,

then the other. She shivered. She thought perhaps she wouldn't go in, but Thea was out of hearing distance. She walked to a place where she could walk no longer and began to swim. She hated the taste of the salt, the feel of the cold water, the awareness that the water was stronger, more powerful than she. She flailed at it almost with deep anger. Thea was out *there,* and this moment she refused to be pushed back, kept away. This moment she could not bear to be alone.

The telephone sat on a perfect little Louis XVI bedside table. Luise had been waiting for more than an hour for it to ring. She was curled up to one side of the contessa's enormous satin-tufted bed attempting to keep her place in one of the new books she had brought down with her from London, but the ribbons of yellow sun that came through the green-slatted blinds on the lovely French doors distracted her, and she found herself concentrating instead on their graceful tracings across the polished terrazzo floor and onto the deep-pile cool green area rugs.

Max was to have called by nine as he did each Sunday morning. It was now ten past ten. Of course, the telephone service between Spain and Italy left a great deal to be desired. Max might not get through for hours yet, and Luise was aware of that. She was hoping that he would, sometime before noon, while the girls were on the beach and the house was quiet and there would be no possibility of anyone's picking up an extension. Between the pages of her book she had a list of things they must talk about, and all of them were painfully private.

She had really seen very little of Max these last few months. She had no doubt that his travels were legitimate, since during that time he had secured financing for his script and was setting up a production office in Madrid. Max seemed to feel he could make the film for much less money there, and since the background was Mexico, Spain could easily double. The film was scheduled to roll in September, Max hopeful that they could shoot all the exteriors before the beginning of November and the onslaught of the Spanish winter. This, of course, caused many problems between them. The plans had originally been for the film to roll the following spring, which would have meant Thea would not have to be disrupted from this last year of school. Then Luise, though she disliked the idea, was to join Max in Madrid with the children for the summer. Now Max had settled them in Italy, would be unable to join them for any period of time during the summer as he prepared to meet his shooting date, and Luise would be unable, because of Thea, to spend the fall and winter with him.

This presented a more serious problem than she could get Max to admit.

They were pulling apart, a distance growing between them that Luise feared might be at some future point—some near-future point—impossible to bridge. It had begun in New York a short time before Max's testimony. Nothing she did seemed capable of overcoming it. They were losing the dialogue they once had together. She was unable to speak to him—the things she cared about, worried about, was happy, sad, bereaved about weighed within her like some massive magnet pulling her inward. She knew there were other women in his life. Perhaps that would always be with Max. Certain men were like that. But always before she had been able to live with it because she felt, truly felt, that she would always be the one Max would come home to. Now she wasn't too sure.

Whatever was in Max's heart or on his mind was no longer being conveyed to her. He never wrote letters, and his calls always dealt with specifics: "I've just found a good location. We can roll on September first . . . I've had the accountants forward you your monthly check." When they were together, he seemed to be in a state of constant preoccupation, the kind of self-hypnosis he often resorted to when he was writing. One could not interrupt. As far as Max was concerned, you simply were not there. Only at her initiative did they make love. That had been humiliating at first. Then, as it allowed hostility to breed in Luise, she found herself using sex as a whip. "I suppose the old man can't make it. Not the man you used to be. I'll put on 'Brahms Lullaby,' if you like."

Oh, God, she was losing him. They were losing each other, and she just did not know what to do about it.

The telephone rang, jarring the quiet in the room and tumbling all her thoughts. The blood rushed to her head. Fear clutched at her heart, and her hand shook as she lifted the receiver and put it to her ear.

"Hello?" For several moments there was an overlapping of foreign voices. Then a steady hum. "Hello?" she said again and took out the slip of paper and tried to reread it, but her glasses were blurred, steamed perhaps from the humidity, and she couldn't see through them. She took them off. "Hello?"

"Luise?"

"Max?"

"No, this is Burt. I'm in Milan."

"Oh. Oh, Burt." There was an echo on the line, and she could hear her own voice. She listened to her tone of disappointment and felt immediately apologetic. "I'm sorry. I was expecting a call from Max. He's in Madrid. Where did you say you were?"

"In Milan."

"Oh. So close. Would you and Sylvia like to come down here?"

"Sylvia's in Angmering. I'm alone."

"Well, of course, you're welcome."

"Max is in Madrid?"

"Umm."

"How long?"

"I don't know, Burt. Well, that is, until next spring at least. He's going to shoot the film there."

"I heard. Are you alone?"

"No. Thea is here and—and a friend."

"Could you get away?"

"To Milan, you mean?"

"Not necessarily. Luise, now don't say anything until I'm through. Please. At least give me that. When I'm through, I'll give you equal time. OK?"

"OK, Burt."

"I have a friend who owns a small island off the coast of Greece. It's called Thesaures. We used it as a location once. It's beautiful. I've had a rough week, a rough month, a year, it seems. I came to Milan to meet with the Italian distributor, but he was called away on a family emergency. His mother died. Can you hear me, Luise?"

"Yes."

"There's an echo on the line. You sound so far away. It feels like I'm talking to myself."

"No, I can hear you."

"I have three or four days. I've called my friend. The island house is available, and I can get a private plane out of Rome. Would you meet me?"

"Burt, oh, Burt, what can I say?"

"Yes."

"I can't. You know I can't. But it's the nicest offer I've had in a very long while."

"Why?"

"The girls—No, it's not that, Burt. I'm married, Burt. I love my husband. It's that simple."

"Don't hate me for what I'm going to say, Luise. All's fair, as they say. I just saw Max last night."

"Max? In Milan?"

"No, at Heathrow. London. He didn't see me. He had just come in on a flight from Madrid, and he had Lucy Banner on his arm."

"Lucy? With Max in London? It can't be." Her mind was spinning, and her heart was pounding so loud she thought Burt must be hearing it, too. "Well, maybe he had to go back. Maybe that's why I haven't heard from him. Maybe he met Lucy on the flight."

"Stop kidding yourself, Luise."

"Please, Burt. Don't mention this to anyone else."

"Of course not."

"It could be misinterpreted."

"Luise—"

"Equal time, you said, Burt."

"Yes, of course."

"Even if you hadn't told me what you just did, I couldn't meet you. It has no bearing. You know that. I love you, Burt. But not *that* way. You're one of my favorite people. My best friend. But I don't feel that way. Not about you or anyone else, Burt. I love Max. I do. I love Max most desperately." Unaccountably her voice was shaking, and it had a touch of hysteria. She was crying, and for some reason it felt good and she couldn't have stopped if she tried.

"Luise?"

"I . . . can't . . . talk . . . Burt."

"I'll come to where you are then. I got all the information from Edyth. I told her I had something from the charity premiere I had to send you. Luise, are you all right?"

"Y-yes."

"I can be there by late tonight."

"No, Burt."

"Hell, haven't you learned no one says no to Burt Winters?" He laughed.

"I do."

"Sometime around ten or eleven. I've already looked up the schedules."

"No, Burt."

"So long, Luise."

"Bye. Thanks for . . . calling."

Burt was gone. The telephone was dead in her hand. She didn't believe for one moment that Burt would show up that evening. A private plane. A private island. Luise had to smile through her tears. It was impossible. Insane. But nice that someone thought of her in that way. She managed to put the receiver back on the hook.

She got up and went into the bathroom and washed her face with cold water. Then she came back into the bedroom and waited. At noon the girls came in and fixed lunch themselves. By three o'clock Max had still not called, and the girls forced her to dress and the three of them took a long walk along the edge of the water—all barefooted, loose hair flying in the soft afternoon breeze. From the road or from a boat near the shore, they would have looked like three young girls without a care in the entire world.

Chapter 26

Thesaures was wild, magnificent. It lay about twelve miles off the mainland, south of Athens and north of Crete. The evening Luise and Burt arrived the Aegean was a deep amethyst, and the mountains to the north were distant black silhouettes shivering in the full moon of the warm summer night as if just arisen from the sea, medieval, sinister—beautiful. The yacht the owner had lent them in Athens pulled effortlessly into a small protected harbor. The island appeared totally uninhabited, dark arrows of pine trees piercing the night sky from its gentle hills. The silence was spectacular. Only the sound of the sea and the steady lap of the waves. The sea mist—the island's breath.

They were met by a man with a cart and a mule who seemed surprised at the small amount of baggage. He piled the two cases into the cart. Luise and Burt followed a winding path from the harbor, Mediterranean pines on each side of them, their pungent salt-tipped smell filling their nostrils, the man with his mule and cart behind.

They had seen the house from the boat as they approached the harbor, its snow-white turrets almost blue in the night sky, its red-tile roof turned a deep plum, ripe, alive. But once on the land and in the harbor, only a tip of plum tile could be seen above the points of the pine trees.

Luise was most aware of the silence. It was quiet on the coast of Italy, but the winds always brought the echoes of distant music, the whoosh of the cars and trucks on the highways close by, the gay Italian voices calling out to the passing boats and the foreign shouts issuing back. But the silence here was a rare thing. Never had Luise been a part of such silence before. It was a world seemingly before man. There were no other inhabitants of the island, which was probably no more than two miles square, and the house had been built just above the harbor so that four-fifths of Thesaures was still primeval. There were no wild animals and only a few birds, and they were as silent as the night.

They started up a paved, terraced path, the pine trees cleared here, the ground sloping upward and planted lushly with vines.

Burt, who was slightly in front of Luise, paused and took her hand. "Are you all right?" he asked.

"Yes."

"Not afraid?"

"No. Strangely not." She smiled then, seeing small traces of question in his moonlit face. "I mean this island. This silence. It could be frightening. Probably should be—but it's not."

He grasped her hand tighter and continued up, pulling her slightly, trying to ease the strain of the climb. Finally, they reached a level space. They were on the top, and beyond a vast lawn stood the cool white house, lighted and waiting. Through its many glass doors and wide porticoes could be seen not one but several pools and beyond them the only cultivation on the island, an orchard of lovely silvery olive trees.

There were no roads, no cars, no driveway or garage. The path gave way to stones polished by the sea and the years and sunk into the lawn and leading directly to the front door, which was open. A woman, possibly the wife of the man with the cart and mule, stood there smiling a welcome to them.

Burt stood back and let Luise enter first.

"It's beautiful. Just perfect."

And by any standard it was. The entire house seemed to flow, one room into another, the inside with the outside. It was built ingeniously and with care not to interrupt the island's beauty or its calm. All the floors were a softly buffed pumice color like the sands in the harbor, the tables were of glass, the furniture low and covered in greens and blues. There was a huge fireplace in the main room in the same kind of polished stones as those set in the front lawn. There were bowls of fruit and a bucket of ice and cold meats and freshly baked sweets and liquor and beer set out on a buffet. A round glass table on an open terrace was set for two.

Luise stood on the terrace, seeing now the little cottage that must belong to the peasant couple. There was a cow, some chickens, a goat, and just beyond the largest pool which was built to follow the natural curve of the terrain, three small children were suddenly whipped away by a mother's hand and sent scattering to their own backyard.

They were alone now in that great silence.

"Are you hungry?" she asked.

"No. You?"

"Not yet. I'll fix us a drink."

"Good idea."

She didn't ask him what he wanted because from years of close friendship and of his being a guest in her house, she knew.

"I don't know the brand, but it's scotch," she said as she extended a tall glass filled with scotch and soda over ice.

"You'll spoil me." He smiled.

"I doubt it."

They were outside, seated by the side of the center pool. There were no outdoor lights, but the night was so bright it wasn't necessary.

"Isn't it strange, but it seems natural." She smiled.

"No. It's natural; it isn't strange. We know each other so well. So long. I've imagined us being totally alone like this so many times. I've been able to close my eyes and see the two of us like this vividly. Now that my eyes are open and here we are, it can't possibly seem strange."

"Burt . . ."

"Umm?"

"Please don't count on this meaning more than it really does."

"What do you think it means, Luise?"

"I can't, of course, know what it means to you. To me, it's not an interlude or an affair. You are right. We know each other so well. It is one more time you have extended your friendship to me."

"I feel a hell of a lot more than friendship."

"That's nice. Right now I find that very nice."

They were sitting side by side in two deck chairs, their faces raised to the moon, their hands loose at their sides. Neither of them reached out to touch the other. There was time. That was the beautiful part. They both knew there was time.

"I feel so *released,*" she said. "It has been bad for such a terribly long time."

"You and Max?"

"Only in part. We're symptomatic. Like you and Sylvia. All suffering in our own ways because of the decline of the human condition. I've been feeling so closed in lately, locked up. Guilts, too. I've suffered a lot of those."

"You, Luise?" Burt asked with surprise.

"Umm. Me. I was never as political as Sylvia—or Max. There was always this confusion, this schism between Max and myself. Sylvia and myself. They concerned themselves with governments, and I could only think about people. Shortsighted, Max called it. But I don't know, I'm enough of a cockeyed believer to feel we should go back a little and think just about each other. When we were young, we could do that. What happens when we get older, Burt?"

"The needs set in—money, power, fame."

"I guess so, but I still feel we can go back. What's up ahead for our children this way? It frightens me."

"It frightens them, too."

"Yes . . . yes, I know you're right. Your girls, Burt, what kind of people are they?"

"Not the ones I would have wished. But I can't blame that entirely on Sylvia."

"She's just so militant. So unrelenting. I've always thought Sylvia didn't like men much and rather disliked me because I did and do."

"I think you may be right."

"I'm not insinuating anything nasty."

"I know you're not. Sylvia's not a lesbian. I'm sure of that. But without her causes, it might be a different matter. She is a good mother, though, a tremendous organizer, an intelligent woman, and a most delinquent wife."

"I'm sorry."

"It's my fault. I should have left years ago."

"Why didn't you?"

"Like Sylvia—I had substitutes. In my case, my work, my ambitions, my need to succeed."

"And now?"

He smiled softly. "There's always a taller mountain."

"Oh, Burt, it's all so damned silly."

He took her hand and held it tightly in his own, but neither of them made an effort to rise. They were looking out to the stars, enclosed in their own thoughts, but something was happening, communicating itself between the flesh and nerve and warmth of their two joined hands.

"Did you know I would finally agree?" she asked.

"I hoped. All I could really know was my own desperate need. I could, though, sense yours."

"This will be difficult for you to accept, Burt, but I have never been to bed with any man except Max in my entire life."

He grinned rather sheepishly. "This is a tougher one. My youth was fairly promiscuous. But since Sylvia . . ."

"Yes. I believe that."

"You *do?*"

"Umm. You're loyal. In a way that's why I was so sure you didn't inform."

"Let's not go over that."

"How can we avoid that? All of us will rake the coals the rest of our lives. It's inevitable. All things henceforth will have its roots in the haunts. McCarthy might not have always been in the *befores,* but McCarthyism was—always was, somewhere, some man, groups of men—it is a terrible thought—but there always will be. I say I'm interested in people, not governments, but I know that's like saying which comes first, the chicken or the egg? People *become* government. *Are* government. That's why we have to start with them. But it has to begin elsewhere. Our children. Theirs. Not us, Burt. We had our chance, and we shot it. We won't let ourselves forget that, but we'll spend our lives in the attempt."

"That's a very strong judgment. No matter what my feelings are for Max, he still is back to making meaningful films. Never really was away."

"Yes, that's why I stay, I guess. I read his scripts and I see his films and I say to myself, 'Luise, there is a man there—the man you always dreamed about, and who maybe someday you will come to know.' "

"You call that love?"

"Oh, Burt, you know love is much more complex than that. Sometimes I hate Max and I realize I need that—to feel hate, that is to feel hate *passionately*—and I call that love. Sometimes, I have to have a dream, and Max can fulfill that because no matter what you think, Max may not be capable of loyalty or honor, but he is most wonderfully capable of supplying dreams, and so I call that love. Sometimes I have to have the familiar to hang onto my sanity. And Max, of course, *is that,* so I call that love. And sometimes I need to feel like a woman, and Max is blessfully endowed with the power to make most of my sex feel that way . . . and he *is* my husband . . . so I call that love. Lately I've needed the last variant of love very badly, and Max has simply not been there. In fact, I think if I want to go on sanely, I must accept the fact that often in the future Max will not be there. He will be elsewhere."

"I could be, though," Burt said softly.

"Now you are. I love you for that."

"No guilts?"

"I'll have a million of them." She laughed. "But after all, what would life be without guilts?"

"Heaven."

"Death. It may be heaven by one name, but it is still death."

"God, it's beautiful here."

"Unreal."

"The last time I was here was for Omega, and we used it for location. It represented an island in the Pacific, from the film of the same title. We brought over sixty Greeks and slanted all their eyes. The tanks came from Italy and the costumes from Berman's in London. There was only myself and a second unit crew. No women. We had ten yachts encircling the island, moored in every cove, to accommodate the men. The second unit director, the cameraman and the sound engineer and myself stayed here. It had a distinctly feudal ring to it, and that seemed unreal."

"That's a ghastly thought." She shuddered. "I'll try to erase the image from my mind—war on this island."

"It wasn't real."

"It could have been." She shuddered again.

"Cold?"

"No."

His hand slid up her arm. "You're shivering."

"Not from cold."

"Would you like to take a swim?"

"Oh, yes!"

"Nude?"

"Oh, Burt . . ."

"Neither of us thought we came here to play backgammon."

She laughed. "OK," she said.

He pulled her to her feet and held her close in his arms. "We can be very good to each other," he whispered and then, lifting her face to his, kissed her gently on the mouth. It was the first time they had ever truly kissed. Both of them were stirred by it. Luise placed her head against his broad chest and held him tightly to her.

"Burt," she said with some surprise, as if she had never really known him before, as if she were shocked to find herself in his arms.

They clung like that for a few moments, and then Burt carefully loosened her arms and held her slightly away from him. "The cabanas are there at the far end."

She broke loose, turned away, and started toward the small frame cabanas. Then she paused. "Those peasant children . . ." she began.

"They live in one room with their parents. I don't believe it would come as a shock."

She laughed, her laughter trailing behind her like a heady scent. Then she stopped at the door to one of the cabanas and turned back to him. He had already taken off his shirt by the poolside and Luise was struck by how well built he was. She liked the way he looked. Liked the ruggedness of the man, the look that he had not been polished, finished. His head sat on his sturdy neck like some marvelous natural uncut stone in a hand-hewn mounting. He was not graceful or electric in his movements. He was somewhere in the great in-between. An image flashed through her mind, and she chuckled at herself. He resembled Fonda a lot. Oh, add twenty, thirty pounds, remove a little hair, crook the nose a little, but he did.

"Hurry up," he called out.

"It won't take me long." She went into the cabana and slowly undressed. She heard the splash as he hit the water, the puffing sounds as he swam across the pool. She hung her clothes up carefully.

He was treading water at the end of the pool closest to her when she came out.

"Duck under," she pleaded. "Then I'll join you."

He obeyed instantly, understanding her embarrassment.

The water was cold, and she began slowly to lower herself into it. Then Burt was below her and, with a sure hold, pulled her in all the way and then held onto her.

"I forgot to ask if you can swim," he asked.

"Fine time to ask."

"Can you?"

"Sure. Weren't you ever at our pool in California?"

"I never had time for such pleasures then."

"So you can let me go."

"In a minute." He kissed her wet brow and her shoulders and drew back to look at her. "Not bad after two kids," he said.

She laughed. "Let's swim."

"Let's."

They made the length of the pool twice, swimming side by side, Burt moving with restraint so he wouldn't pull too far ahead. There was no sense of competition. At the end of the second length, Burt rose out of the water and lifted her onto the edge of the pool above him.

"Let me kiss you," he said softly, his hands resting gently on her knees, his own body still submerged in the water. But then he didn't wait for her answer.

It was damned near a hundred degrees, and Max was sweating uncomfortably as he parked the car under the grape arbors that shaded the driveway of the villa and, dragging himself from behind the front wheel, slammed the door, leaving his suitcase in the rear seat, unable to face carrying it.

"Hey!" he yelled. "Anyone home?"

The maid stuck her head out of the kitchen window that overlooked the driveway. She began screaming unintelligibly at him in Italian.

"Screw you." Max laughed and headed back around the house and to the front door.

"Daddy!" Thea shouted.

Thea and Lissa were just coming up the side path from the beach when Thea sighted her father. She was still wet, and the sand was stuck to her skin and the skimpy suit she wore. She ran to Max and threw her arms around his neck. Lissa hung back.

"Hey, you're wet!" He was laughing and he pushed her slightly away from him. "And you look like a belly dancer in that outfit."

"You *really* think so?" Thea clasped her hands behind her head and did a short imitation of a belly dancer; then she broke up with laughter.

Max smacked her on her wet bottom. "Into the house with you."

"Come on, Lissa," Thea called as she made her way around, toward the kitchen, to avoid wetting the front entry.

Lissa nervously started past Max.

"Hello," he said.

"I'm Melissa Bibbs," she said reticently.

"I guessed."

"How do you do." She nervously edged her hand forward to him.

"How do *you* do, Melissa?" he asked with a smile.

"Fine. It's lovely here."

"Lis! Hurry up!" Thea commanded.

"Go on now, hurry up," Max said and then gave her a slight slap on the rear as he had done to Thea.

Lissa stopped and turned and looked at him. "Don't do that, Mr. Seaman," she said and looked him boldly and directly in the eyes.

"I'll remember," Max replied, properly chastized.

He stood and watched her then as she ambled on to catch up with Thea. He was unable to move from the spot for a few moments after she was out of sight. Something in her eyes had chilled and warmed him at the same time.

"Too damned young," he said to himself and then lumbered exhaustedly to the front door.

Thea, wrapped in a huge turkish towel, opened the front door to him before he could even ring.

"Welcome, Allah Ben Kismet," she chanted and bowed and then broke up with laughter.

"Your mother home?" he inquired as he looked quickly around, immediately getting his bearings and heading across the tile entry and down the few steps to the living room which seemed the most likely place to get a drink.

He was right. The bar was set up closest to the living room terrace. Max took out a glass and a bottle of scotch.

"Mom is in Rome."

"Oh? How about being a good kid, Melissa, and getting a dried-out old man some ice?" he asked as he saw Lissa standing in the hallway.

"Yes, gladly, Mr. Seaman." And she was off.

"Shopping?" Max asked.

"Something like that. Mr. Winters surprised us, and he was driving into Rome."

"Burt Winters?"

"Umm." Thea was at the bar opening two Cokes. "He just spent the night, and as he was driving to Rome the next morning, Mom thought it might be nice to join him."

"When was that?"

"Yesterday morning."

"When will she be back?"

"Day after tomorrow."

"Must have a hell of a lot of shopping to do!"

"She loves Rome. The museums and all. I think it's fine she went. She was very lonely, and we had no idea you'd surprise us."

"Who's she shopping with?"

"Well, I don't know. She mentioned a name. But I can't recall. She said she'd call today."

"Decent of her."

"If you are thinking about Lissa and me, forget it. We're not exactly children and there's help here. And I knew where to reach you in Madrid. Mom left that information."

"Here's the ice."

"I think I'll drink it straight."

"Want some rum in your Coke, Lissa?" Thea asked.

"No," Max replied.

"Party pooper," Thea sneered.

"Yeah."

He was already out of the room and starting up the stairs to where he figured the bedrooms were, a glass in one hand and the full bottle of scotch in the other.

Chapter 27

If there was one place Max would have been certain he would not have run into Lou Whitehorn, it would have been on this narrow, stinking, dust-choking street in the severest heat of an August day in Madrid. However, that was not totally logical as he knew he could come upon any one of his former friends anywhere at all in the world, and it would not be out of the ordinary because all of them were rootless now, the same as he was. Still carrying American passports and paying American taxes, they nonetheless had few ties left in the States. Their memories of the past were bitter ones and their recent ones no less disconcerting. The blacklist was still in effect. Only a few had been able to overcome it. There was very little work and a great deal of humiliation. It started when you stepped off your plane at Idlewild and Immigration shuttled you off to one side after that agonizing fifteen minutes it took to locate your name in the huge black book with all the plane passengers lined up gawking behind you. In Europe it was different. They didn't give a damn about the committee or its names. There was work for the truly talented. It wasn't easy for the others. And how many could write in French or German? It had to be English. That meant sticking around where English or American films were shooting and that could mean—hell, *anywhere*—London, Rome, Paris, Madrid, Athens, islands off any coast. Production costs were too high in the States, cheaper abroad, and audiences since the war and the advent of tourism couldn't be kidded. They knew what an Alpine village in

Switzerland looked like. You couldn't give them the Warner backlot.

Max figured that since he never had felt any roots since leaving the States, it was the same way for the rest. They took their flats in London, châteaus in France, chalets in Switzerland, villas in Italy, and apartments in Madrid. But they were always foreigners, always the outsiders. You could learn the language, but it still wasn't easy to talk to the people. So you stayed a lot with your own crowd. And you really never settled in, because this month you might be shooting a picture in Madrid but next month you might have to be in some godforsaken place in Africa and the following year in a section of pig country in Ireland. Max thought of them all as the "rootless wonders," flying from film set to film set around the world.

At first Max wasn't sure it was Lou at all. The old man headed straight for him, elegantly cool-looking even in the face of the torturous heat and the wilting humidity, *resembled* Lou. But he could have been an old Castilian gentleman on his way to lunch at his club. The old man was older than Max thought Lou would look, even though it had been six years since he had seen him last. Thinner, hair grayer—white, really—skin leathered and brown (if it *was* Lou, he had been either shooting a location film in southern Spain or Greece or Italy or sitting out the years in some place in the south of France), and his step painful. If it was Lou, he was not well.

Max cupped his hands over his eyes to shut out the glare of the sun. "Lou?" he said and stopped a few feet from the man, immediately sorry, because if it was Lou, it was possible he could just spit on the ground and pass right by Max. That son of a bitch Gus Cone had done that outside a gambling casino in Monte Carlo.

Lou stopped. "Max," he said in acknowledgment. "Well, I had heard you were in Madrid."

"Yeah. I roll next month. Three weeks to be exact."

"I shouldn't tell you this, but I read the script."

"Oh?"

"No one ever denied you were a very talented fellow."

"I take that as a compliment, Lou."

"It was meant as one." The voice was cold, though, hard-edged.

"How about me buying you lunch, Lou?"

"I don't think so."

"Hell. Dutch then? You don't have to feel you owe me anything."

"I don't, Max."

"You here on a film? Which one? Bronson's?"

"My own."

"Jesus, that's great, Lou." The sun was beating down on them, and they were blocking the street. "You know I mean that, Lou. I'll have a lot to learn before I'm the craftsman you are." He grinned. "Or the gentleman. You sure are a gentleman, Lou."

"How are Luise and the family?"

"Fine. Fine. In Italy on vacation. Too lousy hot to bring them here and make them suffer. Listen, it's hot as hell standing here. Let's have some lunch. A drink at least."

"All right, Max," Lou said.

Max was surprised but extremely pleased. The pleasure dripped from his face. "I was headed for Bernal's. OK?"

"It sounds agreeable."

Max's entire body took on a new animation. Lou turned and walked by his side down the street he had just come and then crossed with him to the cool green canopy in front of Bernal's.

"I could kiss you, Lou. I really could."

"I think we could avoid demonstrations."

Max laughed. "Yeah," he said and led Lou inside and demanded a table in a far, quiet corner, closest to the gasping air-conditioning vent.

"Let's have a drink," Max suggested.

"I don't start until six. That's the new rule."

"Sure?"

"I think you can take my word."

"Campari and soda," Max told the waiter. "I've just learned to drink it. Scotch is just too damned heavy in this heat," he confided to Lou when the waiter was gone. Max was sweating, and he wiped his face with the napkin and then put it on his lap. "This isn't easy for me, Lou."

"I'm sure of that."

"I've been avoided like some goddamned plague. I'm not going to explain it all to you, Lou. A man does what he thinks he has to do, and that's about all there is to it. I felt I had to do it to survive. I've got something very important in me, Lou. I couldn't let that something down. And I didn't introduce one new name. Not one."

"How have you cast this film, Max?"

The question threw Max. "Cast? I thought about Lancaster, Douglas. Julie would have been perfect."

"Garfield?"

"Yeah. I can't believe he's gone. That man played a hell of a game of tennis, among other things." Max smiled, remembering. "Well, like I said, I thought about all the big boys, and then I decided on a young kid. His name won't matter to you now, but it will after the picture's released. It's an entirely new school of acting, Lou. These young kids really have a marvelous quality. They don't look like stars, not even actors. They just look like *people*. Saw this kid in a low budget an Italian outfit shot. Piece of crap. But this kid made even *me* believe the lousy lines he had to deliver."

The drink arrived, and Max fondled it tenderly. "I've been working a lot with the new breed, Lou. The after crop. I like these young people and their new concept of film." He took a deep swallow of his Campari and soda. It was bitter, and his face set for a moment before relaxing. He put the drink down, his palm over the opening of the glass, the cool feeling good. "So you read the script, eh? Any special reason?"

"Yes. American Independent. Your release. I've been what you might call a script consultant. Any script they're thinking of financing and filming in Europe, I read and give my honest opinion. It's kept me in touch. And using me in this capacity, American had no problems about my name. There are no screen credits given a script consultant."

"You OK'd my project then. Thanks, Lou."

"It had nothing to do with you, Max. It is a good script. It deserves to be made. I didn't agree that you should produce and direct it as well. But that decision was out of my hands."

"I had to, Lou. Anywhere along the line a script can be castrated, ruined. This way, I'm there to guard my baby through all stages. In preproduction, production, and postproduction. No hack director can give me static scenes or miles of mountain or sky. And no producer can say you have to use our money *this* way when I know it's better to use it *that*. I control the cutting and the sound and the titles and the choice of music. And I have a right to fight for advertising and decent theaters. It has to be that way, Lou, because that way it's all mine. Anything else would mean I was being prostituted." Max ran out of breath. He leaned back and looked at Lou. Lou was cool, remote, untouched, the gray eyes like cold slate.

"A writer-director-producer is a three-headed monster," Lou said. "I simply don't subscribe to it. Sometimes lines *have* to be cut. And if they're your lines, you might not do it. Sometimes a scene has to be scrapped, and if it's your scene, you might not allow it." Lou shifted in his seat. He was very thin, and Max was now sorry he hadn't selected a comfortable booth instead of this table with its two hard carved-wood chairs.

"How about ordering now?" Max asked.

But the waiter had already sensed that the moment had arrived and stood by the side of the table.

"Fresh fruit salad," Lou ordered.

"The seafood is great," Max suggested.

"No. A salad will be fine."

Max ordered a mixed seafood plate. "Beer, Lou?"

"No."

"One beer."

The waiter disappeared.

"But you're here to do a film for yourself now?" Max began.

"Write and produce it. I haven't lined up a director."

"An original?"

Lou smiled for the first time, but it was a slow smile, weighted, held back. "No, Max, I leave those to you. This is an adaptation. An old classic. Public domain."

"Background?"

"The Spanish Inquisition."

"Very contemporary." Max laughed.

"I thought so."

"Look, Lou . . ."

"I'm not your conscience, Max. Nor your confessor. I don't want to hear it."

"What was it like in jail, Lou? Did they treat you OK?"

Lou sat back and surveyed Max. It was a long moment before he decided to share his thoughts with him. "American prisons aren't constructed to hold political prisoners," he finally said, his voice brittle. "I was treated like any other convict, without much humanity. In the beginning when they locked that cell door the first time and I found myself in a hole six by eight, open toilet, little light, I guess I didn't think I had the stamina to last a full year. But I did, Max. I did. And in the end I made some good friends. Men I'll never forget. Men I hope I'll never *want* to forget. A big black man in for life on a rape charge. He had already served thirty-two years. His name was Pete. Old Pete we called him. I let him have the books I read and he'd ask questions. He had never read a book in his life. He cried when I left. Cried. And the warden, he came to shake my hand that gray morning I left. 'I never met or knew a Red before,' he told me. 'And I can't say I agree with your politics, but I've read all the transcripts on your trial and I can say, Whitehorn, you and your friends got a bum rap and I'm beginning to think the lunatics are running the asylum.' The lunatics are running the asylum," Lou repeated and then swallowed a halfhearted laugh.

"You still in the party, Lou? Jesus! I'm sorry I asked that. I really am."

"No. I'm not."

"You feel OK?"

"Well enough for a man my age."

"Well, you look trim, brown . . ."

"I still play tennis and swim."

Seated opposite any other man, Max might have added, "And screw?" But Lou Whitehorn was a man you could never say such a thing to. Lou Whitehorn was for some unknown reason your father, the President—*God.*

The waiter brought the food, and both men broke off their conversation. Max was conscious of the appreciation Lou showed the waiter. "Oh, thank you . . . That's lovely . . . I would be most grateful for some toast."

They were alone again.

"I read where Tanner's the new king of TV," Max said.

"I never get the trades."

"I know you won't be able to equate this, Lou, but I hate that son of a bitch."

"You don't hate, Max. You don't really know what hate is. Not really. Real hate is something you stuff back inside yourself, into your heart and lungs—organs where it's trapped—because it's too loathsome a thing to pass off, to expose. Hate is cold steel, silence delivered when silence is the deadliest blow. A letter you purposely never answer. A call you don't accept—or one you don't return. An old friend you walk by without recognition—that's *real* hate, Max. Anything less, screams, fights, murder—a sick way of saying 'love me, help me, save me.' " Lou put down his knife and fork and edged his plate away.

"Hate is what you feel toward yourself when a son betrays you," Lou continued. "*I've failed,* you think, and you hate, really hate yourself for that. Hate is when a little Napoleonic evil chairman can sit in judgment of you, and your government allows it. You really hate yourself for that one, because it is your government and somehow you've failed there, too. Hate is when you live in subhuman conditions for a year in a state institution that your countrymen permit to exist. And they *are* your countrymen, and you've somehow failed there, too. That's the true and terrifying quality of hate, Max. Anything else wavers between passion and apathy. I could pause and say hello to you. Break bread with you, converse. But you see, Max, my hate is so rooted, so impacted, so inextricable, indissoluble, unshakable that you cannot move, stir, dislocate, or arouse it. I can't hate you or any individual. My hate is too advanced now."

Max stared at Lou, not believing the words he just heard delivered in Lou's quiet dignified manner. The voice had been more hard-edged than it had been in earlier years, and his expression more riveting, but the years—and the hate—had not ravished the man. He was thin, aging, obviously ill, but the features were still fine, chiseled, the hair silver, the dress impeccable, his manners the same. To all appearances, he was as always: a civilized, intelligent, *unrelenting* gentleman.

The smell of the seafood, of the garlicked waiter hovering now behind him, of the kitchen as the door swung open and closed, of the damp and rot and mildew coming from the air-conditioning vent over his head, of his own sweat, almost overcame Max. He fought to keep from puking right onto the dining table. "Excuse me, Lou," he said and got up and tore across the restaurant to the men's room, making it just in time. He thought it would never stop. That his guts would all spill out into the stinking latrine.

Five minutes later—only five minutes. It had seemed an hour—Max, his face washed, his hair combed, a Tum in his mouth to counteract the vile taste of his breath, came back to the table. Lou was gone. He asked for the bill but was informed it had been paid. He went out into the street, standing in the green shade of the canopy. He could see Lou nearly a block away. He was walking evenly now, his step never faltering, his silver hair a shiny crown beneath the scalding sun. An elegant, cool, fragrant gentleman possibly on his way to a private club. Then he turned a corner and was gone.

It was the last time Max was to see Lou Whitehorn. He died at four the next morning. *Variety* said it was a heart attack, but the overseas *Times* (oh, yes, there was an obituary there, too) said the cause of death had not yet been determined.

But Max knew.

Chapter 28

They were two weeks behind schedule, and Max was pushing. The Christmas holidays were only three days away. That meant an additional loss of time. Christmas was on a Friday. Thursday would be hopeless, and as the Kid, his great nonstar, could be counted on for a lost weekend, he would have to figure Monday a forfeit as well.

"Reschedule the train sequence for Monday," he said to Edyth, who was at his elbow as he prowled the sound stage, waiting for the next setup. "That's the twenty-eighth."

"I thought you wanted to get rid of the principals as soon as possible," she said.

"I can't count on the Kid for any kind of performance at all Monday, and he's got the big farewell scene to deliver. When have we scheduled the train sequence?"

"Thursday. The thirty-first."

"Great. Write in the farewell scene. The Kid will do his best to get out of here early. We can rely on his cooperation that day." Max sat down. Lighted a cigarette. Edyth was still at his elbow.

"You really hate that boy. Why, Max?"

"No, I don't hate him," Max said quietly, thinking back to Lou and his definition of hate. "He bothers me. Like a fly on a summer's day. I'd like to swat him. That's all." He looked around. "Where's Thea?"

"In the commissary."

"It's not safe to eat in there. Last time I did, I had the trots for a week."

"She's just having coffee with the Kid."

"Jesus! She could get a lot worse things than the trots. How did you let that happen?"

"*You* brought her on the set, Max," Edyth accused.

Max got up angrily and began to stalk the set again. He didn't hate the Kid, that was right, but he certainly did feel a deep loathing for him. Something about the Kid made Max feel old. And there was the Kid's insolence, his total lack of professional conduct, of respect for Max as the director, the head man. And yet, Max knew he had used sure judgment in taking the Kid on. He did not have a polished technique. He employed in its stead intuitive nonacting. He came over lifelike, with a kind of slyness. There was nothing clean-cut or juvenile about the Kid. On film you could see the wheels spinning around in his head, felt he was plotting, calculating, assessing. He was a shrewd little son of a bitch, and so was the character he was playing. After one week of shooting, he had forced a confrontation with Max. There was a line in the script where he was supposed to say, "I came to Mexico because there weren't any other alternatives." And he insisted on saying, "I came to Mexico because there weren't any other alternatives *I'd accept*." The line had cost them a day's shooting, and in the end it had remained in the film the Kid's way. And of course, the Kid had been right. That is what that cocky, arrogant, tin god in Max's film would say. Max never forgave his being right. But he lived with his rancor. The critics would say the Kid was a new genius. Max knew what the Kid really had was *chutzpa*. He did what a slick, professional actor would never do. He emphasized his own hang-ups, his own blemishes, gave them equal time. The Kid was a wheeler-dealer, a natural con man. He'd squeeze his eyes up at people as if he were playing craps and you knew that's what he was really doing, what he did do. And he was a cocksman. He had the wardrobe girl seam his pants as tight as possible. Stood always with legs apart, hips back. He made sure his stance was damned explicit. Anyone else might have been embarrassed. But he was a cocksman, and there wasn't going to be a man or woman or kid in the audience who would doubt that. And of course, *that* was just right for the film.

But the Kid and Thea. That was something else again. That was carrying things just a little too far. That was pushing Max just a bit too close to the edge.

"I think I'll get a cup of coffee," he said to Edyth.

"I've got a thermos right here."

"Yeah, well I want a shot in it."

"I have that, too."

He glared at her. "I could kill that son of a bitch kid," he said.

"Thea is a smart girl, Max. Very perceptive. She isn't going to fall for a man with such obvious bad taste," she told him.

"What's she having coffee with him for, then?" he shouted and stormed off.

By the time he reached the seedy commissary, he had controlled his anger, strapped it back. He slowed down at the door and casually, as if his mind were elsewhere, opened it and went inside and looked around. The smell of sweat and stale beer assailed his nostrils.

They were at the far end of the long counter. Thea's back was to Max. The Kid sat facing him on a stool, one leg dragging the floor, the other back. His goddamned cock was practically pressing out of his tight pants! He saw Max but didn't acknowledge him. He dropped a cigarette on the littered floor, crushed it out with the heel of his boot, and then wheeled himself back toward Thea, smiling.

"Hi, kid," Max said with a small, forced smile on his lips. "They want you in Makeup."

The Kid looked over his shoulder at Max. He grinned at Thea privately. "They want me everywhere," he confided.

"Yeah, well, this moment they want you in Makeup and I think you ought to drag your ass over there since the next setup will be ready in fifteen minutes."

The Kid shrugged his shoulders and seemed to step right over the top of the stool. He patted Thea on the head. "See you later, little one," he said smiling gratuitously, eyes screwed up, a laugh somewhere in his lungs, ready to emerge.

Max stood without moving. "Let's go to my office, Thea," he said.

"Reasons?"

"Yeah, damn good reasons."

He turned and started out of the room, knowing Thea would follow, and held the door until she was up to him and then let her pass by him. He watched her as she walked in front of him, heading for his office, which was through a courtyard and up two flights of stone stairs. Her dress clung to the sweat at the back of her legs, and her skirt was too tight.

He closed the door securely after them.

"You like the Kid?" he asked.

"I find him interesting."

"Yeah?"

"Oh, Daddy, *come on!*"

"Where's your mother?"

"Shopping with Tony."

"They went shopping yesterday."

"That was for Christmas gifts. Today they're looking for something for Mom to wear to that dinner party you're going to New Year's Eve."

"Why the hell didn't you go with her?"

"Because I can shop with Mom anytime. Because I love," she changed to a sotto voice, "*being where the action is.*"

"I'll give you a little action if you don't stay clear of the Kid."

"So will he. He promised as much. Great potential, that boy." She looked directly into her father's eyes, her gaze never wavering, the humor resting easily around the corners of her mouth.

Max relaxed. "OK, lady, we have about five minutes before I go down to the set and you order the car to drive you home."

"Aren't you afraid the driver might rape me?"

"At this moment it seems the lesser of two evils. He's seventy-two and suffers from rheumatism. Sit down."

She was looking out the window into the courtyard below and was closest to his desk chair. She sat down in it, and he sat opposite her, reversing the usual order of things.

"Maybe it was a mistake bringing you here for the holidays," he began.

"Oh, no, Daddy. I'm really having a fabulous time. I'm sorry about just now. I was curious, that's all, and he was interested in me. That was rather nice to know. I mean, I am a girl, and come on now, he may be a terrible louse, but you have to admit he is a lot of man."

"I admit it, and so does he." He smiled.

"But he's not my type. I prefer older men. *Dawling, rawley, I do,*" she gasped in her best imitation of Tallulah.

"Yeah, well, maybe I should drive you home myself."

They laughed, and the tension was dispelled. "Really, Daddy, you have to realize you can't keep me in wraps forever. And you also have to give me credit for some good sense. And also trust me more than you do. That hurts—it really does—when you don't trust me. I'm a virgin, I truly *am*. I don't think I have to submit myself to a clinical test to prove the point. I don't think being a virgin's all that sensational either. I am sure there are far more pleasurable things, but my virginity is mine, a part of me like my hopes and my dreams and my fears. It's really my right to do with it what I want. But I can tell you I am not going to give it away to a creep like tight-pants Willy. And anyway, these next few years I want to be selfish. I have *me* to think of, Anthea Evans. You like that? That's the name I decided to use in my career."

"What's the matter with Anthea Seaman?"

"It sounds like a new biological strain."

"That's very nice."

"I don't mean to be rude. I don't mind it *normally*. I really don't. And I think Anthea was an inspiration. I've never met another Anthea in all my life. But I think Evans is just more—more theatrical, I guess. Now admit it. Don't you?"

"It's not bad." Max sat back. They'd be waiting on the set for him, but he didn't care. There was nothing more important he could do at this time than talk with his daughter. "You're really determined to be an actress then?"

"Resolute. I'm not sure I have the emotional depths that, for instance, Lissa has. I do think I have a good sense of timing, and I move well. Incidentally, tight-pants Willy—he's a real stick, Dad."

"In this part it works."

"Right. He's always got his mind on his equipment."

"Mental and physical."

"Umm. He's a shrewdie. You think he'll be a star?"

"Without question."

"I think so, too. But that doesn't mean he's a good actor. I don't care about becoming a star. Really. But I do want to become a good actress. I think I'd like eventually to do comedy. I mean like Carole Lombard—that sort of thing. And you have to be a really good actress to manage that."

"The best."

"If I don't get into RADA, would you let me study with Strasberg in New York?"

"Who says he'd take you?"

"If he took me, would you let me go?"

"Let's wait and see."

"I'd really like RADA better. I'm not sure about the method. I think solid training first might be a better course. I'm sure Lissa will make it. I'm not so sure about me."

"It matters very much, doesn't it?"

"Very."

They were silent for a time, but they were still communicating with each other.

"You do like Lissa, don't you, Daddy?"

"I only saw her for those few days this last summer. But yes, I liked her very much. Intense. A little too intense I think."

"I love her a lot. Like she was my sister. Something like that. She is intense. I'm always afraid, something, any real crisis, will push her over the edge. I worry about that."

"I'm sure she can handle herself. She seems capable."

"There are just such god-awful pressures on her. She really has to leave home. Really. I wanted to ask you about that. I'd like us to take a flat in London. Lissa and me. Next fall, that is."

"You'll only be seventeen."

"*Nearly* eighteen. And in London. Near you and Mom—I want that more than anything, Daddy. And I know it is the only answer for Lis. But it won't be easy. First, she has no money. But none at all. Second, her father doesn't even know we are good friends and wouldn't accept the situation. I don't want to hash up things with you, but Mr. Bibbs is very, very bitter. One day last week I was walking with Lis and we ran into her father. Lissa introduced me, and he refused to acknowledge my presence. Can you imagine?"

"That son of a bitch!"

"Oh, I wasn't hurt. One look at Mr. Bibbs and you know unalterably that he is an injustice collector. But I was angry. It's so stupid. After all, what did I have to do with the two of you? But in Mr. Bibbs' eyes, I was an extension of you. I understand that. I think it's sick, but I understand."

"He had no right—no right at all."

"Well, he did it. It's done. And that isn't important. What is is that he'll never, ever permit Lissa to share a flat with me, even if he contributes no financial support to it or to Lissa. The only way we can do it is if Lissa breaks completely with her father, and that's not easy."

"I think you're going in far too deep, baby. I'm not sure I agree or will support the idea of you two getting a flat. Anyway, your mother has to be consulted."

"You have to be the strong one, Daddy. Mom would never be convinced otherwise."

"Well, there's time. Let's think about it."

"Not that much time. It's almost January. We'd have to make our plans way before graduation."

"That still gives us a lot of time."

"But you will think about it?"

"Yes, I'll do that."

"You see, I want to have something to tell Lissa, something to keep her going, for her to look forward to. Otherwise, I'm afraid—" Her face quivered and she shook the hair nervously back from her face.

"Of what, baby?"

"Not of anything particular. Not of—*for*—I'm afraid *for* Lissa. She could go off the deep end, as I said. Run off with a guy. Something like that. Anything to get out of her house."

"Melissa struck me as being very mature. If she ever goes off with a man, I'm sure it will be because that's what she really wants."

"Uhh-uhh. You're wrong. Wrong, Daddy."

Max got up. "Don't give too much time to this. You have a fantastic year ahead of you. Think of that. I wouldn't mind being seventeen again."

"Wouldn't you really, Daddy?"

The telephone rang, and Max reached over and picked up the receiver. "Yeah? What? Oh, Edyth. What the hell is all that racket? Yeah, I know. I'll be right down. I said I'd be right down, Edyth," he repeated and hung up.

Thea was standing. "I can take a hint."

"Need some money?" Max asked.

"I never say No—to money, that is. From you, that is. Oh, boy!"

Max grinned. "This OK?" He handed her some Spanish money.

"How much is that in real money?" she asked.

"About ten bucks."

"It will do."

He took another bill out of his wallet and gave it to her. "Don't go wild," he warned.

"No, sir." She saluted and stood there watching her father as he left the small, makeshift office. The back of his shirt was stained with sweat where he had leaned against the chair. There were thick bands of flesh on the back of his neck and one showing over the top of his belt. He had his jacket slung over his shoulder, and the weight seemed an effort.

"He's getting older," Thea said to herself, and the thought made her sad, the saddest she had been the entire day.

Chapter 29

By the time the film was off the floor and in the cutting rooms Max swore he would never again hazard the problems shooting in a primitive studio on a foreign location involved. A year was gone from his life. He had started work the previous June (not including the four months during which he had written the screenplay), cameras rolled in September, came to a halt in January, and the film hadn't had a final cut until May. It would be released in September. There was advertising, previews, publicity to arrange, the usual straws to break your back, but fundamentally, the film was completed. In the can. It was time to start on a new one.

Thea had graduated from high school and was enrolled in RADA for the fall. Luise this time had found for the summer a house complete with boat and dock on Lake Geneva. She was certain it would be ideal for the children. They could practice their French, sail, swim, and take short day trips into the mountains. It was not unappealing to Max, but it had become increasingly more difficult for him to anchor anywhere for even a summer. He was grateful for the excuse of the trip to the States the release of the film engendered. But owing to the tax situation, he couldn't afford to remain stateside for more than two weeks. A new script seemed to be the order of the day. But he was tired, mentally beat. It had never happened to him before—a time when the ideas didn't flow, when he was blocked up, stopped. Max was one of those rare barbarians, the writer who couldn't *not* write. He sent Luise and Thea off to Geneva, to meet Tony there, promising to join them shortly. He then went through all his old notebooks.

Nothing hit him. He was irritable, tiresome, foul-tempered. Edyth found him impossible. She wished he would join the family so that she could have the office to herself for a week or two.

There was no peace at the office for Max, and the quiet at home was too much. The fear had set in. It often did at the end of a film. It was like the end of a love affair. You were so damned sure you would never fall in love again. Something was haunting him. At the back of his mind. Buzzing. Fluttering. An idea he had had a long time ago. So long ago he only remembered that once something had driven him, disturbed him for several months (or was it years?), but he couldn't recall what. He reversed the procedure. He was staying home a lot during the day and coming into the office at night.

One such night, to his surprise, the telephone rang. It was after ten, too late for either Edyth or Luise, unless there was some new crisis. He decided to let it ring. But the caller was insistent. He had been counting and picked up just before the thirteenth ring.

"Yeah?"

"Mr. Seaman?"

"Who's this?"

"Melissa Bibbs. *Lissa.* It is you, isn't it, Mr. Seaman?"

"Live and irascible."

"Oh, I'm sorry I've disturbed you. Shall I hang up?"

"You must have had some good reason to call. What was it?"

"I've run away from home."

"Where to?"

"The booth at the corner near your office."

"How did you know I'd be here?"

"I didn't. Not really. But then I guess I did. I called you at home first, and then I wasn't far from your office and I walked by. I don't know why. I just did. And your lights were on. I knew they were your lights because Thea showed me where your office was. Of course, it might not have been you. It could have been your secretary or a cleaning crew. But it seemed a fair enough guess that it *might* be you, since you weren't home and since your car is also parked at the corner."

He laughed in spite of himself. "Fair enough. Well, come up, Lissa. I'll open the downstairs door for you. It's locked. We'll talk. But be prepared I will try to send you packing home because that's really where you belong."

"Impossible. I've just shot my last fourpence in this coin box."

"I can manage taxi fare."

"I'll hang up and come around to the building, OK?"

"OK."

He disconnected. He should have been annoyed, but he discovered he wasn't. Why in the world should he be put in the middle of a Bibbs family dispute? But he was inwardly glad for the interruption and rather pleased that in a few moments he would be face to face with the piquant and provocative Melissa Bibbs.

She was dressed outlandishly in what could only be called Gypsy Halloween, and yet she looked wonderful in it. She was weighted down on both sides with two enormous shopping bags, and her hair, owing to the summer night winds and the preoccupation of her hands, was a dark, stormy cloud about her small face.

He led the way to the lift, and she followed behind him, still holding onto the stuffed bags at her sides.

"What are you pushing?" He grinned once inside the lift, pointing to the bags.

"All my worldly possessions. My suitcase was in my folks' room."

"You mean you left like that, while they were at home?"

"They were in the bedroom. They couldn't have heard anything."

The doors opened, and he took the bags from her. "Go on," he said.

"I can carry them," she insisted.

"Just do as I say. Open the door to the office." He left "all her worldly possessions" in Edyth's outer office and ushered her inside to his own. "Sit down." He waited until she had. "Now, where the hell did you think you were going at this hour, dressed like that and without a penny in your pocket? Don't you know you were advertising for trouble? And your parents, didn't you give any thought to them? OK. It's rough at home. But your folks have tried damned hard. They have, believe me, done their best—or thought they have. They don't deserve this kind of worry. They've had enough." He leaned back. She hadn't moved. "I guess you thought I'd give you a soft ear and a few quid. Sure, I'll listen and I'll give you taxi fare home. No. On second thought, I'll drive you home myself to make sure you get there. How old are you?"

"Eighteen."

"Guaranteed it's a painful age. But you won't die of it."

"You finished?"

"I haven't started."

"Since I don't plan to leave, I guess I'll have to listen. But I would like to say a few things first. Then I'll listen. *I promise.*" She curled her legs underneath her, taking a cigarette from the box on his desk first and lighting it with his desk lighter. She inhaled deeply and for a moment leaned back and watched the smoke. "Firstly, I am not going back. I love my parents, Mr. Seaman. You might not see it my way, but I do. They would never allow me to leave if I asked. After all, I'm a nice middle-class girl of eighteen. But there isn't room or money to keep me at home. They could not, will not admit it, but that's how the cookie crumbles. If I run off like this, refuse to return, make my own way—that's another thing. They can suffer respectably, be martyrs to yet another cause. But it will be easier for them, I assure you. I will really be doing them a favor. I truly feel the only unconscionable thing I have done is to involve you. But at this moment I had no alternative, and simply trust me when I say it had to be this moment. I am well aware of the battle that wages between my father and you. In coming here, I've forced myself to push it into the background. Apart from the fact that you are the viper in my father's bosom, so to speak, you are the father of my dearest friend, one, and two, a man I met this summer and who I knew I wanted to know better. And three, you are the only person I know who could supply the solution to my problem. In fact, who could even have *two* solutions."

"Which are?"

"A job first. I want to be an actress and you are an autonomous producer et cetera, et cetera and et cetera. You can hire who you want. You really wouldn't be taking a chance. I am very talented; really I am. And I photograph better than I look. I'm a type. I recognize that. You'd pick me out of a crowd. People always remember my face. I'm not Elizabeth Taylor, but I do have a young Hepburn quality. I know that. Everyone tells it to me. Maybe it's my voice and my walk and the fact that I'm a bit of a nonconformist. I was that way at three. It's not imitative."

"I haven't got a film to put you in, Lissa, even if I found out you could act. I have no doubt you would photograph well. You have the right bones, the hollows, the curves. Your skin has texture, and you move well and rather inimitably. Your voice is good. I'd have to hear you read to see if your phrasing is right. But as I said, I have no film, not even a script in sight."

"Put me under contract then."

He laughed. "I'm not Twentieth Century-Fox."

She shrugged her shoulders. "Well, then there's the second solution."

"Which is?"

"You can make me your mistress."

"I don't find that amusing, Lissa."

"It wasn't meant to amuse. I understand you are a great one for the truth. If so, though I know you never permitted yourself to admit it before, now that I've said it out loud, you will have to confess that it's a perfectly plausible eventuality. It was from the first moment we met and you patted me on my rear. There was between us—immediately—a familiarity."

"I'm sorry. You mistook my paternalistic proclivities."

"Like hell."

They both sat there in the night silence of the deserted office building, conscious only of each other. She had finished her cigarette, crushed it out, and was considering reaching for another.

"Don't," he commanded with only the flicker of her hand as evidence of her next move. "You're too young to smoke your life away."

She put her hand decorously in her lap, entwined it with the other and sat quietly that way.

"What would you do if I sent you packing, Lissa?" Max asked.

"I don't know. From the moment you opened the door, I never gave it any thought. It seemed unnecessary. I knew you would want me to stay."

"You're right—but I can't allow it."

"It isn't just your decision."

"In this case it is."

"Forget I'm Merwin Bibbs' daughter. Forget I'm Thea's friend. If I were neither of those people, would you send me away?"

"No."

"There!"

"Look, kid. . . ."

"Lissa. Me, Lissa; you, Max." She laughed softly, rolling the words off the tip of her tongue and then holding back the laughter with it pressed on the shiny edges of her teeth.

"Melissa, in all honesty, I don't quite know what to do about you. But I want you to understand that no matter how desirable I find you, and I'll grant you I do, under no circumstances could I permit an affair to develop between us. To begin with, you are too damned young. You need a young man, younger than I am at any rate and certainly one who is not married. But apart from that, I cannot dissociate you from your mother and father or from my daughter. It would lead to irreconcilable hurt on all sides. I will try to help you, though." He stood up and began pacing as he did when he was working out a story. "I'd give you some money if I thought that would do it. But I don't think so. What you need is some time to consider what you should do next. Not what you want to do, but what you should do. I will buy you a ticket tomorrow for Geneva. You can stay with Mrs. Seaman and Thea and Tony for a couple of weeks at least. But you'll have to call your mother tonight and tell her you are going to do that."

"I won't. She'll stop me."

"If she can stop you, Melissa, then you really want to be stopped."

"OK, so I call Mom. Then?"

"Either you go home for the night or . . . "

"Or?"

"You can stay with my secretary, Miss Spalding."

"I see."

"That's how it is. Accept those terms?"

"Do I have a choice?"

"Only you would know that."

"I haven't."

Max dialed Edyth's number. He picked up the telephone and walked with it. There was no reply. He waited in case she was in the bath, but she was apparently out.

"What do we do now?" Lissa asked.

"We go back to my flat and wait until Miss Spalding comes home. She never stays out too late. It's half past ten now. She'll probably be home in an hour or so. Would your parents worry about you before then?"

"They won't miss me for the rest of the night. I guarantee that."

"You'll still call when I have you safely tucked in at Miss Spalding's."

He started out of the office, picking up her shopping bags as he went through Edyth's office and into the corridor. "Turn out the lights and latch the door," he told her.

"You look nice," she said softly. "Nice and familiar." And she smiled warmly and took one of the bags from him as she joined him in the lift.

They sat waiting in the den. It was already twelve fifteen. Television was finished for the day, prayers said, put to sleep.

"I can't understand why you should have such a difficult time finding material to write about," she said.

"Finding material to write about and finding material for the screen are two entirely separate things."

"You should write about Daddy and you. About McCarthy."

"I could write it, but right now no one would buy it."

"I don't believe it. Do it as a parable. Joan of Arc. I don't believe that legend about her anyway. I was reading a book the other day whose author questioned it, and he had good points. I think Joan of Arc could have been an illegitimate member of the royal family, as he said. She could have informed and a suspected witch been burned in her place. No one saw her face, you know." She was quiet. "I'm sorry. But there is some sort of parable there."

"Yes, there is."

She grinned. "I wouldn't be a bad Joan of Arc."

"You wouldn't be a good one, either."

"You don't like my idea?"

"It's not my kind of story."

"No. It's really not. I've seen all your pictures. Really. All of them. I look up in *What's On* and tube out to the theaters that might be playing them in revival. Between Thea, my father, and your films, I think I know a good deal about you. That's besides you seeming *familiar* to me." She smiled. She was curled up on the couch, a pillow tightly clasped in her arms, her shoes kicked off. "You're a voyeur, really. All the people around you constantly being observed, dissected, pinned like a butterfly collection. It's rather spooky. God knows where *I'll* end up."

"Do you like my films?"

"They excite me. But that's because of you, because each film uncovers you a little more, betrays you at times, or me. You really don't tell the truth, you know? You think you do, but you don't. Oh, it's your truth, but not *the* truth if you know what I mean."

"That's not an original comment."

"Mrs. Seaman? Well, that wasn't difficult. Anyway, I know you think your films smack of realism. They don't, really. And even if they did, I don't think audiences truly want realism."

"No? What do you think they want?"

"Magic."

"To quote Blanche du Bois?"

"I hated that picture. So stagy. But Blanche—I will always think of Vivian Leigh that way. Not as Scarlett, but as Blanche du Bois. She was magic, Della Robbia blue, all those things. And she was right. Everyone has a right to some magic in their lives. Film isn't the best of all places to find it, but it's a start, and it can hold out hope, you know what I mean?"

"You use that phrase too often."

" 'You know what I mean?' Umm. You're right. I'll watch it." She scrunched down further on the couch. "Maybe your secretary isn't coming home tonight," she said.

"She'll be home."

"Was she your mistress once?"

"Why do you ask a question like that?"

"Possessiveness is nine-tenths of revealment."

"It's none of your business."

"I'm a virgin."

"That's none of mine."

"Perhaps, but you were dying to know."

Max got up and went over to the bar and poured himself a drink. "As a matter of fact, I already knew."

"How?"

"A roué's intuitions."

"I like scotch with just a touch of Drambuie in it," she said. "Ever had that?"

"Too sweet."

"Could I have one?"

He turned and looked at her, deciding. "Yeah," he agreed.

"I'll make it."

She rose from the couch unsteadily, held onto the arm for a moment, and then walked over to the bar, standing next to him, as she made her drink. "You make it like a martini. That is—just a breath of Drambuie, like the vermouth in a martini." She finished her task and offered the glass to him. "Want to taste?" she asked.

"No, thanks." He walked away, leaving her standing there with the glass extended. They were at least ten feet from each other.

"I have a favor to ask you," she said.

"Haven't you asked enough?"

"Yes. I guess I have." She turned away.

"Well, what is it?"

"I'd like you to be the first," she said softly, away from him as she spoke and then slowly turning back, facing him proudly and with devouring feminine frailty. There was something haunting, vulnerable, almost hopeless about this fey, exquisite girl-woman.

Max recalled Thea telling him how she feared Lissa could so easily be pushed over the edge. Earlier this evening he had doubted that. But this moment, as he stood looking at her, he knew Thea was right. And Lissa was right, too. She was familiar to him. Incredibly, intoxicatingly familiar.

"Please don't call your secretary," she was saying. "Please. You can call my mother in the morning. Early. No one has to know I've been here tonight, if that's the way you want it. And tomorrow, if you still want me to go to Geneva, I'll go."

"Lissa, you know what you're saying is impossible."

She put her drink down on the bar and walked slowly across the room to him. "Please. Both of us so need magic."

She was still barefooted, and it made her appear smaller than she usually looked. She was a full head shorter than he. She looked up at him and seemed about to cry. She sighed almost imperceptibly and her lower lip quivered.

"Please," she whispered.

He knew he would take her in his arms and that she would spend the night in his bed. He knew also in that instant that her life was in his hands, that she had placed it in his hands from the time of the phone call. No. From that first moment in Italy. It was difficult to know how she would destroy her life if he sent her home or away in the morning. There was no assurance that if she remained with him, she still would not destroy herself and him as well.

"One person can't destroy another, not really," she said as if she had tuned in to his thoughts.

"Darling," he said. And then again, "Darling." They stood there clinging together, not kissing, like two lovers who had just been reunited after a very long separation.

"Tell me if I hurt you at all," he said. He was wringing wet, fighting desperately for control.

"You couldn't hurt me. You wouldn't."

"I'll try not to, baby," he said in her ear. It was not a promise. It was more like a plea, an argument in defense of his own primitive nature. Her body clung to him, drew him in further, deeper. He took a deep breath and lifted his weight off her and onto his arms. Her body tilted up to him. "We'll take it easy for a moment." He pushed her cloud of hair back from her face with the side of his cheek, and he kissed the damp skin left exposed, kissed her eyes, let his lips brush her nose, his tongue finding her mouth. She was moaning softly. "OK, baby," he said. "OK."

He began to heave his body. It was a compulsive thing. Impossible to stop now. *In and out. Roll over. Up and down. Lower your legs. Oh, God, God, baby, baby.* He thought it was over, but he began to heave again. The rhythm sustained, the tempo slow at first, accelerating, building. Like Wagner. Rolling, loud, triumphant, accosting the ears and the senses, stirring a music never stirred before.

The light finally came through a corner of the blind. "Are you all right?" he asked.

"I can't believe it."

He kissed her neck, her nipple, her navel. He lay down beside her. Her arm flew out like a small injured bird's wing and she dropped it across his chest.

"Max."

"Umm?"

"Whatever happens. . ."

"Nothing will."

"Whatever does, let it be known you made one virgin *very* happy."

"For a beginner, you fuck pretty good yourself," he said.

And they laughed. And rolled back toward each other and made love again.

He was exhausted, but he figured he ought to ring Edyth before he allowed himself any sleep. She was lying curled up, arms and legs tightly bound around a pillow. She was sleeping wedged between the pillow and himself. Her hair covered her face. He ran his hand over and down her shoulder and arm. She clasped the pillow tighter. The telephone was on her side of the bed. Max got up without disturbing her and made his way into the bathroom. He closed the door so the flush of the john wouldn't disturb her. He washed without ever looking at himself in the mirror; then he came back to her side of the bed and dialed Edyth. He spoke in a stage whisper, and Edyth, who had evidently just awakened, had trouble hearing him.

"Where the hell were you last night?" he grumbled.

"I'm over twenty-one, you know, and office hours end at six."

"Never mind. Listen—"

"I was over at Sheilah's—you know my friend Sheilah—and we were talking and lost track of the time. Anything wrong?"

"No. But I got a call last night. I want to leave for New York tonight. Set up the advertising campaign on the film."

"Oh?"

"Get a suite at the Sherry Netherlands for me and order a car on both ends. Get me on any night flight that's flying fairly empty, first class, to New York. I want to work and I don't want to be bothered."

"I *see*."

"What the hell do you see, Edyth?" His whisper grew strained.

"I didn't mean anything by it. Coming into the office, or shall I come by before you leave?"

"I'll come in. About five."

"Want me to call Luise?"

"Yeah. Good. What the hell time is it, anyway?"

"Eight seventeen."

"Jesus."

"Shall I tell her you'll be at the Sherry Netherlands?"

"Of course. Damn it, Edyth—never mind. Tell her I'll call her from New York tomorrow—about eleven P.M., her time."

"How long will you be gone?"

"I don't know. Two weeks."

"Want return reservations?"

"Not yet."

"Mind if I do this from home and go into the office about ten?"

"No."

"See you at five then."

"Yeah. Thanks, Edie," he said and disconnected.

Then he walked all the way around the king-sized bed and got in from the other side and slid in close to her to where the sheets held her warmth and, careful not to waken her, pulled her gently to him so that her body meshed with his. He pushed her hair aside and settled in and promptly fell asleep.

Chapter 30

The last time Max had been at the Sherry Netherlands it had been in Harry Steiner's suite. He had not forgotten one moment or detail. Nor did he want to. He could somehow shrug off Gus Cone's indignity, Merwin's hostility, Lou's cold detachment, even Luise's silent accusations, but he could never erase from his mind the loathsome image of Harry Steiner's condescension. But he had desperately needed Steiner then, needed his backing on a project, and so had to swallow the bitter pill—for Max, at least—of humility. The sound of Steiner's voice: "You couldn't use your own name, Max. You'd have to use another name . . . I can't offer you lunch. I have an appointment with some of our Wall Street boys. . . ." And the hard, cutting feeling of that priceless star ruby ring grinding into Max's flesh as they shook hands in greeting and in parting was like a concentration camp number indelibly tattooed on his brain.

The suite Edyth had gotten for him, admittedly on short notice, but still all right, was not on the same floor as Steiner's had been, not at the top, and only one room faced the park. But it had the same spaciousness and class. After the bellboy had left them alone and he had ordered up some food and booze and Melissa had gone into the bathroom to bathe, he had stood in the center of the living room, looking toward the park, remembering how Steiner had stood with his back to a similar set of windows when he had sweated out the story of *Black in Eden*. "Fuck you," he said to the ghost he could see facing him, no emotion on the apparition's face, no clue or giveaway. "I don't need you anymore," he said, and he laughed astringently and then, room service having appeared with his order, made a strong drink for himself and a weaker one for Melissa to have when she came out of her bath.

Melissa. The name tripped down from his subconscious and seemed to purr inside him. Melissa. She had, of course, been right. It had been inevitable from the first time he had seen her in the front garden of the villa, standing there, the sea behind her throbbing in at high tide, her hair still damp, her skin stung with the smell of sea salt, that delicate pink skin, the wild uncontrollable hair, the steady knowing intensity of those massive dark eyes. The first time they had spoken, "Don't do that, Mr. Seaman," she had said when he had patted her on her rear, as he had done Thea. "Don't do that, Mr. Seaman." She had known. Somehow she had known.

But it was too late. It was too late even then, and there was no way of turning back the hands of the clock, moving backward through time, and had there been, it still would not have mattered. They would have met no matter what the circumstances. Max had never been a fatalist before. He believed too intensely in his own power. He was his own man, a seaworthy vessel not needing a captain at the wheel, crossing uncharted waters and charting them himself, fending off sharks, balancing his sails in all winds, sailing a straight course in all storms, through any troubled waters, tidal waves, hidden ice mountains, taking on the whole world—sea and sky. This was different, though, and Max was wise enough to know it.

He remembered when he had been a kid in Bridgeport. Hell, no more than four, but he damn well remembered it. It was a holiday, and even at four, he knew it was *the* holiday. His parents had been up since dawn, and Papa had gone to *shul* to pray. He hadn't been permitted to go with Papa. He was ordered to stay home with Mama, but Mama had been ill and only appeared in the front room to place food in front of him. "You must eat," Mama had said.

"You're not eating. Papa won't eat."

"That's different. It's Yom Kippur. We are fasting for our sins. You're too young, Maxie, eat, eat. The sin at your age would be not to eat."

And Mama had disappeared again, leaving a bowl of hot cereal, swimming in butter and sugar and cream, in front of him. He had taken the cereal and, spoonful by spoonful, fed it down the kitchen drain, washing it away with water as he did. He had fed his lunch out the window to the cat next door and his dinner to the O'Reilly kid downstairs, and as he was supposed to be asleep when Papa came home, he had had nothing else, not even water, until the next morning, although he could smell from his bedroom the herring and onions Mama and Papa always ate to break their fast. He had sinned and he had survived, and the next year, though he had not gone into *shul* with Papa, he had sat on the steps the entire day and was still there when Papa came out. And his mother and his father had not even commented. Mama had asked, "Why, Maxie?" And he had simply replied, "I've sinned." And a look had passed between his parents and that night he had had herring and onions and a slab of fresh yellow *challah* with them.

Max took a swig of scotch. Why he was thinking about that incident at this time he couldn't imagine, but his mouth had been dry as it had been that day without water, and as he waited for Melissa to appear, the pangs of hunger seemed the same. He took a piece of buttered brown bread and a slice of smoked salmon from the room service cart, and then another thought entered his head, pushing out the other, and he went over to the telephone and called the florist shop and told them to send up about five dozen of the best roses they could find.

"Make that six," he added and then hung up.

She came into the room then. Her beauty startled him. Her simplicity terrified him. Her face had been scrubbed clean and was a soft glowing pink. She wore no makeup, no pins in her hair, her feet were bare, and her body was free beneath a loose white robe that seemed to be a sheet that had been tied at her shoulders and allowed to fall at its own direction to her ankles.

"Smoked salmon," she cried and went over to the cart and made herself a generous sandwich. Before she began to eat it, she remembered him. "Shall I make you one?" she offered.

"I've had some. That's your drink next to the platter."

"Umm."

He watched her eat, was fascinated by the performance. It was as if he had never seen another woman eat in his entire life. She breathed deeply as she ate. The pleasure lighted her face and filled her eyes. He could think of her only in the bedroom, in his bed. She had never pleaded, never been supplicant. The next time it would have to be by daylight so that he could see her face, her expression. See that same pleasure tear at her face. She wiped her hands on the sides of her robe as a small child might do and licked the last bit of oil from her lips. She was still breathing deeply, and she had thrust her fingers in her hair as if holding on to her head and crossed to the window and stood looking out. She was only about five feet away from him. A few steps and she could be in his arms. He stood unable to move. He was his own prisoner.

"I used to hate New York when I was a little girl. We came here when Daddy was in prison, Mom and me. She grew up here, and she didn't mind it at all. But I hated it. I was about ten, and we had been living in the valley, not luxuriously, but I had had a room up in the eaves and a giant elm outside my window, and there was always the smell of jasmine and orange, and we had a large backyard, and as the land had once been an orange grove, Daddy had left rows of the trees at the rear of the property so the neighbor behind us wasn't visible and so we weren't visible to him. So I truly hated New York."

She turned back into the room and took a long swallow of her drink and closed her eyes and breathed deeply again until all but the taste of it had gone and she ran her tongue up on the roof of her mouth as if to dissolve the last remnants of taste as well. When she opened her eyes, she smiled at him in the same way she had that very morning when she had awakened and found him lying next to her already awake and studying her.

"Am I boring you? Shall I stop?" she asked.

That morning she had said, "Did you like me? Shall I go away?"

"No. Never," he replied.

"We lived in one room in a hotel on West Seventy-second. I remember the people across the court screaming, fighting. At night, because we had a rear room, you could lie there in the dark and look out and across the court, and it was like a hundred television sets going at one time, the singles and the doubles and the groups. I could see them all in all those lighted windows, screaming, fighting, loving. I hated it when any lights went out. Someone left, and I wanted to follow them. Someone was loving, and I wanted to be loved by them. Someone had died—like the electric light had in a way—and I didn't want them to be alone, to die alone."

She put down her drink and turned and worked to open the

window herself. "It will ruin the air conditioning," she said. "But it's not fair to bottle this cool air this way."

He stood quietly, allowing her the physical labor of opening the window herself, watching as her arms strained and her legs stiffened. When the window was finally opened, she let out a little gasp as though freeing the air inside herself as well. She sat on the window ledge and squinted up at him, through a blinding ray of summer sunlight.

"I remember Mom taking me to the corner, to the park. It was the Fourth of July, and they had stocked the pool with live goldfish and let the children fish with nets for them. I remember bringing home a marvelous large metallic-looking one in an empty jam jar and then sneaking back later in the day and putting it back into the pool and watching it as it arched with happiness and swam away from me. I knew it would have been a terrible thing to keep it bottled up forever in that jam jar. I always knew it wouldn't live forever and I didn't want to think about that, didn't want it to die while I had it, where I would be so close." She cupped her hands over her eyes to see Max better and grinned. "I called him Ambrose. You like that?"

Call me Melissa. No one does anymore. You like that? Try it. Melissa.

"Yeah. I like that."

"Then Daddy was released from jail, and somehow we managed two rooms, and he went to work in some hamburger place, though Mom would never tell me where. Actually, she never told me what he was doing, either. But it wasn't difficult to know. He smelled from hamburger and fried onions all the time. His skin. His hair. I could never eat a hamburger since that day. I mean—a man like Daddy."

She blinked her eyes as if the sun had made them tear and slid off the ledge and walked back across the room and eased herself onto the couch, raising her legs, hugging them to her.

"Someone lent us some money to go to England. I think it was Mr. Winters, but I never heard Daddy actually say so. It didn't happen just like that, though. There was a problem about Daddy getting a passport. They weren't going to issue him one, and Mom and I went ahead of him, and he didn't join us for several months."

She stopped there. Moments went by, and she said nothing else. He knew she was sparing him London. Sparing him her friendship with Thea. Sparing him any more of her suffering. At this moment anything outside this time and place, this young woman, did in fact seem irrelevant to Max. This was no time to explain to her what he knew about her father, about why her father had gone to prison, about how her father had cared about the welfare of his country and how this had to mean he placed mankind above his own family. About how that decision, that year in jail, had been the high point, the glory in her father's life. He wore that year now, would wear it always like a badge, a medal, a trophy for the world to see and nod their heads about and smile proudly at him. *Merwin Bibbs. One of the ten. How dare we ever forget?*

There was a knock on the door, and another bellboy entered. He was loaded down with six dozen roses, his face hidden by them and his voice muffled.

"Where shall I put them?"

"Ask the lady. Where do you want them?"

"Oh. Who are they for? Who are they from?"

"Over here?"

"Oh, Max. I love the thought. I really do. But I can't bear to see them. They'll die. It's like you had had them killed for me."

"Don't be silly, baby. They had already been cut. In the florist shop. Before the florist. They've been in cold storage."

"Please, Max. Take them away, please."

"Here. Here's a five. Keep it. Take them back, but tell the florist he can still charge me. OK?"

"Sure, boss."

The bellboy left. *Crazy people*, he was thinking.

"I'm sorry, Max."

"It's all right. But you can't do anything about all the cut flowers in the world."

"I don't have to personally see any of them die, though."

"No, but even if they weren't cut, they would soon die at the end of the season."

"Yes, yes, of course. But they would have the season. Their own private, *natural* season."

He laughed gently. "Yeah, baby. They'd have that, unless the bugs, or a draft, or the rains, or neglect got to them first."

"Let's not think about that."

"Let's not."

She was still on the couch, kneeling now though—on her knees. He came over to her and lifted her up in his arms.

"I'm crazy about you, Melissa. Out of my head. It's never happened to me before. Before this a broad's been a broad and Luise was my wife. But I'm crazy about you."

He carried her into the bedroom, and he felt young, suddenly come to life. His skin was tight and his breath even. And though her suffering was now his, so was her love and her beauty. He put her down carefully on the bed and drew the blinds, undressed and made love to her the rest of the day.

They went to the Metropolitan Museum of Art the next morning. It seemed a nutty thing to do, but she was crazy to go, woke up with the plan in mind, talked about it all through breakfast. She was even more insistent when she found out that Max had never been inside the museum. Disbelieving, really.

"Oh, Max, really? Poor Max. It's so sad. Truly it is a terrible omission in your life."

"There haven't been many." He grinned.

"I'll make a list and we'll try to get to them all. OK?"

"Sure. OK."

"I don't know how you could have lived so many years in New York City and not gone to the Metropolitan Museum of Art."

"It was easy. And anyway, Luise was always the museum goer."

"But before Luise?"

"I lived in Bridgeport."

"Oh, I see," she said as if just hearing about someone's passing. "I used to go to the museum every Saturday. It was a ritual. And I'd go alone. It was the only place Mom ever allowed me to go alone. She'd put me on the Seventy-second Street crosstown and then I'd walk the rest of the way. I had to be home in the winter by four because it got dark early and in the summer by five. I knew everyone in the museum—just everyone. At one time I thought I might like to grow up and be a curator. Then I realized it was so like a church. Rather holy. People whisper and walk lightly and stand prayerlike in front of the paintings. I liked that holy feeling. We weren't the religious sort. I recall Mom taking me to the Easter services at Hollywood Bowl one year, but that's all. I wouldn't go to a church service I'm sure, but I did like the feeling of holiness, of sacred silence in the Met. I'm talking too much. Tell me to stop."

"Stop."

"Of course, there was the theatrical side of it, too. We could never afford theater, things like that. The Planetarium and the Science Museum cost money. Did you know that?"

"I've been to those."

"Have you! They were closest to the hotel. I could have walked and used the fare for entrance, but I just had this thing for the Met. As I was saying, it was like going to the theater. Better, really, because I could make up my own plot. You could stand in front of any of the great paintings and sooner or later, you could be there—in that time—familiar with those people."

"Dirty theater, eh?"

"Umm. Sometimes. Particularly the Victorians."

"The Victorians?"

"You just know what went on behind all those fans. My favorite rooms are the Egyptian ones, though."

"I wouldn't think you would be inclined toward all those mummies."

"But in a way they're here forever, aren't they? Not like flowers, or bugs, or animals in the forest, or you or me. *Forever*."

"When do you want to go?"

"Can we go now? *May* we?"

"Sure. Want to walk?"

"I'd love that." She got up from the chair she had been sitting in. "Could we stay there a long time? Until lunch?"

"If you can hold out, so can I."

"The restaurant's all palm greens and fountains. That was very special, you see? I never went for lunch. Mom always fed me first, but I'd stand by the fountains and watch."

"The restaurant's a must then."

She went to pass him. He slapped her on the rear.

"Don't do that, Mr. Seaman, or we'll never get to the Met," she whispered.

"Is that what you meant the first time?"

"I haven't thought about it, but I probably did." She was over near the bedroom, and she came back and put her arms around his neck and pressed her body to him and kissed him gently on the lips. "There," she said and pulled away, running into the bedroom to get her purse. "That was because you're such a good daddy," she called back to him.

They walked on the park side of the street and she peered over the fence and into the children's zoo. At Seventy-second, they sat down on a bench. She had stuffed rolls and bread into her purse from the breakfast tray and she sat there and fed the pigeons until all the bread was gone. Then she took his hand as if leading the way for him into the unknown and held tightly to him until they reached the giant façade of the museum. She broke from him then and started up the long front staircase alone. Then she stopped and came running back and linked her arm through his.

"No. We're sharing something private. Something of mine. It's my present to you. OK?"

He squeezed her closer to him, and they walked up together.

"We'll start up and work our way down," she said.

He followed wherever she led and watched her in all her attitudes.

"You're supposed to be looking at the art," she reprimanded in a whisper.

"I am," he whispered back.

She gave him a stern look and continued on.

They walked on in silence, cherishing these moments together. She was ahead of him, her back to him, the sun on her back, lighting the wild ends of her long hair. He closed in the space between them and reached for her hand. She took it and raised it to her lips and brushed them against his knuckles and then lowered their hands to their sides. They were standing close together, and she seemed enraptured as she studied a Raphael.

They didn't get back to the hotel until after two. There was a message from Luise, and he realized then that he had forgotten to call her the night before as he had promised. Somehow it seemed possible to discuss anything, say anything to Melissa. He could say, "I have a message from Luise, and I have to call," without hesitation or embarrassment for either of them.

"I'll take a bath so you can have some privacy."

"You took one this morning."

"Umm. But I have so many nice new images to dream about. The tub is the best place."

Switzerland was at least civilized. He was able to get through almost immediately.

"This was a sudden decision, wasn't it, Max?" Luise said.

"Not really. It's been at the back of my mind."

"Is it unbearable there?"

"It's hot. I don't mind. How's the house working out?"

"Fine. Furnished outlandishly. Neo-Russian, I think, but it's comfortable and the view is lovely and the children seem to be happy."

"Oh, is Tony with you already?"

"You know school ended day before yesterday."

"I forgot. How's Thea?"

"She's met some young people and is having a nice time."

"Good."

"Max . . ."

"Yeah?"

"When you're finished in New York, you could take a direct flight to Geneva."

"I'm not sure what my plans will be. I may have to go back to London first."

"We shouldn't be apart this long or this often."

"Well, it's a tough business. It can't be helped."

"I have a good staff here, Max, and the children are really very reliable. If you go back to London, I could meet you there and then we can come back to Geneva together."

"Let's worry about that when the time comes."

"All right, Max."

"I'll call you in a couple of days."

"I've been thinking, Max."

"Yeah?"

"Well, while you're in New York, you should check into a hospital and have a thorough examination."

"What for? I never felt better."

"You've been looking tired."

"The damned picture just dragged on so. I feel fine now."

"Thursday? You'll call on Thursday?"

"Yeah."

"Max, I love you."

"That's good, Luise. Give my love to the kids. Tell Thea to write me at the Sherry Netherlands."

"Max . . ."

"Me, too, Luise."

"Say it, Max."

"I love you, Luise."

"Good-bye."

" 'Bye."

She had come out of the bathroom, and she was wearing another one of her crazy outfits.

"You want to buy some clothes? We can go shopping this afternoon," he suggested.

"That would be fun. We could get you some really mod clothes. We could get matching pea coats at the Army and Navy Store."

"That wasn't exactly what I had in mind."

"Do you hate the idea?"

"No, I don't hate anything you could think up, but this afternoon let's go to Saks' or Bergdorf's and then tomorrow if you like, we can patronize the Army and Navy."

A fly had managed its way into the room and was buzzing around Max and he smacked at it and missed.

"Oh, don't," she said.

She cupped her hands and ran around the room trying to corner it and finally succeeded. "Open the window," she told him.

"It carries disease, contagion, infection—didn't you ever hear about the Black Plague?"

"Open the window, please."

He did and she thrust her hand out and freed the fly.

"Now he's homeless, poor fly," Max joked.

"But safer."

She went in and washed her hands. "I'm ready for Bergdorf's," she said when she joined him again, "so you'd better bring lots of money."

She bought very little. An umbrella that caught her eye in robin's-egg blue ("Della Robbia nearly," she said in a laugh), a humorous daisy-patterned suitcase, a flowered chiffon scarf, one rather elegant white jersey Grecian dress, a pair of gold slippers to wear with it, a white cloth gardenia for her hair, and a small music box with a dancing couple in it who did the tango to the strains of "Temptation." She let them send everything but the music box to the hotel. She insisted on carrying the last unwrapped, and as they walked, she would wind it up to listen to and to watch the little man in his black tails and the little woman in her orange gown twirl and dip and pop up and down and she would look at Max and they would laugh uproariously, not caring that the New Yorkers that pushed past them thought they were mad.

Chapter 31

"Why aren't you socially conscious anymore?" she asked.

She had just joined him in bed after her third bath of the day. The lights were still on, and he had been reading, as he waited for her, a book he had bought that day when they had passed a bookstore. Stone's *Lust for Life*. She had bought a volume of Emily Dickinson, and it rested now on the bedside table on her side of the bed. He put his book down, and she never picked hers up. Her body was still slightly damp from her bath, and she was lying on top of the covers while he was underneath them. They had been to the theater that evening and seen a big, brassy hit musical which had been her selection but which both of them had hated equally. She had worn the white jersey dress. They had not run into anyone he knew. But he realized if he had, he wouldn't have cared. They had been in New York for three days and had spent their evenings until this one, curled up together, talking, making love, watching television. Tomorrow he would have to tend to some business and leave her alone part of the day. He was already concerned about that. He really didn't like the idea of her being alone in a city like New York, even for a few hours.

"Who said I'm not?" he replied to her question.

"Me." She rolled over on her stomach and put her arm over his chest. "You're not involved. None of you are anymore. None that I know, that is. You're violent about the past, about what happened during the haunts, before—*to you, your friends*—but how about all the kids who might have to go to war, all the issues now, happening now, about to happen, things that might not happen if you all got involved?"

"I care a lot about those kids, Melissa, about the advent of future wars. Once, when I was young like you, I joined groups, protested. It would be impossible for me to do that now."

"Why?"

"Just take me on my word. It's impossible. But I think my films have social content. I'm not interested in making films that don't."

"Well, we're into a discussion on semantics. What you call social content, maybe I don't. Certainly there is a lot of self-revealment in your films, and you lived during a period in which certain things were happening and it's still pretty relevant, but it still isn't *now*. I want to ask you a question."

"Shoot."

"Did you vote in the last election?"

"Yeah, I did."

"Well, I'm glad of that, at least. Daddy didn't. I couldn't believe it. He said it didn't matter one way or the other. But how could that be so? Of course, it matters."

Her hair was falling over her face, and he pushed it back for her, anchoring it behind her ears. "You wrote your parents, as I asked you to do, didn't you, Melissa?"

"Right away. Before we left London. They had it the next day as I sent it express. I told them that I had a job and was taken care of and that I needed to be left alone to find myself but that I was OK and that I loved them. I wrote that over and over, that I was OK and that I loved them. I do. Very much. They're just so desperate. I guess because there is so much truth and reality for them to face. Great disasters and losses in life do that—bring all the truths and realities boiling up to the surface."

"Yes," he said gently. "They sure do. Come on, get under the covers. You're shivering."

She crawled in beside him and huddled close to him. "I guess we have to think about tomorrow," she said.

"I'll only be gone a few hours. You can go shopping if you like. Take in the Army and Navy surplus."

"No, I didn't mean that literally. I meant after we leave New York. When we go back to London." She held him tighter to her.

"I won't give you up, baby."

"It will be terrible for you."

"It will be just as tough for you."

"Only insofar as Thea is concerned. I love Thea. I don't want her to hate me."

"Some things none of us can prevent. Thea is my daughter. She'll understand."

"Oh, I hope so. I do hope so." She pulled away to turn out the light and he drew her back in close to him.

"Leave it on."

"All right, Max. Anything you say."

She had said that she wouldn't mind being alone, but now that she was she minded very much. It occurred to her that she had seldom been really alone before. As a small child she had been able to spend hours she considered alone in that warm and comfortable room of hers under the eaves. But her mother and father were always downstairs, and though she couldn't see the neighbor's house, she knew it belonged to a Mr. Lake, who was a nice man, who from time to time let her ride one of the ponies he owned. In New York she had gone to the museum on Saturdays, and in a way that was being alone, but, of course, she always carried the telephone number of the hotel they lived in, and the museum guards could be more or less counted as friends. London had been different. There was no time she could ever be alone. It had been one of the things she had thought she had been the most desperate for—that feeling of aloneness. She had felt so unbelievably cramped, trapped. But this moment she realized she was truly alone for the first time in her life. She knew no one in New York. The museum guards had not even recognized her, though she had remembered the few from her childhood who were still working there. She knew no one at this hotel, and the small hotel where she had once lived with her parents had been torn down and a high rise built in its place. She had had Max ask the taxi to swing by there on their way home from the theater the night before. It had made her sad that the place was gone. The fact was that she had inwardly cried, and of course, on the surface that seemed ridiculous. The hotel had been old and beyond repair and the guests were forced to take shelter there (for no one would have remained there by choice). It had been an unhappy time in her life, bleak really. (But when had there been happy times? Oh! There had! California. And that summer in Italy with Thea, and these last three miraculously happy days with Max!) Still, the hotel had been a part of her life; little bits of herself had been left behind there. She remembered now her mother crying when she found out their possessions in California were being sold by the storage company to satisfy the bills, and she understood. For the first time she truly understood.

If she wanted to call Max, she would have no place to reach him. And if anything happened to him out there, in the world beyond, would anyone even tell her? She doubted it. He was married. He had a wife. No one even knew she was here in New York with him. If he died out there in the wilderness of this city, the first she might know of it would be when the hotel manager came up or called to ask her to vacate the suite. Where would she go then? What would she do?

Max had given her a hundred dollars before he left in the morning, in case she had wanted to go shopping. But then, a hundred dollars wouldn't get her back to England. Anyway, she would not want to go back to England alone. A hundred dollars would not go very far in New York. Still, it would mean she wasn't destitute. She went into the bedroom where the five twenties Max had left on the dresser for her were and took them and tucked them into the pocket of her dress. It was of sheer material and the bulge the new, stiff money made scratched reassuringly against her thighs. She would not go shopping. She would keep the money. She would stay right here in the hotel suite where everything was familiar and where the scent of Max's after shave still lingered and where the ashes from his endless chain of cigarettes filled the ashtrays and where the remnants of his lather still clung to the enamel of the bathroom sink. But of course, the maid would soon come in, and all those things would be gone, scrubbed and brushed and emptied and disinfected. Gone. *Forever*. His clothes would still be there. But they weren't the same. They were not truly evidence of his livingness.

She crossed over to the telephone and called the housekeeper and told her she had a slight headache and wanted to rest, and would they mind not cleaning the room until after lunch sometime? It had to be before three, the housekeeper told her. And she replied that that was fine. Three o'clock would be just fine. And she had disconnected and breathed with a sense of relief. She had time then. Maybe Max would be back by then. He'd be angry the place was still a mess because she really wasn't terribly organized or neat, and besides Max's cigarette ashes and his soap remains, there seemed to be a lot of her own clutter in the room. She began to pick up after herself, and she was immediately glad for something to do.

When she finished, she decided she had done a pretty good job. She ordered herself a fresh pot of coffee, and when it arrived, she took the tray into the bedroom and got in on Max's side of the bed and put the tray down on hers and propped up all the pillows behind her and drank the coffee slowly.

She could, of course, play Scarlett O'Hara and tell herself she would think about it all tomorrow. But it was no good. It really wasn't in her nature. Before she had called Max that evening, she had thought about it a lot and for a very long time. It was all very difficult to understand or to explain—even to herself. She had never been boy-or-man-crazy in her entire life. In fact, no other male had ever attracted her. She hadn't been like Thea assessing, testing, playing out little scenes with every guy she met. There were always so many things on her mind that there seemed to be no place or room for games. Her head was always so crowded. Sometimes she wished she could drill a little hole in her brain and let out all the thoughts crowding it. She thought of sex, of course. But it had been a dissociated thing, not having anything to do with the male faces and bodies and voices that walked across her path from time to time. It was really a private emotion—sex—like happiness or excitement or sadness or tears. Max had changed that. She had been conscious of its happening long before she met him. When Thea talked about him, and her father cursed at him, and she had gone secretly to see his films. His presence just seemed to be all around her. She'd sit in the movie house watching his people, his thoughts, through his eyes—because the camera was Max's eyes, and that wonderful-terrible tightening in her chest would begin, the drumming in her ears, the flush, the strange ache between her legs. There was something magnetizing about a man who made such films, who had a daughter like Thea who loved him so, who could trigger such hate in her own father. And of course, when she met Max that first time, she understood. It was in the depth and mocking and battle in his eyes, in the timbre and stir and challenge in his voice, in the stalk and the pursuit and the decision in his step. Max was a life-force, as though his presence and even his nonpresence were a source of spiritual adrenaline. Max brought out the best and worst in you. The feelings you hoped but did not know you were capable of until he had touched your life.

Somehow, before she ever met him, Max represented a solid rope to get her up the mountain, even though the cliffside was falling away and into the sea. And after she met him, he was the giant shade tree at the top of that mountain—a God-like man who could grow on top of a mountain and still give a person the feeling that there was a more tortuous but rewarding climb ahead that only he could reveal. From that moment, it had seemed impossible to live without Max. What had taken her a year to decide was whether it would be possible to live *with* him.

She was not sorry she had finally made her decision and left her parents' house and gone to his office. No matter what happened, she was certain that she would never regret that decision.

She began to weave fantasies—or were they?—as to what the future might hold. They might not have to return to London. Maybe they could go back to California, away from Thea and her mother and from her own parents. Time would heal all the hurt. Or Max could quit films altogether and write novels and they could go to some mountain place or some ocean place or some forest place and she would tend and love him and he would write about her, about them—as he had always written for the screen about all the other people in his life.

She knew they were fantasies, though. It wouldn't happen that way. Max was compulsive about film. It was by now an incurable habit. He could exist only if he went on feeding it, and as his existence meant so much to so many other lives, she knew there was no way out. They would return to London. At least they had the summer. But in September, Luise would be back and what then? More terrifying, Thea would be back, expecting her to go to RADA with her, and of course, that was impossible. It was impossible for her ever to be a girl again, rooming with another girl, attending classes. She could become an actress all the same. It mattered to her as it always did, but not in the same way with Thea. Thea had felt, did feel about acting as she had felt, did feel about Max. What seemed all wrong, mixed up, totally out of sync, was the fact that she would be able to succeed as an actress without RADA, without any further training really, and Thea had to have it, and it meant so much less to her than to Thea. She would have liked to give Thea her natural talent, just pass it on to her, as she had given the moments of her girlhood to Max when they had gone to the museum together. But had she really? She didn't know. It seemed terribly important, but she didn't honestly know and could never know because one could not crawl into a man's brain and know what he was thinking, or feeling, or retaining.

The coffee was cold by now, and she had forgotten to drink it. She put the cup down and moved the tray away and squashed herself down in the bed, pulling the covers up tightly over her. When she tried, she could remember the night before, could tune in flashes of remembrance that seemed to fill her completely. *Max*, she thought, *I do love you. Truly, truly love you.* She concentrated on those words, trying to blot out everything else. Then she said over and over again to herself, *Love me, love me, love me.* And then, turning over and clutching the pillows which still held the scent of his hair and his skin, *Come back, come back, come back.* It was like an incantation, a form of voodoo. *Come back, come back, come back.* She insisted to herself that she was in effect attempting to will him back to her side, to the bed, before she had to get up, before the maid came. But she was more aware of the real truth than she cared to admit to herself. She was afraid he might not come back. Always she would be afraid he would not return. Happiness had never been hers to keep, or security, or warmth. It seemed the natural course of things that this pattern would in fact persist.

Come back, come back, come back.

The telephone rang beside her, and her first instinct was to answer it immediately in the belief that her chants had been somehow miraculously successful and that Max was on the other end of the wire just wanting to hear her voice, or asking her to join him, or finding out if she was still there so that he could join her. Then she dropped the arm that she had raised to lift the receiver, and even she laughed because it looked so comical, dropped so suddenly that way.

It could be *for* Max. Could be a business call, in which case Max might not want her to answer, might not be ready for people to know about them. Of course, that was silly. She could be a secretary doing some work in the suite for him, could be the maid. No. A secretary seemed more likely. She thought she recalled that hotel maids were not permitted to answer the telephone of guests.

It was still ringing, and in a quick decision she picked up the receiver.

"Mr. Seaman's suite," she managed in a convincing secretarial tone.

"Overseas calling Mr. Seaman."

"He isn't here at present, but he's expected back later this afternoon."

"Just a moment, please."

Melissa switched the receiver to the other hand. She was for some reason sweaty and nervous. It was taking quite a while. She thought she might hang up, but then they would just ring back, keep ringing. She lighted a cigarette and took a deep puff.

"The party will speak to whoever is at this end."

"But I'm only a temporary secretary, the hotel stenographer."

"Hello? Hello?" It was Thea and she seemed to be coming through a long tunnel. She was whispering. Or at least it seemed as if she were whispering.

Melissa reached for a voice to use. Something with New York in it. Something foreign to Thea's ears. She pretended she had a wad of gum in her mouth. "This is the public stenographer. Mr. Seaman isn't here."

"Lis, is that you?"

"I said—"

"Lis, oh, Lis, I've been worried sick. Your mom called here last night. They seemed to think I might know where you are and I told them I hadn't known you left home, that you hadn't contacted me. But after I hung up . . . all night . . . Lord, it's six in the morning here and I've been up all night. That's why I'm talking so softly; everyone else is asleep. But I can't explain how, Lis—I just *knew*. It was incredible. I *knew*."

"I am afraid—"

"For God's sake, Lissa, *stop it!* I'm sorry; truly I'm sorry. I didn't mean to yell. I *daren't* yell. In terms of you, Lis, please understand. I'm not angry. I don't blame you. I'm worried about you, Lis. I'm terribly, terribly worried about you. Lis, are you there?"

"As I said—"

"Lis!"

"Yes, yes, Thea. I'm here." Unaccountably she began to cry.

"Now, Lis, don't cry. Just listen to me. I love you. I'm not angry, and I don't blame you. And I love my father, too. Is he there?"

"N-no."

"I love him, too. But I am angry and blame him. I may never forgive him. If anything happens to you, I know I never could forgive him. Don't cry, Lis. Please stop it. Listen to me. You see, I understand, Lis. I truly do. Always have. I was just hoping and praying you would hold out, be able to hold out, until this fall, when you would have been out of the house anyway. Then you would have had your studies and I would have been there and I was hoping that would have pulled you through. You see, I *do* understand. All that anxiety in you. All that life being bottled up, held back. You had to cut free, but you've been sick, Lis. I've seen it, know it. I think you've been having a nervous breakdown, may have already had one—Lis? Lis?"

"Umm. . . ."

"Now look, Lis, I know you probably think you're in love with my father—all my life I've thought I was. Maybe I still am. Will always be. He's that kind of a person. And I'm sure—oh, God, I hope—he believes he's in love with you. But you could decide it's not right, or he could decide that. And if that should happen, I'm not saying it will, *but if it should*, I want you to call me instantly. I have some money of my own. I'll cable it to you. I'll meet you someplace. Wherever you think you want to go. Lis? Lis? Are you there? Are you all right?"

Melissa had managed to subdue her tears by then. Her body felt hot and her head heavy, but somehow she was glad Thea's voice was so close. "You don't hate me, Thea?" she said softly.

"No, no, of course not, Lis. I could kill my father. Just kill him. But I don't hate *you*. Believe me."

"I never wanted to hurt anyone."

"I understand that."

"I'll write you, Thea. Is that all right?"

"Yes, of course. Take down this number, too. You have a pencil?"

"Yes."

"Geneva . . . 022-23-26-12 . . . Got that?"

"Yes."

"You have the address. I gave it to you before I left. Remember: Cable or call collect if you need me. OK?"

"OK, Thea. Thea! Oh! I just wanted to say, to assure you, Thea—I love your father very much, and I would be very sad if I thought I had come between you two."

"You just worry about yourself. 'Bye, Lis."

" 'Bye, Thea. 'Bye."

She lay there for nearly a half hour unable to move. Her legs were throbbing, and her head was heavy, and waves of leaden pain moved across her stomach. She was hot, and the air conditioning didn't seem to be working. She kicked off the covers. She thought she was going to be sick, and she stumbled off the bed and into the bathroom. Her period had begun, and the blood came before she could do anything about it. Warm and sticky, distasteful, blemishing the white flesh on the inside of her thighs. Twisted and deformed as it writhed down the inside of her legs. Staining, discoloring. *Hideous. Hideous,* she thought. She was in a state of terror, and only the terrible pain she felt shocked her out of it. She was doubled over with it. She worked with convulsive motion as she turned on the shower and managed somehow to step inside. She knew it wouldn't be possible to stop the flow of blood, but she felt as if she had to attempt to wash herself clean. She turned the shower on full force, and the pellets of water stung her, and she concentrated on their steady bee-sting assaults trying to wipe out the other pain, the other terror. The blood was paler now, diluted, but only until she turned the water off. She was crying. Perhaps she was even screaming. They wouldn't hear her. She wasn't sure she could hear herself. She leaned against the wet tile wall. There was nothing to hold onto, and she felt as if she were about to fall. She held her breath, trying to hold back the pain, the blood, the fainting spell she sensed possible, and reached out desperately for the security of the towel rack beside the shower. She touched it and exerted all her strength and pulled herself over the rim of the shower cubicle. She stood there breathing deeply, not knowing what to do. The telephone was ringing, but she knew even if she could have gotten to it, she would not have been able to lift the receiver. Never. Ever. She stood shivering (though curiously she did not feel cold) until the ringing finally stopped.

Then she wrapped herself in towels, all that the hotel had supplied. She looked like a mummy. She looked terribly funny, and if she could have laughed at herself, she would have done so. She felt the warm, oozing trickle of blood travel down the inside of her leg again and to her ankle. It remained there crazily as if unable to make the short fall from her ankle to the bare tile floor. She hobbled into the bedroom and fell down on the bed. And she sobbed. She could hear her sobs. They filled her whole conscious-ness. But she knew no one else could. She was alone. The maid wouldn't come in until three. Max wouldn't be back until then either, for he was meeting some men for lunch. She drew herself up into a fetal position, and that didn't help, so she lifted herself into the prone-knee position, but that made her nauseated. She dropped flat on her stomach, and somehow that was better. The pressure helped. She sobbed some more, and finally she fell asleep.

By the time Max came in at five she was cool and collected and dressed. The maid had gotten her some pills, and whatever they were they numbed the pain. She sat stiffly on the edge of the couch, fearful that any sudden move would impel another gush of blood. She sat there like that, not getting up to greet him, not rising as he bent to kiss her.

"I'm only going to be here long enough to shower and change," he said. He was sweaty but smiling and happy. Things had gone well with him then. "I have to meet Art Frankel for drinks down-stairs in fifteen minutes. I would have asked him up here, but I thought you'd prefer it this way. I'll only be an hour at the outside."

He was already in the bedroom. She could hear the plunk as his suit jacket hit the top of the bed, then his pants.

"You'll be OK here, won't you?" he called.

"Goodness, it's only an hour."

For a moment the terror rose in her again. What if all the blood had not been washed down the drain? What if little particles clung between the tiles, around the drain? She heard the rush of water. *He was singing. Good God! He was singing.*

He came back into the living room, one fresh bath towel tied around him, drying his hair with a smaller one. "You OK, baby? You look pale."

"I'm fine. Just reflective."

He started back out of the room, and she picked up the hotel magazine off the coffee table and opened it, but she caught him out of the side of her eyes, looking at her, studying her. She instantly directed her entire attention to the magazine.

"We can go out tonight if you like," he suggested.

"That would be nice." But she never looked up.

In a few minutes he reappeared dressed coolly in a tan, lightweight suit. She thought he looked handsome. She liked the way he smelled. She was refreshed by the touch of his cool hand and his cool freshly shaved cheek.

"Only an hour," he whispered and kissed her on the forehead.

And then, suddenly, more violently, she was alone again.

They had gone to a play, and it had been so dull he had fallen asleep during the second act, and they had left before the third. She wasn't hungry and asked if he wouldn't mind eating in their room.

"Of course not, baby," he had said and squeezed her body to him in the taxi.

She felt swollen and heavy and sick again, and she hadn't asked the maid for any extra pills. They ordered dinner, but she couldn't eat. She drank several cognacs, and they helped. At least she thought they helped.

She wore a nightgown when she came to bed. He smiled. "Oh, that's it." He grinned.

"Do you mind?"

"Sure as hell do, but that's life, and sometimes the old girl gets the upper hand."

He patted her gently on her nylon-covered rear and pulled the cover over her and tucked her in. Then he rolled over and away and was asleep almost as soon as his head settled on the pillow.

Chapter 32

Max woke up to the jangling, jarring sound of the telephone by his ear. Before he lifted the receiver to stop the infernal ringing, he glanced at his watch. It was ten ten. He had overslept. He was to have met Arthur Frankel at his office at ten. Probably him calling now. Melissa stirred, turned. She looked disconcerted in her sleep. Her forehead was furrowed unevenly, and her mouth seemed to be trembling. But she was sleeping soundly enough not to have heard the telephone.

"Yeah?" He yawned into the mouthpiece.

"Merwin Bibbs, Max."

It was Bibbs all right. The voice was filled with the same old cold hostility, but it was edged with something new. A driving force. Max played for time, angry at the operator for putting an overseas call straight through. Melissa could have answered. It could have been that close.

"What can I do for you, Merwin?"

"Tell me where Melissa is."

"Melissa?"

She stirred, opened her eyes. "Umm?"

Max reached under the covers for her hand and held on tightly to it.

"*Melissa.* I can't voice my fears, Max. But I've been calling everyone I know. Everyone. Her mother's frantic. We got a letter. But she's only eighteen, Max. *Eighteen.* About the same age as your daughter. I finally heard—someone saw her at the Metropolitan Museum of Art. *Thought* they saw her. An old friend of ours.

303

She thought it was Melissa but was too far away and she couldn't catch her eye. She got back to London and called. 'Melissa in New York?' she asked. It made sense to her mother and me. It was a strong possibility. That had been one of her favorite places when she had been a girl. So I came to New York."

Jesus!

"Flew in last night. God knows how I'm going to pay for it, but as I said, her mother's frantic, and I'm just as concerned. Melissa is what you might call an overemotional girl."

"Well, Mer"—he grabbed her hand tighter—"if I can help in any way at all. I could loan you some money. I could certainly do that."

"You bastard! Never mind all that bullshit, Seaman—just tell me where Melissa is? With you? Is she there with you? I saw Art Frankel early this morning. He said he heard you were—God help me—shacked up with a young girl."

"Well, Mer, I've never been a paragon of virtue. But there is young and there is *young*."

"I'm coming up to your room."

"You downstairs?"

"I am."

"I'll come down. Just wait there, Mer. I'll be right down."

He dropped the receiver back into the cradle, but it was askew, and the phone wasn't disconnected. He swore as he straightened it and jumped out of bed at the same time.

Melissa seemed unable to move.

"Come on, baby. Get up. Get dressed." He was slipping into his pants. "I'll handle it. Don't worry. But it's best if you're dressed at least. He's never going to stay down in that lobby."

"I can't see him. I just can't."

He threw on the same shirt he had worn the night before and buttoned it as he headed for the bathroom. "Maybe you won't have to," he called back, "but I think you had better be prepared."

She lay there in the bed perfectly still.

He came back in the bedroom and sat down on the edge of the bed to put on his stockings and shoes. "Up, baby, *up!*" He leaned across the bed to her, brushed back her hair from her face, lifted her hand in his, and kissed it. "It will be all right. Now believe me, it will. I love you. Just remember that. OK? I love you." He straightened, stood up, grabbed the tie he had slung over a doorknob the night before. "If your father does come up, I'll keep him in the living room, but in the meantime, pick up all your things and stuff them under the bed if you have to and get dressed. If he does find you here, I'll handle it. OK?"

There was a knock on the door to the suite.

"Jesus! *Melissa—*"

She rolled over and slowly swung her feet over the edge of the bed. She sat there as if still half asleep. He patted her on the knee. "Try to be quiet, baby. And remember—*I love you.*" He smiled to reassure her, and she tried to smile back and must have succeeded because he seemed relieved and easier as he left her there and went toward the bedroom door. "You OK?" She nodded, and he went out and closed the door securely.

"She's not here, Merwin. You'll have to take my word for it. But she is in New York, and she is all right."

"You bastard!"

Merwin came at him with clenched fists, but Max sidestepped him and then grabbed hold of him, holding him in a tight vise.

"I was brought up in the slums, Mer. You're no match for me. Don't try to be heroic." Merwin was struggling to get loose, and Max pitched him away and free. Merwin stood in the middle of the room breathing heavily, his face a dangerous high-blood-pressure red.

"Some things happen, Merwin. Like the tide or night. You can't stop them happening. I won't lie to you. I don't want to or need to. Melissa is eighteen—and I said, there is young, and there is *young*. She's a woman, Mer. And goddamn, I love her and she loves me. Now that's how it is. I haven't had time to figure out what to do about Luise. She'll have to divorce me. There's no other way. But I'll protect Melissa to the best of my ability. And even you, Mer"—he grinned, looking up through the tops of his eyes, flicking his hand against the side of his nose, looking like a winning fighter—"even you have to admit I'm pretty damn good at infighting and keeping some distance between myself and my opponents. I'll keep Melissa *behind me.* She'll be all right."

"Where is she, Max?" Merwin asked sharply.

"Safe. Protected."

"Where?"

"In one of the best hotels in the city."

"Here?"

"You're pushing it, Mer."

"In that bedroom? Behind that door? Melissa?" He started toward it. "Melissa?"

There was silence. Merwin stood there undecided.

"OK, Mer, open the door. Go in. If Melissa *was* there, what would you do then? Grab her, take her by force with you? You couldn't do it, Mer. No way. She wouldn't go, and I wouldn't let you lay a finger on her, so that's how it is."

Merwin stood there. His face grew redder and then seemed to pale suddenly. Max thought the man might keel right over, might be seized by a heart attack. He moved toward him.

"Don't dare touch me," Merwin said. Slowly he caught his breath and with great dignity came back into the room and faced Max. "I'm staying with Sol Levitz on West Eighty-sixth," he said. "It's in the book. Ask Melissa to call me. I just want to talk to her. I want to assure myself she's all right. Her mother's a nervous wreck. She should call her, too."

"I'll make sure she does that."

"I'd like to see her."

"That's up to Melissa."

"Not really, Max." Merwin kept his gaze steady. He was shorter than Max, and he had to raise his chin at an angle. "You are a terrible man, Max. I don't know how it's possible for you to live with yourself."

"Are we talking about Melissa?"

"In part." Merwin stood there staring at Max.

Max moved away, toward the window. As he stood there he was conscious of the image of Harry Steiner standing just about where he now stood and he where Merwin was. It unnerved him, like the feeling of witnessing a scene that is all too familiar. He was conscious of falling back on an old habit of cracking his knuckles. The sound was the only one in the room. The way Merwin stood there, unmoving, eyes never flinching from the light behind Max, he had the queasy sense of being on trial, on the witness stand. He seemed forced to open up an offense.

"Merwin, I think you'd better face it. If you weren't one of the first, one of the ten, do you really believe you would have had the guts to take the stand you did?"

"Of course."

"Your hand trembled just now, Merwin. I saw it. Somewhere deep down at your nerve endings you're not sure. And you're an honest man, Mer. I really do believe that. You don't lie to yourself. That's why you're so constantly tortured. As a Jew, Mer, I sympathize. Hell, there isn't a Jew alive who isn't tortured. *You think I would have stood up to the Nazis?* Fact is, Mer, none of the living are sure. And that same thing applies to the haunts, Mer. You're not sure."

"Like hell!"

He was more in control now. Something morbid forced him to continue. "You hate me, Mer. Actually you don't like anyone too much, including yourself. But you hate me and it makes sense to me. Because I represent your conscience in a way—your own guilt. You'd like to be where I am today, Mer, and you figure if you hadn't been one of the ten, you might be. That's why you wear that year like a badge, for your own sanity you have to."

"It would be a waste of time to answer you, Max. A man like you couldn't possibly understand."

"Shit, Merwin. That's all a mouthful of shit. And I have to tell you one thing more; it's been bottled up in me for a hell of a long time, Merwin. If you *hadn't* been one of the ten, you still wouldn't be where I am. You see, you were a hack, oh, a reliable one—but a B-picture man, with pretensions and intelligence. The worst kind. You were never very talented, Mer. And your self-crucifixion made you unpleasant to be around as well. You're a bore and a drag and old hat as a writer as well."

"Through?"

"You want to turn the other cheek?"

Merwin started to the door. "I wouldn't even waste my spit on you," he said.

Something worried Max. He wasn't sure what it was. Not Merwin Bibbs. He could handle Merwin Bibbs in his sleep. No. It was Melissa. He began to move uneasily toward the bedroom door.

"Tell Melissa I'll listen to anything she has to say. I'm not an unreasonable man. I will most naturally try to persuade her to come home with me, but I'm not unreasonable."

Then there it was. Somewhere at the back of Max's brain, somewhere buried in the back of his hearing, stabbing him deep from inside his chest. *A scream!* It nearly shattered his eardrums. It did blur his vision, but it did not cripple his reactions. He ran toward the bedroom and swung open the door.

"Melissa!" he shouted.

Merwin had followed closely on his heels. "My God, what is it? *What is it!*"

The window was open wide, and Max leaped toward it. He looked down. She hadn't screamed. No one had even heard her. She was lying crumpled up on the pavement close to the hotel, and no one had even seen her yet.

"Don't look," he commanded Merwin.

But the father pushed him aside. "My God, oh, my God! *Melissa!*"

He turned back into the room. He was ashen. Max went to put his arm around his shoulders, needing the human touch, instinctively thinking they were bound together this moment in despair.

Merwin shook loose. "You louse," he said, fighting back the convulsive sobs that would soon come. "You louse!" And he walked out of the bedroom and across the living room and into the corridor before he permitted himself the release of his anguish.

Just outside the window, a fly was buzzing.

She wanted it to be free, Max thought. And for some insane, inexplicable reason, he knew he was right.

Chapter 33

DEAR DAD,

I am not sending you back the check you sent me mainly because money really has little meaning and you are my father and somehow, I think I am entitled to an education. I did not, as you suggest, *miss* you in Geneva. I made sure I was on my way as soon as I knew you were coming. And I am not in New York City, as you seem to think, to see shows and forget. I am here to be reminded that I may never forget and to line myself up for the fall as I have decided against RADA and in favor of Mr. Strasberg if he will accept me.

I don't know yet what I feel for you. It is too early and the wound still too fresh. I do know that I never want to see you again and hope you honor my decision in this matter and don't force a confrontation in any way.

You knew! I warned you. But I can't help feeling *you knew*. You are too sensitive, too tuned in, too knowing. *You knew*, and still you allowed it to happen. Encouraged it. I can never forgive you, and I can't see how you can ever forgive yourself. I hope you don't. I mean that. I hope you are never able to.

I hope you know what is happening to Tony, too. Can see it. I never knew Tony before this summer. I don't know why that's so, but it is. He's a beautiful human being and I love him. But he's damaged and I think he's beyond repair, and it's your fault. And even if it's late, I think you owe it to Tony to try to make amends in some way. Though I don't know how, because he hates you so.

And I also want you to know one of the first things I did when I arrived back in the States was to take a train to Washington and go to the Congressional Library and look up the Congressional hearings on the House Un-American Activities Committee—I read your testimony. And then I understood.

I understand how a man who could betray all his friends and himself could have also done such a thing to a small wounded animal like Melissa.

ANTHEA EVANS

BOOK V

Tony

And his soul mocked him and said, "Surely thou hast but little joy out of thy love. Thou art one who in time of death pours water into a broken vessel. Thou gavest away what thou hast, and nought is given to thee in return. It were better for thee to come with me, for I know where the Valley of Pleasure lies, and what things are wrought there.

OSCAR WILDE,
"The Fisherman and His Soul"

Chapter 34

Whichever newspaper Max picked up, he was forced to read about Burt Winters. Forced was perhaps not exactly honest. No one held a gun in his back. Still, once he had seen the name in print (the formal "Burton Winters" generally used unless it was Sheilah Graham or Earl Wilson—then it was "Burt" Winters, as in "Larry" Olivier or "Doug" Fairbanks, the initial C somehow lost, unnoticed years before—B. C. Winters—*Before Christ*, and he hadn't even noticed *that*), it was as though someone had a hammerlock inside his head, a master puppeteer who pulled the strings and who, if he decided Max must read an article, would not release Max until he had. "Burt Winters, that dear man," said Sheilah, "has given over his beautiful home in Angmering, England, as a vacation home for orphan children." (Tax deduction.) "Burt Winters," said Earl Wilson, "has hit the campus circuit here and in England lecturing at his own expense on film as a form of communication. Recruiting young people into film. 'We need young enthusiasm,' says Burt," says Wilson. (Tax deduction *and* ticket seller.) "Burton Winters has established a fund"—the New York *Times*. (Tax deduction.) "Winters Wings to Four World Caps. 'We have to understand the audiences' needs worldwide if we want a universal audience for English speaking films!' says Winters." (*Variety*. Tax deduction and publicity grabber.) If he couldn't win an Oscar (and on the commercial crap he was making, all he might come up with was Best Sound Effects or Visual Effects), then he would buck for a knighthood (Sir Larry, Sir Doug, and Sir Burt). Or, at least, someone's good neighbor award.

Burt's success was a thorn in Max's own success. There was no pat explanation for it, but Max felt decidedly hostile to Burt. No matter what the name of his film, Burt always publicized himself. It was always *his* film, *his* production. "When I was making. . . ." Reviewers and critics referred to Winters' film, Winters' work, and yet Burt did not write, direct, cut, or, even in the working sense, produce his films; he had an associate producer to do that. And that killed Max, because even though the final product was a portentous piece of crap, it always did carry the fetus of intention—one of the leads was black, an unmarried mother, a Jew, a good German, a revolutionary fighting a dictatorship, et cetera, et cetera. So Burt was congratulated constantly on his *intentions,* which never really found their way as more solid stuff on films. He was also held in esteem for the various talent that did suffer through one of *his* films. The script of *Going Home* (Otis Miller), the direction on *Lot's Wife* (Stanley Nimmerman), and the camerawork on *The Final Battle* (Ellis Soames). But generally all other credits on a Burton C. Winters production were swallowed up in the publicity and good intentions of Burton C. Winters himself.

Burt's talent was the art of putting a deal together, of packaging, promoting, and selling. He was still in effect an agent. Now for himself and his own product and at that was the best in the business. Max was in New York trying to secure the final go-ahead from United Artists for his next film. They hadn't approved his budget, and they thought he needed a bigger star. He was sweating and it rankled him and there it was in print: "Winters Pax's 3 Pix Omega Deal" (*Variety*). It had to hurt.

Max hated these trips to New York. The place had become a garbage dump, an open sewer. Newspapers littered the city. ("Burt Winters" staring up at you from a gutter at Lexington and Fifty-third.) Dogs fouled the streets. The smell of urine clung to asphalt and cement and crept into hallways and elevators. People weren't clean about themselves. Restaurants were careless. And everywhere you looked, there were those stinking trash cans with human scavengers hovering over them. *The rubbish collectors. Jesus!* That was what New Yorkers had become. *A pack of rubbish collectors.* And he was a fastidious person. Always had been. Disorder drove him mad, but dirt upset him, made him nervous and itchy, in constant need of showers and a change of fresh underclothes. He loathed the idea of stepping into the back seat of a taxi where *God knows* anything could greet him. He had a limousine waiting whenever possible, but there were times when he miscalculated his needs or had to have an unscheduled meeting. He had always been sensitive to smells. That, of course, was another thing. And it was growing worse. The excrement—sexual smells came like gushers of stinking gas from the streets, the parks, the people.

Yet Luise liked it here. Actually liked it better than London. She had convinced him that they needed an apartment in New York, as well as London, and he had finally agreed. He knew damned well she really wanted an excuse to be close to Tony and Thea, who were now living in New York. That was OK. It gave him and Luise their own private worlds. Maybe, after twenty-five years of marriage, that was the best of all ways. At any rate, it had evolved into a most suitable arrangement. It meant he never had to be in New York alone, never had to stay at a New York hotel, and could hear all about Thea, remain in that way a part of her life, and he was often in London alone, where being alone did not necessarily mean that.

There had been many girls, *women*, since Melissa. It was, after all, nearly seven years since her death. He never could admit to himself it had been suicide because then there was guilt involved. Then he stood equally to blame for Melissa's death along with Merwin; with Melissa herself, who, after all, expected too much from life, was obviously too frail to be of the living. And there was the nagging possibility that he had let her down, disappointed her girl dreams of sex. But that didn't seem plausible. He had loved that kid as he had never loved another woman in his life, and hell, he had had no complaints before. He wavered in his feelings about Melissa from time to time. She had been selfish, dying on his hands, as it were, leaving impressions, insinuations worse than Burt Winters' *intentions*. She could not have loved him under the circumstances. Must, in fact, have loathed him. Her father as well. Saw them—oh, Lord—as one. It had been an act of hate. It had been an act of love. She knew she was not capable of bringing unhappiness to others, to Luise, to Thea, to her mother and father, and she knew that because of this, in the end she would have to bring unhappiness to him. She had been gallant, loving; she had taken the only way out.

They had been together only three days, but he would never forget her. She had accomplished that. Her memory, her essence, was very deep inside him, a very personal, private thing. Too private to talk about—not even to that looney headshrinker Luise had insisted they both go to (for Tony's sake, she claimed). He had quit the headshrinker when he realized that. He didn't subscribe to the entire cult of psychoanalysis anyway. "You're resisting me," that bland-faced legal voyeur had told him, as if Max were meant to be hypnotized. Damn right he resisted him! He hadn't been able to write about Melissa either. The years hadn't eased that. He had tried, but he could not. Truthfully, would not. No. She would remain crypto, hidden, inviolable. The dark in the deep of his heart, an essence, an image, *his ghost*.

He had not forced a confrontation with Anthea. He had, though, seen her from time to time. Luise had managed that. Not telling either of them the other was in town or would be at the apartment. Anthea was coldly polite. She managed a detached smile at certain intervals as if smiling at a thought, something, and someone not in their company, not truly at him. She never asked him a question, never inquired about his life, and after a while, and after the unrelenting ambiguity to his questions and inquiries, he asked her none—none at all. She would kiss her mother in parting, and if her mother were standing there, waiting, she would brush his cheek with her tightened lips as though whipping him with the tip of a cat-o'-nine. And her mother would say afterward, "See, it's all in your mind. She really does love you."

It was interesting that Luise had never mentioned Melissa. It was as though it had never happened, that perhaps the girl had merely lost touch and was married and living in Long Beach, California, or in Leeds, England. Places one never really went to or knew people from. In fact, what had happened to Luise immediately after the inadmissible was perhaps worse than insult or accusation or hostility. She became instantly overbearingly solicitous. The old censure was gone. She looked at him now with a maternal compassion that was suffocating. Her eyes said, "It's terrible. Too terrible to talk about. My poor suffering, suffering child."

She was remaining longer periods alone (except for the children, of course) in New York, and he was spending less and less time there. It was not a real marriage in the accepted sense, but it was beginning to grow into a comfortable friendship. Whatever their differences, Luise was a highly intelligent woman, and of course, she was on his side. It was possible to discuss all his business and script and filming problems with her. She was an excellent sounding board, and she knew him so well that she could often nudge an idea, a response, a story turn out of him that he had not been able to evolve himself. Sexually, his desire for her had increased. Perhaps, because they were apart so much. Perhaps, because it was easier to feel something sexual for a solicitous woman (which went back to the very basic need for supremacy) than for one who constantly accused. Luise had aged well, too. She was, after all, forty-five. Or was it forty-six? He always forgot. But she had lost none of her youthful beauty and, in fact, had added to it. Her body was just as trim, the stomach flat, the legs tight, but her breasts were fuller, her hands more expressive, her movement more confident. She had not cut her hair, but wore it long and soft, to the shoulders, keeping the gray out but frosting it, as was the style, with a gleaming blond that flashed under lights and glittered in the sun and framed her face. And it was still a lovely face. The eyes clear, the skin good, the makeup light and well used, the lips still soft and voluptuous, never setting as some women's did when they reached her age. She still smelled good, no sign of decay, and her body was alive, responsive, sometimes eager, never coy. He had written Luise into almost every script over the past twenty-five years and cast her extravagantly. She was Hayworth in one, Loren in another, Darnell once, O'Hara, even Gardner. It was like writing about a particular person and then disguising the biographical facts. He would write about an ultrafeminine, intelligent, cool, collected woman and cast her *lustily* to disguise her visually. Luise was more Hepburn than Hayworth, more Kelly than Loren, more Kerr than Darnell or O'Hara or Gardner. But he refused to see her that way on screen, for the world, for *his* audience. And casting against type like that always brought another dimension to the character, one the audience could see.

He was positive that Luise was faithful to him. Would always be. He had his nagging doubts about the past, London, *Burt Winters*. It was pure instinct, but he did think that bastard might have gotten into Luise. It was the kind of thing Burt Winters would really enjoy, screwing *his* wife. Still, he refused to admit that Luise could have been seduced that easily, that his hold on her might have wavered at any time. She was his wife, the mother of his children; she was, he was sure, to be depended upon, never to forget that.

Anthea. His heart beat faster when he thought seriously about Anthea. A form of mild tachycardia, possibly, but he was sound, fit. He could still last for two hours on a tennis court, still never had a problem getting an erection, holding one, still could make love as of old (though the all-night sessions were out!), still could eat as he always did, and still could work fourteen hours straight if he had to. He had cut his drinking down and his smoking too, but those were cautionary, not curative measures. He hadn't told the doctor about the self-diagnosed tachycardia, but he was certain it all had something to do with Anthea. And there it went again! *Son of a bitch! Jesus!*

She was an actress now. A pretty wooden one at that. Whenever he saw her on the TV screen (she had not yet been cast in a film—his guess was she never would be), he wanted to boot her in the ass to get some reaction on her face. It made him sore as hell. She was mannered, holding back. She looked like a professional virgin, the hands-off-don't-taint variety. But he knew that was a bald-faced lie. He heard stories everywhere he went. They sometimes didn't connect because her name was now Evans, and so he'd hear stories—"Listen, if you want a good lay, I know a good kid." Wasting herself like that. He couldn't stand it. And all those sons of bitches who hated or feared or even envied him, sniffing around her, hoping to get to him through her. Like Bob Tanner and his breed. No. Tanner was another, separate species altogether. If he had picked up Thea's scent, it was not to get to Max. Tanner had nothing to gain by that anymore. No, with Tanner, Thea herself would have to be a genuine need. It was killing him. Damn! It would kill him. He thought enough about Luise to spare her the details. If Luise knew, she never let on. Would not, of course, because her main role and function were to keep some sort of civilized peace among them all.

It all seemed so blotched now, so soiled and unpleasant. It was a dream. A wet dream filled with all that sexual excrement that littered and stunk up the New York streets. The past—not the recent past, the far-back-in-the-beginning-past—seemed the reality. He had no trouble remembering it all now, as if age had made him more farsighted, better able to define distances, and yet created a shortsightedness, *the now, the present*, at the same time. He remembered being young and in love with Luise, remembered his feelings when he came back from Spain, how all of them, Luise, yes, even Burt, and Sylvia, everyone in the New York of his youth that he knew, everyone in the early years of the Hollywood he knew, had felt he was a part of one, autonomous brotherhood, all in one magnificent conspiracy to overthrow all the world's corrupt justice, right all the wrong verdicts. They were young, very young in their naïveté. But their heart and energy and youthfulness were in the right places. They were against the right things. Thought they were strong enough, bright enough, to overcome the rise of Fascism in Spain, of Nazism in Germany, the spread of it throughout Europe. They were going to do something about the passivity with which the Jews were being butchered, countries raped, with which the underdog accepted his fate. They thought these things were new, that their youthful opposition, their intellectual violence were new. They joined the party. It seemed the answer. The party appeared to offer a solidarity. It was, after all, against all the things they were against. So they became Communists together, and there was a sort of lyric justice in that, some sentence for their youth, their naïveté, their arrogance. But of course, some of them discovered very soon that they were being used. Max had been one. He got the hell out. Or rather thought he had. But of course, he couldn't. It was impossible. Once you had ceased being a virgin, that was it. You just weren't a virgin any longer, and since you lived in a world of labels and advertising and supersell, you had to be *something*, and so you were always a Commie, or a Pinko, or a Red. Of course, that wasn't true anymore. None of them was a member of the old conspiracy anymore. Even Lou had resigned before he died. But the label remained: A man was a Commie, a left-wing writer, he was on the blacklist, one of the named, one of the witnesses, one of the nineteen, one of the ten. No one had thought up a new label yet, and until they did, that was it.

Melissa. One of the last things she had asked him was why none of *them* was socially conscious anymore. It was on her mind. It worried her. It meant she was. And that was right. The order of things. Social consciousness was for the young, the naïve. What the hell right did an old fart like Russell have to go on a strike for disarmament? It wasn't his world. He had had his chance. He failed. Otherwise, there would have been no reason for a strike. Money, endorsement, that was one thing. He still gave, still endorsed. *Jesus*, he was still a human being, but a strike! That was ludicrous, unforgivable.

At this point Max always and finally came around to thinking about Tony. Of his two children, he would have said Anthea would have been the one with a social conscience. But Anthea was more interested in art and music and beauty and, hell, in screwing. He had had fears that Tony would have been a dilettante or a goddamn fag interior decorator. Well, hell, Tony *was* a fag. Even if his mother refused to see it. Even if Tony himself didn't see it. Max did. Had for years. That was his mother's fault: coddling him, shopping with him, confiding in him. He had tried, Lord knows, he had tried. But he didn't blame Luise entirely. He should have fought her even in Europe, sent the boy to more of a man's school than to that pimply place she had selected.

Still and all, Tony had not ended up too badly. He had some of the old man's stuff in him, after all. He had not taken a dime from Max or from Luise (as far as Max knew) since he was eighteen. He saw himself through college, making good grades, on partial scholarship all the way, graduated with honors, got a master's, and, at twenty-two, was teaching in a school in Spanish Harlem— his choice. History was his main subject, but he taught a smattering of everything. He was dedicated completely to the kids he taught and talked about their lives and their housing and home conditions constantly. He marched on City Hall for better housing, rat control, you name it, Tony had marched on City Hall for or against it and had marched on Washington as well and would have gone to Mississippi if the school term and his kids had not intervened.

The fact was that in spite of Tony's feminine inclinations (the emphasis in his voice, the occasionally fluttering hand) and his seeming asexuality (Max would have preferred a professed fag to Tony) Max really quite liked Tony. With it all, the kid had spunk. He was standing up to his mother, rejecting, fighting Max. Max baited him knowingly, enjoying the battles that followed, proud of Tony's fury and anger and the smell of battle under his armpits. But they had no camaraderie at all. This ate at Max. He really wanted very much to reach Tony, to have some kind of dialogue. In the end, though, he was fully aware that a heritage had been passed on. Tony hated Max as Max had hated his own father. And maybe that was where the truth lay and the bones were buried. It was a hate of passion, after all, and passion was a living, a vital, a *moving* thing. Maybe his hopes could rest well with Tony.

Tony, Tony . . .

Thank God, there was not even a mild tachycardia there.

Chapter 35

It was a dark October afternoon. Somewhere, most places, the leaves would be turning a deep autumnal red, and even a storm-crossed day like this one would have its beauty. The somber silhouettes of trees in the distance, the intermingling of ashen chimney smoke and gray cloud, and the scent of damp leaves, wet pine. Here in Spanish Harlem, the gloom was wraithlike, mopping and mowing, here a gnomed hydrant, there a Gorgon building, a bent-over troll woman, a black rime giant. Tony walked as fast as he could without running—a running man in these parts could find this street pulling right out from under him—to the subway. This was always the worst part of the day for Tony, the walk from the school to the subway at the end of the day. He minded it less in the morning. It seemed safer then. Not that Tony was afraid for his own safety. He really was not. But you didn't see the same things at eight in the morning. There were sleeping drunks and hagridden women, junkies leaning against buildings, but the shouts were friendly. "Hey, amigo!" a greeting, "*Como estas,* Mr. See-man," the mothers, the grandmothers, the workingmen, the kids themselves. By half past four (Tony always remained an hour after school to work privately with any students who wanted help—they all *needed* it, but only a few would stay) it was a different matter. They were in the alleys and the doorways then, under the stairs, the addicts and the junkies, the whores; they were gathering on the corners and swaggering down the streets. The hostile, the bored, the hate pickers. Four thirty was a bad time, a time of aimlessness, before a target had been sighted. No one was really safe at such an hour.

Tony just made it down the littered stairs to the train. Above his head came the shouts *"Pato! Pato!"* Laughter. Not for him, Tony was sure. In another direction. But it unnerved him, and he was thankful his train was pulling in and hurried to board it. There were empty seats, but Tony stood. He could never bring himself to sit on a subway train or to rest his hand on the back of a seat. He'd hold a strap with one hand but carefully avoid touching his face with the same hand until after he had had a chance to wash. The subway was the worst part of the job. But there was no alternative. The bus was worse because it took longer, and taxis were too expensive. Tony stood leaning against the wall next to the doors. You had a little room to breathe there. He watched the stations going by, checking them off in his mind. He lived in a new building in a small apartment on East Ninth. It was a long ride, but even by the time he got to Eighty-sixth, he felt a little more relaxed. He'd been doing this for a year now. It was a crazy thing. He hated it, but he loved it. The analyst at the clinic he went to two nights a week (how lucky he had been to get on the list in the first place!) had told him he felt it necessary to do penance for his father. But that opened up an entire avenue of disagreement he had with the analyst—*his father*. He was certain the selection of his job had nothing to do with Max at all. He felt called to teaching, as some men did to the church or to medicine. He hated seeing how these people lived, and yet his greatest joy was when he found he had communicated to one—just one—small child. Though it wasn't on his schedule and he knew he could catch hell from the front office, he took it on himself to insert a short course of Puerto Rican history each term. He wanted his students to feel some dignity and pride, and he thought he was succeeding. He taught the third grade, where he felt they were still young enough to be reached. But then there were the heartaches he couldn't help taking personally. Little Angelina, who had died two weeks ago at age eight and a half from an overdose of the drugs her addicted mother had given her. Roberto, who at ten years was on the borderline of being retarded and whom Tony had given special instruction to, long tedious hours he felt were helping. But Roberto had been removed from his class and sent to a school for the retarded. The list went on and on.

He saw his mother when he could, his father infrequently, but he did see him. He would tell himself he did it to please his mother, but deep down he knew that was a lie. When things were at rock bottom, he needed to see his father. He made him angry, bitter, able to continue the battle. It was better than any upper you could buy. He wasn't sure how long he could teach in Spanish Harlem, but he felt he had to be doing something that made some inroad, served some purpose. His life, however, had fallen into a fairly monotonous pattern. He was up at half past six, on the train by half past seven, when in the winter it was still pretty dark out. He got home after five. He had made friends on the weekends with some of the guys on the same marches and campaigns that he'd been connected with, but he seldom saw them in the evenings. He was aware that most of the men he was attracted to were fags. Aware, too, that he was latently leaning in that direction. At this point in his life he was fighting. There was the free clinic and his work and something in those infrequent meetings with his father that made it important for him to fight.

The train pulled into his station, and he stepped onto the platform and rushed up the stairs, onto the street. It was past five, already dark, and it had begun to rain. The water hit the strewn newspapers on the street, making an empty, frustrated, exhausted sound. He didn't have an umbrella (hated the way he looked in the mirror when carrying one), and he began to run across the intersection and up Ninth. It was still fairly safe to do that in this part of town. People ran to get out of the rain, to catch a bus, weren't suspect when they ran. He stepped into his lobby and took out his clean handkerchief and wiped his face with it, then his hands. There were a few wet spots on his jacket. Not bad.

The doorman must have been in the basement, where he always went for a drink or a smoke. The television set over the doorway showed a deserted lobby except for Tony. What the hell kind of security was that! A television set. And Pete, the doorman, boozing it up in the basement. Tony crossed the ugly red-patterned carpet, the white tile specked with dirt along its sides. He wasn't paying for a stylish lobby, but protection was another thing. The elevator smelled from disinfectant. At least it was clean. It stopped on the fifth floor, Tony's floor, and he got out.

His apartment was pitch-black. The blinds were down and all the curtains closed. He heard a soft moan from the far side of the room and remembered then that Thea had appeared just before he'd left for work, hung over, looking lousy. She had been doing this often lately, coming to him after she got blasted, and he would put her up on the couch in his living room (because as much as he loved her, he couldn't bear the thought of her vomiting over his bed. The couch was different). No smell of vomit, this time. He turned on the overhead light. Thea was sprawled half on and half off the couch, a pillow bunched beneath her, her long golden hair tangled and covering her face.

"Turn it off," she growled and buried her face deeper into the pillow.

"Good God! Diana Barrymore! How nice of you to stay for tea!" Tony walked across the room, flipped up the shade and drew back the curtains. "I am paying for a view of the city, you know, dear; let's get our money's worth." The apartment was a rear and faced a court.

"What the hell time is it?"

Tony was standing, surveying the room. Her coat and bag were thrown carelessly over the stereo, but otherwise no damage. "Well, at least this time you didn't trip over any lamp cords. I rather miss the white sculptured lamp that was on the entrance table."

Thea managed to raise up into a sitting position and open one eye as she still clasped the pillow to her. "Oh, Tony, did I break that lovely lamp last time? I'm sorry. I could cry. I'm such a beast. I'll buy you a new one. Ohhh . . . " she moaned.

"I'll put the coffee up."

"You're an angel."

Tony paused in the door frame. "And you, dear, are making Sadie Thompson look like Rebecca of Sunnybrook Farm."

"Ha-ha—*ohhhhh*."

Tony flicked on the light in the tiny utility kitchen. His eyes immediately darted to the small drainboard surface. No roaches. It was October, after all, but those little bastards were tenacious. Even in a new building and under Tony's ever-watchful eye they would appear. He got out the lovely teak tray he had bought the previous week and as the coffee heated (there had been some from morning), he set it with a tray cloth of his mother's (she had given him a number of her household things when he had moved out to set up the apartment) and one of the white Rosenthal cups and saucers and a matching creamer and sugar and a silver coffeepot (also Luise's). He liked things to look, well, *elegant*. It always helped. He often felt that if breakfast could be served to a Puerto

Rican mother just once in a while in this manner, it would do a good deal more than the social worker could do.

The coffee was strong and pungent. He filled the silver pot with it. He liked it fresh and seldom drank it when it was left over, but it was just the trick for Thea. He carried the tray to her and set it down on the cocktail table in front of the couch.

"Now don't spill it on the couch."

"Did I do that, *too?* I really am getting to be a slob." She was wearing her crumpled-up dress from the night before, and a button was missing from the top. It rolled off the couch and onto the rug as she sat up to pour her coffee. "Aren't you having any, Tony?"

"I like to take my shower first."

"That means you'll be among the missing for at least an hour. Come and sit down. I want to talk."

"Well, at least let me take these clothes off." He went into the bedroom, undressed, hung his suit up carefully and threw his underclothes and his shirt into the hamper, sprayed himself with some cologne, and put on a white terry robe before returning to Thea.

He was distressed seeing her this way. Beautiful golden Thea. He had always been so proud of her, and here she was making a bag of rubbish of herself. He studied her from the doorway. She was sipping her coffee delicately from the fine cup. She was sitting with her profile to him, the finely carved forehead, the straight nose, the full open mouth, the delicate chin and throat. She was still beautiful. Still golden. Thank God. There was still time. He went into the room and sat down by her feet at the edge of the couch.

"Well, who was it this time?" he asked gently.

"That's it, Tony. I've been sitting here obediently drinking my coffee and trying to remember, but I just can't."

"Bob Tanner?"

"I don't know. I just don't know."

"It's incredible how fast the grapevine travels."

"We're not having an affair. We're *nothing*. He's my boss man, that's all." She had been studying her hands. Now she glanced up at him, her gaze riveting. "Tony, I just can't explain Bob Tanner. I mean, forget the fact he's a married man, all that *garbage*. He was an informer, right? And you can forget that, too. I just don't want to be reminded about all that ancient history anymore. But he's pompous and vain, egocentric to the point of madness. Yet, somehow, when he enters a room or comes on the stage when I'm shooting, I feel like I've lost control somehow. Like a child when a parent surprises him—worse. Oh, Lord, imagine me having hot pants for Bob Tanner. I can't be such an idiot that I'd walk right into a tiger's cage like that!"

"Poor baby." He meant it. He understood. She turned her misty eyes away from him. "Thea, look—you really have to do something right away. I'll speak to the clinic."

"You think I'm a drunk?"

"Hell, no. You only drink for dramatic effect. But in the meantime, it's making you lose your own self-respect. And dignity. That, too, Thea."

"You're right, right, *right*."

"And aren't you proud!"

"Oh, Tony—no, not really." She put down the cup, being very careful to do it gently, to set it right. "I'm just not very happy, Tony."

"Well, who the hell is? You should see what I do every day."

"I know, I know, I *know*."

"You don't. No one could unless they've been there." He got up angrily and began to pace. It struck Thea suddenly how so like his father Tony could look from time to time. An attitude, a sudden movement would bring Max flashing into your brain. She once mentioned the fact to Tony. Never again. It had upset him dreadfully, and Thea liked Tony to have as much peace of mind as possible. Yes! But look what she was doing to him now. He was truly, truly upset, unnerved. She knew it could bring on one of his itching spasms. These inner conflicts often did. She watched him stuff his hands into his pockets, turn his back; his shoulders heaved. He was built well. Like his father. Tall, broad-shouldered, small-hipped. The way his hair grew on his neck, the stance—his father. Not *hers*. She never said "hers." "Your father is leaving for Europe," she'd say. *Your father.*

"Tony. . . ."

He turned to her. That wasn't his father. Not that expression. Gentle, tender, the soft, soft gray eyes, the vulnerable mouth, the chin raised at a perfect angle for someone to strike it a killing blow.

"We are such a fucking mess, Thea. We can't let this happen. Hear. We can't let this happen."

"You're doing great, Tony. It's really just me. If I was even a whore, I'd have respect for myself." She got up unsteadily from the couch. "All right if I use the bathroom?"

"Of course. But don't get makeup all over the sink."

"I promise. If I take a bath, will I use up all the hot water?"

"No. It's fine. Go ahead, Thea."

She picked up her purse from the stereo. He was standing close to her, and she put her hand on his arm. He was strong; this always surprised her. Tony's bodily strength—the fact that she always felt she could lean on him.

"Hey, let's have dinner out? OK? Someplace really elegant like Pavillon? Or the Forum? You like the Forum."

"I'm busted."

"Uh-huh! But I have instant money." She flashed her Diner's Club Card. "All right? We can charge to the hilt. I've just paid the bill."

Tony smiled. It lit up his face. "You'll have to go back to your place to change. You could wear your blue velvet."

"I will! And you wear that smashing blue suit of yours. It brings out the blue in your eyes!"

"They're gray, and get the hell into the bathroom."

She ran into the bathroom and then poked her head out again. "Tony?"

"Yeah."

My God, he sounded just like "his" father.

"You're a good kid."

"You're not so bad yourself."

Thea was looking wan and painfully thin. Tony hadn't noticed it so keenly earlier in the evening, but in the hard artificial light of the restaurant and with the reflection of the blue velvet dress under her chin, she looked like an exhausted gaunt lady from Picasso's blue period. Her eyes were heavy with fatigue, and though she had been laughing a lot, reacting, attempting to convey high spirits, she appeared more like a blue butterfly, pinned but still fluttering in a display case, than golden Thea. Tony had always thought of both of them as remaining eternally young, going through life looking as they always did—that is, as they had seemed to each other in the golden summers of Italy and Switzerland. But of course, Thea was no longer young. Not as she was then. She would never be young like that again, even though she was only twenty-five. How many strange beds had she slept in in the seven years she had been in New York? How many strange men had slept in hers? Two a week? A hundred a year? Put them all together and they would overflow the Forum, fill a small theater. She was glancing wide-eyed across the room right now. Whom did she see, think she saw, half-dimly recalled? Fitzgerald wrote about the Daisys—the "golden girls"—of the twenties. The films immortalized the ladies of the forties—the Crawfords and Hepburns and Davises and Stanwycks—the war and postwar glossy independents. Here she was, *Thea*, child of the fifties, the malcontent generation, no Prohibition, Depression, or war to free her, to fall back on, use as a crutch, an excuse. Brought up in an easy economy with easy morals, in a time when family and country had lost their meaning, their solidarity. What could one expect of a twig growing on a loose-rooted tree and faced with a hurricane? Who would chronicle the Theas, the Melissas, the love seekers, the malcontents? He thought about it often, but if he ever took to writing, he didn't think it could be him. It would have to be someone with more objectivity. Right now he was more involved with the Robertos and the Angelinas—until Thea had walked into his room, as she had that morning. Was that the fifth time already this month? Drunk, clothes crumpled even before sleeping in them, thrown down or just crushed back somewhere, smelling—how?—sexually. How many times this month? Five? No. Six. *Good God, beautiful, beautiful, golden Thea.*

The food had been cleared away. The white tablecloth was stained but brushed clear of crumbs. The coffee steamed in cups in front of them. Thea was writing abstractly without conscious exertion with a spoon on the tablecloth. She held her fragile hand delicately on the spoon handle, but he could still read the impression.

"*M* for Max?" he asked.

"Or mother, or mayhem, or marriage." She looked up at him wistfully, without defiance.

"Or Mark, or Mal, or Marv, eh?"

"Right, brother dear, right, right, right." She pressed heavily on the spoon as she blotted out the *M*. "Tell me about your kids, your people," she said.

"They're not mine, Thea. They're not anyone's. That's their problem."

"The line forms on the right."

"Stop wallowing. It's disgusting."

"You mean that."

"Damned right, I mean that."

"OK." She sat up straighter, bringing herself to attention. "Tell me about little Angelina."

"I don't want to, Thea. I really don't want to—not here—not now."

"OK. Shall we get the hell out of here?"

"You want to go home?"

"No. I thought we could try someplace in the Village. Have a nightcap. Something like that."

"I have to be up by half past six."

"Just a nightcap. One."

He called for the bill, and Thea passed him her Diner's card discreetly.

"You can sign my name," she whispered. "No one can read my handwriting anyway."

They hailed a taxi and went down to the small club in the Village where Larry Adler was appearing. They didn't really know Adler, but because of his political proclivities, his English period, they felt he was a friend, someone they should, in fact, come down to see. The place was small and dark and crowded. It was almost time for Adler to appear. Thea sat down at the bar, and Tony stood behind her. He put his arm protectively around her shoulders. There was a guy standing, staring at them from the end of the bar. Actor type. Good-looking son of a bitch. Jewish or Italian or Greek. Too thin, though. But even in the dim light they were in, his good looks were evident. The thick dark hair, the broad face and square chin and huge probing dark eyes, the dramatically straight-edged nose. Thea was aware of his looking at them, too.

"Maybe we can get a table," Tony said.

"I like it here. It's like home."

"Coward writes *wonderful* one-liners."

"That was *not* Coward. It was authentically first-impression Anthea Evans." She leaned back slightly. "That cockteaser at the end of the bar reminds me of someone I met in Madrid once."

"*Met*, dear?"

"Now that *was* Coward."

The guy was headed toward them. He smelled too heavily of cologne. He brushed Tony's shoulder and smiled down at Thea as he paused beside them.

"Anthea Evans, isn't it?" he asked.

"Oh, God! I have met you!"

"No, not really. I'm what you might call a fan."

"Really!" Thea batted her false eyelashes.

"I could vomit," Tony said, but remained holding onto Thea.

"Uh, *Professor* Seaman. Mr. . . . ." Thea began.

"Toscini. Vic Toscini. I'm an actor myself: *Lawrence of Arabia, 55 Days in Peking.*"

"How interesting." Thea smiled expansively.

"I just came back from London. Winged over for the preview of *55 Days*. A dog, but hell, that's life."

"Umm." Thea wet her lips and leaned forward so that her cleavage was directly below his arrow-sharp nose.

He never glanced down. "Seaman, Seaman," he said. "Any relation to Max?"

"His son," Thea piped up. Tony could have killed her. "You know him?"

"Met him once at a party at Nick Ray's. Great man. *Great*." He patted Tony on his shoulder as if it was Tony's accomplishment.

"Which?" Tony asked.

"I'm sorry?"

"Which one's a great man? Seaman or Ray?"

"Now that you ask, both!" Vic grinned displaying his Dentyne-white teeth.

The little light there was in the place went out, and a spotlight came up. Larry Adler walked out to tumultuous applause. Being a harmonica player was the thing this year. He began to play. He was good. Damned good. Tony lifted his arm from around Thea and turned toward the podium to give Adler his full attention. Vic Toscini was staring at him. Not Adler. *Tony.* Tony averted his eyes. In a moment a fresh drink was handed to him.

"I didn't order . . ." Tony whispered.

"On me." Vic Toscini grinned. He was standing next to Tony, almost blocking Thea's view.

They left right after Adler's performance. It was beginning to rain, a soft, indecisive rain. There was no taxi in sight, and they began to walk.

"You know, Tony, I was thinking—little Angelina . . ."

"We're back to her?"

"Well, for some reason inside there, I was thinking. You should write about her. And about all the others."

Tony didn't reply. She was walking beside him, her coat loosely over her shoulders, her hair beginning to fall from the dampness.

"Why not, Tony? Why the hell not? You could do it. You really could."

"I've thought about it, too."

"Have you? That's good, Tony. I'm pleased."

"I'm not sure. Maybe I'm too close."

"Oh, yes, and that's just it. You're close, and yet you can be detached because it's not your life. Well, anyway, you'll think about it? We'll talk about it another time. OK?"

He just smiled appreciatively down at her. Then he sighted someone getting out of a taxi and pulled her along as he ran toward it. "I'll drop you uptown first, if you like," he said as they waited for the driver to give his passenger change.

"No. Look, you take this cab. I'm not ready to go home yet."

"Thea . . ."

"Please, Tony, please . . ."

The taxi was free now and the driver impatient.

"You can come back to my place, Thea. Spend the night with me. I'll take the couch."

"No. No." She pulled away and threw him a kiss and began to walk quickly back to the club they had just left.

"Hey, Mac, I haven't got all day," the driver growled.

Tony slid inside and closed the door. He gave the driver his address.

"We can't win them all." The driver grinned. He was pleased. Tony's apparent rejection by Thea, whom he had assumed to be a date, had pleased him. He straightened. His shoulders seemed to broaden, and he drove Tony home with an air of self-assurance.

Chapter 36

It was dinnertime, and the three of them were sitting around the old oak table Luise had just recently found in a Third Avenue antiques shop, drinking their coffee and pretending to be a family. Luise ran her hand along the well-worn rim of the table. She felt rather pleased with herself. It would have seemed more complete, a truer picture, she insisted to herself, if Thea were sitting in the seat alongside her to help clear the dishes, to keep things light and happy between *their* men. It was Sunday evening, and the maid was off. Outside, a gentle rain washed against the windows. There was a fire in the fireplace, nearly down to embers now. The candles on the table burned low. It had been a very successful dinner, Luise thought. The roast beef had been done to a turn; the salad had been crisp; the soufflé had not fallen. And best of all, Tony and Max had not exchanged a cross word, had in fact been most congenial. Luise leaned back in her chair and smiled with satisfaction. Her two men were lost at the moment in their own thoughts. She could dare study them. They were both handsome. And they did so look alike. No one could mistake that they were father and son, Luise thought proudly. Both children, she realized, looked like Max. Tony sometimes had an expression of hers, but that was all. She was happy that they favored Max, for in that way he was never truly absent. Tony had matured a lot this last year. He was beginning to look terribly manly. A Hemingwayesque, manly face. *A Seamanesque face.* His eyes weren't Max's, though. He gazed so often, as he was doing now, off into space, avoiding eye-to-eye combat when he could. Max's eyes were different, the same flinty gray, but different. Max spoke, persuaded, seduced with his eyes. He was leaning on the table, his eyes closed for the moment, his chin resting on his hand. When he did open his eyes, he raised his glance instantly to Luise. "Good dinner, Luise," he commented.

"I do wish Thea had been able to come. She had to redub something, I believe." Luise smiled uneasily at Max.

Tony immediately reacted. He wanted to say, "What's all that shit? It's Sunday. No studio redubs on Sunday. She's screwing some guy, who the hell knows and who the hell cares because she won't be screwing him tomorrow, and even if she only had Ed Sullivan for Sunday night company, she sure as hell would not be here!" He did not say any of that. First, he never used words like "shit" and "screw" in front of his mother, and second, he avoided talking about Thea. In fact, the only time he ever lied to his mother was when she forced an issue about Thea. He'd say anything then in Thea's defense and get the subject changed as soon as possible. "How about having our coffee in the living room, Mom?" he managed now.

"That's a nice idea." Luise stood, and the two men immediately rose.

"I'll put another log on," Tony offered.

The living room was actually the long section of the L that made up the living-dining area of the apartment. Tony put his coffee cup down on the cocktail table and began to rebuild the fire.

"I never can do that well," Luise said from the dining area. She was always happy to be able to compliment Tony on something in front of Max. "I'll just get the dishes organized. All right?" No one objected and so Luise left the two men alone and disappeared into her sanctum sanctorum, the kitchen. She reappeared for only one moment. "Tell your father about that Puerto Rican child, Tony. Angelina." Then she was gone.

Tony jammed a log onto the grate and then stood and attacked the live coals with a poker to stir them into flame.

"Thea's out screwing around, isn't she?" Max said.

Tony whipped around, facing Max. "How the hell should I know?" he said quietly, so that Luise wouldn't hear.

"She's turned into one of those broads who cry themselves to sleep. You can see it on her face. In her tenseness. She's a Maggie cat, if there ever was one. When she doesn't cry herself to sleep, hell, she's got to screw herself to sleep."

This was usually the kind of opening Max made in private confrontation with Tony—"Fascist son of a bitch you've got running the school board . . . Did you read that stupid statement that little shit at Columbia made? . . . Thea's out screwing around, isn't she?" All of a piece, used like a poker to stir the live embers in him as he had just used one to stir the fire. The fire had caught, and it was roaring and cracking behind him, the heat singeing his neck, but he stood solidly, refusing to move. Max was looking at him intently, slightly mocking, but Tony could see the pensiveness in the expression. He wasn't sure about too much where his father was concerned, but he was certain that where Thea was involved, the old man cared. Yes, his father truly cared about Thea. What she was doing to herself was eating at his gut. He had put his cup and saucer down and was standing seven or eight feet from Tony. The fire made his full face red. He looked like a wounded man and he was standing there hoping Tony would give him a shot of morphine.

"You see her often?" Max asked.

"No. We both keep pretty busy," Tony lied.

"I heard she was fucking around with that son of a bitch Tanner."

"You hear things I don't then," Tony said and moved away from the discomfort of the heat. He started to sit down and then changed his mind. It always rattled him to sit when his father was standing.

"You're loyal, Tony. I like that. Your sister needs loyalty right now."

He wanted to say: "You don't have to tell me that. And you don't have to coerce me into loyalty for Thea." But he didn't. "Thea keeps very busy as I said. She's been doing a lot of shows lately. Tanner's is one of them." He could see the pattern now. The old man wouldn't let go. He was going to try to get as much information from Tony as his chisel mind could dig out.

Max lowered his voice so that Tony had to concentrate hard to hear his words. "I'm not saying Thea's a whore, Tony. She's a mixed-up kid, and punks like Bob Tanner can only mix her up more. In case you've had any doubt, let me make it perfectly clear to you that because Thea seems to have cut me out of her life right now does not mean I've cut her out of mine. You can't put a brake on loving, Tony. Sometimes you get over it, go on, but once you've given some love and taken it, it's always with you, down there where it's three o'clock in the morning. It's always with you."

Something in his father's voice, in his attitude, moved Tony. Max sat down wearily in the nearest chair. He was no longer in the reflection of the flames, but his face was still flushed. Tony wondered if he was suffering from hypertension or if he had been drinking too much lately. Max sat there, curiously vulnerable, looking up at Tony, a small, thoughtful smile on his face. He was thinking about Thea. Thea when she was still young. Thea when they still were open about their love.

"Thea will be all right, Dad."

"You do see her?"

"Yeah."

"Often?"

"Yeah."

Max smiled. "She's a really lousy actress, you know?"

"She's just afraid to let go and be *Thea*."

"Maybe it's better that way, eh? Maybe she'd lose control otherwise."

"I never thought about that. You could be right. I've been trying to get her into therapy."

"And?"

"No go."

"I wouldn't have thought so," Max said, an edge of pride crusting his voice. "Anthea's like me there. Some voyeur monitoring your thoughts, hell! That's worse than tapping your telephone!"

"I think it could help Thea."

"That isn't what's going to help Thea." Max turned aside, looking off into space. "Tell me about this Angelina," Max said when he faced Tony again. It took Tony a little off guard.

"You don't want to hear about Angelina."

"Of course, I do."

Tony leaned forward. "Angelina was a little Puerto Rican girl, bright as hell, eight and a half and in the third grade. I teach third grade, you know?"

"Yes, yes . . ."

"Angelina Guerretez. She had eyes that burned right through you, and she was so frail that you were always painfully conscious of it when you looked at her. In the very beginning—the first day of the school term—all the faces in the room looked unfamiliar to me. But not Angelina's. She was straight out of a Poe poem."

"Lenore?"

"Yes. Lenore."

" 'Deep into that darkness peering, long I stood there wondering, fearing—doubting, dreaming dreams no mortal ever dreamed before.' " Max's voice was quiet, feeling, full of cadence. From time to time he enjoyed quoting the classics—Shakespeare, Shaw, Poe. He would recite his own work at times with this same serious attention. " 'But the silence was unbroken, and the stillness gave no token,' " he continued, " 'and the only word there spoken was the whispered word, *"Lenore!"* This I whispered, and an echo murmured back the word *"Lenore!"* Merely this and nothing more. . . .' "

"Yes. Yes, that was Angelina. An echo. A memory. A child from some former childhood you might have lived."

"And you gave her special attention."

"Well, she was so damned bright. No, perhaps 'wise' is a better word. She was agonizingly wise." Max nodded his head knowingly, and Tony, pleased at his father's interest, went on in a rush. "The class was very difficult in the beginning, and I had a serious problem gaining the upper hand. Angelina would catch my eye. She knew. She understood. She silently begged me to be patient. It was incredible. Then her homework began coming in. Her short essays. For eight and a half, they were absolutely incredible and terrifying." Tony shivered and got up and moved closer to the fire. "She would write things like, 'My mama she is pretty and a whore. I love her very much, but the men they love her more.' Can you believe that? She would refer to red as blood-colored, to black as night-colored, to gray as shadow-colored. She was certainly disturbed, but she had this almost devouring need to learn. She'd sit in her seat after class and wait until I was finished correcting papers or giving extra help. She'd just sit there waiting. 'Yes, Angelina?' I'd ask. 'Can I help you?' 'Is that all you're teaching today?' she'd ask. 'Yes, that's all. I'm getting ready to go home,' I'd tell her. *'Buenos días.'* She would smile, and then she would get up and leave." Max was listening carefully, with full attention.

Tony relaxed a little. "I spoke to the social worker who dealt with her family," he continued. "The mother was a whore. She also burned and beat the children and was an addict. There were four other children, all younger than Angelina. Welfare removed them from the home three weeks ago. For some inexplicable reason, Angelina was left alone with this terrifying mother. The day after her sisters and brothers were placed in a center, Angelina didn't come to school. I spoke to the social worker. They said they would check into it. But the next two days she wasn't in class, and I decided to see for myself."

"That was a dangerous thing, Tony. You could have gotten into a lot of trouble."

"Yeah, but I had to. That was all. I just had to. I won't describe the hole they lived in. It was typical of Spanish Harlem. But Angelina's mother had an obsession against light, and she had covered the few windows there were in the place with red tissue paper. It made everything the color of blood. Everywhere was this horror of blood. When I got there, there was the mother pulling down all the religious pictures in the two rooms and making a fire of them in the stove. She pulled a little wooden cross from around Angelina's neck and threw that in as well. And all of it in this blood-red light. The child asked me to wait outside, and in about five minutes she joined me. 'They shouldn't have taken the others,' she cried. 'They shouldn't.' I suggested that perhaps she should speak to the social worker and offered to call her that moment for her. Actually, I was hoping they would remove Angelina from the home as well. I guess I thought if she spoke to the social worker, it would remind Welfare of her situation. But Angelina wouldn't have it. The next day she was in class and remained afterward. 'You see, it is like theese,' she told me. 'Mama, she really love the leetle ones. She theenks Jesus, he is punishing her . . . She theenks he let me stay just to remind her.' "

Max shifted in his chair. Sat back. He seemed to have lost himself to Tony completely. Tony stood looking down at him. His heart was beating rather wildly. Inner anxiety. God knew he wasn't frightened of his father. No, that wasn't it. It was just that he felt closer to his father this instant than he ever had before. Why that should unnerve him so, he wasn't sure. He thought it was because this meant that a whole, new, unfamiliar situation extended now before him—one in which his father could no longer be counted as an enemy. He would have to speak to the therapist about it.

"The mother killed her to end the eternal judgment," Max said softly.

"The mother didn't mean to kill her. I'm certain of that. She took the needle herself. It hadn't killed her. She just wanted to close Angelina's eyes—wanted to grab a short reprieve for herself, I'm sure." Tony was nervous now. He lit a cigarette and then began to drink the cold coffee. "I was thinking about writing it all down," he said after a while.

"For yourself?"

"No. I thought about it first as a book."

"It might stretch."

"Do you think it would be a basis for a film?" Tony asked.

"No. I don't think so."

"It's so full of images. The apartment, Spanish Harlem. My schoolroom. Angelina. Somehow I think through all those images, there is an important statement that could be made."

"Yeah?"

"Well, there are all the obvious things. But you know Angelina's mother was right. Angelina *was* there to judge her. I'm not too sure about it all yet. It's still too soon, and I'm still so close. I have all her little poems, her essays, though."

"Maybe you should try an article."

"I thought for Angelina—well, I thought a film."

"Not so easy."

"What is?"

"Not too many things in writing. You been thinking about writing a lot lately?"

"Yeah. *Yeah.*"

Max raised himself slowly from the chair. He and Tony were about the same height. He looked evenly into his son's eyes. "You're not ready to try a screenplay yet, Tony. If you were, you could detach yourself and see the truth." Max paused a minute and then leaned down and took a cigarette from the table, lighted it, and then walked slightly away. "You see, the main issue here is not Angelina, but the teacher, Tony. He sees himself pretty much as a Christ figure. That poor kid's death means damned little to him in terms of the kid, but in terms of himself. Ah! That's something else again. He could have given her life. Ordained her with beauty, shown her the way home. But that frigging whore cheated him, which in a way is some sort of justice. He was crucified like Christ, after all."

"I don't agree. It's Angelina's story."

"Then, kid, you haven't got a film. Then you'd better write an article for one of the educational journals. Something like that. Good way to get a feel for words, anyway."

Tony felt the anger mount. "I'm going to write it as a screenplay," he said.

"Can't hurt. It will be a good exercise."

"It will be a good *screenplay*. Not that claptrap they toss at you now. Not these incredible epics. Real people in a real place. A hellhole. Spanish Harlem. *No* actors. No sets. The real thing. I bet you could make it for under a quarter of a million." Tony was perspiring. He moved away from the fire toward the front windows.

"Television film."

"Inexpensive doesn't have to mean Klein's. And expensive sure as hell doesn't always mean taste," Tony snapped.

Luise walked into the room. She was drying her hands on a kitchen towel. Tony's raised voice had alerted her. "Well"—she smiled uncertainly—"I'm so glad you two can be so enthusiastic. Now! How about some fresh coffee?"

"How about a walk?" Max suggested.

"That's a nice idea. I'll get my coat. Tony?"

"No thanks. I'll be getting home." He went out into the hall for his coat, and his mother followed. "Thanks for dinner, Luise," he said and kissed her lightly on the cheek.

"Your father's proud of you, Tony. I'm sure of that," Luise whispered. "As I am."

"Well, I'll see you next week."

"You'll call, Tony?"

"Sure."

"If you see Thea . . ."

"Whatever you have to say to Thea, please do me a favor and say yourself."

"You're very edgy, Tony. I think you're working too hard."

"Yeah," he said and went out into the hallway and, without even looking to see if the elevator was there, made the five flights of rear steps two at a time and then cut down a side street to Madison.

He was damned if he'd have his father looking down at him from a window on Fifth Avenue.

Chapter 37

Thea had promised to have dinner at Tony's. She was to have been there by eight. Tony had said it was something special. A celebration. But it was now close to nine, and they still had one more setup to complete. The director was incredibly slow. Nothing seemed to have been blocked first. Just sloppiness passing for improvisation—for realism. The script wasn't too bad. Not for a half-hour series segment. *The Streets,* the show was called. Twenty-six minutes (after commercials—Kleen, "the fresh odor soap") each week in the life of plainclothes cop—"the one you know who bleeds when he's cut, a socially aware, feeling, fermenting, fighting front-office-cop"—in the streets of the Upper East-West Side of Manhattan. His exact beat was never clarified. Each week it depended on if they were to shoot a Puerto Rican story, or a black story, or a Jewish or Irish or Italian story. This episode was Puerto Rican, and Thea had been hired to play a whore (typecasting, ha-ha). She didn't know if her agent or the director was to blame for that, but she had been baking under the lights for six hours now and the heavy makeup and the damned black wig were driving her up the wall.

"How long, Harry?" she asked the lighting man.

"Quarter of an hour."

"Ten minutes!" the director screamed, overhearing.

"I'm going to make a call." She started across the sound stage.

"Hey!" the director yelled. "You heard. Ten minutes."

Thea kept on walking, and the director ran to catch up with her.

"One more shot and we're done, baby. Even you can wait that long."

Something inside Thea snapped, and she slapped the fat, smiling face before her. Hard. It seemed to collapse like a balloon that had been pricked.

"Why did you do that, baby?" he moaned.

"I don't know. I really don't know." And she didn't. She couldn't really give two hoots in hell for what this baboon thought or said. "I'm just hot and tired. And I had an appointment, and I have to call to say that I can't make it, and keeping it really meant something to me. I'm sorry." She moved away and then turned back. "Actually, I am sorry. I apologize." She walked away quickly to the telephone out in the corridor and without thinking, as she did, she tore the wig from her head and swung it at her side.

"Thea, baby!"

She stopped. She immediately realized what she had done. "Oh, Lord, I'm sorry. I'm sorry." She thought she might cry, but thankfully, mercifully, she was able to control the flood of tears she felt welling up inside her. The director was alongside her again.

"No. That was good. We'll put that in. You come through the door, and the wig is swinging in your hand, just like that. You finished work. Off with the come-on. Off with the wig." He was grinning as though he'd just discovered a cure for the common cold.

"I'm Puerto Rican, for crissakes, and my own hair's blond. Doesn't that strike you the least bit odd?"

"Beautiful! Beautiful! You bleach it. You don't *really* want to be Puerto Rican, but out there on the streets, you *have* to!"

"*Oh, Lord!* I'll be back in a minute. You want to shoot without the wig. I don't care. Honestly. I don't care." She walked away as quickly as she could and prayed he wouldn't follow her.

Tony was disappointed, and she felt like a heel. "I won't be through here for another hour. And I'm beat, and then I'd have to get all the way downtown to you. Tony, darling, please forgive me?"

"Sure."

"You don't. It was special. I can tell it meant a lot to you."

"Don't be ridiculous. Champagne. Caviar. Chicken Kiev. The perfect TV dinner."

"Oh, Tony. I'm sorry. Listen, why don't you forget it and taxi up here . . ."

"Another night, Thea."

"It won't matter."

"It matters. But another night."

Bob Tanner was on the floor when she returned. "What are you doing with the wig off?" he asked crossly.

"I'm sorry, sorry, *sorry!* Dolly!" The hairdresser came running. "I'm sorry, could you please . . ."

The director had joined them. "No, leave it off. I thought it would have a tremendous impact, Bob." He explained his idea to Tanner, who was the executive producer.

"That's the most ludicrous thing I've heard yet. Dolly, get that wig back on Miss Evans. And hurry it up. We're chewing up golden time as if we were shooting an old MGM musical." Bob Tanner walked away but stationed himself to one side where he still had a good overall view.

A different attitude always pervaded the set whenever Tanner chose to put in an appearance. Suddenly there was dignity in making a twenty-six-minute potboiler. He stood there very erect, freshly showered and shaved. Here it was after nine at night, and he looked rested, vital, just ready to begin. He was still a handsome man, but he seemed less conscious of it now than he had when he was younger. He wore his good looks casually, comfortably, as he wore the expensive hand-tailored suit, the silver in his hair, the glowing tan and the slim, well-honed body. He looked successful and secure. But there was more to the respect his appearance commanded than that. Whatever his private ghosts, his public image was one of impeccable and unimpeachable correctness. He had exorcised the past completely. He was no longer a man who had married a woman with connections. He was an executive producer. "King of TV," they called him. Three shows running, a talk show of his own. At least one Emmy every year for the last four. Recognized on the street and in restaurants as if he were a star. No one any longer seemed to recall his appearance before the committee. Reference was made at times to his problems during the McCarthy period, but in the face of his current praiseworthy involvements (the workshop for black actors in Harlem, the fund for young writers, the donations and endorsements, speeches, articles, time spent in behalf of every *sympathetic* liberal organization), the wording of such references immediately made one believe Bob Tanner had stood proud, girding his loins, and had surmounted even the committee.

It was not known if his marriage was happy or unhappy. He had been most careful to keep his private life private. He and Kate were most often together, and he was infrequently seen with other women and never was known to involve himself with an actress or a secretary in his employ. There had been some rumors about Lady Atmore and some speculation about the Duchess of Stanhope. But only that. There was something, though, in the way he now stood and studied Thea. The director, the lighting man, the cameraman, the dresser and hairdresser all seemed alert to it. Only Thea appeared not to notice.

They went through the scene twice and then filmed it on the third try. It was a pretty good take, but Thea was prepared to go through it again.

"That's fine, dear," the director complimented her and then moved off to confer with the sound engineer, who had signaled him. Everyone stood around waiting.

"OK, kids. That wrapped it up," the director called back, and cast and crew began exhaustedly to leave the stage as the lights were killed. Bob Tanner stood by the door saying good-bye to the members of the show and thanking them individually.

"I've taken the liberty of ordering a car for you, Miss Evans," he said as Thea started past him.

"It wasn't necessary."

"You've been kind in giving us several hours of overtime. We appreciate it."

"You do. Great." She smiled facetiously, drew her hand away from his, and headed for the dressing room. If she felt Bob Tanner's eyes on her retreating figure, she gave no outward sign.

She came out of the stage door about ten minutes later. Her face was scrubbed clean, and her long blond hair pulled back. It was cold and windy, and she wore a camel-hair coat tightly belted, the collar up around her ears. A chauffeur tipped his hat to her.

"Miss Evans, this way."

Thea followed and stepped into the rear seat of the limousine. Bob Tanner was pressed back in a corner.

"I guessed. Surprised?" She laughed and collapsed onto the seat. "And I am too tired to object. In fact, I'm too tired, period." She leaned back against the upholstered seat and closed her eyes. The car had moved out into traffic, and the window between the rear seat and the driver had been closed.

"Thea . . ."

"One twenty East Eighty-first."

"I know."

Thea opened her eyes. "Oh, Lord! I think you are what I *thought* I forgot last week."

"After the audition . . ."

"Lord, yes! After the audition. I'm too tired, Mr. Tanner. Tired, tired, *tired*."

"I know you are. Lean against me. You can rest better that way." He drew her closer to him. There was a curious tenderness to the action. Thea lowered her head onto his shoulder, and he pulled his arm around her protectively. They drove in silence, Thea not quite asleep but not quite awake either. He glanced down at her from time to time or stroked back the short broken ends of the hair around her face. He was treating her like a child, and Thea seemed comforted by it. When they reached Thea's building, he woke her from her half sleep gently and helped her out of the car.

"Would you mind waiting for me, Patrick?" he asked his driver compassionately. "There's a fairly good hamburger place around the corner on Madison."

"No, sir. Of course not. Shall I wait there?"

"I think it's wiser."

The man tipped his cap and rushed to open the front door of the building for Thea, who was having a problem doing so, and then held the door open as Thea and his employer went inside.

"As I said, I'm tired," Thea insisted. "I mean I didn't want you to lose face with Fairbanks out there, but boss man, ah'm tired." She extended her hand as Tanner stood in front of the elevator. "And ah thanks you. If mah mama, papa, and brothah was here, they'd thank you, too."

The elevator door opened, and Bob Tanner pushed her gently inside, stepped in after her, and pressed the button at the right number for her floor.

"Umm. Well, that clinches it. You *were* the one." She leaned back against the artificial wood paneling and closed her eyes.

When the elevator jolted to a stop, she opened them and walked past Bob Tanner and down the corridor to the door to her apartment. She never looked back over her shoulder. She knew he was there, right behind her. " 'Just me and my shadow,' " she began to sing. He took the key from her hand and opened the door and clicked on the inside light for her.

"I'm coming in—but not for the reason you think. I want to speak to you." He came in, closed the door, locking it after them, and helped her off with her coat.

"The bar's over thataway." She gestured. "But of course, if you've been here before you know."

"Sit down."

"Is that an order?"

"A suggestion."

"I'm on my own time now."

"Sit down."

"You're serious. You want to talk." She seemed to fold up as she sank down into one of her own chintz-covered living-room chairs. "Is this going to be in the form of some kind of lecture? Oh, I've just tuned in! We're on *Candid Camera*!"

"So you will never be in doubt, I was here last week. And for your information, it is not the sort of thing I often do."

"Oh, but boss man, what a relief! You actually do *do it*."

"For your further information, I do—but not last week with you. You were drunk and passed out."

"I do that from time to time. Well, there aren't any refunds due at this time, are there?"

"I haven't been able to hold another thought in my head all week. Anthea Seaman—a lush . . . and an easy lay. I've known you since you were a child. I never was able to forget you. You were the most beautiful child I have ever seen. The kind of little girl one only sees in Renoir paintings. Gold and orange. Warm and round. Those exquisite tortoiseshell eyes and the golden hair and skin. And here you are—all respect for your own body, your own beauty lost. I looked at you at that audition last week and it was like seeing a great painting destroyed. You were drunk already, you know. You could hardly stand up. The director's an idiot. You were auditioning for a drunken tart, and he figured you were giving it your all. But I knew you were really drunk and that somehow I couldn't let you fall flat on your face in front of him.

Not in front of *him*. So I took you by the arm and managed to get you home."

"A belated thanks."

He was pacing in front of her now. She looked at him, truly looked at him for the first time. She realized she hadn't really looked at him before. She had noticed his good looks, of course, had been aware of his maleness. No more than that. He was a lot older than she had originally thought of him as being. Probably mid-forties. She had forgotten that he had been in and out of her home, that he had known her as a child. Until this moment it had not even connected that this was *the* Bob Tanner that her father had always called that frigging son of a bitch. She began to laugh.

"I assure you, Anthea, that none of this is a laughing matter."

"I'm sorry. But you look so ridiculously pompous and I was just thinking that my father used to call you that frigging son of a bitch." He paused and stared down at her. "Again—I'm sorry. They do say on your sets that you have fired men for gentler language than that."

"Are you close to your father?"

"We don't speak. At least not so anyone would notice."

He seemed relieved. "Does he know you carry on like you do?"

"Haven't a clue."

"And you don't care."

"Not a whit."

"You're a liar."

"Oh, you play that game, too?"

"I don't know what you're talking about."

"The game of truth. It's my father's most passionate hypocrisy."

She noticed a strange, flickering smile cross his face, then fade immediately. Mention of Max had stirred him.

"Your father's one of the great film men in the world."

"Really?"

"I always admired him." The flickering smile again. "Though I don't think the feeling was ever mutual. Once that was important to me."

"Now?"

He avoided answering.

"Oh, Christ! I want you to know you can't get back at my father through me. I want you to know that," she insisted.

"You're wrong. I could. But I told you, I admire your father."

He turned away, and for a moment she saw his shoulders sag. Then he braced himself again. Thea's hand rose as if to reach out to touch him. He caught the gesture and leaned down, resting his weight on the arms of the chair and in close enough for her to smell his good, clean, expensive smell.

"Anthea—"

"Thea. Friends call me Thea."

"I'm in love with you," he said softly, but his rich brown eyes were riveted on her face, his square chin set. "I think I have been since you were a child. You are an incredible life force, you know? Always were. Like your father. He'll always get up off the canvas. I knew that. I knew that," he repeated steadily. He pushed himself back and away from her and then crossed the room and sat down in a chair facing her. He sat stiffly, as though in a dentist's chair, and he looked pained as well.

"I had an intuition. 'Anthea Evans is auditioning,' they told me. I never go to casting auditions. But I had to go to yours. I remembered that vital child, and I hadn't been spared all the ugly men's locker-room stories. I've been torn ever since. 'She'll bounce back,' I told myself. 'She'll get right up for the next round.' But I found I was in a panic. 'What if she doesn't?' I asked myself. 'What if somehow she can't?' "

Thea sat the length of the room from him, spellbound. She was thinking—somehow, this was *it*. Her judgment, her price. They seemed to be acting out some new, yet untried and yet predictable Dürrenmatt play. Her exhaustion drained from her body, and she sat up straighter. She could feel the fire rise in her cheeks. Her head was completely clear. There was a crazy moment in which she felt they were reliving some moment in both their lives.

"I am going to send you to a private sanatorium, Thea. Very discreet. No one will know. All these sexual and alcoholic tantrums of yours—they've been screams for help. Well, I've heard them, Thea, and if you'll now take the help you've been shouting for, you are going to lick this alcohol problem, and you are going to get yourself into a good physical and mental condition. It won't be easy, but I have made all arrangements for you. You can tell your mother and whoever else needs to be told that you're going on a cruise. No one who cares about you could deny just by looking at you that you need something like a cruise. When you're *graduated* from the Farm, maybe we can arrange a cruise as well. You'll have to steel yourself to six weeks at the place, at minimum. I'll come up as often as is possible. I'll call you every day—but I don't think it's a good idea if anyone else knows."

"Why are you doing this?" she asked softly.

"You'd kill yourself inside a year if I didn't."

"But why *you*?" she whispered.

"I told you. I love you."

"You might cure me by just loving me."

"Or kill you. I'm not willing to take such a chance."

"I mean that much to you?"

"That much."

"It's scary. You frighten me."

She began to shiver uncontrollably, and he got up and walked over to her, but he did not touch her.

"Thea," he said quietly, the color fading from his face, "you are going to live—*for me*. And you are going to care about yourself and lift yourself out of this muck you've slithered into." He looked as if he might lose control. Hit her. Cry. Scream. She wasn't sure. Instead, he walked away to the door. "Patrick will pick you up at half past seven in the morning. You'll have a two and a half hour drive. You don't have to pack too much. You'll find just about everything you want waiting for you."

"What makes you think I'll go?"

"You'll go."

"Don't count on it."

"I'm counting on you."

"The coach talking? Papa? Who are you playing? God?"

"If it does the trick, does it matter?"

She pushed herself out of the chair and crossed the room to him. He was not a tall man. She was barefooted, and she was still as tall as he was. "I think this is a worse game than the kind Max Seaman plays," she said sharply.

"This is no game, Thea. This is an emergency operation."

"You're so damned pompous. So damned correct. You come in here and tell me I'm a hopeless drunk, a whore, dirty, too dirty for you. Make arrangements in advance for me to be shipped somewhere like a contaminated package. For what reason? What kind of thanks do you expect *if* I do go? If, if, *if?* What are you trying to do? Manufacture yourself a fully sealed antiseptic, publicly acceptable mistress?" Her voice was shrill, and a small blue vein pumped erratically on the side of her forehead.

"I have not said anything to indicate—"

"Huh!"

He turned to open the door. Her arm shot out in front of him, preventing him from reaching it.

"How could you leave me now? How could you?"

She began to tremble, then to cry. He took her in his arms and held her tightly to him and brushed his lips against her warm forehead.

"I'll stay if you want me to."

She was sobbing and unable to answer him. He was afraid to move for a long time, afraid that she might somehow harm herself by falling, by moving if he did. But after a time her sobbing quieted, and he lifted her in his arms and made his way with her into her bedroom and set her down gently on the bed. He helped her undress and put her under the covers and then sat there, fully clothed, keeping vigil over a time of high temperature and crisis.

Eventually she fell asleep, and he got up very carefully, so as not to wake her, and, leaving a small light in the hallway for her in case she should wake up during the night, turned out the other lights, locked the door, and then went to meet Patrick. Patrick waited while he ordered and ate a poached egg on toast and some coffee. And then the chauffeur drove him home to his penthouse on Sixty-third Street in silence.

Bob Tanner liked coming home. It filled him with a sense of well-being. Kate had immaculate taste. From the soft-muted colors of the Aubusson carpet in the entry to the gentle beauty of the two women in the Clausen painting over the fireplace, there was an elegant, delicate understatement. But none of the rooms lacked the strength that a man liked to see around him. There was not a chair that wasn't sturdy or a table that could not hold a large ashtray and a script, if necessary.

The lights had been left on for him, and he turned them off as he walked as quietly as possible down the long corridor to the bedroom, familiar with this dark, having walked the length of it quite frequently lately. More and more, his work was eating into his life with Kate. It was beginning to drive him rather than the other way around. He was yearning lately to return to films and was on the lookout constantly for a proper reentry. No matter how large his success in television, the medium never seemed to have enough stature for him. They wrote about "the World of Orson Welles" or of Chaplin or of Ford in magazines like *Sight and Sound*. Films warranted legends, television did not. American television audiences, of course, knew his name and his face; he had worked overtime to ensure this. But to the American critics, to the arts, he was Robert Tanner, the television producer with the insatiable ego. No matter how worthy his programs were, the press and industry dismissed them scornfully on the premise that he was cashing in on social injustice (the general theme of all his shows).

Perhaps what hurt most was that in Europe no one knew him at all, and so much a part of him was still an Anglophile. If not in France, he would have at least liked to have been recognized in England. Though he had lived only a few years of his life there, he still spoke with an accent that was strongly English. His clothes were still tailored on Savile Row, his shirts and ties came from Sulka's, his shoes were handmade in the West End, his raincoats came from Aquascutum. He found occasion to fly to London at least once every three or four months, to keep abreast of the European market, he would say. Meantime, he had hired a public relations firm in London to ensure that when he arrived, there would be recognition in certain quarters at least.

There had not been many women in his life since his marriage to Kate. He had had little desire to spoil the tranquillity of his home, and the fact was that though he perhaps did not truly love Kate, she pleased him mightily. She was the most intelligent woman he had ever met, and she had an inbred dignity that made her carry herself regally. The Kennedys, Margaret and Tony, Picasso, Becket, Chaplin—Kate knew them all and was accepted in all their homes. She had been of consummate help to him, and although the general belief was that she had helped him with her connections in his rise in the industry, the fact was he was totally responsible for his own business success. But Kate was responsible for his social acceptance, and of the two, the latter still meant more to him.

Yet here he was placing it all in jeopardy. It was incomprehensible. He desired Anthea more than he recalled desiring a woman before. But he had yet to go to bed with her. It was something deeper. Indefinable. Anthea touched a sacred, private area no other person ever had. She moved him. It was that simple. She truly moved him. Just looking at her, he wanted to cry, to scream out, to protect. She was dead set on destroying the most beautiful thing he felt moved to possess—*herself.* And he knew he wouldn't permit it. He knew he would have to love her, knew she would in turn love him. It was inevitable. She would go obediently with Patrick in the morning, and she would stick it out. He would somehow have to rearrange his life because he knew also he could never let her go. But Kate, that was another matter, another side of his life. What he did not know was if he would ever be able to shut the door forever on this elegant penthouse, on the life he and Kate led—on Kate herself.

She was not asleep. She was sitting up in bed, her dark hair brushed back, her olive skin glowing, her broad shoulders covered by a rich gold satin bed jacket. She looked up from her book as he entered the room and smiled. She was reading a new translation of a Hermann Hesse novel.

"I'm sorry I'm so late," he apologized.

"Shall I get up and fix you something?"

"No. I've eaten."

"Sure?"

"Of course."

He crossed over to the bed and kissed her lightly on the forehead and then went into his dressing room to ready himself for bed. He took longer than usual. When he returned to the bedroom, she was still holding the book.

"Good?" he asked.

"Very."

He got into the bed beside her and turned away to one side.

"I'll turn off the light," she suggested.

"It won't bother me."

She put her book aside, turned off the light nonetheless, and brought her body in close to him. She said nothing and did not move. Yet five minutes later, Bob knew they were both still wide awake. He turned over and took her in his arms, and they made love silently, exchanging only their small moans when the loving had been satisfied. He pulled her close to him then and held her tightly in his arms.

"Bob . . ."

"Shhh. Let's go to sleep."

She was still for a few moments longer.

"Bob . . ."

"Shhh."

"I don't think I could ever live without you. You are just so much a part of my life."

"You won't ever have to, Kate," he said gently, squeezing her affectionately and then patting her on the shoulder. "Now go to sleep."

It wasn't long before Kate's breaths were even and she was, in fact, asleep, but Bob Tanner lay there wakefully beside her for almost the remainder of the dark night.

Chapter 38

Outside, a monotonous wind droned on, caught in the small area of courtyard between the back ends of the apartment houses. The sound was unendurable, and although Tony had tightly shut all the windows, it still stole through the cracks and crevices. It was the end of November, and winter had settled in; a grayness like dirty water seemed to be drowning Manhattan. For more than a week it had been like this, and Tony, though he knew it would really not go away until late March or April, out of some desperation had flipped the pages of his Manufacturers Hanover Trust calendar backward to August and was right now staring at sunshine over Miss Liberty, the waters at her feet a cool, clear postcard blue, and attempting to *will* the grayness to disperse. It was nearly four o'clock, and the winter day would turn to dark soon. He was certain he would welcome it with hope and thanksgiving.

It was Saturday and he had been seated at his desk since nine. He had, of course, found interminable reasons to leave it and had been up and down—how many?—at least fifty, a hundred times. For the eight or ten cups of coffee he allowed to grow cold. For the sandwich he had forgotten to eat. For the fresh cigarettes, though he had an extra pack in his pocket. For matches. For the mail. To go to the john (ten times, at least). To get a sweater. To take it off. To stand by the window and look down at the workmen in the courtyard huddling together and shifting in the cold wind from one foot to the other. He didn't know what they were supposed to be doing, and he thought of opening the window and yelling down to them to find out, but he decided against that and went into the kitchen to make still another pot of fresh coffee.

He had been working on the screenplay for five weeks now. He had begun immediately after returning from his parents' apartment that last agonizing Sunday night when he had told his father about Angelina. Max had returned to England two days later, and though he knew his mother was on the brink of despondency owing to his neglect and Anthea's absence, he was Spartan in his resistence to her. Somehow, at this point, the sharing of even the knowledge that he was writing a screenplay about Angelina might endanger its completion. Anything could really, because he was still in awe of what he had set out to do and still not able to determine if he was, in fact, accomplishing anything worthwhile at all.

Thea had called before she left for the Farm and confided the truth, that she was going away for six weeks for the cure. He promised not to tell Luise, who believed she had flown to Italy for some television film or other. Since she had not even received a card from Thea, Luise was growing steadily more concerned, and Tony had been forced into the sort of lies Thea's doings always seemed to engender. "Yes, I heard from her. She's fine. She said she wrote you. The letter must have been lost. Well, you know the Italians." In reference to his own defection, he would only tell her that he had taken on an extra job.

He was now living an entirely ritualistic life. Up at six to correct whatever work he had done the night before, dressed and fed and on the subway by seven thirty-seven, in class by eight fifteen, lunch in his classroom making notes for later in the day, back on the subway by four ten (he had cut most of his afternoon tutoring), home by five, showered by five thirty and at his desk eating and drinking as he worked until he fell into bed somewhere close to midnight. Saturdays and Sundays he never left his apartment at all. He had ninety-two pages to show for it. Past the halfway mark, but not yet into the homestretch.

Thea had called him once after arriving at the Farm (she had asked him not to call her, and he had both welcomed and respected her request), and though she complained bitterly about "the Fascist bastards who run this asylum," she still sounded more like the old Thea, and he had felt happy and reassured that once again there would be an old Thea. Still, at this moment, he found himself dreading her return in a matter of ten days or two weeks, fearful that he might be wrong and her homecoming, her freedom, might send her off on a terrible tear, which usually meant she would end up on his doorstep. And Tony knew, Spartan though he had been these past five weeks, he could never throw Thea out. And so today, Saturday, and tomorrow, Sunday, he was determined to get himself over the hump, so that even if he lost time when Thea returned, he would be past the point where he would lose his way.

Except it had gone very poorly today.

He really wasn't sure why. The workmen maybe. That was it. What the hell were they doing down there, just grouping, standing there, disappearing from time to time into the rear of the buildings like a line of touring interns? Maybe they were surveyors. Maybe they were going to pull down the whole block. That would be all he'd need, to have to find another apartment that was habitable for the money he could afford! Maybe it was the wind, the grayness, the fact that it was Saturday. Perhaps it was guilt that he had neglected his mother so, not given his students enough time, been happy Thea was away. Whatever it was, he was completely blocked. He had been sitting there all day unable to write one damned acceptable word. Well, at least he knew what writers talked about when they claimed they had a writing block.

The coffee was perking steadily. The aroma warmed him; the rhythm nearly hypnotized him. He'd work through the evening. Maybe he had fallen into a pattern of being creative only in the evening. He poured himself a cup of coffee and decided to drink it at the small table in the living room. Then he would take a shower and go back to work.

He was away from his desk a total of forty-eight minutes, during which time he felt like a small boy playing hooky. It should have made things equal that he had been thinking about Angelina and the script during every second of that forty-eight minutes. But it did not.

Angelina. The most extraordinary thing had occurred. He had had new images. *Angelina* seated on a tall stool and presiding over a courtroom like a judge. *Angelina* burning and beating her sisters and brothers herself so as to get them removed from the home. *Angelina* giving the needle to herself. Something was drastically wrong.

He had been back at his desk for only four minutes when he realized what it was. He had made her too good to be true. There was good and bad in all of us. Even in an eight-and-a-half-year-old child. That was it, of course. The last act of the screenplay. One switched to the mother's point of view as she saw her world, the streets of the slum she lived in, the rat-infested place she lived, her children growing like animals, and her oldest child—always her judge, accusing her, hating her—yes, hating her for bringing herself and her sisters and brothers into such a world. And what else could she do but kill that child, end her misery? She had brought the child into this world. It was, it seemed, her right. And in the end you showed the mother being led by the police from her slum dwelling, but you held the camera in the window of her living-sleeping room, the filthy net curtains flapping in a hot wind while down below on the streets of Spanish Harlem the camera would focus on the dirt in the streets, the children in the gutters, the junkies at the corners, no one caring as the mother is led away, the mother praying as she enters the police car and catches sight of the police hearse pulling to the curb, of the men in white and the stretcher going up the stairs to her building. And then the camera would pull back to *that* room, to Angelina, as though sleeping peacefully, to the men in white and the stretcher as the door opens.

Tony began to write feverishly. The words simply came pouring out. He could not type quickly enough at times to keep up with their impatience. He'd get up to heat the coffee, to grab a biscuit or a slice of cheese, to go to the john, always in a hurry, always irritated at the intrusions of his body needs. At two in the morning, a downstairs neighbor hammered on his ceiling. Tony left the typewriter and picked up a pad and pencil and sat writing on the edge of the bed for several hours more. Sometime around five he just leaned back to close his eyes for a moment and fell asleep. By nine he awakened with a start, stripped, and stepped into a cold shower. He got into a pair of jeans and a sweater and made a fresh pot of strong coffee and waited resentfully for it to perk. Then he took the pot and a clean cup and saucer into the bedroom and took up on the typewriter where he had left off in longhand the night before. He worked straight through until just after three, when his telephone rang. His first instinct was to let it ring, but he had never been able to do that. He answered. "Yeah?" he grumbled with annoyance.

"It's Mother, dear."

"Can I call you back?"

"I thought you'd make a special effort to come over for dinner tonight. It is Sunday."

"I can't."

"Your father flew in and surprised me this morning. It would be quite nice."

"No, maybe tomorrow night. OK? Tomorrow night?"

"Oh. He had a surprise for you."

"It will wait."

"Tony . . ."

"OK. OK. You win. But I don't know what time. When I get there. OK?"

"Of course, dear. That will be fine."

Tony banged the telephone down and went back to work. At six o'clock he wrote the words "the end" and felt as if he might just cry from relief. But he didn't. He poured himself a stiff drink instead and then stacked the pages neatly and put a weight on them to keep them that way. He'd proof them when he got back, and somehow he'd have to find time to type a clean copy the following week. One hundred and forty-two pages, and though it now seemed incredible to him, he had written fifty of them inside twenty-four hours. His arms and hands and shoulders and back ached. He stripped again and got back into the shower and turned the water from hot to cold and cold to hot full force, making the water pellets knead out his tired flesh.

Where to submit the script was another matter. Perhaps he could ask his father about that. No. Better not. Better to keep the entire thing to himself. Not to say anything until he had sold it. That probably meant he would need an agent. He knew some of the big ones through his father. That guy at William Morris, the one he'd known since he was a kid. No. Not him. Not anyone in any way connected with Max. On his own. A smaller agent. When Thea got back, he could speak to her about it. Yes, Thea would be the logical one to discuss it with.

That brought his mind to Thea, and he began to feel restless about her. He should have made sure she was all right. He should have gone up to that place to see for himself. But she had sounded good. He repeated that to himself as he stepped out of the shower. He wrapped a towel around himself and dialed her number. There wasn't any answer, and of course, he had not really expected there would be. Still, it didn't seem a strange thing for him to have done, and it did ease his conscience a bit. He could ask the long-distance operator to get the number of the place she was at, but he decided he would wait for Thea to call him. He lifted the weight and picked up the script just to glance at a few pages and sat down and began correcting it, changing small things for more than an hour. He put it back against his true desire and anchored it with the paperweight. It was after eight, and he wasn't dressed. He'd have to take a taxi.

He didn't arrive uptown until just past nine. Luise made no mention of the hour, and indeed both his parents seemed pleased to see him. They had a leisurely drink first and exchanged small talk. Luise then went into the kitchen to ready dinner. A special television program began at ten that Max had wanted to watch, and so for a change they were going to eat in the living room in front of the set.

"Dinner!" Luise called triumphantly when she entered with a huge tray laden with food and plates. Tony took it from her. "Put it on the cocktail table, dear. We'll just all help ourselves."

Max was adjusting the television. His program was about to start. Though Luise had said they would all help themselves, she still stood there serving the food. It was some kind of curry—a dish Tony didn't care for, but he accepted his plate without complaint. He wasn't too hungry anyway.

The program was a special report on the South American countries. As those things went, it wasn't bad. It was a bit hypnotizing in its sameness, and at least allowed Tony some time for his own private thoughts. It had turned into a very impersonal evening. It was better that way. Max was probably exhausted from the flight and not yet adjusted to the time change. It was in reality the middle of the night for him.

Max got up and turned off the set as soon as the program was over. "Interesting," he commented blandly.

"I have ice cream for dessert, if that's all right," Luise said as she rose and stacked the dishes on the tray.

"Not for me, Mom," Tony said, conscious that he only called his mother Mom in front of his father and Luise all other times. He took the tray from her and carried it into the kitchen.

"Your father looks well, don't you think?" she inquired when they were alone.

"Fine," he lied, knowing she hadn't really thought so and was trying to trip him into saying out loud what she was silently thinking. They went back into the living room with the coffee.

"Oh, did you tell him?" Luise asked Max as she poured.

"Not yet." Max was smiling with some small-boy embarrassment.

"Tell me what?" Tony asked.

"Well," Luise began after glancing at Max and seeing that he was going to remain silent. "Your Angelina. She disturbed your father so that when he got back to London after you two had spoken, he sat right down and wrote a treatment. Isn't that correct, darling? A treatment?"

"Yes," Max agreed. "A treatment."

"Based on *exactly* what you told us about that god-awful mother and so on. What did you call it, Max?"

"*Little Angel*, tentatively, that is."

"Yes, and Columbia OK'd it. Tony, isn't that marvelous. Angelina is going to be your father's next film." Luise glanced proudly at Max. It was obvious she felt that this somehow brought her two men closer together, that now they shared something. That Max, by writing about little Angelina, had finally given *their* son his approval.

Tony sat as though suddenly paralyzed. He was unable to speak, unable to move, and for a moment he thought he might actually be having some sort of seizure. He just kept staring at the dead television screen, seeing only its ghosts, not his own.

"Well, of course, it isn't exactly Tony's story. It was that son of a bitch teacher that interested me. I was thinking about the Kid all the time. How that little shit could play the bejesus out of that role."

"It's wonderful, isn't it, Tony?" Luise smiled.

Tony somehow found his voice. "Great," he said. He stood up. "Listen, if you two don't mind, I'm beat."

"It's all this tutoring you've been doing, Tony," Luise insisted.

If that was what she thought, Tony decided to leave it at that. "Yeah," he agreed, "I guess you're right."

He shook hands with his father and kissed his mother on the cheek. This time he waited for the elevator as Luise stood in the open doorway of the apartment, watching him. He could see his father crossing to the bar in the room behind her.

"Night," he said when the elevator came and got inside. Luise still had the apartment door open as he began to descend.

He walked over to Eighty-sixth and took the subway. It was empty, but he still stood all the way to his stop. It was bitter cold, and the wind had grown icy, but he didn't hurry across the intersection or up his street. He even said a casual hello to the doorman and exchanged the usual nonsense.

"Cold."

"Yeah."

"Maybe it will snow."

"Looks like it."

Mrs. Rabin from 5C rode up in the elevator with him. She had apparently been down in the basement collecting her wash and stood guarding the huge wicker basket filled with towels and faded nylon. It was a crazy hour for anyone to be doing their wash, particularly on Sunday night, but Tony didn't comment.

"You missed Ed Sullivan," she said. "Such a delightful show."

The elevator stopped on Five, and as that was Tony's floor, too, he carried her basket to her door for her.

"Thank you so much, Mr. Seaman." Tony turned to continue on. "Mr. Seaman . . ." Tony turned. "That blond actress you were seeing, the one who had the drinking problem. Well, I couldn't help noticing—she got sick once right outside my door—you've broken up, eh?"

"I don't know who you mean," Tony said stiffly and continued on and went into his apartment without looking back at the disapproving Mrs. Rabin.

He stood there in the dark, just making out the outlines of the furniture. The curtains were open, and the lights across the court shone in between the slats of the blinds making the gray patches appear striped. He went into the kitchen and stood there for a long moment, and then he did something he could not explain. He took the long butcher knife he always left hanging on the magnetized board over the stove and walked with it into the living room and directly to the couch and then with a most terrible heaving of his body, he thrust the knife into the back cushions, ripping the material apart, thrusting the knife in again and again, pulling it apart, disembowling it—the back . . . the arms . . . the seat. Over and over and over and over. There was no other sound in the room. Just his grunts and the whir of the knife and the thud as the insides were exposed. He finally dropped the knife and stumbled into the bedroom, where he picked up the paperweight and cast it through the window and fastidiously ripping all one hundred and forty-two pages into shreds, threw them out into the court as well. Then he fell down on the bed, and since he knew it would have been impossible for him to have fallen asleep so quickly, he assumed later that he had passed out.

Chapter 39

The Evans chick was not the first person Vic Toscini had thought to call. He had a long list, and Anthea Evans was fairly far down at the bottom. But he had zeroed out on those above her, and this was what he called desperation time. He was down to his last ten bucks. He hadn't worked in more than a year—*55 Days in Peking*, for crissakes!—and the old dame he had been living with had taken an overdose and left him homeless. Kicked off with no will and only the ten lousy bucks he now had in her pocketbook. Sure she had jewelry, minks, but that wasn't his speed. He wasn't a thief. In fact, he never took anything from anyone in his entire life. The ten spot, that was something else again. The old crow owed him carfare at the very least.

Well, he thought, *I'm on my way again.* Vic Toscini believed wholeheartedly in himself. He was positive he was going to make it through the States, the world, through all the forces out to get him, through all the problems that were out to entrap him, through all his limitations—his lack of education, his shitty family, all the languages he didn't understand, the things he didn't know. He was going to make it, and if that lush actress Anthea Evans could help him, well, hell, break the ten bucks and put a dime in the coin box!

To his surprise, she was sober, and in fact, she sounded rather groovy, top-drawer, class. Yes, now that he thought about it, even when soused, Anthea Evans had had class. That was a hot one. A classy drunk!

"Hi, baby," he had said.

"Who is this?" Hepburn, strained right through the nose.

"Vic Toscini."

"I'm terribly sorry. . ."

"Vic Toscini, baby. About two months ago in the Village. That joint Adler was appearing in. You were with that Professor Seaman."

"Oh! *That* Vic Toscini. I'm not in."

"Hey! Don't hang up. Baby. . ."

"Mr. Toscini, I'm rahley chahmed, rahley, but you see, I rahley don't care to talk with you, rhaley. You're yesterday—all my yesterdays—and I rahley, rahley must hang up."

"Hey! All I want is the professor's telephone number."

"Tony's? Good heavens, why?"

"Remember you told me about his work and about this story you wanted him to write?"

"Honestly, Mr. Toscini . . ."

"Vic."

"Honestly, Mr. Toscini, I don't, but in all probability I did. So?"

"I have to speak to him, and I find his number's unlisted. I think I know a cat who could be interested. Someone who wants to film a low budget, with that kind of slant, right here in New York."

"Who?"

"You wouldn't know him. He doesn't know you."

"I'll ring Tony and get his agent's number."

"His agent? Come on now, baby!"

"Well . . ."

He heard her doorbell ring in the background.

"I can't see that it would hurt."

And she had rattled off the number and then, the doorbell ringing in the background again, had rather abruptly disconnected.

Vic was calling from the lobby of the Plaza, where he had left his suitcases at the desk before checking in with an excuse that he'd be right back, he had to make a call. If he got nowhere with Tony Seaman, he'd check in and figure out a way to pay for it later. "Live now, pay later" had become his motto. It wasn't by choice. It seemed to be forced on him. He really could do this Tony Seaman a big favor. Now there was a constipated character if he ever saw one. But he legitimately had background for a good, cheap film—and Vic had Len Rogers. Put them both together, they spelled promise. He had already hooked Len by convincing him Tony was a friend and that his father—hell, who didn't know Max Seaman?—would be willing to help with a little bread to see him on his way. And Len was a smart kid, an underground filmmaker who had worked with Warhol but had this itch to go on his own.

Vic dropped the dime in the slot and dialed Tony's number. He sweated it out until Tony answered, which seemed a hell of a long time. That must be some spread-out pad.

"Professor!" Vic cried enthusiastically to Tony's less-than-cordial "Yeah."

"You have the wrong number."

"Hey, Professor *Seaman*?"

"*Anthony* Seaman speaking."

"This is Vic Toscini."

"*Who*?"

"A friend of Anthea Evans." That seemed to work. "We met once, but I guess you don't recall. However, I'm an actor—in films. And I had been telling Anthea I was looking for a vehicle for myself, because this seemed the only way today and she mentioned an idea you were working on, and it's been bugging me all week. Now so happens, I know a young director . . ."

"Miss Evans misled you. I don't write, I teach."

"I, of course, would speak to your agent regarding any business, but I thought, Professor . . ."

"I'm not a professor."

"Couldn't we meet, have a drink, something like that?"

"I'm afraid not."

"It doesn't have to be this evening, though I happen to be in your neighborhood at this minute . . ."

"Miss Evans should *never* have given you my address."

"She really didn't. She just mentioned that you lived close by."

"You just spoke to her?"

"Yes."

"Well, I'm on Ninth. Where are you?"

Crissakes! Ninth!

"Five minutes away, but I do have some business to finish up. Could I just see you for ten minutes, say, in half an hour?"

"I have a nine o'clock appointment uptown. I can only spare about ten minutes."

Vic got the address and hung up. Then he went over to the head bellboy.

"I'm Mr. Toscini. Just checking in. Could you get me a car and driver pronto, like five, ten minutes top? And hold my bags until I get back. I don't want to be put in some dog of a suite. I'll want to see my accommodations myself. OK?" He handed the man a five-dollar bill, leaving himself exactly four bucks eighty to his name.

"Which is your luggage, sir?"

"The Gucci." And thank you, oh, dearly departed, for the going-away gift! (Well, that wasn't stealing. She sure as hell wouldn't need Gucci luggage where she was going.) "I'll be in the Oak Room bar."

"Yes, sir."

He went into the cool dark Oak Room. Outside it was all snow and cold wind, but he was hot and sweating. The cool air felt good. He ordered a Chivas Regal, leaving four bucks on the bar and not glancing at his change when it came. He was paged in ten minutes flat. A long sleek Lincoln Continental limousine was waiting. He got in and leaned back comfortably in the richly upholstered rear seat. Whenever he could, Vic Toscini rode in limousines. He hadn't been in a bus or subway in about five years. He'd walk rather than do that. He generally took taxis, but he delighted in finding times like this when there was every reason to hire a car. A taxi would have been three bucks each way, leaving him shit. And who wanted to go flagging down a taxi on Ninth Street?

For some reason he had refrained from checking in at the Plaza and making these calls from his suite. Something had been buzzing around in the top of his head. Something he remembered about this Seaman cat. It had been the memory of that one moment when their shoulders had brushed in the Village club that night. *Not fag. Not yet*, he had thought. And the telephone conversation. Seaman really did not want to talk about any story ideas. Yet, his manner had changed in midstream.

Vic smiled to himself and straightened his tie and absently removed a speck of lint from his expensive trench coat (Madrid period—the English deb who wanted to learn about life).

"Wait for me," he told the driver when they had reached Tony's.

Tony could not imagine what had possessed him to allow Vic Toscini time. Particularly this evening when he had to be at the clinic by nine and when he knew his session would not be an easy one owing to his mental state the last three weeks—ever since that ghastly evening when he last saw his father. He didn't want to think about it at all, but every time he glanced at the empty space where the couch had been, he was reminded. Getting the couch out of the apartment had been no easy task. He had taken it down to the incinerator in the basement cushion by cushion, feeling like a murderer disposing of the body. Then he had to ask the janitor to help him get the frame out, telling him he had dropped a burning cigarette on the cushions.

It was incredible that Vic Toscini should materialize now. Tony had not actually remembered his name, but during this entire low period, the man, the face, the eyes, would flash in his mind. Tony knew somehow that it would happen one day. That Vic Toscini would reenter his life. But he had not been prepared for its happening so soon.

He had avoided seeing his father for the remainder of his stay, and he had avoided the usual Sunday night with Luise as well. Now that Thea was home, that was easier. Clearly, Thea's health on her return was the only good thing that had occurred that year. And she was happy too. Tony knew she'd entered into an arrangement with Bob Tanner (though, of course, Luise did not), and though he did not approve, he was thankful for anyone in her life who could keep her sober and bring back some semblance of the old Thea. Tanner was at least doing that. So he was married. Who was Tony to criticize?

But right now all he could think of was how to postpone Vic Toscini's arrival. He had been in the shower when the call first came and yet he had gone back in and, knowing that Toscini was arriving in a matter of half an hour, remained in the shower until the doorman had just called to report that the man was on his way up. *Oh, God! On his way up.* Tony hurried into his bedroom and, throwing the towel he had wrapped around himself into the hamper, got into some shorts and a bathrobe. He wouldn't answer the door. What right had Toscini to come straight up? Why hadn't the doorman asked Tony if he wanted him up in the first place? He'd have to speak to the doorman about that. This week. Before Christmas. Next week after the small Christmas gift Tony would have to give him (he had ordered a new sofa which had eaten into his savings) he couldn't expect any service at all. No, he'd have to answer the door, but the man could see it was an inconvenient hour. He'd ask him to come back another time.

Tony stuffed his feet into his slippers and brushed his hair. He couldn't let go of the ugly images of the past few weeks, of his father's face as Luise told Tony about *Little Angel*, the horror when he got home, the destruction of the couch, the painful discussions about it at the clinic with his analyst, the deep, deep anger and frustration and loneliness these weeks. *Oh, God, yes—the loneliness*. The night he went to the bar around the corner and some fag propositioned him. And the lavatory, that was worst, the black male hand sliding a message under the door—"Roger" and a telephone number. Oh, God, and he hadn't thrown it away. That was the worst thing. It was still under Thea's picture in the bedroom. He was sweating again and wished he could get back into the shower. He thought about it. He wouldn't hear the doorbell if he was in the shower.

"Are you a virgin?" the analyst had asked.

"If you mean have I fucked anyone, I am in that sense a virgin."

"What else could I mean?"

"Semantics are a pain. But I consider myself too used up to be considered a virgin. Anyway, it's a ridiculously coy phrase."

"Have you ever made love to a woman then?"

"No."

"A man . . . a *boy*?"

"For crissakes, no!" He had stood up, angry, his heart pounding wildly. "You know, you're sick. You know, I think you're sick," he had shouted at the analyst.

"Well, then, have you ever thought about doing that with a man?"

"Look, just because I'm twenty-three and . . . No! For crissakes, no!"

"Sit down, Tony. Please sit down."

"Voyeur, that's what that son of a bitch my father calls analysts. I hate to admit it, but he just *might* be right." Still he sat down, and he had felt a little calmer, a little better.

"Have you been able to speak to your father since the incident?"

"With some luck he might never speak to me again! Son of a bitch!"

"Do you think he knows how his betrayal hurt you?"

"Damned right! Son of a bitch!"

The doorbell rang. Tony's heart sank. "Just a minute," he called. He stood there looking at himself in the bathroom mirror, unable to draw his eyes away from his own riveting stare. The doorbell rang again. Tony splashed some Guerlain Vegetal on himself and slowly went to greet his guest.

Vic Toscini seemed of smaller stature than he remembered, younger. He looked hungry for that matter, but if that was so, he wasn't disturbed by the condition. He moved electrically and shot out his hand. "Good to see you, Professor." He grinned.

"I am *not* a professor." Tony stood aside, though, and let Vic enter.

"Nice pad. Good taste."

"The couch is out being re-covered."

"Uh-huh. Look, I have my car waiting downstairs. My driver will take you wherever you want to go and we can talk on the way."

"That would be all right. As you can see, I'm late. The telephone . . . things . . ." He stood nervously in the center of the room staring at Vic Toscini.

"I didn't interrupt anything, did I?"

"No. Why?"

"Your prick, baby. It's standing right up at attention."

Tony thought he might get ill. He felt faint, thought he would keel over. He excused himself and headed for the bedroom, but Vic Toscini was following him. He stood in the doorway as Tony sat down on the edge of the bed.

"I know how it is, Tony. Hell, we can't get up on a rooftop and scream down at all the lousy indifferent people, *'Hey! Someone down there, love me.'* "

Tony studied the handsome face so close to him. There had been tenderness in the voice, and strangely, there was tenderness in those brown velvet eyes. Tony felt a strong wave of compassion for the lean, hungry face. Vic Toscini was what all the Robertos he taught might grow to be. And Tony knew exactly what that was—calculating, desperate, clawing humans—but, yes, for the emotionally and physically starved, compassionate, tender.

"Hey! Someone down there, love me."

Roberto on the roof of a tenement.

Angelina from the window of her derelict apartment.

They had silently screamed that. So had Vic Toscini. And so Vic Toscini could easily see in a minute that Tony was, in fact, screaming that, too—this moment . . .

Tony never did get to his analyst that night. And Vic Toscini did not leave. Tony gave him ten dollars to have the chauffeur pick up his luggage at the Plaza and Vic gave the man Tony's address to send the limousine bill. Vic Toscini had come to stay, and Tony knew he was going to do everything he could to keep things that way.

BOOK VI

Golgotha-The Place
of the Skulls

I dreamed I had a child and even in the dream I saw it was my life, and it was an idiot, and I ran away. But it always crept into my lap again, clutched at my clothes. Until I thought, if I could kiss it, whatever in it was my own, perhaps I could sleep. And I bent to its broken face, and it was horrible but I kissed it. I think one must finally take one's life in one's arms.—Holga

ARTHUR MILLER, *After the Fall*

Chapter 40

It was on the occasion of Max's fifty-fourth birthday that he got it into his head to go to Peru. The thing was that his own life seemed to be crowding him, and when he tried to push it away, to breathe with some ease, he'd get that damned pressure on his chest and be unable to concentrate on his work because in those blinding flashes his parents, Luise, the kids, Lou, Edyth, Melissa—the commitee—would attack him, suffocating him, allowing him no fresh whiffs of air. All that unpolluted, come-and-get-it air on those mountains in Peru. He didn't kid himself (now that was one thing he never did!): his parents, Luise, the kids, Lou, Edyth, Melissa—the committee—he'd never shake them. They were his. Like his talent, his drive, his habits, his brutalities. *His life.* He couldn't kill them without killing himself. All he hoped to do was create a little less interdependence. Anyone else might have thought him mad. But he had awakened this morning of his fifty-fourth birthday—April 19, 1969—and decided he would at least check into the possibilities of Peru.

Edyth called before he was out of bed. "Happy birthday," she chirped.

The truth was that until she had congratulated him, he had not recalled that it was his birthday. Somehow the information seemed to cinch things for him. "Edyth, would you call Albany Travel and ask them about flying arrangements to Peru?"

"Peru? Mind if I ask why?"

"A story's been bugging me. I think it could only be shot in Peru."

"I'll have the information for you as soon as possible."

"Appreciate that."

"Max . . ."

"Umm?"

"Considering how long it is since we've been alone, I mean as friends. Out somewhere or together—as friends—this may seem out of place, but it is your birthday and you are alone . . . have been really for quite a time . . . Well, I thought . . ."

"Sure, Edyth. We'll celebrate together."

"I thought I'd like to cook dinner for you if you'd let me."

"I don't think . . ."

"It was just a thought. I understand."

"You never listen, Edyth. You always answer your own questions and refuse your own invitations. You're welcome to share my birthday, but I buy."

"But I thought . . ."

"Edyth, I buy or forget it."

"OK, Max. Thank you very much. Peru! I'm dying to hear that story!"

She was gone and Max dropped the telephone receiver back into place but remained in bed. He really did have a story forming in his head, and the crazy thing was Peru did seem the perfect and only place to shoot it. The whole damned thing was a chase up in those mountains. Just two men. Who the men were, or why one was running away and the other in pursuit, would not come into focus until the climactic moments. The running man would not be sure of anything. Why he was running. Why he was being pursued. He just knew he couldn't stop or he was dead. And the stalking man would not know why he must not turn back, why he must track his victim on. He just knew if he stopped, there would be no going back or going on. He was dead. And so the two would continue treacherously over the brutal, violent mountains of Peru. Just two men. One with a black sombrero, of course, so score could be kept. But from time to time, the camera would explore their thoughts, fears, memories—the story leaving Peru then—but always mystically, never in full focus. And then other characters would be introduced. Not until the climactic moments of the chase would the stalking man be revealed by these flashes of truth and nightmare and reverie. Sympathy would immediately be reversed. The stalking man must get his prey. He has been in life the victim, as the running man has been in life his false judge.

Max took a pad and pencil from the bedside and began to make a list of titles.

The Running Man (used)
The Stalking Man (*The Stalking Moon* just out—too close)
The Chase (used)
The Quarry (Dürrenmatt novel—no good)
The Pursuit (not bad, not good)
The Edge (not bad)
The Outer Edge (better)
Edge of Fear (too melodramatic?)
Truth Is the Hunter (giveaway)
Run, Man, Run (?)

He stopped there. He thought he liked the last title. *Run, Man, Run.* It had a modern feel to it (*Burn, Baby, Burn*), and it moved, implying action, saying a lot, saying nothing. He circled it heavily and, leaving the pad and pencil on the far side of the bed, threw the covers back and, walking in the nude and arrow-straight, headed for the bathroom to start the day.

The two men in his new story never left his thoughts the entire day. He spent an hour on arrival at the office looking through the American and English Players Directory: Male. He was looking for faces—the just-right faces for his stalking and running men. There really weren't any he liked. He toyed with a Fellini approach. Find the faces, anywhere. Then dub real actors for the voices. It could be done. Fellini did it brilliantly. Yeah. But that was Fellini. He was Seaman. He'd find two just-right faces somewhere, actors, and *get* performances out of them. For a few minutes he toyed with the idea of a black man for the stalking man and then dismissed it. The emphasis would shift that way. Though Sandy Mayberry would make a hell of a stalking man. *No.*

"OK," Edyth was saying.

Max looked up. Edyth was standing in the doorway reading from some notes.

"Here's the information. BOAC has a flight every Tuesday, leaving at ten A.M., arriving in Lima at nineteen fifteen. The flight actually takes fourteen hours and fifteen minutes' flying time. Then Peruvia has two flights—eight forty-five A.M. on Thursday and Saturday arriving in Lima at twenty-three fifty-five."

He sat there staring at Edyth, not really hearing a word she was saying. Fellini would have used Edyth in a film. She had a truly arresting face. Maybe he'd even cast her in this. What was it in Edyth's face that so commanded his attention? Even in the beginning. Whatever it was was still there nagging at him. Restraint, resignation—alone these two were deadly traits, but in Edyth they held a form of fascination. The thing about Edyth was that one knew in an instant that she was of the predator species. No need for Edyth to swoop or attack. Edyth hovered and waited, vulturesque. If the stalking man didn't succeed, there was Edyth at the end of the mountain pass, at the end of the running man's endurance—there was Edyth, restrained, resigned . . . smiling.

Edyth was smiling.

"What?"

"I said do you want the one-way or round-trip fare?"

"I'm not planning to rob the Bank of England, Edyth. I'm thinking about looking at locations!"

"Single or double?"

"Maybe with a whole camera crew. How the hell do I know? All the information I want right now is how often the planes go and how long it takes. File the rest."

"Of course, Max." She turned to go.

"Why the hell don't you tell me to my face that I'm a bastard?" he shouted.

She came gently back into the room. Her voice retained the same even tonality. "You're not, Max. By your own definition you're not. You are, though, quite thoroughly through and through a son of a bitch."

"Why don't you leave me then?"

"Why don't you fire me?"

"Damned if I know, Edyth."

She smiled again. "I do, Max. And that's why I don't leave." She turned then and went to the door. "Would you like me to reserve dinner?"

"Yeah."

"Where?"

"Wherever you want to eat."

"It's your birthday."

"Yeah. How old am I, Edyth?"

"Fifty-four."

"An old man, eh?"

Her eyes twinkled. "Old and gamy."

"I stink, eh?" He was looking up at her.

"When not refrigerated. Like all the other wild animals in the jungle."

"Which one? A lion, would you say?"

"*The* lion, Max."

He laughed. He felt happier now. Some of the crowding pushed back. "How about Mirabel's?"

"Too posh."

"White Elephant?"

"Too tame."

"Where then?"

"We could do something crazy. Fly to Paris."

"For dinner?"

She just nodded her head.

"I'm surprised at you, Edyth. A nice middle-class American girl like you."

"The Horse?"

"Where?"

"It's a new place. 'Swinging London,' that kind of thing."

"Been there?"

"Unh-unh. But I thought it might be fun for you."

"The Horse then." He was smiling at her as she nodded and then turned to go. From the rear, nothing at all had changed about Edyth. The same tight ass, long legs. "Hey, and Edie, keep the incense burning at your place."

"You didn't used to need it," she threw over her shoulder and then left him alone.

He was really alone. Well, that was the apparent order of things. Neither of the kids was in contact with him anymore. He hadn't seen Luise since that violent evening in New York almost a year now. He couldn't even recall how it started, but suddenly a volcano had erupted, and the words like searing hot lava had burned a path between them, finally—*finally*, after thirty years, engulfing them, and ending with their screaming obscenities at each other on a public street about some girl who had only been in his life a few months and whom he hadn't even seen since. *Melissa had been in his life only a few days, however.* That was something else again. Melissa had always been in his life and even now—even now. That was the point. Of course, he was really alone, but then again, he was not. There, they all were pushing, crowding, closing in on him.

Max got up and poured himself a straight scotch on ice from his office bar. Eleven in the morning. He had been doing that a lot lately. The entire year for that matter. He used to always wait until six. It had been a rule, self-imposed, self-kept. No drinking until six. But this year all previous conditions, maxims, discipline seemed to collapse.

Going to see Burt Winters as he had. That was a totally mad and self-destructive act. What the hell did he care now, after all these years, what Burt had really said before the committee? Or if he had slept with Luise? Or that Burt was pulling in money like fish in season on the Klamath River? And writing Rossellini that letter telling him that in thinking about it, he thought Rossellini's films with Bergman and his biographical films—*Stromboli, The Greatest Love, Strangers,* and *Fear*—were great art. He had also written Kramer and said he thought he was a phony, had called Foreman and asked, "Now just for the record, who the fuck *really* wrote the screenplay on *River Kwai?*" Who the hell cared anyway? And Fellini—he had written him suggesting a meeting (those Fellini faces), and the bastard hadn't even had the courtesy to reply. It ate at his gut, and why the hell should it? That was the point. Why should it?

And here he had agreed to have dinner with Edyth after an entirely sensible cease-fire had been respected for more than fifteen years. Another irrational act. All his acts irrational acts. It was the crowding. That was responsible for it all.

What seemed the most irrational was the trip he had taken to Washington last time he was in the States. He had stayed at the Shoreham, walked in the little park behind it where he and Henry Green had once walked. And then he had gone to the Congressional Library and taken out the transcripts of his own appearance before the committee and sat down with them in that scholarly place just sitting there with his hand on top of the nineteen pages (only nineteen pages!) that represented his entire testimony. Just sat there with his hand resting that way. What was that—a caress? Who the hell did he think he was comforting? And why had he just sat that way, never reading the transcript he had come all the way to Washington to read? Irrational—totally irrational. The ground was slipping from under him. They all were closing in on him.

And yet he had not felt bad when he left Washington. That was the odd thing. He had in a way even felt comforted. There had been a demonstration of young people in Washington at the same time he had been there. And he had left envying them. Yes, envying them. They cared. They felt akin to this country. Dissent passionate enough to march itself right up to where the heart was. "Beat for us a while," they screamed. "Listen to our voices," they shouted. They cared. They belonged. This was their country, and they were still young enough to fight for it, their way, still hopeful it could be what they dared to dream it could be. He had felt that way once, when he had insisted on fasting when he was a kid just four. He had felt Jewish then. He felt a part of a Jewish family. When he went to Spain, he went feeling like the emissary. He was part of a largehearted country—a country that had been pressed down but whose bounty still spilled over. He had felt American then. All the time in Spain he had realized how American he had felt. And when he had returned home and after. It had been a bad time in his country. He was young, and yet he was older. He was a writer, and yet he was to be a father. What he had seen wrong, he felt he had to fight to correct. He had done it his way, which seemed the only way at that time. He wrote articles to expose the wrong things, trusting in his countrymen to see and to act. Then he wrote screenplays. In the beginning it was really for that same reason. He was a writer, and that was how he could fight—and dissent. He joined organizations. He joined the party. But then the party had been a terrible shock—a disillusionment. He had felt used by it, and he had felt his ideals and his talents were being used by it. So he got out. And then what was there? *The Committee.* The rise and fall of Joe McCarthy. For fighting for his country, for what he believed idealistically his country should be, he had been branded an outcast—pariah, leper. He was no longer a part. Not that that was the reason for his return to Washington, his testimony in front of the committee. Or was it? He was confused on that point. He was trying to be honest, but he was confused. Whatever his subconscious motivation, consciously he had believed he had not betrayed any one of his friends or colleagues (they all had been named before. That was what no one took into consideration—*they had been named before*—and if he could continue writing, he at least could continue fighting with words. No one took that into consideration). What the hell! He wouldn't look back over his shoulder. This was no time to feel sorry for himself. But he assured himself it wasn't self-pity. Max Seaman wallowing in self-pity—impossible! He was just attempting to put some order to things.

So, he became in the eyes of his world, an ex-patriot. He was also, for all intents and purposes, an ex-husband, ex-father, ex-Hollywood filmmaker. *Jesus.* He had ex'd out his whole frigging life. But one just couldn't leave things at that. Being an ex-anything had to be a transitory stage. Before you became something else or returned to the familiar. It was purgatory. Living apart from Luise and still feeling married, living away from the States and still feeling American. Not seeing his children and still regarding himself as a father, not having made a film in Hollywood in more than twenty years and still considering himself a Hollywood filmmaker . . . *abroad.*

It was right back to the game of truth. If he was truly none of these things, then he had to admit it to himself and do something about being . . . what? . . . Max Seaman. Perhaps, in the final analysis one had to become more a part of oneself.

Edyth was standing in the doorway again, waiting.

"Yeah?"

"It's after one."

"So?"

"How about lunch?"

"Bring me back something."

"All right."

"And disconnect the switchboard. I'm working on the new story. *Run, Man, Run.* You like that?"

"It's easy to remember."

"Yeah, well, I think it's good." He sat down at his desk. He had a straight glass of scotch in his hand, and she was staring at it. He downed it. "I want to rough out the plot construction. Tough job on this one. You have to keep the action, the conflict up in every scene. It's a chase. Beginning to end—it's a chase. But it's more. It's a man's last drowning minutes. Yeah. That's what it is."

"We can talk about it when I come back. I'll bring my lunch with me. We can bat it around. OK?" She was gentle, almost tender.

"Good idea."

"Would a hamburger be all right?"

"Sounds great."

She smiled benevolently at him and closed the door to his office gently, as though he were a child being put to sleep.

He sat there until he heard her leave her office, too. Then he picked up the telephone. She had disconnected the switchboard. Good. He took out a fresh lined legal pad, turned back the cover, and, using a finely sharpened pencil from his desk holder, wrote at the top of the first page:

RUN, MAN, RUN!
Original Screenplay by
MAXWELL ISAAC SEAMAN

Then in the lower right-hand corner he wrote:

1st Treatment
Property of Elektra Productions
London, England

He flipped the page over and in the upper left-hand corner he wrote:

CAMERA FADES IN:

Then he pushed the pad aside. He felt better. Committed. He had started a new screenplay. "What is your current project," Mr. Seaman?" the reporter might ask. *"Run, Man, Run,"* he'd say. "What category does it fall into?" He'd look up seriously. "Action. It's a chase from beginning to end. Takes place in Peru. The mountains. I'm flying there shortly to scout for locations."

That would be a good start, whet their appetites. Hell, everyone loved a chase, and Peru was pretty much virgin film territory.

He still held the pencil and, taking a note pad from his drawer, scribbled a few lines to Edyth:

GONE HOME. NO CALLS. STARTING
THE TREATMENT AND NEED QUIET.
PICK ME UP AT EIGHT.
Max

That was the way it had to be. Edyth picking *him* up. The way it always had been. He was starting a new screenplay. No time for drastic changes.

The Horse was a confusion of psychedelic colors: gas blue, traffic-light red and green, blinding, glaring, alienating, distorting, bringing the scope of vision down to about the six inches before one's nose. Max couldn't read the menu. It hardly seemed to matter because he would not have been able to convey to the waiter what he wanted anyway. Everyone in the room seemed to be tightly preserved in sound. It pressed in on all sides. The sound. Loud, deafening, brass-mouthed, trumpet-tongued, a carrillon blasting enough to waken the dead, a din tumultuous enough to silence the living. At first it oppressed him. When they had entered the main room and the sound had first lashed out at him, he had wanted to turn right around and leave. But Edyth had already made her way to a table at the rear, presumably following someone, though Max had not been able to determine who it could be. Once seated, and with a scotch in his hand, he felt immeasurably better. Even liberated. It was impossible to carry on a conversation with Edyth. All he could do was smile at her through the cloud of flamelight between them. She looked a little like a Modigliani painting. Long planes and distorted hollows all splashed with red and flecked with millions of white dust particles. After a while he was not conscious of the sound. But he was aware that words were no longer necessary. Were, in fact, superfluous. He sat there, then, smiling when he thought his face needed exercise, glancing at his own Modigliani from time to time and otherwise enjoying the intelligent company of his own thoughts.

Edyth had pointed to the menu a couple of times, and he now picked it up. There were only five selections. The numbers in large Roman numerals stood out alongside them. The numbers were all Max could read. He decided to gamble, what the hell! And held up three fingers to the waiter. Edyth held up five. Dinner was going to be like the prize in a crackerjack box.

He had sat down to write as soon as he had returned home that afternoon, but the words had not come. The thoughts had not ordered themselves. His attention had always been pulled away by an incredible magnetic force. His life again, compacting, compressing, squeezing in on him. He allowed it to happen. He didn't fight it off this time. Somewhere, in all those desperate moments, with all those desperate people, somewhere was the hook for his story. The peg to hang his hat on. When he found it, a door would open, and another world, new and changing, touched with the magic of all newness would be his.

Somewhere there was a far-off horn, a clarion in the wilderness, in the dark of forgetfulness. Thousands of familiar moments panned past him, faces animate, inanimate. The familiar, the loved, the vaguely remembered, the lost but faintly recognized. One face in particular. One moment. Though he had not been able to bring it into clear focus. Yet there it was. In everything he looked at. It was in the distant voices, the faces, the silence. A face. A moment. Coming in for a flickering instant, then mixing with the other faces, drowning in the sea depths of the past. Lost. And then somehow found again.

He was on his fourth or fifth scotch. Actually, he had lost count. But the face. The moment was clear. What was shattering was that Max could not place either of them. The face seemed to him like some floating red balloon, a blood-washed moon with a gloating eye. Then a red-hot coal. One thing, it never remained still, never long enough to allow recognition.

It was growing late in the afternoon, and the light had gone in the sky, and his room was dark where he sat—a sodden, chilled gray. It was cold, and he should have risen, closed the window, turned on the heat and flicked on the light. There were ice tongs gripping his shoulders. He was frozen and not able to move.

Then, there it was!

The chairman!

"Do you solemnly swear . . ."

The moment . . .

It shook him at first. He had been unable to write a word the entire day, and he knew enough about himself to know why. He had not known who one of the men engaged in that chase really was. He had recognized by the time he had left the office that the stalking man was to be himself—but the running man, that was another matter. Now he knew. The chairman. That little demonic, red-faced Kafkaesque man who was evil incarnate. And why? Because he pushed men to the edge of the cliff, and that was all. Now it was his turn. An allegory then, but it had to have an easily acceptable and simple plot. The running man was a judge; the stalking man, a witness who had come before him. The truth really.

He had put it aside, not wanting to think about it, not really ready. But he was stung with the impact of the identification of the running man. He was in the battle once more. He had sighted the enemy. He was approaching the enemy camp.

But then he had not been able to let the thing alone, and just before Edyth had picked him up, it had come to him. He had been able to identify the face of the chairman and the moment as the hearing room, but the witness in the chair had not been himself. No. The witness had been Bertolt Brecht. He was, therefore, happy that traffic was too heavy for Edyth to talk much on the way to the Horse and relieved that it was impossible to converse once inside. Because it was all clicking into place. *Why Brecht?* he kept asking himself. *Why not Seaman?* (And when had this happened? This thinking about himself in the third person?) And then one moment when his Modigliani looked distracted, when he had nothing to focus on but flamelight and white dust, the answer hit him. It was not because he had been a witness before the chairman that the stalking man was in pursuit. No. It was because he had been denied being a witness when he was ready. Yes, of course, that was it. If it had been Seaman, not Brecht—if the Hollywood ten had, in fact, been the Hollywood eleven, Seaman's life would have been entirely different. The life that mattered. The life where one's private ghosts are housed. The point was that there was a time in every man's life when forces around him prevented him from thinking in the singular, when one became either a lemming or a battle hero. That had happened to the nineteen, to Seaman. But the chairman had decided to call the ballgame before Seaman could testify. Brecht's testimony had unsettled the chairman. And so that was it. The ball game was over, and Seaman had not been allowed his time at bat. When that time came, he was alone in the ball park. The spectators had gone home, and the score stood in his favor. Or so it seemed.

So that was it, then. The stalking man was an uncalled witness during the trial of the century (it would have to be a crime of course, not political in nature). The appearance that had been denied by the running man had twisted and destroyed the stalking man's life. There it was. The hook. The peg. Max felt jubilant. Edyth was trying to say something to him.

"What? What is it, Edyth?"

"Let's go."

"What's the hurry?"

He wanted to stay and be a part of the celebration. They all had to be celebrating something. He tried to get the attention of the waiter to order another scotch. Edyth had risen and was standing next to him.

"You can take care of the bill outside, all right?"

She was smiling apologetically over him. Waiting for him to rise. Edyth would always be waiting. He got up and followed her lead through the crowded room.

"Thank you, sir," the waiter said as he handed the check to Max. "Are you a member?"

"Yes," Edyth said. "Mr. Seaman is a member. Just sign, Max. They'll send the bill to the office."

Max signed.

"Thank you, Mr. Seaman." The waiter smiled, before even looking at the size of the tip.

"Mr. *Maxwell* Seaman?" the girl asked.

She was young. Eighteen. Nineteen. Beautiful. She seemed to be alone. But that wasn't why he stood there looking at her. He was remembering. She looked like a young deb. Dark hair, worn long and straight but groomed impeccably, and wearing the best of the boutique clothes. Not at all like Melissa. And yet he was overwhelmed with how much she did remind him of Melissa. She had, however, the slight trace of an accent, though it had almost been masked by a carefully cultivated English inflection.

"Yes." He grinned encouragingly. "*That* Seaman."

She extended her hand and he took it in his. "I'm very happy to meet you. I'm Bonita de Miralda. My mother is the Contessa de Miralda."

"Oh, *that* De Miralda."

She laughed, and she had small pretty, very white teeth. "Umm. You once had our villa for a summer. I hated you then. We had had to let it. My father had just died. We couldn't afford the upkeep. I was a very little girl, and it mattered to me then."

"I'm sorry."

"Don't be. It changed my life. For the better, I think. I'm Bonnie Lewis now. An actress. Louis was my father's Christian name—spelled *ou*, but my agent thought it looked better with an *ew*. I loved my father a lot. I don't think he'd mind."

"No. I don't think so either."

"Max . . ."

"Sorry, Edyth."

"The car's in front."

"Oh, oh, good. I'll be right there. An actress." He smiled at the girl. "Any credits?"

"Not that you would notice."

"You have a good face. I'm looking for faces right now."

"Bonnie . . ." a man called.

"I have to go. I work in the checkroom here. I recognized you and just wanted to say hello."

"When do you finish work?"

"Two o'clock."

"I'll pick you up."

"A little late for an interview, isn't it?"

"Haven't you heard about producers yet?"

"I've even dated a few. But not at two in the morning."

"Call me at ten in the office then."

"What? After seeing you later tonight?" She laughed wide-eyed.

"Bonnie!" The man again.

"It's a date then."

"Shhh. I'm not supposed to date the customers."

He watched her as she walked away. She was tall and lean. Her perfume lingered as he joined Edyth in the car.

"I'm sorry about that place, Max. I didn't think it would be so noisy and crowded. But of course, it's the weekend."

"It was perfect, Edyth."

"Well, I'm sorry."

"I loved it." He leaned back extravagantly. "And you look beautiful, Edyth," he commented. "I think I neglected to tell you that."

Edyth reflected on that all the way back to his place. It gave him time to consider. A new film and a new woman. It tasted good. Life was his again.

She had dark hair and alabaster skin. Her father had been Italian, but her mother was English. After her father had died, she had been sent to boarding school, then finishing school, and then a theater school in England where her grandparents still lived. Her mother had remarried and divorced twice but was living again as a widow in Italy, retaining her title of Contessa. The villa was gone. Most past glories were gone for that matter. Her succeeding husbands had been younger and poorer than she. She now earned her living as an estate agent devoted to finding elegant living quarters for elegant people. The grandparents lived in Surrey, where they had a small cottage. The grandfather was a retired postal clerk. Bonnie had a bedsitter in Chelsea, but she spent most of her time at Max's, redecorating the flat for him (she had pretty good taste) and cooking for him. (Not bad in that department either.) She had a good story head, and he could use her as a sounding board. She was actually twenty, certainly not a virgin, and knew exactly what she wanted—money, stardom, a career—in about that order. She was not vastly talented. She was quite beautiful and incredibly photogenic. She could possibly make it. Max was determined to help her. Somehow, it seemed important. At first he wrote her into the script, and then her character began to develop, to snowball. He knew full well it was Melissa he was writing, Melissa who could have carried the role. He had never seen Melissa act, but somehow he had known she was one of the God-given. It wasn't going to be easy for Bonnie, who was not. She'd need a lot of help and a minimum of dialogue. Keep the camera on those haunted, troubled, preoccupied brown eyes. The emotion was there. Whatever depths she had and was capable of were there. In the eyes. Something of the wounded animal. Her eyes were what had reminded him of Melissa. Bonnie was a wounded cat, not dying, but hurt, and she would crawl, if she had to, out of the jungle for help—for life. That portrait she had given him had caught it. Painted by some artist she'd had an affair with. The artist had seen what was to be seen. So had Max. And they both had been fascinated with the same thing. Bonnie was a magnificent survivor.

The script was developing at a fast clip. He had decided not to go down to Peru until it was completed. It was June already. He'd have a first draft by the end of August.

He felt exceptionally good. His old self. Self-generating. The only setback he had had came from an unexpected source. The news release of Harry Steiner's death. He had, he felt, been acting entirely rationally up till that point. But Steiner's death hit him, and that made very little sense, if any. The old boy was nearly eighty. And certainly there was no love lost there. Yet the old man's death meant the death of something for Max, too. He felt he should mourn, pay the old man some respect, which was unexplainable as he had been certain he had dismissed Steiner from his life many years before. For about eight hours after reading the obituary, he had struggled with the thought that maybe he should fly to Hollywood and attend the funeral.

"Why in the world would you want to do that?" Edyth had asked him.

"To make sure the son of a bitch is really dead," he had said, smiling.

But of course, even Edyth knew differently. That had been a Friday, and he had asked her casually, and after he had decided not to fly to Hollywood, to check out where the nearest *shul* was. "Not a temple, Edyth, a *shul.* I was never comfortable in those higher establishments."

She had stood in front of his desk quietly. "Yes, of course, Max. But if that's how you feel, maybe you should go to the funeral."

"It's Friday night. I just thought I might like to attend services. So I'm getting a little religion in my old age. Don't make a big thing out of it, Edyth."

She had gone silently out of the room, but five minutes later she had all the information on *shuls* in London.

He had gone alone. It was the first time Max had been inside a *shul* since his father's death. He had, for some reason, through all the years, with all the moving, held onto his father's *yarmulke* and *tallis.* They were folded neatly at the back of his underwear drawer and smelled sweetly of the wood of all the drawers where they had been resting through those many years. He had sat in the rear of the small male congregation at the *shul.* The faces all seemed old and wise. At fifty-four, he was certain he was the youngest man in attendance. He had remembered the prayers. He said them under his breath, but he hadn't forgotten one word.

"Gut Shabbos," the old bearded gentleman seated beside him had said when the service had ended.

"Gut Shabbos," he had replied and nodded his head.

And somehow, though as soon as he had returned home, he had refolded and stuffed the *yarmulke* and *tallis* back in its sweet wood darkness, and though he knew he would not return to the *shul* ever again, he had felt better. And he had done it for a son of a bitch like Harry Steiner.

Irrational.

But the incident had made him think about the past. Particularly about Luise. He found himself thinking about Luise a lot for that matter. And thinking about her comforted him, too. But it was different with Luise. Luise was like going home. Luise was home. After all his adventure had been spent, he would go back to Luise, and she would, of course, be there, and they would comfort each other. Thinking about Luise that way pleased him and put his mind at rest where she was concerned. He really did love Luise then, after all. He had heard she was pulling together a retrospective of all his work. He felt good about that. When the time came, he would write Luise a letter and thank her for that.

The twenty-seventh of June was a Friday. It was a rare, warm day, the kind where gentle breezes blow. Bonnie had seemed restless the entire week. He had been thinking about driving down into the country with her for the weekend. She was a good kid, and he'd been so hard at work on the script ever since they had been seeing each other that they really hadn't spent much time just being together. He planned to have Edyth check out inns but decided that wasn't too good an idea. They could just play it by ear. Get into the car and go. They could leave that evening, for that matter, giving them two full days. But it was June 27, and he first had a decision to make.

June 27 was Thea's thirtieth birthday.

He had come into the office early, figuring he would call before Edyth got in. But of course, it was five hours earlier in New York, so he had had to wait. Then he realized he did not have Thea's telephone number. He'd have to get it from Luise, or worse, Thea's agent, or worse still, Bob Tanner's office. He knew she was still sleeping with Tanner, even though Tanner had remained with Kate. Things like that could hardly be kept secret. Nothing could have hurt Max more than Thea's liaison with Tanner. Not even her rejection of himself. He'd always be there if she needed him. He knew that, and in his heart he was confident that Thea did, too. But he never discussed these matters with Edyth. So at lunchtime, when she was out of the office, he went to her desk. He had guessed right. Edyth had the number. He got the operator, but there was several hours' delay. He left the office early and went home and tried from there. Thea was out of town, the answering service informed him. He was on his third scotch and it wasn't even six o'clock when Bonnie came in.

"Hi, kid." He grinned at her.

"Oh, hello."

"What kind of greeting was that?"

"I wasn't expecting you'd be here yet."

"Yeah, well, it is home."

He went over to her and lifted her chin and kissed her lightly on her full mouth. She didn't wear lipstick, and he liked that about her. She smiled weakly at him and went over to the bar and made herself a drink.

"That's unusual, isn't it?" he commented because Bonnie seldom drank.

"A bit."

"Feeling that way, huh? Well, I'll tell you, I've noticed you've been a little out of sorts lately and I have been thinking we could drive out into the country for the weekend . . ."

"I don't think so."

"Oh?"

"Oh, Max, I'd love to go, I really would. It would be a terrible mess, though. Really. It just . . ."

"I'm a big boy. I know about those things." He laughed a little to himself and sat down.

"It isn't that. I wish it was. I—" She put the glass down because her hand was trembling.

Max seemed not to notice. He was staring into the dead fireplace, away from her. "What is it, kid?" Then he turned to her, and as he studied her, it began to dawn on him. He sat there startled for the moment. It was not the surprise or the complications of what Bonnie was insinuating that startled him so. It was something else. Something he couldn't put his finger on for the moment. But here a twenty-year-old kid was trying to tell him she was pregnant with his child—a married fifty-four-year-old tortured Jew, for crissakes—and he felt as if someone had just shot him with a full vial of adrenaline.

She looked as if she might cry, and so he got up out of the chair and went over to her and put down his drink on the bar top and placed his hands gently on her shoulders.

"You know for certain?" he asked. She just nodded. He kissed her again and then held her close to him. Then he held her slightly away from him. "You got a good doctor?"

"Wolfie David." She was trembling.

"Wolfie David? That son of a bitch!" he shouted.

"I didn't tell him it was you. I didn't have to tell him who the . . ."

"Let me get this straight. You went to that son of a bitch to arrange an abortion?" He was still shouting, and she moved instantly away to close the window.

"Yes," she said softly as the window banged shut.

"What right did you have?"

"Right?"

"Yeah, that's what I said. *Right*?"

"I thought you'd be pleased if I arranged it all. If you weren't troubled . . ."

"This is *my* kid you want to let that son of a bitch, murdering . . ."

"Max, Max, darling. Please. Don't get so upset." She had come back to him and was stroking his face. "You . . . you want me to have the baby?"

"Damned right!" He pulled her hand down from his face. "When were you going to . . ."

"This evening."

He looked at her coldly. "That was a terrible thing for you to do, Bonnie. Make that decision yourself. Now you call that son of a bitch up and tell him you've changed your mind. Then you go home and pack a small bag. We'll go away for the weekend just as I planned. We won't talk about this until we get back. Then I'll make the plans."

"Yes, Max."

"I don't want to hear you talking to that son of a bitch, David. I need some air anyway. I'll take a walk."

"OK, Max."

He headed immediately for the front door.

"Max . . ."

"Yeah?"

"You'll forgive me. I thought . . ."

"Get your ass into that bedroom and do as I told you," Max said as he went out.

He didn't walk. He took the car and drove down to the office.

He had it in his mind to try to reach Thea anyway, to find out where she was, just to say, "Happy Birthday, kid," even if she hung up on him. And he needed a place to sit down and digest the new turn in his life. But Edyth was still in the office.

"Forget I'm here," he told her. "I just have a few thoughts I want to put down on paper."

He went into his office, leaving the door open, not because he'd meant to, but because he was so distracted. He still couldn't make head or tail out of his reaction. He was, yes, elated. He knew it was important to him that Bonnie have this child, was looking forward to watching the child grow inside her, was pleased at the prospect of fatherhood. And at fifty-four! Damn! That was pretty good. But Luise— Well, there was not going to be any alternative. Luise would have to divorce him. His child would legitimately carry his name. He'd put Bonnie in the hands of the best OB he could find. He suddenly felt very benevolent.

"Edyth," he called.

"Yes, Max?" Always ready.

"Edyth, I just want to thank you."

"For what, Max?"

"All the years."

"Don't be ridiculous."

"Well, I still want to say it. *Thanks.*" He got up then and left the office. He felt better than he had for one hell of a long time. He was damned sure Edyth would leave him as soon as she knew. Yeah, no doubt about it. Edyth would definitely leave him now.

They had a wonderful weekend. They drove down the coast, stopping wherever they saw a place they thought looked interesting. They didn't talk much, but Max could tell that she was happy, and he felt good about that, too. Sure, she loved him. But he didn't lie to himself when it came to such things. Bonnie knew she had just made it. If that was her plan in the first place, he didn't care. Not really. Financially, Bonnie was close to being secure now. That's all she was really interested in. Max made a mental note that as soon as they got back to London, he would attend to this. A doctor, a new will, and then Luise.

They got back late Sunday night. He had decided on the weekend that he would now move Bonnie into his place. Monday, he'd arrange for all her things to be moved over. They'd stay there temporarily until they could find suitable larger accommodations.

For the first time she seemed embarrassed to get into the bed beside him. He had been preoccupied at that moment, but he had noticed it. A thought had come to him. Several, rushing in. The last section of the screenplay. Wrong. He'd tear into it in the morning. And the title. Wrong. He leaned over and wrote on his bedside pad, *The Game of Truth!* Yeah. That was it. Then he turned over to Bonnie. She had the sheet drawn up tightly under her chin, and he drew it gently away and down. He ran his hand over her flat belly and her small breasts.

"You'll be beautiful." He smiled.

Bonnie clicked off the light. He was stroking her and felt her trembling.

"What are you going to do, Max?" she said softly. She meant about Luise and the divorce, and he knew it.

"Fuck, baby. You can't get pregnant twice." He grinned.

And he mounted her. There was moonlight coming through the blind and Bonnie could see his face: the shaggy hair, the broad forehead, the strong nose and full, sensuous mouth. He reminded her of a lion. She smiled at that idea. And then her body took over. *Oh, my God*, was all she could think. *Oh, my God.* Then she heard him moan. She thought she had as well. But she wasn't sure. Max grew heavy on her. "Max," she whispered, "Max." Then with some impatience, "Max, please."

But there was only the sound of the shade as it fluttered in a sudden breeze.

Epilogue

Chapter 41

It was incredible how beautiful Thea was at times. She had left the door to the apartment open and was sitting in front of the window with the great weight of the unrelenting July sun settled on her shoulders as he entered. She wore the dense sunlight like a golden shawl. She sat there rather primly, dressed in a loose lemon-yellow silk robe, her hair unbound but brushed back from her face, cascading like falling sand down the gentle slope between her shoulder blades, which protruded as she was poised, with shoulders back, head tilted, hands clasped tightly in her lap. She wore no makeup. It was still morning, and she had not yet bothered to prepare herself for the day. Perhaps she could not, Tony thought.

He had rung the bell, and she had called out in a voice slightly deeper than normal. "Yes?"

"Tony, Thea."

"Oh." A catch in the voice. "Come in."

And when he had entered, she had looked up at him silently, never moving.

"You all right, Thea?"

"I'm yar."

"Oh, Lord, we're to have Katharine Hepburn again."

"Was it Hepburn who said that?"

"The Philadelphia Story."

"Hm. I didn't remember."

Tony came across the room to her and sat down on the arm of the chair, facing her. "You called?" he asked dryly.

She attempted to smile, but the smile was never quite born. "I called, and thanks for coming." She reached out, touched his hand, and then pulled slowly away. "I told him I never would see him again. 'Give me back my key and take your Chivas Regal,' I said."

"What a coincidence. He drank Chivas Regal, too."

"Discreetly."

"He'll be back. You'll let him in. The door isn't locked, you know."

"No. He won't ever walk through that door again."

"Don't be so sure."

"When you have lived with a man for five years, there are no surprises." She was looking directly into Tony's eyes, and yet with the sunlight between them, Tony doubted that she could really see him, not clearly, at least. She was an aureole blur before him, and he stood up and moved away to bring her into clearer focus.

"Have you eaten anything? Shall I make you some coffee?" he offered.

"Do you know what I said, Tony? Well, he was shaving and I stood in the doorway and looked at his reflection in the mirror—isn't that a hell of a place to end an affair? In the loo. 'I don't need you anymore,' I said. No. He'll never come back."

"I'll make us both some coffee." He went into the kitchen, which was as disorganized as always, and began to wash out the coffeepot. Thea appeared in the doorway.

"He had left Kate, you know. Incredible. He had finally left Kate. But she'll take him back." She came into her kitchen and edged herself onto the kitchen stool and watched Tony working as she talked. "Yesterday, Tony, I thought I was the happiest girl in the world. Imagine! Anthea Evans thinking she was that happy. It had to be an illusion." A small smile finally crept over her face. "Damned if it wasn't." She breathed deeply and studied her hands. "And it was nothing that he did. Nothing at all. It had all been over just like that. In twenty-four hours. He hadn't changed. But suddenly I really didn't need him anymore. I know you don't mind my saying these things to you. Sexually, forget it. I never heard the cymbals thundering. I don't know if he did. I mean, how does anyone really know about someone else? But I don't think that ever mattered to Bob. It didn't matter to me."

Tony went to the refrigerator to get the cream. It was sour, and he had to spill it out. He found some powdered cream on a shelf and took that out. Then he stood, awkwardly, waiting for the coffee to perk, hesitant to lean against the drainboard, which wasn't exactly clean.

"But I am terribly beholden to that man—Hepburn again, eh? This is my Hepburn period, I think." She folded and refolded her hands. "I am that—beholden to him. I did need him most desperately once, and he was always there. But it is just as I told him this morning. I don't need him anymore."

"Maybe he needs you now, Thea," Tony reminded her.

"Yes, yes, yes." She sighed. "I am a terribly selfish, spoiled . . . lady." She grinned sadly. "But ain't that nice? I really am a lady!"

"Luverly."

"You're supposed to say, 'Well, what are you going to do now, Thea?' "

"OK. So what are you going to do now, Thea?"

"Gird my loins, as the old book says. And I can and will. I don't know, Tony, suddenly I feel as though I can finally do all the things I never could before." She turned pensive. Her eyes misted, and she raised her chin. "We haven't really talked about it, but we should. I mean, my gawd, our father just died." She sucked in some air and held it. It was several moments before she could go on. "Well, of course, we weren't speaking at the end, but I know he'd never go out without leaving me money. I'm speaking about . . ."

"Yes. I know. I follow the script."

"I don't know how much it will be, but at least I'll feel . . . *cushioned?*"

"It's a good word."

"I want to act again. Well, let's just say I feel I finally can act. I read a play last week that was submitted to Bob for backing. He turned it down. But I liked it. There's a minor role, hear that? A minor role, well, that's show biz."

"Yeah, well, you never were much of a supporting player anyway."

She laughed uneasily. The coffee was ready, and he took two cups out and wiped them first before filling them.

"Let's go back into the living room," Tony suggested. "Kitchens are not my best environment."

He handed her the coffee, and they walked back into the living room and sat next to each other on the couch. They were silent for a long time. The telephone rang. Thea ignored it, and Tony finally started to rise to answer.

"Don't. The service will get it."

"It could be Mom."

"I don't think so. I spoke to her already. I told her I'd ring back."

The telephone was silenced in mid-ring.

"He called Friday night, you know?"

"Who?"

She drew a deep breath. "Dad," she said. Her eyes filled but she maintained control.

"Oh?"

"I was in Puerto Rico, as you know. It was my birthday. My thirtieth."

"Yeah, I remembered."

"Oh, yes, you did! The lovely pale-blue chiffon blouse. I've worn it already! I loved it."

"Good."

They were silent again. Suddenly she smiled. "Della Robbia blue," she said.

"What?"

"It's a line from *Streetcar*. I just thought about it. But you've been wrong about me, Tony. I may look soft on the outside, but inside, I'm a rock." She put her hand out and placed it on top of his. "Rahley, dahling," she cooed.

Tony stood up. "We might as well end all this slobbering confession. In my case, he left *me*, and I'm not at all sure I don't need him anymore!"

"Vic?"

"You know what his real name is? *Henry*. Now if I had known that in the beginning, the thing might never have started."

"Shit."

"I hate it when you use words like that, Thea," he said with genuine distaste.

"You'll have to accept it. It's me."

"No, it's not, Thea. That's the point. It's not. You are a lady, with or without Robert L. Tanner, and ladies don't use *those* words."

"Sorry."

He walked to the window and stood looking out. "I really should move. All I ever see in the daytime is that grim rear face of the building backing mine. I don't mind it during the night, the lights have a certain magic, but during the day it's truly upsetting."

"He'll be back."

"Yes, I'm sure he will be. He went off with that fading whore who was once married to a Ford or Rockefeller—some rich son of a bitch—well, he thinks she's going to finance a film for him. He wants so intolerably hard to become famous. 'You don't know the difference between famous and infamous,' I told him. I screamed a lot, as I think about it."

"He'll still come back."

He turned to her. "I hope he doesn't, Thea. For my sake, I hope he doesn't."

"I hope that, too, Tony," she said softly.

She rose from the couch and went over to him. He turned away from her, and she put her arms around him from the back. "Poor baby," she whispered.

Tony straightened immediately and stepped away. Then the two of them stood looking at each other. It was Thea who broke into sobs first. Her body seemed convulsed with them. They were silent at first. Giant heavings. Her body thrashing inside the yellow silk robe. When the sobs finally did become audible, they were the beginnings and ends of her inward screams.

"Oh, my God. Tony! . . . he's dead . . . he's dead. Oh, my God, my God . . . Da-da-daddy . . . is dead, my God . . ."

And she seemed just to collapse to the floor, her body appearing to have been swallowed up beneath the wide lengths of the soft billowing yellow material.

Tony walked away from her and to the window, looking out, away, not wanting to, not able to look at Thea at this moment. The sobs rose in him then. He took out a clean white handkerchief and covered his face with it, trying to hide them.

"Yeah, he's dead. The . . . lion . . . is . . . dead," he muttered between sobs, but he wasn't sure that Thea heard him.

Chapter 42

Bonnie stood in the living room of Max's flat for a long time after Luise had left. The events of the past week had simply been too swift for her to deal with dispassionately, but the cobwebs were finally being swept away, and she seemed once more in control of events, of herself, her own future.

Luise Seaman had given her the keys to the flat.

Bonnie had known immediately. She had won some manner of battle. But at the moment it had happened, Bonnie had not known what the battle had been, what she had, in fact, won.

Luise Seaman had given her the keys to the flat.

It had been conceded then that the premises and the furnishings were to be Bonnie's. Bonnie smiled serenely. *Thank you, Max.* She knew Max owned a long lease. It was not really a large flat, but it was terribly elegant and very private, very impressive. The fireplace in the living room, the unusual circular dining room, the American kitchen, master suite, guest room, three, not two, but three full baths—worth at a minimum, twenty to twenty-five thousand pounds. And the furnishings another five thousand, easy. She sat down and took a quick visual inventory.

She would be all right now. Though the first thing she had to do was make sure that the flat was legally transferred to her name. That would take time, and in her condition she didn't have too much time to waste. She would first have to see to it that Luise Seaman *assigned* all rights in the flat to her. That would be easy. Then she could move in until the title was legally hers. She could sell a few things for some cash in the meantime. No, under the circumstances a small settlement would not seem too much to ask. She had gone through Max's personal bank statements when he had been out of the flat. He owned the flat, the car, had more than fifty thousand dollars in one American bank alone, ten thousand pounds in Barclay's, eighteen thousand dollars in the Bank of America on Davis Street, and one paid-up insurance policy of a hundred thousand dollars made payable to Anthea, his daughter, and another of twenty-five thousand dollars payable to his son, Anthony. So they were taken care of. Then, of course, there was his business, his films, the office, stocks, bonds, God knew what else. He had died a very rich man. Bonnie gently stroked her stomach. Plenty of money for everyone, she thought. She had even found a copy of his will. Everything besides the policies had been left to his wife, except for a pretty generous bequest to that old spinster secretary who hated her so. He had given a percentage from all future revenues on his films to her as well. But his wife got the largest share. She only had to deal with Luise Seaman then.

Bonnie got up and went over to Max's desk and, using his desk pen but a piece of plain stationery, began a letter to Luise.

DEAR MRS. SEAMAN,

This is, of course, the most difficult letter I have ever had to write and, I am sure, one of the most trying you shall ever receive. We have hardly spoken and just met once, but this terrible time in both our lives forces me to discuss things with you which, out of consideration for myself and you, I normally would not bring to your attention so soon.

I am actually Bonita de Miralda. You once, in fact, rented my mother's villa for a summer. All that is lost now, and my mother, who is now a widow, is working as an estate agent in Rome. I was intent on becoming an actress until I met Max. I am sorry if this hurts, but we were very deeply in love, and Max had intended to ask you for a divorce so that we could marry. You see, I am carrying Max's child. He was very much excited about this. It is a strange thing to say, but I do honestly believe he died a happy man.

Now I want you to know that my sincerest wish is to insure dignity for all of us—Max's unborn child as well. My pride refuses to ask for more than I need to begin a life for myself and Max's child.

If I could retain this flat in my own name (this has, in fact, been my home), I would feel the child and I have at least a roof over our heads. If you could assign the lease to me, I would be terribly grateful. Max and I had discussed his will, and he planned to rewrite it to take into consideration this new turn of events. He was never able to do this, but I do know that you and your children and Miss Spalding, who he considered so loyal and a part of his family, are well taken care of. I am happy for this and, because of it, do not feel I would be taking anything from you in keeping the flat. So, if you could write such an assignment before you leave London, it would relieve my fears for the safekeeping of Max's third child.

I only have two other requests. I will need five thousand dollars to care for myself during pregnancy and for the expenses of the hospital. Afterward, I hope to return to work and be independent once again. And could you see it in your heart to let me keep Max's diamond ring to pass on to our child?

I will now pack a box with all of Max's other valuables, his watch, which I know you would want Anthony to have, and his cuff links and such, and all his personal papers. Shall I send his clothes to anyone in particular or any charity? That won't be an easy task for me, but I will somehow cope.

I assure you I am indeed with child, and it is indisputably Max's child. I bless that fact.

My sorrow extends to take in yours. We have both lost a truly dearly beloved.

Sincerely yours,

BONITA DE MIRALDA

(Bonnie Lewis)

P.S. I will not allow the world to intrude on this, our shared secret. It might be difficult for your children and for you. Max's child shall carry only his first name. If it is a boy (I pray for that), it will be named Maxwell Lewis. If it is a girl, Maxine Lewis. I assure you of this.

I wait your reply.

Bonnie folded and sealed the letter and wrote "Mrs. Luise Seaman, Claridges. Private" on the front. Then she went into the bedroom and, taking Max's jewelry box, opened it and removed the diamond ring. Then she reconsidered. It would be better if Luise sent it back to her. She wrapped the box into a parcel and secured the letter on the top. Then she took the keys to Max's car, which were still on the dresser, and left the flat.

She hadn't asked for the car, but perhaps they would overlook it. (If Luise asked for its return, she could make a magnanimous offer for it.) That would work.

She gave the parcel to the head porter to take up to Luise. Then she turned around and drove to her place, where she packed all her possessions and returned with them to the flat.

She was actually only six weeks pregnant. She could afford to wait about two months, no longer. She'd tell Luise, if she ever asked, that all the grief had caused a miscarriage, but she had a feeling Luise Seaman would not inquire further.

She wished for a moment that the car was a convertible. It was such a beautiful day, and the mirror over the dashboard reaffirmed that she was a very beautiful girl. She was only twenty years old, and the world was a ball of butter.

Thank you, dear Max, she thought and then parked the car and moved all her things into her new home.

Chapter 43

Luise took the parcel from the porter, tipped him, closed the door, and then stood there uncertainly. Something in the childish handwriting on the envelope alerted her. At first she thought she might open the package later. She came inside to the living room of the suite and set it down on a table. She thought she might shower. She needed a little time to unwind. Even so, she knew she wouldn't be prepared for a meeting with Merwin Bibbs. She sat down and picked the parcel up, loosening the envelope from under the cord and putting it aside as she opened the package. All the pieces of Max's jewelry were familiar to her. She sat there, staring at the contents of the small box, unable to touch anything, afraid for the moment she would be violating an unspoken, unwritten law if she did. She knew immediately the letter would have to be from Bonnie. She opened the envelope carefully and without any premonitions. She assumed the girl had simply sent the package to Luise, not wanting to be responsible for the jewelry or thinking Luise would want it. She read the letter with growing shock. When she had finished, she laid the letter back on the table and, then unable to see it exposed that way, refolded it neatly, replaced it in the envelope, and, folding the envelope in half, slipped it into the pocket of her robe.

She believed most of what Bonnie wrote. Mainly that Bonnie carried Max's child and that Max, knowing this, had planned to ask her for a divorce. Max would be loyal only to what was his, and she was sure that the child Bonnie bore was that. Something told her it was the truth. She closed her eyes, fighting back the searing fire in them. This made things quite different, made the future a new and unfamiliar world. A world truly without Max Seaman. Before the arrival of Bonnie's letter, she had been Max's widow, all the years of estrangement blotted out, erased, obliterated—gone. Max had simply been away—out in the fields, fighting the wars, in combat. She had, she had to admit, been feeling for the past forty-eight hours very close to Max again. She had wanted to return to New York with Max. To comfort herself with the memory of their life, their love. Before, no matter who the woman had been in Max's life, Luise had known he would eventually come home to her.

But not if *his* child was involved. No, he would have deserted Luise to ensure the possession of his newfound child. To the world she might still be considered Max Seaman's widow. In her heart, for the first time in her life, she felt like the ex-Mrs. Max Seaman.

Yes, it was now a totally new and possibly unbearable world.

The telephone rang, and she picked up the package and took it with her into the bedroom to answer. She was gripping the jewelry box with one hand as she picked up the receiver with the other. She hoped whoever it was would not call for too much from her. She did not want to break down, did not think she would, and yet she was feeling so odd that any behavior on her part would not have surprised her.

"Yes?"

"Luise, are you all right?"

It was Burt. She breathed a sigh of relief and sat down on the edge of the bed, finally releasing the jewelry box from her grasp. She could feel its weight against her hip, and she edged away from it.

"A bit tired."

"Would you like me to ring back later?"

"No. I'm glad you called."

"Look, I just want you to know I have everything in hand. The funeral arrangements, I mean. I won't discuss it with you, but between Edyth and myself, it will all be taken care of."

"Here?"

"Why, yes. Isn't that what you want?"

She thought about Bonnie and the child. "Yes, of course. Here."

"Luise, would you like me to send a doctor over? Not Wolfie David. A reputable man."

"No. Really," she assured him. "Burt." Something was disturbing her.

"Yes, Luise?"

"Please, understand this, but I would prefer you didn't get too involved in the arrangements."

"I had thought I might read the eulogy."

"No. Please don't."

"All right, Luise. Would you rather I not inquire why?"

"It's hypocritical."

"You mean the island? I'm sorry, this is no time. I apologize."

"That and, well, I'd just prefer you didn't."

"As you wish, Luise."

"Ah, when will Sylvia be home?" she asked, simply fighting for casual conversation.

"She won't."

"That's— What did you say, Burt?"

"Sylvia isn't coming back. She's remaining on the Coast."

"You mean until her mother recuperates?"

"No. I mean Sylvia is divorcing me. Listen, Luise, this isn't the time to burden you with the problems in my life."

"But after all these years! How could she have decided that after all these years!"

"It seems as though Sylvia has fallen in love."

"Oh, Burt. Burt, I'm so sorry." She felt awkward, not knowing what to say. "Would you forgive me now, Burt? Merwin Bibbs is coming up, and I'm not even dressed."

"Merwin? Why?"

"I don't know. He said he had to talk to me."

"He's an idiot, that man. Call down and leave word you can't see him."

"No. I already said I would. It's fine. Really. Believe me, Burt." She smiled, for the first time in days it seemed. "I don't think Merwin could even throw me a curve now."

"If you're sure."

"I am."

"I'll deal with Edyth on the funeral. Is that agreeable?"

"Very."

"Good."

"Thank you, Burt."

"Nothing I ever said in the past has changed at all, Luise. Will you remember that?"

"Umm. Yes. Thank you again, Burt." She lowered the receiver into the cradle. She had changed her mind about the shower. There was something more important to do first.

She got up and went to the little desk in the room and sat down and took out a pale blue sheet of Claridges' stationery. She was careful to write in a very legible hand:

TO WHOM IT MAY CONCERN:

This letter is to state that I, Luise Haydyn Seaman, in sound mind do assign any right bequeathed to me by my husband Maxwell Isaac Seaman in the property at Number 11 Kensington Crescent, with all its contents therein, to Miss Bonita de Miralda (known professionally as Bonnie Lewis) from this day forward.

July 2, 1969
LUISE HAYDYN SEAMAN

She would inform the attorneys about the letter as soon as she met with them and make what further legal provisions had to be made. She got up and got her pocketbook, took out her checkbook and came back to the desk with it. She wrote out a check for five thousand dollars, payable to Bonita de Miralda. Then she wrote a short note to the girl.

BONNIE,

What can I say? The enclosed perhaps says it better. I felt even without this information that the flat truly belonged to you. I will contact my attorneys and inform them of what I have done. I am enclosing the ring as well. I trust all goes well with you and for you and the child.

Sincerely,
LUISE HAYDYN SEAMAN

She placed the two letters and the check in an envelope and took out all the jewelry in the box except the diamond ring; then she redid the package, addressed the envelope and rang for the porter. *Later*, she thought. *There is still time. I will arrange part of the estate for the child. Not now, later, I can't think any more now . . . In a few months, maybe when the child is born.*

The doorbell rang, and taking the package with her, she went to answer it, expecting it to be the porter. She was still in her robe, warm, and needing fresh makeup.

It was Merwin Bibbs.

"I'm sorry, Luise. Should I have called up first?" he said.

"No. It's all right, Merwin. I just had some letters to write and didn't watch the time. Come in." She stepped aside and let him pass by her.

The porter now stood at the opened doorway, and Luise handed him the package, along with the two-shilling piece she had ready to tip him. "If you will see that this is sent by bonded messenger as soon as possible, I would appreciate it. Just put the charges on my bill."

"Is it valuable, madam?"

"The package? Yes, I would say so."

"Perhaps, madam . . ."

"Please." Luise felt distracted. She was sure she didn't look well, and the porter instantly reacted to it.

"Yes, most certainly, madam. I was only going to suggest that you ring the desk at your convenience and tell them the value of the package. Only for insurance purposes, of course, madam."

"Yes, yes. I'll do that."

"Thank you—"

She closed the door before he had had a chance to call her "madam" again. The inflection in the word had disturbed her, the arch to his voice, as though mentally he were clicking heels.

"Pour us both a drink, Merwin. It's after five, and I suppose under the circumstances it's permissible. I drink scotch on the rocks. I believe there's still ice in the bucket. I'll be right with you."

"Certainly, Luise."

Luise went into the bedroom and closed the door. She called the hall porter and told him the package contained a piece of jewelry, worth probably between five hundred to one thousand pounds. He suggested they insure it at the latter, and she agreed. She thanked him and hung up. Then she put a little lipstick on and touched up her eyes. She sprayed on some cologne and went back into the living room to join Merwin.

She had forgotten what he looked like until she saw him standing in her doorway. It had, after all, been more than twenty-two years since she had last seen him. He was making their drinks very fastidiously. A very meticulous, conscientious, and censorious person was Merwin Bibbs. He had his back to her as she reentered the room. His quick, darting actions made him look mechanical. His head with its carefully slicked down sparse gray hair looked a bit like an oiled knob. *Funny*, she thought, *he's all knobs and nuts and bolts. If he loses one, he is apt to become inoperable.* He could just collapse into a pile of carpenter's fittings at her feet. Planes and nippers and pegs and knobs and nuts and bolts. And, of course, a motor.

"Here you are," he said as he turned.

He had found the bar napkins and had one wrapped securely around the base of the glass.

"Thank you," she said as she accepted the glass and immediately sat down on the couch. His face was flushed, and his hand trembled. *Slow the motor*, she thought. *Turn down the steam.*

"This isn't easy," he began.

His voice was the most memorable thing about him. Pedantic, equal attention given every word. The low-droning-never-missing-machine-perfect voice of a motor.

"Not for me either, Merwin. You have chosen to see me at a most difficult time. The truth is I am not at all sure I will get through this meeting without totally breaking down into a sobbing, hysterical, uncontrollable . . . widow."

"I am sorry, Luise."

"For what, Merwin? It is just too late in the game for any of us to apologize for anything—*anything*—Merwin. And I really can't imagine what you have to say to me, but whatever it is, I just don't want to hear it. I think I have that right. Because you feel you have to say something that you need to say does not mean that you have the right to expect me to listen."

"It is a bad time. I am aware of that. I deliberated because of it for a long time."

"I have only been here two days. Max has only been dead three."

"To me it seemed a long time."

"To me as well." She put the glass down to allow the ice to melt and dilute the scotch. "Merwin, my husband has just died. A good chunk of my life has died with him. We were married thirty-one years. That is a very long time. Very long. I am aware of his shortcomings, his weaknesses, his transgressions, his lusts, his anger, as if they were my very own. They were part of my life, too. Should I hate Max for those human foibles? No one will give me a new life in exchange for the old. I will go on living, I will be making additions, but that is all. One's life is like one's child, Merwin. Nonreplaceable. You can have another child, two, three. But each one takes up so much of your life. If you lose them, the space is always there."

"What I came to talk to you about, Luise"—it was as though he weren't listening—"was the business of the *minyan*."

"The *minyan*?"

"Well, of course, it is not exactly that, but for all intents and purposes that is what Burt meant it to be."

"Burt?"

"He has arranged for a group, all who knew Max, of course, to carry the coffin, to sit together. A tribute. Of course, ten men are required for a true *minyan*, you might not know that. There will be Burt, and Henry Green, Gus Cone, Milton Stevens, and Saunders Mayberry. Burt had expected me to be the sixth man. Not a true *minyan*, as I said, but . . ."

"I won't permit it."

Merwin seemed visibly relieved. "I had a feeling if you knew, you would say that."

"It's a lie. Max would never have countenanced such a terrible, terrible, lie." She shivered. "I'll call Burt later."

"I refused, of course, to take any part in it."

She looked up at him with some surprise. "Is that why you are here? To tell me that?"

"Yes, Luise."

"Did you realize what you were doing?"

"Why, of course."

"I don't believe you did, or do. No. I don't believe it, Merwin. Because you think yourself a man of good conscience. No, you could not have been aware of what you were doing."

"I felt it important to you, Luise, that you know exactly why I refused Burt's, ah, request. I have felt a good deal of sympathy where you are concerned. Not always, of course. As you say, a man and wife are in many respects considered one. You find a man is your enemy, his wife has to be as well."

"That is one incredibly liberal viewpoint, Merwin." She stood up, angry and unable to shout. She paced nervously, her drink clutched in her hand, the napkin torn from it so that she could feel the sharp cold of the bottom of the glass in her palm. "For your information, I had my own mind to think with, my own heart to feel with." She turned to face him. "But I loved him. You accept evil and good when you love someone, Merwin. But you still have your own standards."

"What I thought it was important for you to understand, Luise, when you saw my five colleagues at the funeral, was that my not being with them had nothing whatsoever to do with Melissa."

"Oh, my God!"

"That is important. Melissa was an entirely separate matter. She was, after all, a consenting adult. I see that now. No, the major issue still remains. Max was an informer. My absence from Burt Winters' *minyan* must be recognized as my protest . . ."

"Protest? Who cares anymore, Merwin? That's the point: Who cares? Are you saying that if Max had not been an—an informer, you would have appeared by the side of his coffin? You never did like Max. Even in the early days. Never. A wife senses those things. Would that have been less of a betrayal of yourself, to stand in death by a man you would not have stood by in life? And coming here, satisfying your selfish needs. How can that be excuse for what you are doing to me?"

"I am sorry, Luise, but there are some things a man must do."

"Yes, yes, I understand. Like your protest in Washington twenty-two years ago. Well, you had a *minyan* then, I guess. Ten. Isn't that what you said? Ten men for a *minyan*."

Merwin smiled. "That's strange. I never thought about that." He put down his glass. "I am sorry I intruded, Luise." *The mental clicking of the heels.*

"You're not, Merwin. The scene has pleased you. You'll play it over in your memory for a long time to come."

Merwin went to the door. "I do wish you a good life now, Luise. I want you to know that as well."

"Good-bye, Merwin."

"Good-bye, Luise."

He let himself out and closed the door behind, very surely. Luise stood there unable to react for a time. Not sure of what had really just happened. Then indeed she did break down into sobs.

She managed to make her way into the bedroom, where she threw herself onto the bed, clasping the cool exposed pillow to her, and she did a very strange thing. She kissed the pillow. It was her country. It was Max. It was her life. She kissed it again and held it suffocatingly close to her.

Chapter 44

The plane did not depart until ten, but owing to the circumstances, Edyth had to check in no later than eight forty-five. She was accompanying Max back to California. The change in plans had been Luise's idea. At first Edyth had resisted. But then it all began to make good sense.

Of course, Max should reach his final rest in Hollywood (calls had been made and arrangements secured at the resting place directly behind Paramount Studios). And of course, she should be the one to accompany him.

"I think he'd want to go home, Edyth," Luise had said. "In the final analysis, I do think that would be the case. He gave no instructions in the will, but I think that was because Max had no idea where he would ever be tomorrow. Not since we left California. That was home, the only home we had really. That is where the past is buried and where today, tomorrow was born. And I would consider it the greatest kindness, Edyth, if you accompanied Max home."

Of course that was how it should be.

It was the Fourth of July, and when they arrived in Los Angeles there would be fireworks lighting up the sky. That pleased Edyth. She smiled at the thought.

She had gained permission to stand at the landing platform as they raised Max into the dark belly of the giant plane. She stood there now. A heavy fog threatened to blanket the airport, and she was fearful the flight might be delayed, but the airline had reassured her that it was a low fog and that the plane could lift above it.

It was a leaden gray morning, though, and cold. Not anything like July. Feeling more like November. Edyth buttoned her suit jacket under her throat and slipped her hands into her gloves. That was better.

They were sliding the coffin out of the open truck now. Carefully lifting it up and in. Edyth felt she should cry, but there were no tears. She had shed so many lone tears on dark nights that there were no more left. She did not move, though the wind was strong and biting and she was chilled. She stood, immobile, at attention until the coffin had been swallowed up inside the plane and the yawning doors had been closed.

The pilot had come around to her side.

"Miss Spalding, there is no sense in your going back to the departure lounge. We will be loading in five minutes, anyway. You can wait in the cabin, if you wish."

"Thank you kindly." Edyth smiled bravely.

The young man took her arm, led her around the plane, and helped her up the stairway. A smiling stewardess stood at the top. She took Edyth's hand luggage.

"Would you like to sit in the front?" the stewardess inquired.

"Yes, please."

She was given the first seat.

"I'm sorry, I can't give you a drink until takeoff, but I could manage coffee."

"That would be fine."

The stewardess disappeared immediately into the first-class galley.

Edyth sat looking out the window as the passengers filed out on the field. She took the coffee when the stewardess returned and drank it slowly, turned to one side, avoiding the other passengers' glances as they came on board.

Then Edyth leaned back in her seat and closed her eyes. Her heart rose as the motors sounded and the plane began to lift.

They were going home, and incredibly, they were going there together.

"Oh, Max," she whispered beneath her breath. "You knew, I'm sure you always knew I'd be there at the end."

When she opened her eyes, it was as the airline had assured her. They were above the fog. There were endless, lovely white clouds all about them.